RISE OF THE BLACK MARKET

The Wizard Hall Chronicles

SHERYL STEINES

The Day of First Sun
Black Market
Wizard War
Prophecy
Rise of the Black Market

Cover Art: Damonza
Editor: Rachel Porter

Rise of the Black Market

Copyright 2020 Sheryl Steines
All rights reserved.

ISBN 10: 0-9858652-9-6
ISBN 13: 978-0-9858652-9-0

ACKNOWLEDGEMENTS

THIS IS THE last installment of The Wizard Hall Chronicles. I write this with a heavy heart.

I lived with these characters in my head for the last ten years. Thinking for them, breathing for them, crafting their lives, all in hopes of entertaining readers and making them think,or feel or simply enjoy.

I couldn't have done this without the help of A LOT of people.

This is for me, then, a thank you letter to the following people:

Thank you to:

Joy Meredith, you are the one who re-sparked my desire to become an author because you were published and I was green with envy. I took that jealousy and turned it into my first book.

Pavarti Tyler, believe it or not, meeting you changed my career as an author. Because that day, you introduced me to other authors, marketers, editors, and book cover designers. I am where I am today because we met.

Melissa Storm and Briana Clark, my earliest marketing help. You are still in my corner and offer encouragement when asked.

Ashley Egan, Kira McFadden and Rachel Porter, my editors. Each of you has supported me on my journey. I trust you more than I trust anyone else with my work.

Chrissy, Alisha, and Damon with Damonza.com and Mallory Rock with Rock Solid Designs, you bring my vision to life in brilliant, beautiful ways.

Ed and Jamie White. While we have never met in person, I trust you with my babies as ARC readers and reviewers. You're always supportive and there when I need an extra set of eyes.

Marilyn Mages, Jim Pearson, and Bonnie Litch, my friends and marketing help. For EVERYTHING, I am grateful.

My brother, Brad Aronson, for being my first editor and making my books less Harry Potter-ish.

To my friends and family for purchasing the books, attending events, liking my posts, and sharing them with everyone they know. I appreciate the time and support.

For without all of you, I wouldn't be where I am today.

Sheryl

PROLOGUE

Middle East 1347

STURTAGAARD RAN WILDLY through the black market, hiding himself in the horde of traders and buyers. He didn't dare turn to see his pursuers, though he was tempted to gauge their distance. While he ran, he stumbled against a customer and pushed himself off of him. The vampire couldn't care less, even when the man glowered at him and sent a fireball in his direction, barely missing his dark, black hair.

The vampire was stronger, faster, leaner than the men that followed. Though he didn't possess their black magic, he was cocky and therefore certain he would make it through the portal before they could reach him.

Those in the market knew he was a vampire. Perhaps it was the icy chill that radiated off of his skin as he skimmed against them that gave him away, or perhaps it was his incredibly pale skin, which seemed to glow in the shadows. Either way, everyone around him steered clear of him and stepped out of his path, making room for him and the men who were bearing down on him.

Sturtagaard had been alive for over two centuries. It had been plenty of time for him to learn survival tactics. But more importantly, he had learned how powerful he was as a vampire and how much his presence instilled fear in those around him. Because of that, he had never worried about what they could try to do to him. Until today.

He forgot himself and anxiously glanced behind him, sure they couldn't possibly be gaining speed—and yet there they were, less than five tents behind him.

Damn! They're vampires, too!

He hadn't thought of that possibility, he realized as he crossed into the market center. Here, men, women, and evil creatures looking to do wicked things conducted private business, rested from a day of trading and buying or consumed food from stands that lined the perimeter of the open park. Sturtagaard jumped over a small cart and continued running for the other side of the market. He slipped inside a passageway teeming with customers.

The vampires chasing Sturtagaard lost sight of him as they spun around the market center searching for him, leaving Sturtagaard what could have been considered a bit of breathing room, had he actually breathed. Once ensconced in the crowd, he jumped over a table covered with merchandise and lunged inside the owner's tent, pulling the flaps closed.

The tent owner, whom Sturtagaard recognized as a man named Ezra, startled. "What are you doing here?" he demanded.

Sturtagaard ignored the question and peered through the slit in the tent flaps, guardedly watching Asher and Raziel searching the crowd for him—more specifically, searching for the Chintamani stones that weighed down his pockets.

The magically imbued stones were so ancient that they were said to have belonged to King Solomon. While Sturtagaard generally doubted the truth of the story, he now couldn't help but consider it, given that these men were so doggedly chasing him in order to retrieve them.

Absently, Sturtagaard placed his hand in his pocket and rolled the cool, smooth stones around his fingers. He wasn't about to lose valuable artifacts when he had a perfectly willing buyer waiting for them.

"I asked you, what are you doing here?" Ezra demanded. He glared at the intruder with crossed arms. If he was trying to appear menacing, it wasn't working. Sturtagaard returned his glare, revealing his black eyes and fangs.

"You're a va... va... vampire," Ezra stammered.

"Shut up, pig," Sturtagaard growled and looked back through the tent flaps. Raziel and Asher were one tent over.

Sturtagaard glared at Ezra, placed a finger on his lips, and ducked below the tent's back wall, shimmying his way into a narrow alley that separated the tents along the next passageway. He crouched low and slunk toward the end of it. There, he peered out and glanced down both sides of the passage to see clear aisles. Believing he had escaped, the vampire stepped onto the main thoroughfare and ran to the left, away from the Fraternitatem of Solomon.

Just as he was almost to the portal exit, so close he could see the shimmering magic, Sturtagaard made a grave mistake and glanced back, if only to confirm he was truly free of the them. Seeing no one following him, he slowed his pace. When he turned back toward the portal, he crashed into David.

Shit!

Even with Sturtagaard's vampire strength, speed, and smarts, he was no match for the leader of the Fraternitatem of Solomon. David was a formidable wizard, who practiced the darkest of magics.

In two centuries, nothing had truly frightened the vampire—nothing until he met the Fraternitatem. A stake he could avoid, but the Fraternitatem had a far reach across the continent. Not wanting to become snared in their web, Sturtagaard scrambled away from the wizard, sliding across the silky dirt and hiding himself under the table. Not ashamed by his retreat, Sturtagaard slithered from booth to booth, dragging himself through the dirt. David, undeterred by the vampire's hasty departure, patiently strolled along the passageway.

At the end of the row of tables, Sturtagaard scrambled up and ran into Asher. To his left, Raziel closed in on him, trapping him.

"I do not have what you seem to think I have," Sturtagaard pleaded.

David seized the vampire's arm, ignoring the icy cold that radiated from the demon. He yanked Sturtagaard's arms behind his back and tied them with a magical rope. Sturtagaard struggled against the bindings and was rewarded with a jinx to the shoulder.

"I think you are lying," David said. He shot another jinx, Sturtagaard fell to the ground, unconscious.

"That was easy," David said as he teleported the vampire from the black market.

❦

Sturtagaard woke with his hands bound behind his back. He struggled to release the rope and found his shoulder was stiff from being held so long in that position. He stared at the stone floor beneath him, gingerly turned his head, and spit out a mouthful of dirt.

"It's about time," David quipped. As ruler of the Fraternitatem of Solomon, David surrounded himself with the trappings of wealth and power. His wooden throne was built with wood from the farthest reaches of the world and hand carved with the Fraternitatem seal: a six-pointed star surrounded by four dots that created the shape of a square. He crossed his legs under his heavy velvet robes and glared at the vampire.

"Untie me!" Sturtagaard grunted through his fangs.

David held out his hand and showed Sturtagaard the four Chintamani stones he had been hiding in his pocket. "I don't think you are in any position to demand anything."

Sturtagaard looked on with horror at the stones he worked so hard to steal, which glistened in the dim blue light of the cave. "I... I was not aware those rocks were the ones you sought. See? You can let me go. You have what you want." Sturtagaard rolled over, still pulling on the magical ropes binding his arms together. The magic was impenetrable. He stared at the cave ceiling.

"I do not think it is wise to let you live." David gracefully stood, then knelt beside Sturtagaard. He summoned an acacia stake and tossed it in the air. When it hit his palm, Sturtagaard jumped.

"No. No. You see, I know people and places. I can get you whatever you want. I can kill for you. Please let us not have it come to that," Sturtagaard pleaded.

David looked thoughtfully at Sturtagaard and stood. He paced along the back wall of the cavern known as the Cave of Ages, a cave system that once belonged to King Solomon, once held his vast treasure. He stopped after traversing the path several times. "What do you have to offer in exchange for your life?"

Sturtagaard smirked. He had lived a long life, collected much knowledge, and had filed away his secrets in his brain like a filing cabinet;

information to be used when it suited him the most. There was only one piece of information he believed would save him from the stake. He jerked his body as he tried again to loosen the ties that bound him. Still stuck, the vampire jeered, extended fangs. When David didn't respond, Sturtagaard asked, "You hoard power, yes?'

David's eyebrows rose. "Go on."

Sturtagaard sniffed the iron-scented air. As David's blood coursed through his veins, his heartbeat pounded in the vampire's ears, a sign of his anxiety and curiosity. The vampire felt the upper hand had shifted.

"Release me and I will give you the ultimate power," he said calmly.

David shook his head and laughed a deep, throaty laugh. "I do not expect that a scum vampire such as yourself would have any knowledge of an ultimate power."

Sturtagaard studied his adversary carefully as he contemplated his options. Not many people or creatures had an opportunity to find them-selves inside the Cave of Ages. As Sturtagaard lay on the stone floor, he scanned the cavern; the iridescent blue of the walls shimmered and played tricks with his eyes. To his left, an open entrance in the side of the cliff showed the way outside. Two passages on either side of the stone room led deeper inside the cliff. As he took in his surroundings, he wondered if it were true about the Fraternitatem, that there were hundreds of members across the continent, or if those numbers were exaggerated. He glared at David.

"It is the strength of power that will allow you to control the entire black market, maybe even the entire continent," Sturtagaard explained.

With wide eyes, David stared at the vampire. "And how did you learn of this... ultimate power?"

Sturtagaard pulled on the ropes. "I will tell you when I'm released."

David frowned. "And what guarantee do I have that you will not run out when you are released? You have not given me a crumb of information. No. I do not think it wise to let you go. Now tell me where this power is and how I can retrieve it. Maybe then, I will discuss the possibility of releasing you."

Sturtagaard cringed and rocked himself upwards, struggling to right himself. Once upright, he stared at David. "A girl will be born in a future time. When she is of age, she will accept her destiny. In return, the ancient ones will bestow upon her a power unlike any other." Sturtagaard glanced at David; his face was stony and controlled. "With this power, she will have control of water, earth, air, and fire. But most important of all, she will have control over the dead: the ability to conjure and turn ghosts corporeal."

David listened patiently. With his hands behind his back, he took several steps while staring at the vampire. "I do not think you are smart enough to know this," he finally said.

Sturtagaard laughed.

David watched the vampire, assuming he was mad.

But Sturtagaard knew the truth. He had been in Jorvik when Anaise arrived. His family had died because she did not act quickly enough to save them. When she finally fulfilled the prophecy and killed every last demon across the land, she did receive that ultimate power. While he hadn't physically watched it happen, he had heard how she rose in the air, sputtering and flying above them. He had scoffed when he heard, but the Vikings who regaled him with the tale were frightened by the events, and those warriors were not easily frightened by little girls. Anaise's power had scared them.

For years after, they whispered about her conjured ghostly father and how she turned him corporeal before she went back to her time. They believed it, so he believed it. More than anything, Sturtagaard hoped the Fraternitatem would believe it too.

"I was there when she received her powers. I saw a dead man come to life." He kept his voice calm and steady as he wove the lie.

"There is no such power that allows all of that," David said with disbelief.

Sturtagaard stumbled up and walked to David, their eyes now level. "Yes. There is. Anaise was sought from the future to rid the demons from England. There are now no more regenerating demons in England, and she received her powers before returning to her own time. She has done these things."

"And you saw the power of this Anaise?" David asked skeptically.

Without hesitation, Sturtagaard replied, "Yes. Release me and I will tell you when she receives them."

"If you are lying—"

"I am not."

David observed the vampire cautiously before releasing the magical ropes from Sturtagaard's wrists. The vampire shook out his arms as if the bindings had blocked the circulation he didn't have.

"When?" David asked.

"She returned to the twenty-first century. There are stories of her great heroics. She will be more powerful than you." Sturtagaard sneered at him.

"If you are wrong, or if you are lying, we will find you and kill you."

Sturtagaard nodded with understanding.

"When she is born, you will contact us here. You will keep an eye on the girl as she grows and keep us updated on what she has learned and accomplished. And when she returns with the power, you will report to us immediately," David ordered.

Sturtagaard nodded, relieved David was taking the bait.

"If we catch you with King Solomon's belongings again, this deal will be considered broken and you will be staked."

CHAPTER 1

ANNIE SAT ON the window seat in her bedroom, observing the deep shadows that crossed the flower beds in her backyard. A fat billdad popped out from the garden and hopped across the grass. She smiled wanly at the momentary respite from the itching that bubbled under her skin, as the magic she received in ancient England possessed her body. Her skin now burned with raw, red scratches from her incessant rubbing, so much so that she had taken to wearing cotton gloves. If she were to be truthful, she would admit that it did little to ease her discomfort. She set her hand in her lap and sighed as she wiped away frustrated tears.

"Come back to bed, baby," Cham murmured as he turned toward her.

Annie looked at his form in the moonlight. "I can't sleep with the tingling and itching." She leaned back against the wall.

The bed creaked when Cham sat up. "Did the potion help at all?" He moved to the edge of the bed and took her hand.

The potion was a stop-gap measure to relieve the itching. Annie had been hopeful when she left the past that Zola, her Aloja Fairy, would have found the answer to removing the magic from her without killing her. But when Annie returned, she was disappointed; in eleven hundred years, a solution hadn't been found. For now, Annie knew she'd have to live with the itching if it meant the strength of the magic could help to defeat the Fraternitatem.

Annie squeezed Cham's hand and then let go, returning to scratching against her stomach. "It helped and then it didn't." The magic coursed through her veins from her feet, traversing up her legs, through her body, down her arms, and to her head like clockwork, spreading the itch and pain.

Cham knew better than to stop her. Holding back and not relieving the itch increased her anxiety more than scratching it did. In the meantime, Cham continued to work with the doctors to adjust the potions and lotions to keep the magic from consuming Annie. Unfortunately, the last batch didn't last long enough to get her through the night.

"Want me to fetch some more to help you sleep?" Cham asked.

She smiled at him, though in the darkness, he couldn't see. She placed her hand on his knee and patted it.

"Can you add a sleeping draught. I'm exhausted and tomorrow's my first day back. I'm investigating two locations tomorrow night," Annie said.

"Yeah. I'll get it for you." He touched her shoulder and shuffled from the room.

Annie returned to peering out the window; the billdad's shadow moved in and out of the garden.

Since returning from the past, Annie kept herself busy. It was easier to ignore the intolerable itching when her mind was occupied with something else. Tonight she was anxious about her first day back, the first time she would see the black market leads that Kathy's son, Robin Price, had given her.

What if they're nothing and we don't find it?

Annie sighed. She wasn't solely responsible for finding the market; this was a top priority for all Wizard Councils across the world. For Annie, though, finding the market was merely a way to keep busy. Her priority was closer to home: her own life and the threat of it ending at the hands of her mother, who Annie believed to be dead, up until three months ago.

Lights switched on downstairs as Cham pulled ingredients to create a sleeping draught that he would add to the anti-itching potion. While Annie waited for him to return, she stared at a picture of her family taken weeks before her mother died. At first glance they seemed happy, smiling broadly, hugging each other for the camera, unaware that their lives would forever change in a matter of weeks. Skilled in reading people, Annie began to notice how her mother's body faced away from them, her hands rested loosely on Annie's shoulders, not firmly gripped like Jason, who leaned into his girls. But what she noticed most of all was that Emily's smile was too broad, as if she was trying too hard to appear normal, or was hiding a secret.

Or maybe I'm reading more into it.

She placed the picture back under the seat cushion.

It had been such a shock to Annie and her sister, Samantha Pearce Chamsky, when they discovered their mother hadn't died and was alive, living across the world. Even today, Annie continued to have difficulty coming to terms with the fact that Emily Pearce had made the choice to leave them. Left them because she was a naïve nonmagical who was duped into believing her actions protected her daughter.

Always skeptical, Annie believed the Fraternitatem of Solomon would use her mother to come after her, having started the plan decades ago as they waited for Annie to come into the power. But what they failed to understand was simple: Annie had no emotional connection to the woman who had left long before a connection could be established.

The two weeks since returning home had been difficult for Annie. Bringing Gibbs back to the present and attending his funeral had drained her, and she missed him terribly. But after his ashes were laid to rest in the Wizard Guard mausoleum, she experienced the constant reminder of the magic under her skin. But more importantly, the magic reminded her that Emily Pearce would strike soon. Not knowing when that would be left Annie feeling vulnerable and out of sorts. She longed to jump in, find her mother, and finally end the Fraternitatem of Solomon. As much as she wanted to strike first, Annie knew the best course of action was to learn all she could about them, not just where they made their headquarters but also how they operated and the magic they used. She believed that knowledge would help her defeat them. She spent much of her time since returning reviewing their Book of Shadows and rereading her father's notes, learning nothing new. Annie sighed.

The downstairs lights flicked off as Cham made his way back upstairs. Annie climbed into bed and pulled the blankets over her bare skin. Though it was the middle of summer, she shivered under the coolness of the sheets.

"Here, this should help you sleep," Cham said.

She grimaced at the liquid before swigging it down and placed the glass on her bedside table. "Bah. That tastes horrible."

He chuckled lightly and climbed in beside her, wrapping his arms around her. His natural body heat warmed her, and she squirmed beside him.

"Me or the itching?" he asked.

"Itching." Annie yawned, the sleeping draught already taking hold.

"I love you," he whispered in her ear.

"Hmmm," she said as sleep overtook her.

⚜

There wasn't an official classification for Annie's trip to the past. While it was considered a case, there was something far more that couldn't be put into words. It rewrote wizard history, it exterminated a species of demon, and Annie had returned changed. All of the artifacts, notes, and case files had been packed away at Artifact Hall as Annie used her compensation time to heal.

While she remained holed up at home, secure and away from most people, she did allow a few visitors. Kathy, Ryan, Samantha, John, and even Marina and Don Chamsky stopped by with dinner. Their visits were light and enjoyable, and allowed her, for a short time, to forget the pain and itching.

After a restless night, Annie woke early, giving herself time to dress and eat. She still had difficulty using her hands after they were broken by the evil wizard Everard while in the past. While mostly healed, they were still stiff and sore, another reminder of what she had suffered while in ancient England.

Alone for the first time in days, she sat in her den and watched the Witch News Network as she sipped her tea.

"Hey. I'm on my way. Meetings all day. Need anything before I leave?" Cham asked as he shrunk his field pack.

"Nope. I'll be in later to check messages before I head out with Robin." She glanced at the notebook Robin had given her prior to her trip to the past. He'd promised Annie multiple leads to the new black market. She had circled the two locations for the night.

"Text me if you need something. Go home if it's too much."

"Will do, boss." She offered a smile.

Cham should have left. He stood still and watched her.

"What."

"Boss. That sounds funny."

"Why? It's what it is. Besides, I've known for years that Ryan wanted you in that position. The council let me stay there even though we were dating."

Cham frowned. "Now that we're engaged, the Wizard Council isn't too keen on you staying my employee."

Annie stood and walked to him. "I never had a problem with you becoming the manager. If I did, I would have said something."

"But it's your career. You always wanted to do this."

Annie wrapped her arms around his waist. "I love you. As much as I wanted this growing up, I always knew once I became a parent, I'd quit. I never wanted to do this as long as I had kids."

Cham kissed her forehead. "You don't have kids yet," he whispered.

Annie pulled away. "I'm smart, I'm good at what I do. I'll find something that makes me just as happy." Cham touched her cheek.

"I was going to petition the council to let you stay as long as you need. I had an idea."

He piqued her interest, she raised her eyebrows. "How?"

He chuckled. "You can't report to me. Doesn't mean you still can't be a guard."

Annie laughed. "That's just working around the problem. Though… who would I report to?"

"I haven't thought of that yet. Once you're a wizard guard, you're always a wizard guard. If I'm not directing you or giving you performance reviews, you can stay. Until you're ready to leave."

She gave him a kiss. "Go be a boss." She watched him leave for work, before checking her phone again. While she didn't have to leave until late afternoon, she was feeling anxious for her first day back. She finished her tea, still chuckling at his plan. When she finished, she placed the notebook in her field pack and found herself roaming through the house, rearranging items on the shelves and organizing the spice cabinet to keep busy.

"Excuse me. What are you doing?" Zola asked. But when Annie looked at her, the fairy took up a wash rag to wipe up the counter. From what Annie could see, Zola's eyes were still bright, emerald green, but they were crinkled at the corner as if she were either worried or annoyed. Annie assumed it was a little of both.

"I need to stay busy," Annie said as she scratched her leg.

Zola glanced at Annie and quickly turned her head to the side. "I wish I could have found the solution to removing the magic," she said, not making eye contact with Annie.

"You've been avoiding me since I got back. Are you upset or embarrassed because you couldn't find the answer? What aren't you telling me?"

"I can't. I'm…" Tears rolled down Zola's cheek.

"What?" Annie reached for Zola, but her fairy pulled away and wiped her cheeks.

"In order to keep you safe, I… I had to make some… choices. I can't tell you."

Annie firmly held Zola's hand, not allowing her to leave. She stared at her fairy, held Zola's chin steady so she could look her in the eyes. "Thank you for saving me. However, you had to do it. Please don't shut me out because of it. I still need you." Annie let go of Zola's chin and placed her hand against her own stomach, feeling the heat of the magic as it traveled upwards. She closed her eyes and took a breath.

Zola rolled up Annie's sleeve and stared at her burning skin.

"I'm sorry. I wasn't aware I had pulled away so far. I promise I am still working to keep you safe, and I'm trying new potions to keep the itching at bay." Zola touched Annie's cheek. "Your skin is hot. Are you okay to work today?"

Annie pulled her arm away, rolled down her sleeve. "I need to get back to work." She turned and began to empty the dishwasher. "I'll be fine."

They remained silent as Zola pulled plates from the dishwasher putting them in the cabinet. "Who are you working with?"

"Actually, Robin is coming with me tonight. He wants to find the market as much as the Wizard Guard. Finding it will help him do his new job as well," Annie said.

Zola took the glass from Annie's shaky hands. "I am so happy I was able to accomplish my biggest task," she murmured as she patted Annie's hand.

Annie thought back to her hospital stay, when Zola had admitted that Annie's lifeline had been cut short; she was supposed to die in the past. Zola was able to fix that in eleven hundred years, though Annie didn't know what she had done to accomplish that.

"You never did tell me how you saved my life. Is that what you can't tell me?" Annie asked.

Zola nodded. "I was sworn to secrecy. Though if it will help you find peace, I can tell you that I worked with my sisters and petitioned the Fates to help."

Annie looked at Zola with concern. She knew better than to press Zola any further. If Zola had gone to the Fates to save her life, that meant she had given up something in return for Annie's life.

"Thank you."

"You're that important to me. It was your life, and I'll be damned if you were going to die so young and for them," Zola said.

Annie wrapped her arms around Zola and lay her head on her shoulder. Zola rubbed Annie's back with soft, cool hands, just like she used to do when Annie was a child.

"I will never let anything happen to you," Zola murmured in Annie's ear.

Annie hoped Zola really felt that and wasn't just trying to convince herself.

⁂

Annie stepped through the employee entrance accessed through the courtyard. Manny, the new assistant manager, was on the desk. "Welcome back," he said with a wide smile.

"What are you doing behind the desk?" Annie asked as she shot her spell through the security box at the end of the tabletop.

"Oh, well, I missed my old job and thought I'd pick up the slack. We're down a guard today," he said as he opened the security gate for Annie to step through.

"It's always good to see you," Annie said on the other side.

"Glad to have you back to the future."

Annie waved as she entered the hall and headed down the back entrance into the main building.

The familiar buzz of Wizard Hall was comforting to Annie. In the present moment, she relished in feeling like a cog in a very big machine, without others noticing her. She slunk to the back hallway and took the stairs to the fifth floor.

It was harder to hide on her home floor, where she knew so many people after working there for six years. She waved to some and greeted others. When she reached her cubicle, she glanced inside. Her desk was covered in piles of folders, notepads, scribbled-down phone messages. Her eyes roamed to the cubicle next to hers, where Gibbs had spent a better part of thirty years. It was spotless, just as he had left it: his inbox, his outbox, the top of his credenza. Annie entered and looked inside at a box that was sitting on one of two visitors' chairs. It was empty, as though no one had the desire to box his things up.

"You didn't have to come in today. Not with the market investigation tonight," Cham said from behind her.

"I'm restless at home. I thought it was time to check my messages and files." She leaned against Gibbs's desk. "I miss him."

"I do, too. He was a great resource and a loyal friend."

Annie picked up a jar filled with liquid and a small elf ear floating inside. Annie had once asked Gibbs why he had it. He had responded simply that it was a reminder that evil was in the world, and he was determined to make sure all creatures had the opportunity for a good life. She placed the jar into empty box, then thought better of it and placed back on his desk.

"Zola intervened with the Fates to spare my life," Annie told Cham.

Cham frowned. "The Fates? Why would they interfere in the process at all?"

"I expect there was a deal of some kind," Annie said.

Cham looked at her carefully. "You think Zola made a deal to save your life?"

"Zola said I was supposed to die in the past. Why else am I alive?"

Cham leaned against the cubicle wall, his arms crossed, his face crinkled in worry. "Maybe she did something else to change the future. The charm she gave you before you left?" Cham offered.

Annie grimaced. "Maybe. Whatever it is, she's acting funny, like she can't look me in the eyes. I'm concerned there's something else going on."

"Give her time. She'll be honest when she ready," Cham said.

"I hope so. Because right now, I think I need her the most."

CHAPTER 2

ALONG THE BORDER between Georgia and Florida, a creeping spiral of Spanish moss hung from the trees and slowly choked the life from them. Annie sighed woefully and yanked a handful of the parasitic plant down before stepping onto the trail that should, if the coordinates were accurate, take them to a black market.

Annie blew wayward hair from her face as she pushed vines from the trail. "I wish I had a machete to clear this path."

Robin, walking beside her, summoned a small machete. "Like this?"

Annie held her stiff hands up. "Maybe you could?"

He chuckled, stepped in front of her and began hacking at the green foliage.

"Glad you're back to work?" Robin joked as he cut through a large swatch.

"Honestly?" Annie swatted away a large mosquito. "I needed to get back. This is a little out of the ordinary, but at least it's 2019." She ducked under a branch.

Robin stopped and pulled out his phone.

"How far are we?" Annie asked.

Robin swiped and checked the coordinates. "I hate to say it but we're about a mile away. I didn't want to teleport too closely to the portal in case we're spotted." He showed her the map on his screen.

"I'm with you there. I guess we just look for the telltale signs of a portal: atmospheric changes, humming, buzzing." Annie switched on her flashlight and swept the path in front and beside her, glad she was searching for the portal with Robin. He was a good friend, the closest she had to a brother. As an adventurer, he searched the globe for magical, antique, and rare items, either at the request of wizard councils or on his own. Annie reminding him of what to look for was nothing more than foolishness.

"Not my first rodeo kiddo," he said as he took a few steps ahead.

"Blah, blah," Annie replied as she wiped her forehead with her arm. While it was midnight, it was the middle of summer in the South, and the heat and humidity were heavy. She smacked a mosquito on her face as they followed the overgrown path.

Robin reached for a handful of Spanish moss. "Feel that?"

Annie reached for the magically charged air. Goosebumps traveled up her arm, and the magical itching grew more intense. She grimaced and tried to refrain from scratching. Taking several steps forward, she touched the icy portal. "Got it." The portal hung in the air, across from a large oak tree. Annie shone her light on the energy that shimmered wildly. She flashed the trees and bushes around them, searching for anyone hiding near the portal. Several footsteps pattered across the ground as animals scurried away. She turned toward the sound of a branch cracking.

"Are you okay?" Robin asked. He glanced in the direction of the footsteps.

"I thought I heard something," Annie said.

"Probably animals feeding," Robin said.

Annie scanned her location. Seeing nothing ominous, she pulled out her cursed knife and jammed it into the anomaly. They stepped back; air blew out at them, churning like a violent storm. Lightning struck rapidly. Annie glanced inside the portal, expecting it to burst open.

"You're not going to break this one," Robin said. Whether she wanted it or not, most people who worked at Wizard Hall knew about the magic tearing down the portal home.

"Still, it makes me nervous," she admitted as she waited for the portal to react to her. When it didn't, she glanced inside and sighed.

"It's small. Let's check it out and hit the next location," Robin said. Annie nodded and stepped through, Robin following closely behind.

Tonight was Annie's first market investigation. She had been advised that the markets were nothing more than a handful of vendors selling nothing stronger than protection potions or the ingredients to make such potions. This market consisted of three short aisles of booths. Annie and Robin strolled through the market, taking a passageway at a time and noting the stall owners; nearly all were unfamiliar to both of them. She stopped to inspect one booth and checked the wares stored in the many baskets on the table. The baskets contained nothing odd, dangerous, poisonous, or imbued with black magic.

They turned down the second aisle.

"Doesn't look much different than my last three," Robin commented. He followed Annie as she turned right and took the outer pathway around the smaller, quieter, and cleaner market. More than anything else, it lacked the low-hanging dust cloud that covered them with the stench of dung and the musty aroma of wild dogs, dragons, and other nefarious creatures.

"This is weird," Annie whispered to Robin.

He walked to a booth. The owner glared at him over the United States magical newspaper, *The American Sphinx*. Robin perused the items and joined Annie at the end of the aisle when he finished scanning the table.

"These are real markets, and they're popping up all over the world. There's nothing dangerous or evil about them. You're right, it's weird," Robin said.

"You can get these items at any new age shop," Annie said. "And they've all been like this?"

"This is my seventh. I feel like we're either missing something or they're intended just for show," he said.

Annie observed the workings of the market. "Do you think someone is hiding the real market?" she asked.

"I have tracked every market that's been searched. I've saved coordinates, pictures, names of wizard guards who investigated. More leads come in every day. It feels like a wild goose chase. Yes, I'm starting to think it's being hidden on purpose," Robin said.

Annie turned down the final aisle, checking the stalls and noting the vendors. While the market was hidden in another plane of existence, it was still surrounded by an unnecessary cinderblock fence covered in colorful graffiti. Annie turned to examine what appeared to be small glyphs.

"Has anyone recorded the graffiti? Do you think it means something, or are there just a bunch of magical vandals roaming about?" Annie took out her phone and did a quick recording of the wall.

"Not specifically. I took pictures of the market in general," he said. "I'll take a look at what I have and see if any of the graffiti is odd or similar."

She turned and took in the small market one last time. "Thanks. I don't see anything here. Let's hit the next stop."

Annie and Robin exited the market through the only portal and landed themselves again on the trail between Georgia and Florida, where they teleported to the next location, an inlet in the south of Florida. Annie was surprised by the highly populated area. "Is this the right location?" she asked. Streetlamps lined the street, which looked out over a small bay.

Robin checked the coordinates again. "Yeah. It looks like we follow around this way out of the residential area."

It was after midnight when they landed; the street was silent. Annie and Robin followed the road to a dead end and stepped onto a dirt road parallel to the narrow waterway. It led away from the residential area. Annie switched on her flashlight as they walked closer to the water.

"You're not worried about being seen?" Robin followed.

"I'm more worried about gators," she said as they headed toward a small bridge where two red eyes stared at them. She moved her flashlight over the drain beneath the bridge and took note of the alligator that lay half submerged in the water. "Like that one," she said, scanning the area. Annie returned to watching the alligator, who seemed uninterested in their presence. Robin glanced at his own map.

"Head up the hill toward the left. From what it looks like, this is industrial. It should be somewhere in there," Robin said.

They climbed the hill, leaving the alligator behind, and entered into the industrial park where several buildings sat crumbling. The road was marked with pot holes and shattered glass. Annie paced herself as she surveyed the exterior walls and ground for a shimmering anomaly.

At the crossroad, Annie and Robin took opposite directions. Annie used both her arms to feel for the portal; she stopped at the center of the road and listened for the humming and buzzing of magic.

"I found it!" Robin called out as he plunged his knife inside. Annie ran for the open portal and glanced inside. She shuddered as the whirling mass of air knocked her backwards.

"Did you see inside?" Robin asked as he helped her up.

"Looks like the last. Let's take a quick sweep and go home," Annie suggested as she stepped inside.

Even smaller than the last, this market contained one row of four booths with a corrugated steel fence surrounding them. While all of the booths were jammed packed with items, there was no one tending to any stalls, no customers, no animals—no life inside whatsoever.

"It looks abandoned," Annie said, checking the perimeter of the market. She scanned the walls and noticed same graffiti painted there. On first glance, the drawings meant nothing to her, but she took pictures and continued around the market. When she and Robin returned to the portal, she said, "I think you're right. There're a lot of fake markets to throw us off. Though this one almost looks like a storage unit."

"When I mark it on my spreadsheet, I'm noting the amount of poison I found in those booths," Robin stated as they headed to the portal and out to the industrial park.

"Thanks. I'll see you tomorrow," Annie said. She gave him a hug before teleporting herself home.

∽

When Annie landed on her porch, the hairs on the back of her neck stood straight up. She turned cautiously and glanced inside the darkened forest behind her house. The feeling of being watched was so strong in her since she returned from the past. It was too dark in the forest; she couldn't distinguish between shadows and silhouettes. Sighing, she entered the house where Cham was awake and working at the kitchen table, sorting through a case file. She shuffled over and sat beside him.

"Hey. Find anything?" he asked.

"More of the same. Small nonthreatening markets. The second one was abandoned and the stuff was left in the four stalls," Annie told him. Sitting for the first time in several hours, she felt the rise of the itching and began scratching. When Cham glanced at her, she stopped momentarily, almost embarrassed by her condition.

Cham played with the folder. "I'm wondering how much longer to keep everyone on this. I've talked to France, Amborix, Germany, India, and Spain. Their Wizard Guard units don't have the resources we have, so none of the European or Asian coordinates are being investigated." He pushed the folder aside.

Annie rubbed her forearm, unable to discern between the magic and the mosquito bites.

It's gonna be another long night.

Cham picked up her arm and looked her irritated skin. "Go take a shower, I'll prepare more potion. It should take care of the mosquito bites, too," he said.

"Is Zola here?" Annie asked.

"No. I haven't seen her. I figured she was at Sami and John's."

"Maybe." Annie patted his hand and took his advice, stripping off her clothes and stepping inside a hot shower. The water pelted her like small stones against her sore skin, causing her to cry out. She quickly soaped and washed her hair from outside the stream of water and stuck her head inside to rinse off. It was the fastest shower she had ever taken.

Cham waited beside the shower when she exited, offering her a towel and a sour drink of sleeping draught and itch relief.

"It's gross," Annie said before accepting the glass.

"Yeah, well, it seems to help a little," Cham said.

Annie drank the liquid with a grimace and handed the empty glass to him. She dried herself off, slipped on her pajamas, and ran a toothbrush across her teeth.

Too tired to pull down the blankets, she fell on top of her comforter.

"Robin thinks the main market is being hidden by all these smaller markets." Annie yawned.

"Is that what you think?"

"I'm not sure what to think. I've only seen the two of them. He's been to seven and has seen pictures from other markets across the country. I trust his impressions." Annie closed her eyes.

"That could be a problem. And saying that, I can't stop the searches. Maybe everyone can do two locations a week. Any more than that and we'll burn out." Cham pulled the blankets around them.

"Then I can start planning the wedding," Annie offered as she snuggled into his bare chest.

"Ah yes, the wedding. I want a big-ass cake, a large sub sandwich, and televisions to watch the game," Cham said.

"You're hilarious," Annie murmured. If she had her way, they'd elope. But, as she was "related" to the Grand Marksman, she was pretty sure their wedding would be a large, formal affair like Samantha's wedding to John had been.

"A big cake?" he asked.

"A big cake with all of your favorite flavors," Annie said, listening to his heart against his chest.

"I know it'll be big like Sami and John's," Cham said.

"Probably." Annie rubbed his chest.

"Sub sandwiches for an appetizer?" Cham asked expectantly.

Annie looked at him. "If that's what you want, that's what you'll get," she said.

He rolled her over. She giggled as he kissed her neck, her chest. She ran her hands through his hair, kissed his cheek, bit his lip. When he entered her, she forgot the itching, the wedding, the market, and the rest of the world that wasn't in their room.

❦

Cham left early; department manager meetings with the Wizard Council were taking up his day today. Annie took her time eating, holding back the desire to call for Zola even though she was anxious to know what Zola had given up to save her life. Annie immersed herself in the most recent *American Sphinx*, reading the week's news.

She glanced up when she heard the chair squeak across the floor; her father sat down with his own breakfast.

"Hi, Dad," Annie said flatly. It had been three weeks since she returned home and conjured her father. While she accepted her responsibility in bringing him back, she was torn between taking advantage of the situation and getting to know her father again, and knowing he couldn't stay because this was not his time. Realizing that last part, she had begun to avoid him when she could, because she knew his eventual departure would leave her as heartbroken as his death had nine years ago.

"Morning, sweetie." If Jason felt her anxiety and the tension it brought, he didn't mention it to Annie and acted as if it were normal to come back from the dead. "If you're back from work early enough, I thought we could have dinner tonight."

Annie had spent the last three weeks in the house surrounded by friends and family. She had rarely spent time alone with her father. She observed him carefully.

"Ghosts technically need food. Besides, we still have dinner together every night," she said.

"Well, as true as that is, I enjoy eating for the sake of the food and it's never just the two of us." He returned her glance. "I mean, I know Cham basically lives here, but I have this feeling you're avoiding me." He offered her a smile, apparently trying to ease any tension. Annie placed her hand on his and sucked in air, holding it as she searched for words.

It's not time to be cautious.

"If you were me, would you feel comfortable with your dead father eating in your kitchen?"

Jason responded to the question with a hearty laugh. "Fair enough," he said.

"You can't stay. You'll have to go back to where you were."

Jason rubbed her hand where it was still swollen. "It's not my time." He glanced at her. "That's why you pulled away."

"Yes."

Jason stood and paced along the kitchen island. "There are two choices. We take advantage of the time I'm here, or you can ignore me."

Annie smiled. "I'm not sure I can give my heart to you again. It nearly broke when you died."

Jason sat beside Annie and took up her hands again. He stared at them. They were still swollen, her joints bigger than they had been. "I'm here because you need me. I am here to keep you and Sami safe. Let me be that for you. Knowing I have to leave puts you ahead of what's to come. My memory won't hurt you this time. It will keep you in the light and happy."

"You understand why I hesitate, though."

"You always did think like a wizard guard. I guess that's why I trained you and not Sami."

Annie had spent her childhood as a classic "tomboy," while Samantha had no interest in sports or the dark magic training. Annie had always enjoyed learning from her dad and spending the time with him, but she often wondered if he would have been interested in training her had she had a brother instead. She frowned at the thought and let it pass.

"I'm glad you trained me," she said. "All that information you gave Cham and me, it helped a lot. We scored really well on the Wizard Guard test." Reminiscing about that made Annie realize for the first time since her dad came back how nice it would have been to share her life with him.

"I heard that. He scored one point higher than you, and you scored like thirty points higher than me." He smiled again. "I'm very proud of you. And just so you remember, I'm here because you summoned me. *You* did. The Fraternitatem didn't, your mom didn't. That means I'm linked to you."

Annie squeezed his hand. "Sami doesn't know to be afraid of you. To distrust this. I wanted her to be cautious. I just... It was so hard for me when you died. Do I let you in and watch you go again?"

Jason looked at his daughter with sadness in his eyes. "It's been hard to see how life moved on without me, how much I missed, how close you are to Kathy and Ryan, as if they're your parents. I realize I don't belong here and I know I'll have to leave again." He played with his fork. "Sami sees this as a good thing. You're just like me and you see the reality of the situation." He chuckled lightly.

"You're not supposed to be here," Annie said.

"I give you permission to let me go. I'll go willingly if you choose to un-summon me."

Annie played with her eggs, shifting them around her plate.

"The Wizard Council agreed to let me work a few cases." Annie glanced up at him. She knew her dad had grown anxious sitting around the house without a purpose. He believed he was here to protect his daughters.

"You're my wild card. I need you hidden."

Jason nodded. "I know. That was the caveat and it's taken care of. Are you okay with that?"

"I'm not going to un-summon you, and I'm not going to tell you what to do. I just need you to stay safe. As long as the Fraternitatem doesn't know you're here, the better chance I have to stay alive."

"As you wish," Jason said to his youngest daughter.

CHAPTER 3

ROBIN PLACED A world map on the wall of the Wizard Guard conference room. All investigated coordinates were added to the map; North America was filling quickly. In the last three weeks, the United States team alone had investigated thirty portals that led to small markets similar to the ones Annie added to the map.

"We have Isaak Denberry and Smith James in the southeast satellite. They sent pictures of baby dragons. They also found graffiti along the perimeter wall in this market here," Robin advised.

Annie stared at the map as if it could tell her something useful about the markets.

"Seeing anything?" Robin asked.

"Just a big old mess. What did your contact say about the coordinates?" Annie asked.

"I have several contacts throwing out locations. They all claim they lead to the market." Robin leaned against the table and crossed his arms against his chest. "I honestly thought we'd have more answers. Instead, it feels like proof they're making fools out of us by feeding us these empty markets." Robin made notes in his small notebook. "Oh, and Stephenson McKay and Eddy Woods from the Northwest found a disturbing quantity of elf parts." He walked to the board and noted it on the map.

"Do you think it's a market to revisit?" Annie asked.

"I don't know. I'm leaving that up to Cham. I'm swamped with Artifact Hall. If it wasn't for Mrs. Cuttlebrink, I'd be drowning in paperwork."

"Welcome to the nine-to-five," Annie joked. Robin grimaced. "Any suggestions on where to go from here?" she asked.

Robin handed her a stack of pictures. "These are all of the walls and the graffiti that we have. I've numbered the pictures and the coordinating number on the map. You think this might lead somewhere?"

Annie stared at the pictures. "I wonder if Bucky Hart in Telecommunications can do something with these. Maybe it's something, maybe it's not. Can I take them?"

"All yours," Robin said. "There's no rhyme or reason to the portal locations, no patterns."

"You might be right about it being a wild goose chase to keep us from finding the real market," Annie said.

"It's a lot of work to hide it this way. So why do that? The last market was what? A thousand years old? Everyone knew how to get in."

"The only thing I could guess about that is that they're hiding something. And it would be big," Annie said.

"That doesn't leave me feeling comfy cozy," Robin said.

"The magical markets are nasty. You've been out there. I don't have to tell you," Annie said.

"One thousand years. Until Gladden Worchester and that djinn tried to control the market, it was pretty much just a place. Dangerous, yeah, but easy enough to maneuver. They left it alone, and it thrived as a business. This hiding thing, it feels like someone actually has control of it."

"If someone does control the market, that's bad news for us," Annie said. "Anyway. I need to check the call list and catch a case. If you hear anything else, let me know."

"Will do," Robin said, and they left the conference room together.

⚬

It was Annie's first full day back at Wizard Hall. She stared in her cubicle at the desk she ignored the day before and sat in her chair. Piles of folders lined her desktop, her inbox was filled, and the stack of phone messages was thick. She moved the piles to her credenza behind her and stared at the phone messages to sort through any urgent business.

"Well, forget the new call list," Annie mumbled, looking at the first message from Headmaster Turtledove at Windmere School of Wizardry. She dialed his number.

"Annie Pearce, how are you?" Fitzgerald Turtledove asked. He was warm and sounded genuinely glad to hear from her.

"Hi, Headmaster. Sorry to take so much time returning your call. I've been out of the office for several weeks," Annie said.

"Did I hear correctly? You were in the past?" he asked.

"Ninth-century England, to be exact. I actually met the original Wizard Council," Annie said.

"Well, it sounds exciting. I'd love to hear about it someday."

"Maybe someday. So, how can I help you?" Annie asked. Her first thought was that he needed an advanced potions teacher for a school seminar. She scowled at the thought.

"Well. If I remember correctly, I told you once you should come back here and teach," he said.

Like she did the first time he brought it up, she laughed. "Yeah. I remember something to that effect. I still don't think I'm teacher material."

"Well, I would very much like for you to come in so we can talk in person. I have some ideas and plans that I wish to discuss," he said.

Well, that's vague.

"I'm good for lunch today if that works," Annie said.

"I'm glad you said that. Come by. I'll see you then." He hung up.

Annie returned the phone receiver to the base and began to sort through the rest of her files. She reviewed the other messages, made a few calls, and sent emails for the calls that didn't need her immediate attention. When she finished, she moved on to the folders in her inbox. Some were case files that needed plan approvals; others needed her opinion, and she made notes where she could. Halfway through the pile, she stretched her arms in the air as she stared at the ceiling where a new tile had replaced the old, stained one. With the pile smaller, she glanced at her phone. It was time to leave for her meeting with the Headmaster.

"Hey, Emerson," Annie said when she reached the end of the hallway. "If anyone asks, I'm at lunch."

Emerson nodded. "How are you?"

"I'm recovering. I'm fine," Annie told her.

No thanks to your family.

"I'm glad. The Wizard Council wants to charge my grandmother with obstruction," Emerson said.

Annie nodded. "I heard that. I'm staying out of it."

"I'm not asking you to comment. I thought you should know."

Annie nodded and said goodbye. She teleported from the courtyard of Wizard Hall to Windmere School of Wizardry.

The teleportation location at Windmere was a flat piece of land surrounded by high privacy walls, a mile from the school property. While it was a magical property, it was still a public location just south of the Canadian border in Minnesota.

Security cameras placed around the teleportation spot captured Annie the moment she landed. She ignored the cameras and stepped onto the ancient stone path toward the school. It curved and undulated along small hills and valleys leading to the fence that snaked around the school property.

Annie pushed the security button and waited for the security officer to answer.

"I'm Annie Pearce, here to see Headmaster Turtledove," she said and was left to wait for a Windmere house elves to let her into the building.

The elf who eventually appeared was four feet tall with grayish-green skin and a school employee uniform of a white cotton tunic over white cotton pants. He nodded quickly and motioned for Annie to follow. School would be starting within weeks, but the building was currently nearly empty. Annie found the silence unnerving as she took a seat in the corner of the foyer beside an unlit fireplace.

"Headmaster Turtledove asked to have you wait here," the elf said. He was not especially talkative; he hadn't even said his name. Annie watched him walk from the foyer through the employee kitchen door and disappear.

The school hadn't changed much since Annie had been here six months ago with Bitherby when they were both hiding from the Fraternitatem. The thought made her shudder as she scanned the entrance foyer that currently resembled an oversized ski lodge.

She lay her head against the hard stone wall, closed her eyes, and listened to the sounds of the old building. Gusts of air blew through the building, whistling through cracks in the rocks. She opened her eyes when she heard the distinct sound of steps against the stone. Headmaster Turtledove climbed down the curved stairs from the second floor. Annie stood.

"Glad you could make it," Fitzgerald Turtledove said when he joined Annie at the bottom of the stairs. He was relaxed in a Hawaiian shirt over jeans with his long hair pulled back in a low ponytail. He greeted her with a kiss on her cheek.

"No problem. You've piqued my curiosity," Annie said. He led her down the main school hallway. "Um, lunch is the other way."

Turtledove chuckled as they passed several empty classrooms. "Patience, my favorite student," he said. The stroll through the stone-lined walls brought Annie back to her school days, classes and homework, the flying team. She passed several scorch marks against the wall caused by wayward spells.

She stopped behind the headmaster at a classroom Annie had never been in before. The headmaster switched on the lights and Annie entered. To her right, a stage was set with a table and a podium. The back wall contained a large whiteboard, clean and ready for use.

To the left, tables were placed from one end of the room to the other on three levels; the chairs were turned upside down resting on the table-tops. It was a small auditorium that could seat possibly fifty students at one time.

"You're still serious about me teaching here then?" Annie asked as she stepped inside. She climbed up one step and stood at the podium, where a syllabus for advanced potion making lay at the center.

"I've always been serious. I heard a rumor and, looking at your left hand, I see that it's true," he said.

She glanced at her engagement ring as it sparkled under the artificial lights.

"Congratulations," he said to her.

"Thanks," she said sheepishly.

She turned to the back wall. Under the whiteboard, a bookshelf was stuffed with books, potion vials, mortar, and pestles. She glanced at the tomes. All of them were new, updated materials—and not just of the magical variety kind. She found chemistry, biology, horticulture, and spell books as well.

"What do you think?" Turtledove asked. He sat on the edge of the stage and watched her explore.

"Once a wizard guard, always a wizard guard," she said as she pulled out a large tome of ancient potions. She sat on the floor and searched for potions from the ninth century.

"Cham will be the department manager of the Wizard Guard within months. You can't work for him. What are you planning on doing?" Turtledove asked.

She closed the tome and looked at her mentor. "We've been engaged all of four weeks and I've been out of town for most of that. Weirdly enough though, we just talked about this yesterday."

"What did you decide?" he asked again.

"I can't report to him. I can report to someone else."

Headmaster Turtledove appeared dejected. "So, you don't like the space?"

Annie glanced around the small auditorium. "It's cozy, it seems well stocked. I'd put a mirror above the table and tilt for the class to see. I assume there's a potions library or storage for ingredients?"

He pointed to a locked door to their left.

"I can't just quit. I'm always going to be a wizard guard. Regardless of who I report to."

Turtledove held up his hand. "What I'm proposing is this: You teach one day a week, a three-hour class. You pick the day. We'll work around you. But most importantly, I understand you are connected to the Guard. Having said that, I'd like you to liaison between the Guard and the school. What you and Cham did your senior year here, taking your first-year Wizard Guard training here—I think we should do that again. Not just for the Guard, but for law, medicine, zoology. All of it." He was nearly breathless when he stopped, sounding excited by the prospect.

"Most schools wouldn't do that. Why here?" she asked.

"Because I know you, and I know you will consider the school in this before decisions are made. You'll give us autonomy yet guidance." He smiled.

"I'd have to talk to the Wizard Council. I know they've wanted to work with the schools more closely for years. No one agreed to it."

"We will agree to it. We don't have a college system in the wizard world. I mean, law and medicine do have one of sorts. I think we waste the senior year and the first year out in the real world is mostly training that would be better completed here."

Annie replaced the tome. "We have students who work in the non-magical world too."

"You help me plan it and we'll educate them too."

She pulled herself up and walked through the seats, sitting in a middle chair across from the podium. The table was scrubbed clean, any graffiti removed and the wood re-stained. "Can I have a few days?"

"Yes. In the meantime, I had the kitchen prepare lunch. It should be in my office," he said.

Annie took one last look at the room and followed Headmaster Turtledove out for lunch.

∽

It was a surprising conversation that left Annie thinking, seriously thinking, about her future. While she had always wanted to be a wizard guard and had never thought of being anything else, her relationship with Cham opened her up to a world of possibilities she otherwise wouldn't have thought of.

Teacher.

She knocked on Cham's cubicle.

"Hey, Annie." He motioned for her to sit.

"It's personal."

Cham placed his hand on his cubicle wall and put a muffle spell around them as she sat. When the walls were shimmering in the spell, he turned back. "What's up?"

She glanced around the space. "A little overkill."

Cham shrugged. "What's up?"

"Turtledove offered me a job of sorts."

"Really?"

Annie explained the room, the supplies, the offer to teach advanced potion making. When she finished, she sat back in the chair and crossed her legs.

"Teacher? Not so far off. You do train new guards. And you do the continuing training. And you train other departments."

She held her hand up. "I got the point."

"Do you want to do this? We never talked about me taking this job. It happened. I accepted without talking to you."

"I told you yesterday, I knew it was coming. I'm good with it. Besides, this might be a good opportunity. I just thought you should know."

Cham whipped his palm out, releasing the spell. "Thanks. You're better than I am."

Annie stood up and waved as she left. Rather than heading to her cubicle, she walked to the executive branch and to Ryan's office. Only the Wizard Council could approve a new department, a new position. She thought she'd start at the top.

"Hi, Megan. Is Ryan in?" she asked his assistant.

"Hi, Annie. He is." Megan led her to his door.

"Annie! Come in," Ryan said when he saw them. He smiled as Annie sat.

"I have something... interesting to talk to you about. Not related to anything else."

He raised an eyebrow and waited for her to continue. Annie explained her conversation with the Headmaster. Ryan listened attentively until she finished.

"That is interesting," he said.

"And?"

"Fitzgerald poses it well. You'd mostly be here. I can create an education department, mostly as a liaison to assist departments in creating programs for students in their senior year. It's not a bad idea," Ryan said thoughtfully.

"It gets me out of reporting to Cham," Annie said.

He nodded in agreement. "Is this what you'd want to do?"

Annie drummed her fingers on the arm rests of her chair. "I've always wanted to be a wizard guard."

"You once told me you wouldn't do it if you had kids. Is that still true?"

Annie took a deep breath and blew it out slowly. "Yes. I won't leave them without a mom."

"You can't directly report to a spouse. The policy is clear on that."

"Kathy can never be in a department manager position because of you," Annie said thoughtfully.

"It comes with marriage."

"Cham suggested I report to someone else and retain my status as a wizard guard."

Ryan chuckled. "That definitely allows you to stay an active wizard guard. I can't make that decision for you. So again, I ask. Do you want to teach?"

"I'd be able facilitate training for multiple departments. Ensure all departments have survival training or basic medical care knowledge. There's stuff that I can do to effect change, to keep witches and wizards safe. I can see this being a good change."

As she spoke, she understood what she could do, and all of the changes for the better. It was an exciting proposition to Annie.

"I'll talk to members of the Wizard Council. We'll put it to a vote at the next meeting. You have the experience and qualifications to be a department manager. We'll see what they say," Ryan told her.

There wasn't much more he could do than that. She said goodbye and headed back to her office to catch up.

CHAPTER 4

IT WAS NEARLY five o'clock when Annie finished reviewing the last folder in her inbox. While she had made headway, there were still several cases, she needed to follow up.

She had wanted to review the Fraternitatem of Solomon grimoire and review her father's notes but was interrupted when Robin Price knocked at her cubicle door.

"What's up?" Annie said cheerfully, though she didn't feel so light and happy inside. It had been a time suck of a day, and she had little to show for her work. She closed her field pack and motioned for Robin to sit.

"I leaned on one of my contacts. He gave me a new lead. Wanna check it out?" he said when he sat.

"You know I haven't seen you in months, close to a year actually, and all you want to do is work, work, work," Annie said. She shrunk her field pack and stuck it in the hidden pocket on her waistband.

"It hasn't been a year!" Robin argued.

"Yes, it has. So where's the location?" Annie asked.

Robin rolled the scroll across the desk. Annie picked it up and straightened out the parchment; written on the scroll was a latitude and longitude.

She grimaced.

"I had to lean on him heavily for that. I think it's worth a look."

"How much do you trust this contact?" Annie asked.

"As far as I can throw him. He's… he's a vampire," Robin admitted.

Annie glanced at him with a raised eyebrow and sighed. "Meet at my house at eleven?"

"I'm there."

⁓

Annie teleported to her neighborhood by way of a cluster of trees at the end of her street. She stepped along the sidewalk and glanced at her phone. It was still early, 5:30 p.m., and the sun was bright and warm. The closer she came to her house, the more relaxed and happy she felt.

Neighbors pulled into the subdivision, rode around the block to the back alley, parking in their garages or finding empty spots outside their homes. Those already home gathered mail, watered plants, or cut the grass. It was a pleasant summer evening, which struck Annie as funny. She wondered what her neighbors would think of her father miraculously back from the dead—until she realized most of them hadn't lived here before either of her parents died.

The din from traffic several streets away hung over the neighborhood like a comfortable blanket, the sound of laughter and music from various houses was familiar and easy. Stopping briefly, she turned and scanned both sides of the street before continuing home. As she passed Mrs. Wexler's house, she waved to the older woman, who was pulling mail from the mailbox and sorting each piece.

"Hey, Mrs. Wexler. How's it going?" Annie asked.

"I'm good, Annie dear. You look like you're working too hard again," Mrs. Wexler said.

Annie chuckled. "Not really. Have a good night." Annie walked up her front sidewalk and entered her porch.

The door was opened a crack. She glanced at the handle and lock. It hadn't been forcibly open, but she hesitated anyway and stood beside the door to eavesdrop. She heard two voices speaking softly.

Zola!

She ran inside to see Zola and her father at the kitchen table. Zola looked tired, her cream skin smudged with dirt, her lip split, dried blood covering her bottom lip.

"What the hell happened?" Annie shouted as she reached Zola.

"I was followed and someone nabbed me. It took a little time to escape his grasp," Zola explained.

Annie grimaced and bit her lip as she thought.

"What is it, sweetie?" Jason asked.

"I feel like I'm being followed or someone is watching me. I'm not surprised you'd be too, but I am surprised they tried to take you," Annie said. She glanced at Jason, whose jaw clenched tightly. "Dad?"

"If they were after Zola, it might be because they took your mom to weaken you. I'm not surprised they'd take your Aloja fairy. She can find you easily, she can heal you. Without Zola, you would be weaker and easier to get at," Jason said.

"Did they take you someplace? I was worried when you didn't come home," Annie said.

Zola shook her head. Her hands were shaking. "I went to my ancient fairy home in the mountains. Someone knew where the Aloja Fairies live and how to get there. I barely got away."

"Why did you go back there? I thought you already made a deal for my life," Annie said. She hadn't meant to be blunt; it just came out.

Zola looked at her incredulously. The wrinkle in her forehead deepened, and she shook her head. "I didn't..." She glanced at Annie, unable to lie, and said, "I was going back there to make sure your lifeline was still long."

"And?" Jason asked.

"It's still long and very strong." Zola looked at her long, thin fingers.

Annie observed Zola carefully. Not only did the temporary gray irises tell Annie that Zola was emotional; the fairy's inability to contradict her theory told her she was correct. Annie sat beside her friend and took her hands.

"The charm you gave me wouldn't have saved my life, not completely. And I won't ask what deal you made to save my life."

"Thank you. It puts me in a difficult position, choosing between my family in the mountains or my charge. I love you. That's all you need to know."

Annie felt a pang of heartbreak and feared Zola gave up something considerable. She chose her words carefully. "I will always appreciate what you did to bring me home, whatever that was. But I need you to be careful. If Dad's correct, they might be trying to take out my inner circle. I can't lose you too."

"We'll stop them," Jason said.

Annie shook her head. "The Fraternitatem had eleven hundred years to plan this. Your files and their grimoire tell me nothing new, no way to stop them."

"I'm pretty sure I know the answer to this, but have you looked for your mom?" Jason asked.

Annie glanced at Jason, not surprised by his question. Of all the people who knew her, he'd be the one to know that she would have started to look for Emily. "As soon as I found the pictures, I asked the computer expert at Wizard Hall, Bucky Hart, to search for Emily. Even with his impeccable skills, we're dealing with the Fraternitatem and he's been unable to find her," she said.

"That doesn't surprise me. I'm sure they figured you'd go looking. They'll hide her until she's ready to come for you," Jason said.

Annie looked at an injured Zola and a worried father. Her own anxiety increased, and the magic continued to bubble under her skin until the itching became unbearable and the world around her spun quickly. She wanted to run and to be free of them, of all of this. Annie pushed herself from the table, pushing the chair with such force, it bounced against the table.

Jason jumped. "Annie?"

Annie walked to the den window that faced the forest and looked inside the trees. For weeks, it had felt like she was being watched. Her breathing became faster and shallow; she couldn't catch her breath or take in oxygen. It terrified her. Jason put his hand on her shoulder.

"Slow breaths."

Annie nodded. "They've been watching me and probably everyone I know, learning how to get to me." She practiced her breaths. "No matter how much research I do, they're still going to come, and they're going to kill me!" Her voice growing high with fear, Annie made a fist and opened her hand; bright, white magic flew from her palms, blowing behind her into the kitchen. It sped across the kitchen table, splintering the thick, wooden tabletop into two halves. Annie, Zola, and Jason watched with their jaws open as each half of the table fell sideways and crashed on the floor.

"Crap!" Annie shouted as she glanced at her table and then her palms, which were covered in large scorch marks. "I love that table."

"What the hell was that?" Jason asked.

Annie held her hands out. A white mist trailed from her palms and billowed upwards as if the magic was leaking from her body. "This isn't MY magic coming out, is it?" she cried out with a wave of panic. She closed her fists, but the magic continued to escape through the cracks of her fists. Her anxiety grew and her chest tightened. Magic hung in the air around her, buzzing and humming as if alive. Jason and Zola stared helplessly.

"Annie?" Jason took her hands. "Are you hurting?"

She shook her head.

The white mist sparkled and rose to the ceiling. "What the hell?" Cham asked, entering the kitchen and racing to Annie. "What happened?"

Through shallow breaths, she explained her anger, the table, the magic. Cham glanced at table laying in two halves and then at her hands. He summoned his crystal and ran it across the magic that escaped from her palms. She hyperventilated as he glanced inside the rock.

"I recognize your signature. This is not yours. It's... it must be the new powers," Cham said.

Annie glanced at her hands, at the magic billowing from her palms. "I still don't know what this magic is. What powers I possess," Annie admitted. She glanced at Jason. "What did they tell you?"

"The prophecy wasn't specific. You know that. You conjured me and made me corporeal. We know that has to be the powers. Has anything else happened to you?"

Annie watched the magic stream from her palms, slowly dissipating, leaving behind scorch marks at the center of her palms.

"I thought I was having prophetic dreams."

"That might be one of the powers. Look at the table. The magic is stronger. Wilder," he noted.

"What do they want with them? What could the powers possibly have that makes them want to kill me for it?"

"Conjuring the dead is a pretty powerful magic. Only the Fates can control life or death," Zola said.

"Necromancers?" Annie asked.

"They animate the dead, much like creating zombies. It's not the same," Jason added.

"Do you know what other powers I have?" Annie stared at Zola, her lips tightly pursed as the magic floated about her head.

"Like your dad said, the prophecy wasn't specific. I'm not sure who would know for certain as you've just received them. I've only heard rumors. Impossible-to-believe rumors of you controlling the elements." Zola chuckled.

"You're right. No one would really know what the magic is. I haven't discovered it yet and there's nothing written." Annie smiled. "I wonder if Sturtagaard lied to the Fraternitatem about how powerful the magic would be."

"To bargain for his life, I'm sure he would've done that," Jason said.

"Awesome. He charmed them with lies and now my life is in danger. Damn vampire." Annie scratched at her arms, grimacing at the pain in her palms.

Cham reached for her hand, turned it over, and stared at the scorch mark at the center of both palms. He summoned a water bottle, floated the water above the burn mark, and healed it gently before repeating the process on the other hand. "How's the itching?"

Annie made a fist and released it, watching the magic burst from her palms. She repeated the process several times until the magic seemed to lessen. "Still there, but not as bad," she admitted as she looked at her newly healed palms.

"Maybe you need to work the magic out. Like repetitive spells, strong magic, fireballs. The magic could be building up," Cham suggested.

"I guess I can go to the lab and use that space." Annie sighed. She glanced at her hands. The scorch marks were gone. "I should fix the table," she said, standing.

"I'll fix it. You rest up," Cham offered.

Annie shook her head. "No. I think I'm done resting. After they came for Zola, there's no more waiting for Emily to come for me." She marched back to the kitchen and stared at the table.

Cham rested his hand on her shoulder. She resisted the urge to move it away. "Bucky is looking for her and you're learning about the Fraternitatem. We will take control of this situation," he said.

"And how's that going?" She took a deep breath. "Sorry. I just need to find her. I don't want any surprises."

Cham wrapped his arms around her. "I expect nothing less from you because I know how you work. Just be careful and tell us what you need. Please."

Annie nodded. She looked at Zola, at her dad. "I promise. No going off on my own. I'll keep safe."

"Then we should eat, I'll make a sleeping potion, and we'll call it a night," Cham offered.

"As great as that sounds, I'm going with Robin tonight. He thinks he has a really good lead on the market," Annie told him.

"Well then, you need to eat," Zola said as Jason and Cham magically repaired the table.

⚜

Annie and Robin landed at the edge of a swamp in Southern Louisiana. The air was heavy, moist, and sticky, hanging over the land like a moldy, stale blanket. Immediately after landing, a swarm of mosquitos descended on them. Annie feverishly swatted them away.

"This is awesome," Annie said as she smacked the mosquito biting her cheek.

"Sorry. It could have waited," Robin said, wiping bugs from his hair.

"Eh. It's the job." They listened carefully, and when they were certain they were alone, Annie turned on her flashlight and scanned the grasses and trees for unwelcome wildlife or someone they may have missed. "Baddies are getting wickedly clever. This location sucks," Annie grumbled. Twigs cracked and water sloshed. Annie turned in her spot, her flashlight highlighting enough to tell her they were still alone.

Robin looked into the trees. "Is there anything out there?"

"Nothing," she said.

While Annie continued to act as a lookout, Robin reviewed the map. "Sorry, but it's only going to get worse. We have to walk through the water to reach the portal. You sure you're okay?"

Annie highlighted their watery path hoping to find the portal magic hanging in the air. From her angle, she couldn't see anything unusual and grimaced as she took a step into the cold water that seeped up her legs.

"Yeah, yeah. I'm fine. For this, you need to tell me the name of your contact. I'd love to thank him." Annie was merely making conversation, taking her mind off of the fact she was in a swamp and not particularly fond of high water.

Robin groaned as he stepped into the water. "You really want me to squeal?"

"I know the game, but it could prove helpful." Those with contacts around the markets were careful to not release their names as being a snitch could be dangerous for them or their associates.

"Don't tell him I've said anything. It's Godfrey and he lives somewhere in the ninth district in New Orleans," Robin said. "He is a vampire, so maybe I should have distrusted his help."

Annie held her hands out, feeling for changes in the air; all she found were mosquitos biting away at her hand. "Don't worry about it. The council really wants to find the black market. It's still a priority, though not at the expense of our other duties," Annie reiterated.

Annie made a fist and released it; small sparks of magic popped from her palm. It was only when she remembered the magic that she felt it boiling up inside her, making the itching unbearable. She scratched at her belly for relief and took another step in the muddy water.

"A good way to keep out the riffraff," Robin joked.

"In this scenario, I'm the riffraff." Annie chuckled.

Robin held his crystal as it searched for the magic. When it glowed dark purple, he glanced inside the rock and showed Annie. "We're here," he said.

Annie read the magic trace.

Dark magic.

Annie illuminated the air space. The hazy anomaly hung beside them. She reached out, though the portal chilled her arm. "Here it is. Godfrey wasn't lying about the portal. Let's see what's inside," she said and summoned her cursed athame, a knife magically imbued with a black magic, to open the portal.

"This could be *the* black market," Robin said.

Annie shrugged and looked at her knife in the light. "How sure are you he's not setting us up in a trap?" she asked. She could feel the chill from the portal.

"You mean the vampire?"

They glanced at each other and then to the portal. Footsteps sloshed through the wet earth. "I think someone's coming," Annie whispered. She shut off her flashlight and climbed up to dry land, hiding behind a tree.

A tall, lanky creature came through the trees, glanced around his location, and stepped into the water. He took out his knife, but just as he was going to plunge it into the portal, he paused and sniffed the air.

Annie recognized the profile, the glowing white skin in the moonlight. "Damn!" She slid from behind the tree. "What the hell are you doing here?" she asked Sturtagaard.

She hadn't seen the vampire since she returned to the present. Everyone, even Annie, had believed she was going to stake Sturtagaard when she returned, but she hadn't. Robin warned her before she left not to let Sturtagaard's knowledge taint her judgment. It had, and she hadn't killed him yet as a result.

He got me again.

"I'm following a lead. And you?" the vampire inquired. He offered an amused smirk. Annie knew he was trying to piss her off.

"Is this the market you claimed to know the location of?" Annie asked.

He pursed his lips and smiled. "You haven't gone in yet then?"

"Deciding if it's a trap. Vampires aren't known to be trustworthy," Annie commented. "So, why the hell are you here?"

"Like I said, this is a lead. As much as I'd like you to finally stake me and put me out of my misery, you won't until you know where it is," Sturtagaard said.

Annie knew he'd drag it out as long as he could. Once he helped find the market, he'd find something else to bargain for his life.

I should have killed him when I got home. But I didn't.

Seeing his family in the past had given Annie an insight to the vampire she hadn't had before. While she still hated the him, she now had some sympathy for the former husband and father who watched his family die. While she carried that sympathy back to the present with her, she realized staking him wouldn't change the past. Her family was irreparably changed; the die was cast, and the story was being unfolded.

Until she saw Sturtagaard outside the portal. Now she felt confused and had difficulty reconciling her sympathy and hatred.

Reluctantly, she motioned for Sturtagaard to open the portal and waited patiently as he slid his cursed athame into the magic. Air whirled violently, lightning sparked, and static popped. Sturtagaard shrugged and stepped one foot into the portal.

"You coming?" he asked.

Annie stepped beside him and looked inside. It was unlike the original market in that the original market had been roughly fifty acres of booths and animal corrals with a large dungeon and elf dormitory beneath the circular market, which had been shaped like a wheel with spokes.

This market was much smaller and consisted of five aisles parallel to each other. The booths were thinner; three booths were squeezed into the same space that would have been occupied by one in the original market. Cautiously, Annie stepped inside, taking in the entire market. For her, this market was more familiar than the last two they'd visited, right down to the stench of dung and burnt flesh. She shuddered, thinking this could be what they were after.

"You coming?" Sturtagaard asked.

She glanced at him with a confused expression. "You want me to see what you're up to?"

"No, but the sooner I hand you the market, the sooner I'll be free of you," he jeered.

"I'm sorry your family died and I'm sorry that caused you to destroy mine. But you playing the martyr doesn't inspire me to kill you. I'd just as soon let you wallow in your pain long after I'm dead."

Annie and Robin exchanged glances; Robin bit his lip to keep from laughing. Sturtagaard stormed off to the left, past a booth filled with several large baskets holding a variety of large eggs. At first look, Annie thought they were ostrich eggs. As she followed the vampire, she noticed the purple and green striations throughout the shell.

Dragon eggs. It's not the time to raid the place.

The outer passage contained four booths busy with customers, selling nothing of consequence to Annie's quick glances. She assumed they'd be stopping at one of the booths, but Sturtagaard had a specific location to which he was searching.

As they passed the final booth at the end of the aisle, Annie stopped short. Sitting inside was a man named Joseph, whom Annie had met while investigating the murder of Princess Amelie almost a year ago. He saw Annie and smiled.

"Give me a second," Annie said to Robin and Sturtagaard as she turned to Joseph's booth.

"Hi Joseph," she said.

He looked at her and offered a large, wide smile. "Annie Pearce. What a surprise," he said.

She glanced inside his booth, which was far different than the one he'd kept at the original market. While that one was a hodgepodge of magical junk in various sized piles, this one was well organized. Shelves lined three sides of his tent, filled with items neatly housed in several baskets. Even the table separating the pair was neat and clean. She could easily tell he was selling herbs and potions, but to her trained eye, nothing appeared illegal or seemed like items that were normally sold at the market. "You've changed how you do business, I see. Selling anything I should be worried about?" she inquired.

He offered a hardy laugh. He was a different man than the first time they met. He no longer seemed fearful of the Wizard Guard questioning him. He waved her across the barrier.

In the corner, he held an index finger across his lips, looked toward the entrance of his tent and then back to Annie.

"There's much I did not tell you the last time we met," he said in a low yet booming voice.

"I gathered something was up," Annie admitted.

Hearing footsteps come to the edge of the tent, she turned. "It's okay, give me a sec," she said to Robin, who discretely moved away.

"Okay, what's up?" she asked, looking back at Joseph.

She watched Joseph hold his hand on his tent wall, applying a muffle spell. It flew from his hand and whipped around the canvas walls, keeping their conversation private. When he finished, he tossed a spell into a locked box; a drawer sprung open. He reached inside, pulled out what looked to be a law enforcement wallet, and passed it to Annie. She opened it, revealing his wizard guard ID in the name Joseph Agrante, wizard guard level one.

He's too old to be first level...

She glanced at the other side of his wallet and saw a shield stating he was from the Wizard Guard, South Africa. She looked at him.

"I estimate you're about forty-five or fifty years old. You're too old to still be a level one. When did this happen?" she asked, handing back his identification.

He chuckled as he tossed the ID back in the drawer, slamming it shut. "Well, Annie Pearce. When I first met you, I was in the black market as an informant to the South African Wizard Guard. They pulled me from the market before it fell. After that, they felt I had something to offer and trained me as a guard, and here I am." He opened his arms wide and welcoming, and laughed again.

"Well, congrats. So you're back at this market. I'll leave so I don't draw attention to you." She nodded once.

He grabbed her arm. "Actually, Annie Pearce, I am here because of you."

She frowned. When she returned to the present, the United States Wizard Guard had sent word to all of the Wizard Guard units across the world, explaining about the Fraternitatem and what it was planning on doing with Annie's powers. She looked at Joseph. "How much do you know?"

"I know that you met the Fraternitatem of Solomon in March. You quite possibly know more than anyone about where they are, who they are, and what they look like. We are also aware that you went to the past to fight the demons and were rewarded with a power. How am I doing so far?" He chuckled again.

"You're right on. We've been letting all wizard guards in on what happened," she said.

Joseph sat on the edge of his wood desk and folded his hands. "Exactly. All Wizard Guard units are mobilizing the best we can. While we're not as big as you in the States, we are trying to find as many of the markets as we can. We found this one, and I've been working here, learning as much information as I can."

Annie glanced around the tent. His training appeared to be helping.

"What's the biggest thing you've discovered?" she asked.

"Nothing specific. But it's a new market system. There are rumblings of different factions wanting control and the Fraternitatem of Solomon wants your power..." he shrugged.

"To be honest with you, I'm not exactly sure what this power can do. I don't know how it's different than the magic I was born with."

Joseph looked at her. The magic slowly trickled from her palms. "I'm rather surprised you hadn't researched that." He pointed to the magic rising from her hands.

Annie glanced down before matching his gaze. "You're right. Though, I've only been back a few weeks and they've been rather hectic."

"So have you learned of any new powers since you've been back? Anything out of the ordinary?"

Annie chuckled.

I can't tell him all the truth.

"Yeah. I conjured a ghost and turned him corporeal without knowing how I did it."

Joseph offered a serious stare. "That's major power. You do you know what the Fraternitatem could do with that?"

Annie looked at him questioningly and then shuddered. "Raise an army of the dead." Wolfgange Rathbone tried to raise an army of zombies in an attempt to gain control of the U.S. Wizard Council. It had been a slow process for him because reanimating the dead was tricky. The spells were complicated and you needed to have the necessary numbers of dead bodies. In contrast, Annie had easily conjured Jason. She'd simply whipped her hand across his ethereal form and he became corporeal.

"If they had the numbers, they could surely control the market," Joseph said.

"He who controls the market could in effect control the whole wizard world." Annie glanced through the tent flaps and saw both the vampire and Robin watching her. She held up her finger to signal one more minute. "That doesn't leave me with a good feeling."

"Well, I'm sure, Annie Pearce, you will learn in time what powers you have. It has to be written somewhere. In the meantime, you should go. I can't have the Wizard Guard hassling me." He chuckled and pointed to Sturtagaard and Robin.

Annie handed him her phone number. "Welcome to our side," she said. "I'll admit, I'm not sure why the vampire dragged us here." She smiled, shook his hand, and returned to following Sturtagaard down the passageway.

⁓

Sturtagaard closely reviewed each glyph along the perimeter wall as if he were searching for something in particular. He punched the wall and grumbled to himself as he moved to the next section. While he anxiously searched the graffiti, Annie and Robin took pictures of the glyphs until they met back where they started. They observed Sturtagaard for a moment and glanced at each other.

"Is he losing it?" Robin asked.

Annie shrugged and found Sturtagaard tapping the wall. "What the hell are we doing here?" she asked impatiently.

"The portal is here somewhere," Sturtagaard announced.

Annie looked at the vampire incredulously. "You're losing your touch. These glyphs are in all of the markets," she said.

"My contact promised there was a portal to the main market in this market. These pictures lead to it," Sturtagaard said.

"Dumb shit. If the market is hidden, why the hell would the portal be out in the open?" Annie asked.

"Then where is it?" Sturtagaard shouted, drawing attention to them.

Annie glared at him before glancing around the market.

"Well?" Sturtagaard snapped.

"Oh, shut up," Annie said as she scanned the walls.

"I doubt there will be any in the booths." Robin followed Annie's gaze. "The outbuildings?"

Annie and Robin walked to a storage building in the far corner, a five-foot-by-five-foot shed tucked so closely into the corner that there was only room for one body in the space. They shimmied their way around the structure, scraping against the steel wall. "Do you feel a portal?" Annie asked as she turned the corner, exposing them to the market.

"No. I'm just hot and cramped," Robin groused.

"And Godfrey was positive it's here?" Annie asked.

"Just as sure as Sturtagaard is." Robin faced the back wall. "There's enough room to open a portal." Robin poked against the back wall searching for an anomaly. "I don't feel it though."

Sturtagaard came to them. "Is it here?"

"No chill or magic anomaly," Annie said.

Sturtagaard pushed her aside and searched the wall himself, falling to his knees. "My contact said this was the location of the portal to the market. It was drawn on the walls. Are you going to help look for it or just stand there like an idiot?"

"Did your contact tell you what to look for? I see lots of glyphs here," Annie said.

"You're so fucking smart, figure it out!" Sturtagaard jeered.

"Get out! Now!" Annie pulled the vampire up and yanked him from the narrow space and tossed him on the ground. He sneered as he watched them work.

Annie and Robin used their crystal high and low as they searched for magic. With no magic, their crystals remained dull. "Okay. Where the hell is it?" she asked.

"And that's the conundrum, I would say." Sturtagaard smirked as if it were a joke and stood to face Annie.

"You want me to punch you, don't you?" she said. Behind her, Robin chuckled lightly.

"Not so smart, are you?" Sturtagaard said.

Annie leaned against the storage unit and stared at the pictures, noticing two of the same.

What does this mean?

She stared again and found a third glyph like the other two. "See this picture. It's here… and here," Annie said as she pointed to the three.

"Maybe there's a pattern," Robin suggested.

They searched for multiple glyphs, attempting to find any patterns. Robin summoned a thick piece of chalk and began to mark the first picture, which appeared to be a dove. Four of them were randomly scattered across the wall.

"No pattern," Robin said as he erased the marks and tried again with a picture of a triangle. Again, no pattern emerged. Robin and Annie tried several more glyphs, none of which formed a pattern that piqued their interest. They moved on to a picture of a square with a dot at the center. After finding three additional pictures, they discovered the four glyphs formed a perfect square.

"And that's a pattern," Annie said as she snapped a picture of the wall.

"What is that? A square with a dot at the center?" Robin moved closer but saw nothing of consequence in any of the pictures.

"I'm not sure what that is." Annie reviewed all glyphs inside the supposed square. The steel was cold and lacked magic of any kind. "I still don't see or feel a portal," she said.

"It's got to be here, somewhere between these symbols. Only a limited number of people know how to enter," Sturtagaard said with a self-satisfied smile.

Annie rolled her eyes. "You're such an ass. I wish I'd staked you when I came home," she said.

"So you keep saying," Sturtagaard said as he slunk away.

CHAPTER 5

WARM, SOAPY WATER slid down Annie's body and pooled at her feet, removing the stench of the swamp and market. She closed her eyes and dunked under the water, washing away thoughts of Sturtagaard and symbols and black markets. As the water pelted her, the magic drifted from her palms and hung around her head. Annie swatted at it, watching it dissipate.

An army of the dead.

She shuddered in the warm water as she tried to wash away that sinking feeling of danger, of what the Fraternitatem of Solomon could do with her power.

The bathroom door squeaked opened. "Hey, baby," Cham said as he sat on the toilet beside the shower and held a towel for her. "How was tonight's search?"

"Open my phone and check the last picture." Annie went back under the water to rinse off.

"What is it?" he asked.

"Not sure. I sent it to Bucky. Hopefully, he'll can tell me something about the glyph." She shut off the water and stepped outside, shivering and covering herself with the towel. "By the way, Sturtagaard was there. He claims the portal to *the* market is somewhere in that smaller one." She used the towel and wiped off the water, before wrapping it around her hair.

"Okay, that's a little distracting." Cham smiled.

She shrugged and pulled on a T-shirt hanging from a hook on the back of the door.

"Any humming, buzzing, popping?" Cham swiped through the pictures on her phone and followed her to the bed.

"Nothing. The portal to the small market was in the water at the edge of a swamp. Sturtagaard thinks he knows the portal is related to the glyphs on the walls." Annie climbed under the covers while Cham stared at the picture of the four symbols that created a square on the wall.

He dropped the phone and kissed her, soft and slow, cupping the back of her head. "So nothing conclusive?" he asked when he pulled away.

"What do you expect from a bunch of vampires." She sat up and dried her hair with a spell, leaving wild curls. When she finished, she lay on her pillow and pulled the covers to her chin to warm up.

"How's it going with your dad?" Cham asked.

Annie grimaced and said nothing.

"He wants to bond with you. You're throwing up brick walls." Cham wrapped an arm around her.

The tension he referred to and his body heat made Annie's skin burn as the magic traveled through her body; she threw off the covers and sat up.

"I told him it was hard enough to live through his death the first time. He's a ghost in a time not his. If I get close to him and watch him leave again, I'm not sure I can handle that. Again." Annie raised her legs and set her head on knees. "It's really hard."

"I'm the messenger only. I see his point, though."

Annie glanced at him.

"Baby. How many people get a second chance to be with their dead loved ones? Even if it's only for a short time."

Annie reached for his hand. "Would you want see your grandpa again? You had a tough time at his funeral."

"But I had a great life with him. He died too soon, and I'd love to spend an afternoon fishing with him and telling him about you. He's the only one who really thought I should be a wizard guard. I'd definitely do it, if I could."

Annie gave him a gentle kiss on his lips and placed her hand on his cheek. "Point taken." She wrapped herself in the blanket and yawned.

"Get some sleep. It's been a long day."

"Thanks," she murmured. She slid to her back and closed her eyes. "I almost forgot. Joseph from the market. He's back. And he's a level one from South Africa."

Cham chuckled. "I remember him. He didn't seem to know much when we knew him. And it's real?"

Annie nodded. "As far as I can tell he's legit. Wizard guards are heeding our message and mobilizing across the planet. He implied the Fraternitatem is going to use my magic to make play for the market."

"No one group has ever owned or run the market. That could be really bad for the magical world," Cham said.

"I thought so too." Annie yawned again.

"Since you found the symbol, can you pass it on to the team and see if anyone has seen it? We may need to backtrack at the markets we've already investigated."

"Robin said most teams took pictures of the glyphs. He's going to have Bucky search them for the symbols. I'll ask around tomorrow."

Despite how hot her skin was against his, he remained beside her. She closed her eyes, took in his scent, and drifted to sleep.

When the bubbling and itching woke Annie, the sun was still below the horizon. As Cham lay sleeping, she shuffled herself out of bed and curled in the corner of the sofa in the den. She pulled her family's Book of Shadows toward her. The large tome contained all the spells, creatures, potions, and magic that the Pearce family had come across over many lifetimes. It was passed to her through her father and his mother before him. As often as Annie spent reading the passages, she recently discovered that her study hadn't been as thorough as she believed it was. Many of the spells, stories, and entries in the book had been placed there by a long-ago ancestor named Bega. She was the same girl who had helped Annie in ancient England. Some of the potions Annie remembered using in England. She chuckled over Bega's notations in the book.

Annie touched the ancient ink and turned the page as she sipped her coffee.

"You're up early."

Even after three weeks, Jason Pearce's voice made Annie's heart stop in surprise and anxiety. She glanced at her phone; it was five thirty in the morning, almost time to get ready for work. She took another sip of coffee. "Morning, dad. There's coffee in the machine."

"I saw Sami and John last night after you left," Jason said while pouring his coffee. His footsteps were heavy against the wood as he entered the den and sat beside her. He glanced at the Book of Shadows. "Damn that book got thick."

Annie smiled and turned to the first page. "I met her. In England. Bega and Svenson." She showed Jason the first entry.

"I never noticed that before," Jason said.

"The magical book is a little more fluid than I thought. After my trip, some things changed, I think," Annie said. Some magical objects weren't easily controlled, including a family's Book of Shadows. Those items often changed, as family experiences changed whether they knew it or not. Annie returned to the last passage she reviewed.

"Whatcha' looking for?" Jason moved closer to the book. Annie passed him the picture of the glyph she found in the market and explained what they thought it was.

"I've never seen this. I'm guessing it's not in the book," he offered.

"How do you know Great-Grandma never saw this?" She chuckled and passed him the book. "Be useful. I'll make breakfast."

Annie was a potion master, an expert rank of someone who had completed extensive study and performed well on a difficult test. She had an affinity for mixing ingredients and often times used that skill to cook. Today she thought she'd try omelets. She pulled the ingredients from the fridge, lay them out like she was preparing a potion. Gently she blended the eggs, adding salt and pepper and a bit of garlic. She poured the mixture slowly and stirred until fluffy. She folded in the gruyère cheese and mushrooms.

"That smells good," Jason said. He sat at the table and returned to the book, perusing and snooping through the pages as he learned what Annie had done over the years.

"Thanks. I actually like cooking," she said as she scraped the eggs onto a large platter and carried it to the table. "I have toast coming," she advised, popping several slices in the toaster.

"Where'd you learn to cook?" he asked as he took a bite.

"I'm a potion master. It's the same principal." She took her own bite of eggs. "Anything in there?"

"No. Great-Grandma never saw that symbol. I'd be happy to research it for you at the library," he offered.

"I have Bucky searching for it. Though the internet might not have an ancient magical symbol listed." She closed the Book of Shadows and slid it across the table.

"I just want to get to know you while I'm here."

Annie held her breath and let it out slowly.

I explained this to him.

"I know. Cham presented me with two options. I'm trying to open myself up to you."

"You conjured me," he reminded her.

She took one last bite of eggs and started on a slice of toast. "I can't be held responsible for the magic I perform in my sleep." She winked.

Jason laughed. "You need me to keep you safe and I need you to let me," he said.

Annie knew she had called for him because she was afraid of Emily, of the Fraternitatem. She needed him here.

"Just remember, I'm twenty-four years old. I can take care of myself," Annie said firmly.

"Fair enough." He placed the last bite of eggs on his toast and took a bite. "It's good."

"I know."

❧

Though Jason promised he would remain hidden while living at Annie's house, he quickly grew bored. He longed to get out and be useful in keeping his daughters safe. When it came down to it, he essentially begged both Cham and Milo to be allowed to work.

Originally, Milo was dead set against it, worried that Jason being here would upset the magical balance. What they came to realize was that, as a corporeal ghost, he didn't need to breathe, or eat, and he didn't produce any magical energy. Milo finally relented, and ideas were thrown around on how to keep Jason hidden outside of Wizard Hall and out of the sight of the Fraternitatem, who watched Annie carefully.

Ryan, preferring to keep his government transparent, held a mandatory, secret meeting of the Wizard Council, where he informed them that Jason Pearce had returned as a corporeal ghost and was going to work at Wizard Hall on cases. It went as well as Ryan could expect. There was several witches and wizards who had reservations, who worried about Annie's safety, and who refused to vote in favor.

In the end, it was agreed upon with stipulations.

First, Jason was not to walk the neighborhood around the house. There were no exceptions to the rule. Second, he could teleport from the house to Wizard Hall without a disguise. Any other wizard location required one. Third, he was given a new name, Michael Shine, so that employee records could be forged in the computer system and identification issued. No one really believed the Fraternitatem could hack into the system, but they took the precautions just in case. The final stipulation was that Jason's presence would be known as needed, which primarily extended to managers and above, as well as any employee that would be working with him. Jason agreed without complaint.

Jason glanced at his wizard guard ID. "Is this really necessary?" he asked Annie as he stood inside her cubicle.

"Dad, seriously. You know all cases have to be documented. Technically, you're dead. Can't document it as Jason Pearce," Annie said pragmatically. "And that name isn't one you used before. We checked."

"Fine." He sat in her guest chair and put his legs on her desk. "I really can't go back to my old life. I gotta say, though, it was great seeing Bertha again. She looked like she saw a ghost when I showed up."

Annie chuckled. "You're such a dork."

Jason flashed a smiled. "So, what are we doing next?" Jason asked.

Annie took what Cham has said to heart, that she needed to try with her father and include him in her life. She'd let him shadow her for now, until they could get him into his own investigation. She glanced at him. "Bucky Hart sent me a text. He's got something. We'll see him first. Oh, and this." Annie summoned a phone. "I programed everyone's number into this. I wasn't sure if you wanted something more substantial. It's a burner phone, so it should make it hard for anyone to find you. You'll be able to call and text." She handed it to him.

"Thanks. This will help." He turned on the phone and stared at the screen. He sighed. "I'll need to play around with this. Not sure how much has changed." He pocketed the phone.

"Ready?" Jason followed Annie through the passageways of Wizard Hall. She led him downstairs to the basement and the telecommunications department, where Bucky was waiting for them.

"Some things are exactly the same. Other things, I'm not sure I'll get used to," Jason admitted as they entered.

"You'll love what Bucky can do," Annie said.

Jason followed his daughter to the back end of the department. He watched in fascination as packages were received through magical tubes, landing in large wheeled containers. His jaw hung open as employees quickly typed on small laptops, scanned police radios, magically used nonmagical office equipment, sent emails, and floated notes back and forth. Annie gently tugged his sleeve to have him follow to Bucky's cubicle.

"Sorry. It's changed," he said as Annie knocked on Bucky's cubicle wall.

"No worries." She smiled first to him and then to Bucky. Bucky nodded, placed his hand on the wall, and cast a muffle spell.

"The family Pearce. I'm honored," Bucky said as he quickly cleared two chairs of stacks of files and loose papers.

"I was surprised to get a text so soon," Annie admitted as she sat beside Bucky and introduced him to her father. After shaking hands, Jason stood beside Annie in awe as Bucky pulled up several screens on all three of his monitors.

"Well, I found something interesting in the symbol I wanted to show you immediately," Bucky told them. On one screen, he enlarged the single image first showing the rectangle with the circle at the center. He continued to zoom in until they could clearly see a dot at the center. Jason moved closer to the screen as Bucky continued to enlarge the picture.

"That looks like chain links. What is it?" Annie asked.

"Glad you asked. I searched and found what I think is a Solomon's knot," Bucky said.

Annie sat back in the chair. "A Solomon's knot. Coincidental?"

"If you believe in coincidences," Bucky said. Annie shrugged. "I uploaded all the pictures from you and the other wizard guards and scanned them. I've been searching for all of these square, circle, Solomon's knot combos to see if they form a pattern or if they're random. While all of the pictures contain the glyph, none of them appeared to be placed in any pattern, that I could discern."

"That's a lot of glyphs on a lot of walls. How are you sure there aren't any other patterns?" Jason asked.

"I'm running a computer program that will find that glyph in a clear pattern. If there is one, the computer will find it. So far, nothing." Bucky pointed to the top computer screen. Annie and Jason watched for a moment as the program searched one picture and looked for patterns. When none were discovered, the computer searched another glyph and repeated the process.

"Okay. If this is the only location where multiple glyphs form a pattern, there might be something there," Annie said.

"Did you find the telltale portal sign?" Bucky asked.

Annie sighed. "Not yet. We were hoping the glyphs meant something."

"If this is how they're hiding the market now, anything's possible," Bucky said.

Annie grimaced.

Jason stepped closer to the screen, reviewing the Solomon's knot. "Can I take the leap and assume that if this a Solomon's knot, that indicates a connection to the Fraternitatem?" Jason asked.

"Have you ever believed in coincidence?" Annie asked.

"No. And it sounds like you don't either."

"No. It scares me knowing they might already have control," Annie said.

"I don't think they do yet. They probably have their hands in how the market will be shaped. If they had control, you would feel it already. Those small markets, Archibald Mortimer, the other Wizard Guard units.

They need your power for an all-out take over," Jason reassured her. Annie wasn't convinced.

"Thanks, Bucky. That's definitely interesting," Annie said.

"About the other thing you asked…" he stopped and glanced at Annie.

"Is there anything on Emily?" Annie asked.

"I still haven't found her per se. But an Emily King earned a degree in archaeology at Tel Aviv University. The reason I mention it is that she's the same age as Emily Pearce and it's the same degree as Dr. Arden Blakely. Is King a name you have a connection to?" Bucky asked.

Annie looked at Jason.

"No. It's not in my family and I don't believe it's in hers either. She could have gotten married. Maybe there's a marriage license of an Emily to someone with the last name King," Jason suggested.

"I made some assumptions. I'll have to rethink those. I'll look for that. I do think she's been living in the Middle East though," Bucky said.

Annie blew out stale air. "Thanks. I think you're right. We'll let you get back to work." Bucky handed her a folder complete with copies of all pictures. They said goodbye and Annie led Jason out of the telecommunications department to the library.

"Mrs. Cuttlebrink for research?" Jason asked as they entered the large basement room.

"Just curious," Annie said.

It was the first time she had been to the library since returning home. She stared at the doors and touched the carving of herself. "I saw these doors hanging on a Viking longhouse in Jorvik. There were only a few carvings; most of this hadn't happened yet."

Jason touched her shoulder. "My brilliant girl. You can see all that you saved, right here," he said.

"I'm still trying to comprehend it all." She let go of the carvings and entered the empty library. Hearing nothing in the stacks, she walked to the office, where she found the librarian reading a thick tome.

"Annie, dear. How can I help…" Though Mrs. Cuttlebrink knew Jason was back from the dead, she hadn't seen him. She held her breath as she stared at her old friend, taking in his young face, his hair, his eyes. "Jason. Welcome back," she said breathlessly.

"It's good to see you, Sabrina." The two friends came together in a hug.

When they separated, Mrs. Cuttlebrink said, "I heard, but I couldn't believe it. I'm so glad to see you." She was a bit teary eyed as she offered them seats.

"So, Annie, Jason, how can I help you?" she finally asked.

Annie passed her the picture of the square, circle, and the Solomon's knot and explained what they learned from Bucky.

The librarian stared at the picture. "I can say I've never seen this particular combination before. Just from researching so many cases over the years, I know the square has been used as a symbol over the course of human history. Things like, community, integrity, structure, balance. It can represent north, south, east, and west as well."

"I wonder if it's like a map to tell us where the portals to *the* market are," Annie said.

Mrs. Cuttlebrink stared at the picture again. "Quite possibly. It can also represent horizontal and vertical planes. The circle with the dot at the center has represented the sun or the alchemical symbol for gold. But that's not a dot per se. So the Solomon's knot," the librarian said.

"Bucky found that clue. It sounds like whoever's responsible for the puzzling disarray of pictures probably borrowed them from other cultures and multiple meanings," Annie said.

"I rather doubt the merchants and the Fraternitatem were interested in the meanings of these pictures. I'm guessing they gave you these clues to distract you from finding the market."

Annie took out another picture illustrating the square pattern. "That particular combo formed a pattern. A square."

Mrs. Cuttlebrink stared at the picture of the wall, the glyph highlighted. "So they do. I wouldn't spend time looking for a meaning to the glyphs. I would definitely concentrate what that pattern represents and how it helps you find the portal. I'll research this and see what we have on the subject. Where was the market you found this in?"

"A smaller market in Louisiana. We think the portal to the main market can be found there. But we didn't feel that humming or buzzing, and there was no chill."

"That is perplexing. I'll get back to you when I have something."

CHAPTER 6

ANNIE STOOD OUTSIDE Gibbs's cubicle. He had been a man of few words and few possessions, so his walls were mostly bare. His books and artifacts that he chose to display were sparse, but neatly lined on the shelves along his wall. His notes were still lying in the in box. The room looked like it did before they left for the past.

She held back the tears as she entered, this time doing what no one else dared do: sitting in his desk chair, an old, well-used seat. She could feel the indentations he had made over the years.

"What are you going to do with his things?" Jason asked as he sat across from her in one of the two guest chairs.

"I don't know. I need to catalogue his stuff. If there's anything really dangerous, we'll confiscate it and lock it up. Anything else..." She looked around at his things. "If there's anything else, I guess we pass it out to his friends."

Spencer stood at the cubicle opening. "Hey, Annie, Jason." he sat in the last chair. "I haven't had the will to come in here."

"I was in here yesterday, but in a different capacity. Today"—she glanced around the small cubicle— "today, it feels weird. Sad. I guess we could wait, though." She summoned a vial of Gibbs's blood, something all wizard guards submitted to on the off chance it was needed. She would need it to get into his locked drawer.

"It's time. We need to find and remove the dangerous items," Spencer said. He glanced at his hands and then to Annie. "I'm sorry I hadn't been out to see you. I was angry and I think I blamed you."

"I understand. I blamed myself too." Annie pulled the nearly empty box with the elf ear inside and placed it at the center of the desk. "I say we remove all of the personal stuff. Dangerous things will go to Artifact Hall, and we can distribute his personal items to those who want something of his?" she suggested to Spencer.

As tears fell from her eyes, Annie placed Gibbs's blood inside his blood lock and listened for the lock to pop open. When it did, she opened the top drawer and looked inside.

"The magic that killed him was ancient black magic," Spencer said.

"The man who killed him used black magic to keep himself alive for over a century, to create the demons that wiped out hundreds of people. Gibbs didn't deserve that kind of death." Annie leaned back and closed her eyes.

"He volunteered to protect you knowing he might not come back. He went because he wanted to protect you and so I could... I could stay with my family."

Annie saw the guilt in Spencer's eyes, his jaw clenched in worry. "It's not your fault." She wiped the tears from her cheek.

"He'd be so pissed at us for sitting around crying over him." Spencer reached for the wooden box inside the top of the credenza drawer and maneuvered his crystal across the wood. It glowed bright white. "Not evil," he said as he stuck the box in the cardboard one on the top of the desk. "Will you be all right?" he asked Annie.

She nodded and returned to Gibbs's items, sorting them into the boxes. The evil magical items pile was smaller than they expected: one personal box and three with magical artifacts, plus a pile of books. Jason glanced inside the items with good magic and pulled out a small amulet, a magical protection necklace in the shape of the Eye of Horus. "I wore this the night I died," Jason said. His hands trembled, perhaps at the memory or the knowledge that it meant enough to Gibbs to keep it all those years.

"You weren't killed with magic?" Annie asked.

Jason shook his head and unbuttoned his shirt exposing a large purple scar where he had been stabbed.

"Oh," Annie cried out.

"Rathbone blocked my magic and stabbed me. To put off the investigation." Jason sat shaken at the memory. "It's so fresh, like it happened yesterday," he said.

Annie reached inside the drawer on the left side of the desk and pulled out Gibbs's personal case file for Jason Pearce's murder. "Gibbs had been working your case for years. There was something off with your body just like with mom's. It's like there was a magical trace, but it wasn't what they expected." Annie pushed the folder toward her father. He pushed it back.

"I was there. What I remember, I remember. I don't want to know anything else."

"It's probably better that way," Spencer said. Spencer wasn't a guard when Jason was alive. He was curious more than anything, but refrained from pursuing any questioning.

"Anything else in there?"

Annie glanced inside the empty drawer and slammed it shut. She opened the bottom drawer where Gibbs stored case files. "These need to be transferred to the Wizard Guard files and distributed. We can go through those on another day," she suggested. "I'll take the boxes to Artifact Hall. Unless you want to come with."

"Three boxes, three of us," Spencer said.

Artifact Hall was an expansive room in the basement of Wizard Hall. It housed and displayed artifacts from the earliest of wizard and witches and documented history with its glass cases and museum quality information cards. They walked through the front door and down the wide main hallway toward the back, where a new exhibit was being built. All the artifacts Annie collected in ancient England would be displayed here, including the talismans that Robin had managed to acquire from the Jorvik Viking Museum in York, England, the sword Annie used to get blood from the demon, clothes worn by the coven, Bega's original Book of Shadows, and Annie's family tree.

Annie placed her box on the floor, opened the back of the display case, and took out the book.

"Isn't that part of the display?" Spencer asked.

"When we were there, we were helped by a young girl named Bega. As it turns out…" Annie took out the letter from Bega and handed it to Spencer.

He read the letter and glanced at Annie. "You're kidding."

"Not every day you get to meet your many times great-grandmother," Jason said proudly.

Annie placed the note back inside the book. "It's weird and a little disconcerting. Her husband was a Viking named Svenson."

"I thought I heard voices out here," Robin said, coming out as he saw them with their boxes. "What do you have?"

"We just went through Gibbs's stuff. They're laced with magic that shouldn't be out and about," Annie said.

"No problem. I'll take these and lock them in the vault until I have a chance to review the items." He glanced at the book Annie held. "That book belongs to you. Are you ready to read it?"

"Yeah. I'll return it when I'm done if that's okay?"

"It's yours. You really don't need to return it." Robin waved his palm and floated the boxes on top of each other. "I'll take these away. If you don't need anything else, I'll talk to you soon," he said as he floated the stack toward the back of the hall. Annie watched as Gibbs's life's work was taken away.

"We still have the other things," Spencer said.

"I know. Still, it's like we're wiping him out of our lives."

"Never," Spencer said as they walked from the hall, leaving behind a part of their friend.

⤝

The day felt long. In Annie's weariness, the magic was overactive, itchy, and rendered her exhausted. Not in the mood to stroll from her teleportation spot at the end of her block, she teleported directly to her back porch and entered the quiet house.

"Zola," she called out, but the fairy didn't answer; Annie assumed she was at Samantha's house for the evening. As she walked through the hallway and checked the mailbox outside her front door, sorting through the letters, she again couldn't shake the feeling she was being watched. There was nothing out of the ordinary as she scanned her neighborhood; two cars drove down the street, one stopped in front of her neighbor's house, another continued further down the street and turned right at the first stop sign.

And yet she sensed eyes on her.

I'd watch if I was planning to kill someone.

Her gaze stopped when she caught movement behind the bushes in the yard across the street. She tossed her mail on the floor and closed the door behind her, stepping out on the small front porch. She crossed the yard and strolled down the sidewalk, realizing it was nearly impossible to be inconspicuous as she was still dressed in a blazer and work slacks. But her curiosity got the better of her. She strolled past the house, glancing at it quickly, and walked to the end of the block, past Janie's childhood home.

Turning right, she heard footsteps clacking behind her. She turned quickly to find herself alone on the cement walkway. Chiding herself for being paranoid, she returned home—but her eyes focused on the house where she thought she saw movement. Annie blinked several times, thinking she saw the top of a head of red hair, much like the color her mother wore. Annie picked up her pace, no longer feeling safe in her neighborhood. She ran up her sidewalk and slammed the door behind her.

༄

"I'll change the protection around the house," Cham said.

Annie paced across the fireplace, stopped at the television, turned and repeated.

I imagined it.

"If I overreact, they have an advantage," Annie said. She didn't want her mother or the Fraternitatem to witness her anxiety or have any sense of what Annie might have planned for them.

"The Fraternitatem is watching you, studying you. They probably have been most of your life," Jason said.

Annie glared at him. It wasn't something she wanted to be aware of, and yet it was probably true.

"Update the protection around here," Jason said.

Annie scratched at the magic under her skin. It reacted to her racing heart and churned up emotions. As it rushed through her, it left her dizzy and nauseated. She lifted her left hand, and the golden mist billowed from her palms. As she moved her hand, the magic trailed after, like a shimmering tail. She flicked her wrist, and the magic flew from her hands, exploding a pillow across the front room.

"Awesome," Annie grumbled as she put her hands in her pockets. Still, the magic wafted out and up.

"It's worse when you're upset, isn't it?" Cham asked.

Annie nodded. "If I had killed the human Sturtagaard, none of this would have happened. None of it." She stomped to the sofa and plopped herself on the cushion.

"He told you he knew where the market was. You trusted your gut like you always do. That bastard came through for you again," Cham said.

"Yeah, he did. I'm still vacillating between letting him stew in his meaningless life and staking him now," Annie said.

"I'd like to stake him. He was a pain in my ass for years too. Now I know why," Jason said. He fiddled with his fingers.

"You look like you have more to say," Annie said.

Jason nodded. "I did try to get Emily out of there, but she was so brainwashed, I didn't know her anymore. I walked away, left her behind. They killed me anyway."

"You didn't pursue it?" Annie asked quizzically. "I was under the impression you pressed them. Put her first to bring her home."

Jason shook his head. "No. I wanted to talk to her. I wanted to understand. But the threat from them was big, and I worried they'd come after you and Sami. You were my priority, and I left like they asked. It didn't matter."

Annie watched him thoughtfully. "You finding her back then was good timing for them. They could get rid of you without having any ties to the prophecy or to them. Eight years later, if I hadn't found your folder, I wouldn't have linked it. Even if you hadn't met her and the Fraternitatem, they would have killed you before I went to the past so you wouldn't get in their way."

Jason nodded. "I believe that is correct. I'd be dead one way or another. But the Fraternitatem underestimated you and the magic. You conjured me. You move your hands, and the magic explodes things." He chuckled and slapped his thighs. "And because of that, I'm here now. That's all that matters. I have a second chance to make things right." He smiled gently and walked from the room. Annie listened to his footsteps as they made their way down the hall and to the basement where he was staying.

It was the first time in weeks his presence didn't make her anxious.

≈

The local wizard bar called the Witches Brew was run out of a house owned by Douglass Rand, an adventurer like Robin Price. He had settled down years ago with his wife Wilma, opened the bar, and entertained young witches and wizards with his stories ever since.

The bar was set up in the front room and dining room of his house; the walls were lined with shelves that showed off hundreds of artifacts that he had collected over his many years of travels. Pictures decorated the rest of the space including nonmagical and magical celebrity pictures he had collected over forty years.

Annie's first weeks back had been hectic, not just with work but with her father and learning to live with him again. She was grateful for the respite as she and Cham entered the front door and were blasted by music unheard by the nonmagical community due to several well-placed muffle spells around the property.

"It's busy tonight," Cham remarked as he and Annie entered the main front room.

"Last time we were here—" Annie started. They had been there a week and a half ago for the dinner following Gibbs's funeral. In contrast, tonight was filled with life and the art of living it. She glanced across the room recognizing several fellow witches and wizards, some of whom she had known as far back as elementary school.

She exchanged greetings as they walked to an empty table in the far corner and took a seat. Annie chose to have her back against the wall with a clear view of the front door and entrance to the kitchen.

Anxiously, she scratched her arm.

"Your dad wants to go after the Fraternitatem," Cham said as he picked up a menu.

"I'm sure he does. He didn't sound happy when I told him what I thought I saw," Annie commented.

"He wants to protect you," Cham said. Milo had made them all promise to keep Jason hidden, out of view of the Fraternitatem. Annie worried he'd go rogue.

"Milo's mostly retired. The decision is yours to make," she said as she perused the menu. Her mood was dark when the music changed to something soft and slow. She didn't want to dance, but the feeling of the drums beating inside of her seemed to overpower the itching. She forced a smile on her face when her best friend Janie and her now, fiancé, Randy, entered the bar and found them in the corner.

"Hey. Look at you guys. Out on an actual date," Janie cooed as she sat beside Annie. They ordered some beers, sliders, and potato skins. When the loaded plates arrived, they dug into their food.

While Cham and Randy traded work stories, Janie glanced at Annie. "You okay? You seem quiet."

"Sorry. Dad, Mom, you know, the impending family reunion," Annie said glibly.

Janie wrapped her around Annie's shoulders. "Sorry. I wish I could help." She stared at Annie's arm. "You're scratching again."

Annie looked down at her left arm and the multitude of red, burning lines.

"I'm struggling with it all. I wish I could share but not yet. Tell me about criminal law?"

Janie didn't have an opportunity to answer; they were joined by Robin. "Hey, Annie and gang." He was received with a hug from Janie and handshakes from Randy and Cham.

"What are you doing here?" Annie asked.

"Oh, you know, a night out. Visiting old friends." He tilted his head toward Douglass. "Do you have a sec, Annie?" She nodded and joined Robin at the bar where Douglass filled several glasses with beer and handed them to Sheila, the waitress for the evening.

"Annie Pearce. How are you holding up?" Douglass asked. He reached across the thin bar and shook her hand. "I hear the guard is anxious to find the market," he said.

"You know something?" she asked.

Douglass Rand pulled a scroll from his pocket and pushed it across the bar. "I hear that symbol you're looking for has to do with that."

Annie unrolled the scroll and stared at a very complex potion. "What is this?"

He shrugged. "I assume it's a potion to open the portal. Those symbols. You'll find them in multiple locations."

"The square, circle, and Solomon's knot?" she asked.

"Yes," Douglass said.

"We're not sure what the symbols actually means though," Annie said.

He nodded. "I've got to say, the evil ones are getting sneakier." He chuckled.

"Putting the portal to the main market inside a smaller one. Yeah, that's getting sneaky," Annie agreed. She rolled the scroll and stuck it in her pocket. "Thanks. Care to share your contact?"

"Not at this time." He offered a grin and turned toward Wilma taking the next order.

"I guess that's it," Annie said and returned to the corner table and her waiting food.

CHAPTER 7

ANNIE AND JANIE linked their arms, like they used to when they were kids, and skipped down the sidewalk, laughing. Behind them, Cham and Randy discussed the coming broomstick-racing season and the teams that had a chance to win.

"Feeling better?" Janie asked when they slowed down. Though there was still a low roar of engines humming on Harlem Avenue, several blocks away, the cool night air blew against Annie's cheeks. She felt light and free, and she smiled.

"Yeah. I do." She held Janie's arm tighter as they headed to Annie's house.

As they neared home, Annie saw her front room light through the window, lighting the yard and front stoop with a warm glow. She stopped completely when she thought she heard footsteps from across the street. She peered into the darkness, scanning the light and shadows.

"Annie?" Cham asked as he grabbed her arm.

"She's watching me," Annie said.

Cham scanned the street. "Let's go." He took Annie's arm as they rushed to their house, opened the front door, and slammed it shut when everyone was safely inside.

"You saw her," Annie said.

Cham looked through curtains, searching for movement on the sidewalks. "I don't know what I saw."

"What happened?" Jason asked as he entered the front room.

"I saw what I thought was a woman—small, thin," Cham said as he closed the curtains.

Jason opened the door and stepped onto the front stoop, visible under the porch light. He glanced across the street where bushes rustled.

"What are you doing?" Cham asked, pulling him inside and slamming the door. "You're supposed to stay hidden in the neighborhood and from the Fraternitatem."

"She was behind a bush. She couldn't have seen me," Jason said.

"Stay hidden," Cham ordered.

"You're trying to be bait?" Randy asked.

Annie nodded.

"Well, I guess that makes sense, since technically he's dead," Randy said.

Annie burst into laughter. They all looked at her as she fell back into the sofa. Cham glanced through thin drapery liners.

"You okay?" Janie asked, concern in her voice.

"Yeah. Peachy," Annie placed her head on the back cushion and closed her eyes. "I can't stop Dad from making the first move. He's a grown man and really not here. Letting them see him might hasten their attempt at me. What do you suggest, Dad?"

Jason sat on the lounge chair. "I'm assuming they have a way to scry for you. So if you teleport, it will take her time to get to you, unless the Fraternitatem is here." He grimaced. "I'm guessing she's trying to find out your daily habits. Change those. Sleep at Cham's, at Janie's, Sami's. Change what time you leave for work."

"That's exhausting. At least I know where they are, more or less," Annie said. She observed her father carefully. For the first time since he'd come back, she noticed that the lines around his eyes, mouth, and forehead had deepened. Gray hair was poking out from his temples.

Why does he look older? Ghosts don't age.

"Annie?" Cham touched her shoulder. "Okay?"

She nodded and returned her attention to her father. He took out a small notebook, and glanced at the back door.

"You going somewhere?" she asked.

"I'd like to pick up the slack and investigate those locations. I've got the coordinates and a picture of the ancient symbol. I'll be careful. They won't know I'm there." He touched Annie's hand.

"Disguise?" Annie asked. Jason handed Annie a picture and a spell.

No magic?

She stared at the photo taken some time in the 1980s. Annie glanced at her father. "You want me to turn you into Billy Idol?"

"That was my go-to disguise. It was good," he argued. "Did you ever use one?"

Annie frowned. "Once. I had to infiltrate a group of witches and wizards who used illegal magical boosts like a drug." She summoned a picture of her in disguise to show him.

Jason frowned. "You look like a severe drug addict."

"I had no choice. She was in serious trouble, I needed to get at the dealer. I had to play a part. Like you do. You are my secret weapon. Don't get caught." She held her hand to her father and chanted the spell. He shimmered and, in an instant, stood before them again. He remained the same size and shape, but his hair was now spiked and bleached blonde, and his eyes were lined with thick eye makeup.

Annie pursed her lips as if she had eaten a lemon.

"What's wrong with it?" he asked.

"Nothing. Nothing." Annie held her hand to her lips and smiled. "How are you getting there? You have no magic."

"See, that's the thing. Robin said he'd go with me. He wants to find the market as badly as the Wizard Guard. I can help and he has contacts," Jason explained.

Cham and Annie exchanged glances. She could no longer keep her reactions in. They all burst into laughter at his costume.

"You're all very bad children," Jason said as he waved them off and headed to the back porch to wait for Robin to fetch him.

"Don't forget your boom box and cassette tapes!" Annie called out after him.

"You're grounded," Jason said as he slammed the door behind him.

"It's weird having him back?" Janie asked.

"You have no idea." Annie chuckled again.

"We should go. You should have the protection spell updated," Janie said. She reached for Annie and gave her a hug.

After saying their goodbyes, Janie and Randy teleported from the back porch. Milo arrived minutes later. Annie opened the back door. "Why are you here?" she asked.

"I'm updating your magical protection," Milo said.

"You're retired."

"Once a wizard guard, always a wizard guard."

"Again. Why are you here?" Annie turned to Cham. "Did you send a text to the whole team and he's the only one who responded?" she asked incredulously.

"Yes and no. Others replied. Milo demanded to come," Cham said.

Annie smirked.

"Where'd you see her?" he asked, his usual gruff self on full display. Cham walked him to the front door, explaining what he had seen.

Milo, with his own way of doing things, walked up the stairs of a house he knew well, after spending much time here with Jason over the years. He entered Annie's childhood bedroom, which currently sat empty. Annie followed and observed him as he scanned the yards.

"If Emily's out there, she's hiding herself well. I'll up the magic around the house and take a tour of the neighborhood," Milo said.

"You still look like hell. Not as bad as before, but it still looks bad," Annie said.

"Thanks. I feel awful," he said.

"Then why are you here?"

"Because if Gibbs were alive, he'd do it. He's not here, so it's me."

"Milo?"

She saw him wipe tears from his eyes. He stopped and stared at her. "I loved your dad. He was a good friend. Gibbs and I promised him that we would look after you and Sami." He walked past her, leaving her in the hallway.

❦

Milo walked the perimeter of the backyard, adding magic along the fence.

He knelt low and glanced inside the flower beds, moving flowers aside, lifting rocks and shaking them.

"What the hell is he looking for?" Annie asked.

"Magical spy objects maybe?" Cham said as they watched through the kitchen window.

Milo strolled through the gate along the side of the house to the small patch of grass that made up the front yard. He carefully increased the magic until he reached the other side of the yard. Satisfied with the additional magic, he entered the house and found them waiting in the kitchen.

"Well?" Annie asked.

"I added more magic to the protection spells. I did a preliminary check for any magical or electronic listening and video devices. I didn't see anything, but it wouldn't surprise me if the Fraternitatem used them. I think the Vampire Attack Unit should do a sweep and verify there's nothing out there or in here for that matter." Milo sat at the kitchen table.

Annie popped open a bottle of beer and handed it to him. "So you're staying tonight?" she asked.

"Yes. You think you saw her across the street. I'll take a look out there around midnight. I'm assuming your neighbors will be asleep by then," he mumbled and took a sip of beer.

◈

"This is ridiculous," Annie said as she climbed into bed. Cham stood in the doorway staring at the darkened staircase.

"Milo will be back soon, and I'll come to bed. He'll let your dad back in," Cham said.

"It's only been three weeks. Emily's not ready yet." Annie yawned. Though she was tired, she didn't think she could sleep.

Cham waited at the door until 12:45 a.m., when the back door opened and two sets of footsteps entered the kitchen. Male voices spoke in soft tones. Cham held his palms up and out as they neared. He and Annie exited the bedroom and switched on the hallway light; Jason and Milo were at the foot of the stairs.

"My first location was near the old portal in Patagonia. The portal opened to nothing," Jason said.

"One more to knock off the list at least," Milo said. He turned to Cham and held out a black bandana. "I don't know if this belongs to Emily or not. But I found it in the yard where you thought you saw her."

Annie grabbed the bandana. It had been tied around her neck or head. The knot was still there, and several strands of red hair were tucked inside. "Either they are really good or this is really her," she said.

"It's the color I remember she had," Milo said and glanced at Jason.

Annie observed her father. His hands shook as he took the fabric.

When her phone buzzed, she glanced at it and chuckled. "Happy Sunday morning. The VAU is here to debug the house."

⚶

Annie stayed out of Graham Lightner's way as he directed his team: Sky Starling, Allen, Bernice, and Monica as they searched for magical and nonmagical bugs. Annie sat at the kitchen table cradling a mug of tea, Jason sat across from her playing with the phone Annie purchased for him. While it was a basic phone, it was far more sophisticated than he knew and he grumbled several times as he tried to make it work. Annie chuckled.

The team worked for an hour, sweeping her house for magic, searching for bugs and other items. Each magical trace they collected was compared to Annie's, Cham's, and Zola's. They found nothing out of the ordinary.

After an hour, Graham sat beside Annie as the rest of his team searched the yard.

"So, what did you see?" Graham asked.

Annie handed him the bandana with the red hair in the knot. "Milo found it across the street. I thought I was being followed from the Witches Brew."

Graham placed the bandana into an evidence bag and marked it. "I'll look at the location just to get a second set of eyes on in. I'll take the bandana to Perkins in the lab. If I remember correctly, Emily's DNA is in the database." Graham looked at Jason, his friend from so long ago. He, too, seemed to have difficulty believing that Jason was here, even as a corporeal ghost.

"You did. We used it to confirm she was—" Jason started. Whoever performed the magic on the anonymous body, did a thorough job, fooling them all.

"We know, Jason. We all failed. Their magic was too sophisticated," Graham said.

Annie observed their exchange and understood the discomfort. "Someone else is buried in her casket. You and Mom were both buried in the wizard graveyard. Maybe we should exhume the body and return whoever it is to their family," she suggested.

"Now that we know more, maybe it will help us with the Fraternitatem," Graham said as he played with his hands. "Are you looking for her?"

"Bucky is," Annie said.

"I expect you won't wait for her to get to you. You're going to strike first," Graham said.

Annie nodded. "I was never happy with the decision to let them go in the first place and it looks like they need my magic to take control of the market. We need to be careful." She sighed and texted Ryan, explaining the night's events. He was through her back door before she put down the phone.

"You were awake," she said as he entered the kitchen.

"I was working on something else," he sat beside Jason. "So, are you asking permission to go after them or are you telling me?"

The rest of the VAU entered Annie's kitchen and stood around the table. "There's nothing out there. No bugs, no extraneous magic that doesn't belong to you. They're taking their time, either to upset you or to make you impatient and therefore cause you to do something stupid," Sky said.

"Thanks for coming in so late. You can go home," Graham said.

"Really? Shouldn't we know what's going on?" Sky asked.

Graham laughed. "Yeah. It's Sunday morning. I'll keep you posted."

Reluctantly, the VAU team left Annie's house. A rush of air swished loudly outside the back door as they departed.

"Too many people," Graham said.

Though it was now two in the morning, Milo, Jason, Graham, Annie, Cham, and Ryan sat around Annie's kitchen table. For Annie, it felt perfectly normal, which made her feel nauseated. Or maybe it was the nature of the plan.

She sighed and went to her locked cabinet, sticking her finger into the pin and drawing blood. The blood sprung the lock and the door opened. She pulled out the grimoire Archibald Mortimer had given her.

"What is that?" Milo asked.

"I got this from Mortimer before I left for the past. He swears it's a real grimoire from the Fraternitatem. I've been reading it. There's stuff in there about Mom," she said. They stared at the book.

"This is what we do know: they kidnapped a nonmagical, probably brainwashed her, and forced her to work for them. They killed Benaiah, one of their own. They're coming for Annie for her magic so they can control the market. We told them not to come back here. If Emily is working for them and she's here, they did not heed that warning," Ryan said. He picked up the grimoire after Milo placed it on the table. "The last bit will hold if we can prove she's here on their behalf. What else do we know?"

Annie pulled out the potion written on the scroll she got from Douglass Rand. "Douglass Rand said this potion will open the portal. I'll work on the potion tom... today and we can test it out this week," Annie watched the scroll roll to the middle of the table. "The other wizard guard units have listened to our warnings about the Fraternitatem. The South African guard has a man at the market I visited with Robin. The portal location is on map in the conference room."

"You've been busy," Ryan commented.

"Priority," she said.

"Get some sleep and stay safe. We'll prepare a full plan on Monday. If you need us before that, let me know," Ryan said.

It was nearly four in the morning before Annie finally fell asleep.

CHAPTER 8

"YOU SAW MOM yesterday?" Samantha asked over the phone with a shaky voice.

Annie rolled over; the clock said 11:30 a.m. Though she had managed seven hours of sleep, she was exhausted and not up for having this conversation with her sister.

"I didn't see her. I heard someone," Annie reiterated. "Did Dad tell you?"

Samantha was clearly pacing across her kitchen; her heavy footsteps across her wood floor resounded in Annie's ear. "He wanted to warn me. Just in case she follows me."

Annie sat up, leaving the warmth of the coverings. Cham, already awake, was busying himself in the kitchen. "Have you seen or heard anything?" Annie ran her hands through her gnarly, ratted curls, stepped out of bed, and searched her closet for something to wear.

"No. But I wasn't looking," Samantha said.

Placing her phone on speaker, she pulled on jeans and a T-shirt. As smart as her sister was, she wasn't trained to fight nor was she hyper aware of her surroundings. Annie glanced at her phone.

Would the Fraternitatem use Sami to get to me?

When Annie was under the most stress, when her heart pounded rapidly, when the realization hit her, she could feel the magic move through her, and the itching became unbearable. She felt all of this now, realizing that Samantha could be a target. Samantha, who was thrilled to have

Jason back. Where Annie had no emotional attachment to Emily, having no memory of her mother, Samantha remembered her and missed her every day.

"Sami. You need to be careful. Pay attention to your surroundings and look out for unknown people. You're not exactly trained to defend yourself," Annie warned.

"Really. She's my mom. I don't expect she's going to hurt either of us. I think she's being used to get close to us. She won't hurt us."

"Don't be so naïve! If she's been brainwashed, she's capable of anything!"

"But, you feel nothing for her. They misjudged her usefulness to get to you. You said so yourself," Samantha said.

Annie balled her hands into fists. If she thought it would help, she'd punch a hole in her wall to release her rising tension. Sometimes dealing with her sister was like talking to a wall that couldn't really listen. "And, you still feel something for her. You are my weakness. They could use you to trap me," she said with a shrillness in her voice.

"Annie... I..." Samantha's voice cracked.

Annie walked out of her room and into the kitchen. "Put Dad on the phone. Now!"

Cham looked at her questioningly. "You okay?" he mouthed.

Annie shook her head.

"What's the matter? Sami seems a bit frightened," Jason asked, taking the phone over from Samantha.

Annie paced. "I didn't think this through. I couldn't figure out why they took Emily so long ago. I have no emotional connection to her. Her coming back makes me suspicious. I'm not longing for my mommy back. My connection's to Sami, and she still has an emotion connection to Mom."

"Oh," Jason finally said.

"No 'oh,' Dad. Sami was never interested in fighting or learning to defend herself. She's not paying attention to what's around her. They need a protection spell up at the house. Remind them to teleport in and out from the roof. I'll be there soon," Annie said and hung up.

"Baby. That's a contingency we hadn't thought of. It would make their plan a great deal more thoughtful if they would go after Sami. That would bring you to them in a much more emotional state," Cham said.

Annie pulled her hair into a ponytail and slipped on her shoes over at the back door. "She's my kryptonite. I need to go. I'll call you later."

Cham held her wrist and kissed her, slowly, passionately, until she calmed.

When she settled, he said, "I'll meet you there. Be careful."

∽

Annie landed on Samantha and John's townhouse roof. She always loved the view of the city from the rooftop, but, today it caused her great stress as she began walking the perimeter of the roof.

Annie walked along the metal railing with her crystal out, picking up any magic. With the perimeter clean, she began to crisscross the roof until the door to the upper hallway opened and Jason walked out.

"Finding anything?" he asked as he met her stride.

"Not yet."

"You scared her," Jason reprimanded. It reminded Annie of her childhood and the many times she frightened her older sister with stories of monsters and demons. Jason had never been pleased with that.

"She needs to be scared," Annie replied as she sat in the outdoor lounger. "She needs to be aware of her surroundings. Sometimes she lives as though she's a nonmagical and none of this stuff happens."

"Well, you accomplished what you wanted," Jason said.

"Don't reprimand me. This is how you raised me. You left it up to me to protect her," Annie spat.

Jason glanced at his hands. "I made a mistake," he murmured.

Annie shuddered and placed her head in her hands. She rubbed her face and then looked back at Jason. "I saw you. Strong and brave. I wanted to be like you. Being a wizard guard was all I knew. All I ever wanted. It's just now…" She glanced out at the glorious sight of Chicago to the east.

"And now," Jason prodded.

"It's like this. In the last year, I've learned the truth about your death, about Mom, about what Sturtagaard did to exact his revenge against me. My life turned upside down because someone else orchestrated it." Annie stood at the railing and leaned into it, looking through the courtyard outside the house.

"Seeing you here now, I wonder if all I was doing was trying to please you." She shuddered, remembering that Sturtagaard had implied the same.

Jason shook his head and chuckled. "When you were eleven, you took one of my case files and reorganized and made notes in the margins. Frankly, you helped me solve the bloody thing."

Annie turned back to him. "I don't remember."

"You don't remember because there were so many times you did stuff like that. You did research for me on your own without being asked. I got permission for you to work at Wizard Hall on summer break to research for the other guards. At twelve, you worked in the lab learning how they investigated the deaths. You asked for that and I agreed. Gibbs took you on a vampire hunt when you were thirteen because he wanted you to learn to fear them because he saw what I saw. You went to the prison on your own because you wanted to see the vampires locked up just before they were staked. I wouldn't have done any of that if I thought you wanted to do anything else with your life. I never took John and Samantha, but I took you, and later, I took Cham—because you both desired to learn."

Air popped behind them. Annie started and turned to see Cham on the roof. "How's it going?" Cham asked cautiously, sensing the tension on their faces.

"I haven't found anything up here," Annie said.

"And down there?" He pointed to the attic door of the townhouse.

"Haven't been down yet," Annie said. "Dad's reprimanding me for scaring her and reminding me I've always wanted to do this."

Cham glanced between Annie and Jason. "It sounds like I missed a lot. I suggest we go down and make sure she's okay." Cham led them inside, through a back hallway to the stairs that led to the front room.

"I hate your job." Samantha scowled from where she sat beside John on the sofa. Her arms were crossed tightly against her chest, keeping Annie at a distance.

"This has nothing to do with my job. It has to do with the stupid powers that the Fraternitatem want," Annie said. She waved her hands and let Samantha see the magic as it floated from her palms.

Samantha refused to look at Annie, keeping her focus on the television. John stared at the magic as it trailed behind Annie's movements. His jaw floated open in surprise.

Annie waited impatiently for Samantha to soften, to look at her. John stood.

"This isn't easy for us either," he said.

"I never said it was." Annie's hands flew up in exasperation. She opened the large glass doors and stepped on to the narrow balcony. From there she could observe the courtyard filled with young families enjoying the warm summer day. Her eyes darted across the grass where children ran and dogs chased balls. A young boy of four learned to ride a two-wheel bicycle as his younger sister chased him and laughed.

Annie focused on the adult women, searching for the only thing she remembered of her mother: the dark red hair. She searched for bandanas or hats that would hide it. She tensed at the sight of a woman in a wide-brimmed hat, who was sitting on a blanket with a thick book. Though the woman held the book close to her face, it was low enough to peer over the top edge. Annie gripped the handrail as she stared at her.

Cham saw her tense and joined her on the balcony, slipping an arm around her waist. "See something?" Cham asked. He followed Annie's gaze and looked away after spotting the slim woman on the blanket. "She's not really reading. She's looking up here," he said.

"I noticed that too." Annie leaned against the handrail and placed her chin in her hand staying as casual as she could, though for a moment, she felt nauseated. She continued to scan the crowd, periodically stopping on the woman not reading, in order to assess her features. Delicate, petite hands held the book tightly; short, thin legs were tucked beneath her. Annie turned her focus on the dog still chasing a ball across the courtyard.

The woman finally placed her book in a tote bag, folded her blanket, and stuffed it inside. She stood and casually glanced at Samantha and John's townhouse before she limped through the courtyard, stopping at a corner townhouse. She typed a code on the keypad on the gate and entered the small front yard before entering the house.

"Maybe she's nothing," Annie said.

"Maybe." Cham took out his phone and texted Bucky. Annie peered over his shoulder. He was asking for the ownership of all the homes at this location.

"What are you doing out there?" Samantha finally turned to Annie, who frowned.

"Just looking outside. Paying attention to my surroundings. For instance, I thought that corner townhouse had been empty for a while," Annie said.

"The sign was taken down about two months ago. We never saw anyone move in though," John said. "Did you see someone enter?"

"Yeah. A woman. Short, slim. Couldn't see much else." Annie continued to watch the crowd.

"You don't think it's her, do you?" Samantha asked.

"No. I just watched a woman enter a house I thought was empty. Just curious." Annie pulled herself from the railing and walked through the living room to the kitchen. She filled the tea kettle with water and set it on the fire.

"You just got back. If it's been two months, the timeline's wrong," Samantha said. It sounded like she was trying to convince herself that her growing fear was irrational and unfounded.

"No. Sturtagaard told them when I was going to the past. They've been preparing for years. Besides, she was reading a book, and just because she glanced up here doesn't mean anything other than she thought Cham was hot," Annie said. She gathered mugs and tea and set them on the counter.

"I can't live here. I can't stay here!" Samantha sounded nearly hysterical. John put his arms around her.

The tea kettle whistled. Annie poured the boiling water into mugs, placed them on a tray with tea and sugar, and brought them to her sister.

"First of all, we didn't say it was her. She glanced up here casually. While she was smallish, I didn't see her face or her hair. The point is, that she was looking up here, and you need to be careful. Watchful. She can't get in here. If you teleport from the roof, you'll be fine. Otherwise, stay with Don and Marina at the farm."

Annie returned to the large window and stared at the corner townhouse. The drapes in the upper window slid closed.

Weird.

Annie refused to back down as she watched the window where she knew the woman was watching her back.

Samantha picked up a mug and looked at Annie still leaning against the balcony. She walked over.

"What are you looking at?" Samantha asked.

Annie kept her focus on the corner townhouse. "I'm just looking out the window. It's a nice day out."

"You think it's her?" Samantha took a sip.

"I think you have a new neighbor who was enjoying the lovely day. I'm sorry. I didn't mean to scare you. I'm less trusting than you and the thought popped in my head. I reacted badly." Annie eyed the curtains fluttering across the way.

"I wish I were brave like you," Samantha admitted. "I still hate your job."

"Take a number."

❧

It was never really dark in the heart of the city. While the stars shined above her, she stepped across the empty courtyard, across the damp grass. She had been to the place countless times, sharing life's experiences with Samantha, and never had cause to fear it. Even in sleep, as she neared the corner townhouse and as her feet grew wet from dew, Annie felt, at least in a sense, fear. She stopped at the gate and turned to look at Samantha's empty townhouse with its darkened windows and no lights at the front door. She sighed and turned back to the corner home.

The gate was cool and slippery with a layer of dew. It yielded easily when she pushed it open and strolled along the short sidewalk to the door. Shuddering at the thought of being watched, Annie glanced at the second-floor window and saw Emily Pearce staring down at her. She swallowed the lump in her throat; it was the first time mother and daughter had eyes on each other in twenty years.

But I'm not really here.

She studied her mother's face. While Emily retained a youthful appearance, she had aged in twenty years. Though Annie didn't remember her, she knew her face from the many pictures stored away in the basement.

Annie pulled her gaze from her mother and glanced at the flowers that lined the narrow sidewalk to the front stoop. At the door, terracotta pots were filled with bright summer flowers in purple and dark pink. They smelled sweet as Annie passed. She held the door handle, took a deep breath, and let herself inside.

She recognized the floor plan, the same as Samantha and John's, and bypassed the small den, taking the stairs to the right. It led to a single large room that encompassed a family room, kitchen, and dining room.

Curiosity overwhelmed her and pulled her toward the fireplace. The mantle was lined with pictures. She scanned her mother's life through the images. The first was of Emily with a baby, whose lips were smooth and curved like Annie's. In the next picture, he was a young boy; his mother hugged him and smiled brightly for the camera. Annie moved to the next, a picture of Emily in a thin, strapped summer dress, carrying a bouquet of flowers in one hand, a man casually draping his arm around her shoulder.

Who is he?

Annie's heart ached. She felt a ping of jealousy as she perused their lives in pictures, as she watched Emily's face age, as the wrinkles appeared at the corner of her eyes, at her mouth as her hair grayed throughout. Annie scanned them as if she would find someone familiar to her. She stopped when she came to a photo nearly hidden. Pulling it from its spot, Annie stared at her three-year-old self, standing in front of the porch outside the house she now shared with Cham. The old front door she recently replaced had just been painted bright red by her mother, hours before the picture was taken.

Though the picture was unfamiliar to her, the lopsided ponytails springing from both sides of her head were all too familiar, as was the one sock at her ankle and the other at her knee.

Annie touched the image of her mother, who was smiling warmly, her arm protectively holding her youngest daughter. Samantha stood beside Annie, almost her twin, wearing the same white dress. Her long, curly hair was pulled into a single ponytail springing out from behind her head. She was neatly combed and both socks stayed at her knees. She was held by her father, who was smiling proudly.

She shuttered and took the picture with her as she turned toward the stairs to the third floor. Absently she climbed, her right hand grazing the handrail as she reached the bedrooms. She turned toward the front room and entered, finally looking up to see Emily glancing out the window. Hearing her daughter, Emily turned. Her light-pink lips curved slightly upwards.

"I've been waiting for you."

❧

Annie flew up. Her heart pounded violently and her stomach roiled. She glanced around the den. The light was low, the television on mute. She could hear two male voices in the back hallway, their footsteps crossing the kitchen to the den.

"Hey, you're awake," Cham said as he entered with Bucky Hart, who carried a case folder with him.

"Yeah. Hey, Bucky. It could've waited until tomorrow," Annie said as she pulled her hair into a ponytail.

Bucky sat in the chair beside the sliding window. "Actually Annie, it couldn't wait. To be perfectly honest, when Cham asked me to look into the townhouses, singularly based on a woman looking up at you, I was curious. I'm glad I looked today," he said.

She exchanged concerned glances with Cham and returned her attention to Bucky.

"I reviewed each house in the complex. Every one checked out except for the corner lot. It was purchased two months ago, cash, a quick move in." He handed them the list.

Annie read the owners' names: Emily King-Solomon and Levi King-Solomon.

"This is a joke," she said. "Could they be more obvious?" She was incensed, as if they were purposely baiting her.

"That's why I'm here. It's too much of a coincidence. And it's brazen," Bucky said. "So I assumed it's her, and with a name, comes everything else." He handed her the folder.

Annie looked at the first document, a marriage license between Emily Worthington Pearce and Levi King-Solomon. She read the document carefully and frowned at the date of the marriage. "She married him after Dad died at least," she spat. "Is it a real marriage license or fake like we create?"

"The document was recorded in Tel Aviv the day after your dad died.

As far as I can tell, it was a legal wedding. Though I've been trying to determine if this Levi had a different name at some point."

"Obviously, they knew when he died. I'm surprised they didn't just change her name and marry her off earlier," Annie said.

Annie perused the other documents. "You were right. She graduated from college with a degree in archaeology from Tel Aviv University." She pulled out the next page and held her breath.

"What's the matter?" Cham asked. Her hands shook when she handed him the printout. "Oh," he said, looking at it. "You have a half-brother named Shiloh."

"You have a what?" Jason asked.

Annie glanced at her dad and shook her head. "You don't have to know this." She closed the items in the folder.

"You found her," he said and reached for the folder, slowly opening the cover. "The house is owned by Emily King-Solomon. She remarried..." he shuffled through the rest of the documents, reviewing the marriage license and then the birth certificate. "I didn't remarry because I loved her and couldn't find anyone else. I couldn't..." Jason sat on the sofa.

"She remarried after you died, if that helps," Annie said. She knew it didn't make Jason any less emotional. "She was brainwashed, probably threatened, and most likely lied to. She's not the woman you fell in love with as much as she's not the woman who gave birth to me. My mom died that day. This is a woman with the same name; she's not my mom." Annie took the folder from Jason and set it on the ottoman. She looked at Bucky.

"I'm sorry, Annie. You needed to know the Fraternitatem has been watching you for years."

"It's not your fault. I appreciate knowing. It will just make it easier to do what I need to do," she admitted.

"Do you want me to broadcast their names? Especially to the Middle Eastern Guard. They might know more," Bucky suggested.

Annie frowned. "Go ahead and send them the list. I wouldn't expect a whole lot, though. They didn't have much about the Fraternitatem when the black market fell, and that group is small and responsible for the entire region. Hopefully, they have outside contacts who can help."

"Yeah, I wondered about that. I'll send it anyway and keep you posted." Bucky took his leave, his expression grim and apologetic.

"Are you okay?" Annie asked Jason after the door slammed shut.

"I know she wasn't the woman I married when I saw her at the Cave of Ages. I knew I would never get her back. But seeing her move on this way…" he glanced at the folder.

"It'll be easier knowing this," Annie said as she held back the tears that threatened to fall.

CHAPTER 9

ANNIE SAT AT the picnic table near the employee entrance of Wizard Hall, letting the sun warm her as she perused her notes. She glanced up, peered inside the entrance as the security day manager, Manny, trained a new security guard.

"Afraid of the new security officer?" Cham chuckled.

"No. Just enjoying the sunshine," Annie said. She put her notes back inside her field pack and slung it across her shoulder.

"Everything okay?"

"Yeah. I had a thought." Annie didn't elaborate as she and Cham entered the hall.

"Annie, Cham," Manny said as they cast their magic spells into the security box and headed inside.

They took the stairs from the back hallway and walked in silence, Annie mostly lost in her jumbled thoughts.

"You going to elaborate any time soon?" Cham asked as they entered the fifth floor. The Wizard Guard department was relatively quiet. Since many guards had been out late investigating markets the previous night, they wouldn't be coming to work until afternoon.

She smirked at Cham and entered her cubicle. "I need to make a phone call first." While her computer loaded, she scanned her phone for Jack Ramsey's number and paced until he answered.

"Hi, Annie. How are you holding up?" While he was sufficiently solemn in regards to Gibbs's recent death, he still sounded far more jovial than normal. Usually a call from her rendered him grumpy with thoughts of magical investigations that could potentially result in the end of the world.

"I'm okay. Work continues and keeps me busy. Which is why I'm calling you. I have a bit of a dilemma I'm hoping you can help me with," Annie said.

There was a moment of silence on Jack's end. Annie didn't rush him; she knew calls from her made him anxious.

"Princess Amelie isn't alive again, is she?" Jack joked.

Annie laughed. "Seriously, are you drunk?"

"No. But since you've asked, Amanda and I are engaged." She could almost see him beaming through the phone.

"Congratulations! I'm happy for you. That explains your dopey demeanor," Annie said. She glanced at her ring finger. Her diamond gleamed in the artificial light.

"Thanks. How's the fiancé?" he asked.

"He's good. We're dealing." Jack had witnessed Gibbs's funeral, so he knew how hard it had hit Annie and the rest of the team.

"You sound preoccupied. What's up?" Jack asked.

"I am. It's just… another case revolving around my dad's murder."

Jack was silent for a moment as he gathered his thoughts. "Does that mean the Fraternitatem of Solomon is back in the picture?" His manner changed, not completely all business, but she sensed his concern.

"Good guess. I'll be dealing with them in time. I was hoping you could get me in to see Wolfgange Rathbone."

She could hear Jack typing on his keyboard. He soon said, "Yes, with the caveat you tell me what's going on. I'll help if I can."

"Deal. Let me know when," Annie said.

They said quick goodbyes. Annie glanced at Cham standing in her cubicle door. "What?" she asked.

"We should have asked Rathbone sooner," he said.

"We've been busy," Annie pointed out.

Cham took a seat across from her. "You okay to face him?"

Annie chuckled. "I should bring my dad with me."

"That would definitely be a sight to see." He smiled lightly. "I ask again, you okay to meet with him, knowing what we know?"

"I'll do what I have to if it helps stop the Fraternitatem," Annie said as she pulled down the first folder in her inbox.

∽

When the elevator doors slid open, Annie jumped at the sight of her father. It was still a surprise whenever he appeared around a corner. She wondered if she'd get used it before he had to leave again.

"Hey, Dad," she said as she stepped inside.

"Where are you off to?" he asked. He stood against the door, keeping it from closing.

"Mrs. Cuttlebrink has something for me about that symbol in the market. If you're not busy, wanna come?" If work was the only way Annie could include him in her life, she decided she would make any attempt to do so. She sensed his happiness when he re-entered the elevator.

"Sure. I have no place in particular to go and I'm not getting paid," he said.

"We should remedy that. You should get paid something," Annie said as she pressed the basement button.

"For what purpose? I'm here to protect you. It's not like I'm buying a new car." He leaned against the shiny metal walls.

Annie chuckled. "You're okay with your daughters giving you spending money?"

Jason shrugged. "I gave you money for years. We'll call it even. Besides, I can't go out, so what's there to spend?"

They exited at the basement; Annie glanced at her phone. It was 8:59. "She is definitely punctual," Annie said of Mrs. Cuttlebrink.

"If anything, Sabrina lives for structure," Jason agreed.

The elevator whirled, the doors opened, and Mrs. Cuttlebrink rushed out. "Sorry, Annie, dear. Jason. There's a back log at the front entrance," she said as she opened the library doors with thick, antique keys.

She did her morning routine, holding the doors open, turning on the lights, switching on the computers. "My office, if that works," she directed them as she logged in to the computer.

"She seems a bit hassled this morning," Annie commented as they sat in the guest chairs in the librarian's office.

She joined them shortly, summoned her bag, and pulled out a pile of folders and a book. "I explained last week some of the representations of a square, yes?" she asked as she sat. She pulled open a book with sticky notes marking several pages.

Annie nodded.

"We missed a really, really big one." Mrs. Cuttlebrink handed Annie the book. She read quickly and glanced up.

"The earth is round," Annie said as she referenced the highlighted section from Mrs. Cuttlebrink. She passed it to Jason.

"Yes, it is. The idea of the four corners of Earth is merely mythical. There's the biblical version, the flat earthers version, and the idea that there are four quadrants of Earth," Mrs. Cuttlebrink advised.

"Let's say no to the flat earth theory. I'm guessing the Fraternitatem won't know about that anyway. What are we looking at?" Annie asked.

"Well, from the mentions in the Bible, it appears to mean bringing people together from all over the Earth," the librarian said.

Annie thought for a moment. Jason said, "It's a nice thought, but that would leave four quadrants. Yes?"

"I would figure you could divide the earth by the western and eastern hemisphere and north and south of the equator," the librarian said.

"So, if that's one of the meanings of the square symbol, could we assume we're looking at four portals, one in each quadrant. If the Louisiana market holds one of the portals…" Annie said.

"Find that portal and that should lead you to the other three. In theory," Mrs. Cuttlebrink added.

"The side of evil has gone through a lot of trouble to hide the market," Jason said.

"They're definitely making it hard to find them and easy to hide whatever it is they're doing." Annie stopped for a moment.

"I think with the Solomon's knot, you're close. I would think that means the Fraternitatem is making a play for the market," Mrs. Cuttlebrink noted.

Jason glanced at his daughter and grimaced with worry.

"I'll keep researching the idea of the four corners and see where the portals might be located. If you find the portals let me know and I can change the parameters," Mrs. Cuttlebrink said.

With the new information, they left the librarian to catch up on her work for the morning.

∽

"Where to next?" Jason asked as they exited the library.

"Well, unpaid help, you want to make a potion?" Annie asked.

Jason smiled. "Lead the way."

The lab location hadn't changed, but over the years, the lab had grown into something sophisticated and far more high tech than it ever had been. At the door, Annie said, "A few months ago, the lab was attacked with a magical bomb. It's been rebuilt and it's very different than what you last saw."

"I'd expect it would have changed," Jason said. He walked through the door, a look of awe on his face.

"Wow!" he murmured as he entered. When Jason last saw the lab, it was smaller, half the size as it was now, and it didn't include the gym that was attached. His eyes darted across the space, taking in the increased number of examination tables, the equipment that was stored on shelves below, the higher number of cabinets and nonmagical investigation instruments. Even the new door to the showers had been upgraded and the incinerator tube no longer existed in the middle of the floor.

Standing at the first table were lab analysts Minka and Roscoe. "Hey, Annie. Great to see you back. And is this *the* Jason Pearce?" Minka asked.

Annie introduced her father to Minka and Roscoe and explained why they were there.

"Busy morning then," Minka said.

Perkins Abernathy walked into the lab from his office and stopped short when he saw Jason standing there. They had been friends nine years ago; he was the one who performed the autopsy on his friend's lifeless body. "Jason," he murmured.

While it hadn't been announced widely through Wizard Hall, word had spread amongst Jason's friends. Perkins was both a friend and a wizard council member, so he was aware of Jason's return. But as it was with most of his friends, the idea he was back was happy and troubling at the same time. Perkins had been one of Jason's closest friends since they were young children. His happiness was clear as the two men embraced.

"Sorry I haven't been by," Jason said. "Originally—"

Perkins held up his hand. "No need to explain. I know why. And I could say the same. I'm just amazed to see you here. And working with your daughter."

Jason smiled and they walked to Annie waiting at the table.

"She brings me the most interesting things." Perkins smile was a mixture of happiness and caution. He pulled out a plastic bag with the bandana Milo found in Annie's neighbor's yard. He sighed deeply. "We had Emily's DNA on file. The hair is most definitely hers."

"And the body we buried?" Jason asked.

"I don't know how they did it. I would guess either they broke in here and tampered with the evidence, or their magic is scary good," Perkins said.

"How likely is it they broke in?" Annie asked.

"Not very likely," Perkins answered.

"It was twenty years ago. How good were our DNA techniques?" Jason asked as he stared at the bandana.

"As good as the nonmagical techniques. That's what we used," Perkins said.

"Their magic is strong, but they're an ancient organization. I don't think their magic is good enough to fool a DNA test," Annie said.

Perkins knew Annie well enough to know where she was heading. He signed into his computer and pulled up the roster of employees in the lab in 1999. He printed off the list. "We had several employees in and out that year. They were all vetted, background checks, criminal records, the works. Some were dissatisfied with the amount of nonmagical techniques we employed to do our jobs. Others... well, one other came and went within six months. Just didn't cut it." Perkins handed Annie the list.

"Thanks. I'll see if anyone on this list has ties to the Fraternitatem. Well, at least what we know." Annie folded the printout and stuck it in her pocket.

"We should figure out who's buried in Emily's grave," Jason said.

"As you're technically dead, I need either Annie or Samantha to sign off on it." Perkins pulled out the standard form. Annie perused the document and signed her name.

"We'll take care of this tonight. Is there anything else we can help you with?" Perkins asked.

Annie pulled out the scroll she received from Douglass Rand. "I need to make this potion. I've been told it will open the portal to the main market." She handed him the scroll. Perkins grimaced and bit his tongue as he read the ingredient list.

"It's... well, huh. These ingredients are something. Each ingredient is dangerous in itself. To use so many in one potion seems a bit overkill, so to speak. But then, the market is inherently evil." He took a breath. "I guess you're making a new cursed athame?"

"That's my plan. I'm guessing pouring the potion in the portal location isn't the way to go, though I'd like to take additional potion with us, just in case," Annie said.

Perkins laughed. "You are a potions master, so I will say this: Yes, we can do that, under two conditions. One I need to be here when you make it, and two, you must promise to be careful with this in your possession."

"Agreed. The biggest question is; do you have these ingredients? Like you said, they're a bit poisonous."

"Who do you think I am?" Perkins asked as he led the wizard guards into the gym to mix the potion.

⚜

Perkins entered a very large walk-in closet only accessible by a small group of people with the correct clearance. He shot a spell into the magical lock, donned his gloves, and sorted through the potion ingredients, pulling what was needed.

While he organized, Minka set up the Bunsen burner, cauldron, and the mortar and pestle on a table set up in the middle of the newly refurbished gym, while Roscoe turned on a large industrial fan to suck up any contaminants released in the air.

"Suits on, please," Perkins said as he donned his contamination gear. When the group was protected, he handed Annie several jars, each containing one poisonous plant: poison ivy sap, giant hogweed, poison hemlock, foxglove, jimson weed, and oleander. She removed one leaf from each container, dropped it into her mortar and began grinding them into a thick, mushy consistency. When the poison was exposed, it was dumped into the cauldron filled with clear water, and the unfinished potion was set on a low flame. She cleaned out the mixing bowl and started on the next group of ingredients, including one small drop of arsenic and a poison from arrow poison frog.

As Annie dropped each ingredient into the cauldron, Perkins monitored her work and carefully mixed the heated liquid as he maintained the temperature. Noxious fumes rose from the cauldron and into the fan through the ventilation system.

"Nice," Annie said through her heavy mask.

Perkins checked the potion again, measured the temperature in the cauldron, and stirred. Patiently, they waited for the potion to shimmer to a clear color. "It's ready for the athame," Perkins finally said.

Annie summoned the knife she kept in a scabbard strapped to her leg. The hilt was a dragon, for Jason's birth year on the Chinese Zodiac. Its eyes were two small emeralds, his birthstone. The tail had been forged to wrap around the ten-inch-long blade, made of elven steel. It gleamed in the artificial light.

"It looks like you've hardly used it," Jason said.

"Look again. I always have it with me," Annie said as she passed the knife to Perkins. He held it with tongs and lowered it carefully in the bubbling potion.

"And the spell," Perkins began.

It was in Latin, so he ran his hand across the words, casting a translate spell. He grimaced when the spell wouldn't translate and took to reciting it in Latin with his hand above the cauldron. When he finished, a black light popped from his palm and hit the potion with a small explosion. They stepped back and waited, but nothing more happened.

"Is that it?" Annie asked as she glanced inside the still bubbling cauldron.

"That's it," Perkins advised as he used the tongs to remove the athame. He lay it on a towel; the knife glowed with magic.

Annie bent over the athame. The potion bubbled against the metal, sizzling as the magic changed the metal, cursing it. When the metal stopped glowing and sizzling, it lay still as if nothing had happened. Perkins dried the knife with the towel, took off his glove, and touched the cool metal.

"Easy enough. Stay safe at the market," Perkins said as he handed Annie her newly cursed athame.

"Thanks. I hope it brings me good luck."

CHAPTER 10

THE KNIFE LAY on Annie desk. She grazed it with her fingers lovingly.

"I remember when I got that. My parents had it made for me when I became a guard," Jason said thoughtfully.

"It's beautiful. Thanks for leaving it to me," Annie murmured.

Jason picked up the cursed athame. "I was going to give it to you when you became a guard. I'm sorry I missed it."

"So am I." She pulled out the Fraternitatem grimoire. "I wonder if the potion was here." She passed the book to Jason.

"You want me to dig for it?"

"You're the unpaid help. So, yeah. By the way, how did you become my partner in this?"

Jason opened the grimoire and began to peruse their spells, potions, and other notes. "Just lucky I guess." He smirked. "I'm sure Spencer would love to have you back." He turned another page.

"I'd love to what?" Spencer asked as he passed her cubicle.

"Miss me?" Annie asked.

He joined them in her office and sat beside Jason. "I do. But it looks like you've had a better offer." He glanced at Jason who was getting lost in the grimoire.

"Eh. He's a hack." Annie glanced at her partner. "You doing okay?"

Spencer sighed. He and Gibbs, as opposite as they were, had been close. Annie understood how hard it was on Spencer to lose him.

"Every day is different. This meeting of the entire Wizard Guard, he'd have hated it. Knowing that hits me hard," Spencer said.

Annie glanced at her phone. "I almost forgot. I suppose we should get there."

They headed to the conference room where Milo was already seated at the head of the table. It made no difference to him that he was retired and Cham was in charge. With Jason back and Annie in trouble, he felt it was his responsibility to return to the wizard guard, however that meant. "It's odd to see you here," he commented as Jason sat beside him.

"Weird for me too," Jason said.

Once a wizard guard, always a wizard guard.

Annie took a seat beside Shiff and Brite where they waited for the other wizard guards to trickle in from the all satellite offices. "How are you?" Brite asked.

"I'm better. Itching seems to lessen during the day when I'm busy," she said.

"Sleeping okay?" Brite asked.

Annie observed Brite carefully. While they had known each other prior to the trip to the past, they grew close while there. She worried about him. He was pale and drawn, and his eyes were encircled with purple. "On and off. You look like hell." Annie tried to sound teasing, though she knew it wasn't funny. What they had been through had been difficult on them. Since their return, they had been avoiding each other and the feelings that came with it.

"Feel like it. I'm sorry I haven't called."

Annie shook her head. "Don't worry about it. I haven't either. Too much baggage to unpack."

She glanced down and saw his right hand graze Shiff's. He pulled it away as the other guards from satellite offices began to enter the conference room.

Annie recognized most of the wizard guards; she had either trained them in some fashion, or she'd worked extensively with them on past cases. When wizard guard partners Isaak Denberry and Eddy Woods entered, they sat on her left.

"Hey, Annie. How are you?" Isaak asked.

"Not bad. Hanging in there. It's good to see you guys again," she said.

"I like Cham's initiative. I forget how fun it is working at the hall," Eddy said as several new recruits made their way into the room, taking seats in the back.

"They look a little scared," Eddy joked.

Annie chuckled to herself as Cham took his place at the front of the room and let the din wind down until all eyes were on him.

"Great that everyone could come in today," he began. "As everyone knows, my plan is to have a monthly meeting with the entire U.S. Wizard Guard. If we need to meet on a more regular basis, we can do that online. So, we have a few issues we need to discuss."

Cham switched on the television with a map of the world on the screen.

"As everyone is aware, Annie came back to the present with a great deal of power," he began.

All eyes were on Annie now. Normally, being the center of attention wasn't a problem for her, and she had no issue speaking in front of large groups, but this situation felt different. She placed shaky hands in her lap. Brite reached over, held her hand, and squeezed gently, not letting go.

"We've contacted all wizard guard units across the world and advised them that we think the Fraternitatem of Solomon is on its way back, not only to kill Annie for her power, but also to use that power to take control the market. We obviously don't want the market in their hands. They're powerful, secretive, and dangerous." Cham pointed to the map. "Here we have all of the markets that we've already searched. The purple dot is the market Annie investigated. This has the symbol in the square pattern." He switched to the picture of the Fraternitatem symbol. "It might be a Fraternitatem symbol based on the Solomon's knot."

Annie raised her hand. "Sorry to interrupt. It's been a long morning, but I've spoken to Mrs. Cuttlebrink. We think we have an answer to the square." She explained the representations of a square in the course of human history. "Yes, I know the earth is round. We think it means the earth is divided into four quadrants: north, south, east, and west. Four markets that probably have that symbol in the pattern of a square." Annie passed out the picture of the wall with the glyphs showing the pattern.

"We couldn't find a portal. No humming or buzzing, no hazy anomaly, no cold air. We're not sure if there's even a portal in the market."

A new guard named Starla Lakin spoke up. "So, what the point of all this?"

Annie knew Starla in passing; her few conversations in the last year with the new guard had been about potion creation after Annie taught Starla's potion class when the younger guard began her training. Beyond that, Annie had never worked with her.

"Well, for starters, we think we have a way to find the portals to the market. We found that pattern behind a storage shed in the Louisiana market. I received a potion from the adventurer named Douglass Rand, the owner of the Witches Brew, who swears it opens the portal to the market. I'm going tonight to verify this. If anyone wants to come, let me know." Before Annie could take a breath, ten hands rose in the air. "Okay. I'm not choosing. You all can decide which three of you are going. I don't want to make a scene at the market." She smirked.

"So. I guess we need a new plan to find the other portals. Any ideas on how to go about that?" Cham asked. He specifically looked at Lial.

Lial unfurled a map of the world and divided it by the prime meridian and the equator. "If that's a correct assumption, here would be the four quadrants." Next, he placed an 'X' at Annie's market location. "So here's Annie's portal. I would think they'd make them all equidistance from each other so the locations form a square. Give me a few hours and I'll pull some coordinates that fit that theory," he said.

They continued on with Wizard Guard business: new procedures, monthly meetings, a new training schedule, and continuing education. "I appreciate everyone coming in for this meeting," Cham finally said. "I have nothing else. If you're staying here to work, we added several small cubicles to the side of the department. I'd like wizard guards to come visit more often. They're fairly large for temporary cubicles and have some basic books and such. If you're heading back to your satellite office, have a good day. When we finally deal with the Fraternitatem, I'll be traveling to the satellite offices. I want to get a good feel for your cases and what you might need. Come find me, I'll be in my cube the rest of the day."

They pushed back their chairs and said goodbye to their colleagues, though all of them decided to stay in main office for the day. Annie walked back with Starla and Monica, inviting them in her cubicle.

"I'll come with you tonight," Starla said as she sat down.

"Great. I'd like to leave around eleven thirty. I can meet you back here. We'll be heading to Louisiana. It's wet, hot, and buggy, so dress accordingly," Annie advised.

"Congrats. I see the ring," Monica said, reaching for Annie's hand.

"Thanks." Annie continued the conversation, enjoying the moment with no thoughts of her father, her mother, or the Fraternitatem.

∽

After a while, they separated, Starla and Monica finding empty cubicles. Annie knocked on Cham's cubicle. "Hey," she said and sat beside Milo, who was speaking with Cham.

"I wasn't expecting you," Cham joked.

"Eh. Just wanted to let you know I'm trying to get a meeting with Rathbone. Jack is working on it now."

"You should take Ryan with," Milo suggested. He glanced at Cham. "Sorry. Habit."

"No worries. I didn't think it was time to tell everyone about Emily. On that account, I'm deferring to you on everything," Cham said.

"There's only a few people I trust with that. I have two thoughts actually. First, I wonder if she might try to get in touch with her mother. Second, I wonder if we could have a team break into Emily's house and snoop a little. Find something that proves it's her."

Cham looked at Milo, who knew Emily even better than Annie did.

"It's easy enough to put a team on your grandmother. We might be able to bug the phones and put a camera on the doors. Who do you trust with this?" Milo asked.

"Brite and Shiff. Brite already knows," Annie said.

Milo patted Annie's hand. "So I suggest Shiff and Brite investigate that house. It would help to know if it's really her. In terms of your grandmother, I defer to the department manager."

"Is there anyone else you trust?" Cham asked.

"Spencer and—" She leaned backwards in the chair. Her eyes teared up; she didn't bother to wipe them away. "Sorry."

"We all miss him," Milo said.

"I feel vulnerable without him," Annie said.

"I'm here to help. I can watch your grandmother with Lial if he'll go," Milo said. He touched her hand.

"I'm a blubbering mess sometimes," Annie said. She started to scratch at her thighs.

"You're still scratching?" Milo asked.

"When I'm tired, sad, angry, or contemplative." She wiped the tears. "It never really goes away. Though I notice it less when I'm busy."

There was a knock at the cubicle wall, and they all turned to see Shiff and Brite standing there. Brite held up his phone, revealing the text Cham had just sent.

"You're quick," Annie said as the two men walked into the cubicle.

"Yes we are. So, how can we help?" Brite asked.

"My mom. We think we know where she is," Annie said.

"Bucky found her. That's a positive step. Where?" Brite asked. He pulled his chair beside Annie.

"We think she's watching Sami." Annie told him what they had seen over the weekend. She described the woman who watched them and the house that was just purchased in the courtyard.

"You want us to follow her and watch her?" Brite asked.

"Break in and look around and verify it's her," Cham said.

Annie passed Brite the address. He looked at Shiff and back to Annie. "I think we can do that."

CHAPTER 11

THE ATHAME SAT in a leather sheath strapped to Annie's leg and rubbed against her skin when she walked. She placed the extra potion inside her pocket and sealed it with a spell, then read the map of the market locations and sought out the portal in the Louisiana swamp.

"Um, that's where we land?" Starla asked.

Annie shook her head. "Actually, we'll land here and trek through the swamp." Her finger trailed the path she and Robin had taken the week before. Annie glanced at the costume Starla chose to wear: a low-cut tank top under a leather jacket, tight jeans, and tall boots. She appeared nothing like a guard, something much in her favor.

"What's the interest in coming tonight?" Annie asked. Starla was from the Northeast region and primarily worked vampire cases in New England.

"I've never worked with the main team. I thought it was time to get out and get my face shown." She smiled widely.

"Welcome. I think Cham wants to rotate everyone throughout the five offices to get a taste of the different cases. The market problem was a great way to get everyone out," Annie said.

"Cham seems cool. I like that he's the new manager," Starla said.

Annie smiled and said, "As much as I got used to Milo's way of managing, it's nice for something new."

"When did you and Cham become engaged?" Starla asked, tapping her fingers against her jeans.

"About four weeks ago." Annie checked her phone.

"You can't work for him, can you?"

"No, I can't. But as the old saying goes, once a wizard guard, always a wizard guard. I'll be around," Annie said. She had known from the beginning, when she and Cham began dating, that this would happen. It had been months since Headmaster Turtledove had asked her if she'd try her hand at teaching at Windmere School of Wizardry. She was intrigued by his new offer, a real offer, and she was curious what the reaction of the Wizard Council would be when Ryan took the plan to them. Annie sighed and glanced up as Spencer entered the conference room.

"Are we ready?" Spencer said as he glanced at Starla. She stared back at him. Neither had ever worked together and they each seemed surprised by the other's going-to-market appearance. Spencer normally dressed in collared shirts and chinos, but tonight he wore boots, tight jeans, and a tight T-shirt showing off his muscles. Over that, he wore a black leather coat. Annie recognized it as Gibbs's jacket. Meanwhile, Spencer couldn't stop staring at the high heels on Starla's boots.

Annie chuckled softly. "Starla, can you magically shrink your heels? You're gonna have a rough time through the swamp."

Starla glanced at her boots and back to Annie, a pink blush on her cheeks. "Sorry, I didn't realize."

"No problem," Annie said as Starla adjusted the heels.

"Ready?" Annie asked, as she led them down the back staircase, teleporting from the Wizard Hall courtyard.

⌁

Shiff and Brite teleported to the roof of Samantha and John's townhouse. While they worked in the Chicago main office on several cases, they weren't from the area and took a moment to take in the cityscape from their location on the roof.

"It's a great view up here," Shiff commented.

"Yeah. It is." Brite walked to the far corner of the roof and took out his binoculars aiming them at the townhouse belonging to Emily and Levi King-Solomon; the shades were drawn and the lights were off.

"They could be asleep," Shiff said as he looked over his partner's shoulders.

"Most normal people would be at midnight," Brite said curtly.

"You seem mad. Care to share?"

"Not now. I've only been back three weeks. I need time to decompress." Brite moved to another location along the roof top and glanced through his binoculars, searching for any visible signs of recording equipment, magical hexes, and jinxes.

"We have to talk about what happened to you. What you saw. I'm your best friend," Shiff said.

Brite pulled away from the binoculars and stared absently into the darkness. "Annie's in danger and I'm really fond of her. You and I, we're still just partners."

Shiff cringed. "It could be so much more," he said. "I touch your hand, you hold mine. I try for more, you push me away."

Brite looked through the binoculars again, scanning the roof across the courtyard. "I felt it before I left. I did. I knew. I knew that you were more to me than just my partner. But I can't do this now. I want Annie safe. I need time to process... everything." He sighed deeply.

"I'll wait. No more pressure. Just tell me how I can help." Shiff raised his hand above Brite's shoulder but removed it.

Brite glanced at him with sad eyes. As he passed him the binocular, their hands touched. Brite made no movement to stop it.

Shiff took his turn watching the rooftop. "I'm not seeing anything up there. We should be able to take them, as they're not magical," he said.

"The husband and kid might be," Brite reminded him.

"Sure. It's possible. Damn, I know we're here to help Annie, but I'd love transfer to the main office," Shiff said.

"A new start." Brite nodded and smiled. "When she's safe, we'll talk. I'll head to the rooftop on the right." He teleported away.

Shiff teleported after and watched cautiously as Brite flashed a light across to the King-Solomon roof top, searching for magical hazes or nonmagical devices. "Anything?" Shiff asked.

"Nothing. Why does that make me anxious?"

"It's like they're baiting her to come after them," Shiff said.

"I sense a trap. Wanna break it?" Brite smirked before he teleported to the King-Solomon rooftop.

"You're getting bolder." Shiff said as Brite jiggled the door handle.

"She's a good friend. And this pisses me off." Brite held his hand six inches from the handle and twisted his wrist until the lock popped and the door swung open. They waited for any sign of a security system. "No alarm," Brite whispered.

Rather than using flashlights, they activated their crystals. A dim, bluish glow highlighted their path as they searched for magic and booby traps along the back hallway. It led them to the bedrooms; they stopped at the first room on the right. Shiff nodded as he positioned himself between the other room and his partner as Brite opened the door. The room was small. A young teenager lay in a twin bed along the far wall. His digital clock blinked 12:30 a.m. Above him, a large Chicago Bears mural took up the entire wall. Brite backed out of the room and closed the door.

"Shiloh King-Solomon," Brite whispered. "We should come back when no one's here."

The next room was open and empty; they entered and closed the door. A decorated bed sat under the window and two pillows lay against the headboard. Family pictures hung along the far wall covering most of it. Shiff and Brite perused the photos of Shiloh from baby to teenager. Apparently, the family had traveled extensively through Europe, Israel, and Africa. Brite and Shiff took several pictures of the family with their phones.

Beside the individual pictures were two large collage frames. They studied each of them, getting a sense of Emily's life with Shiloh and Levi. At the corner of the left collage, Shiff found a picture of Annie and Samantha with Jason. He snapped a picture. "Either a part of her never stopped loving them, or it was a reminder of what she had to do," Shiff said.

Brite pointed to the closet and found a small filing cabinet. He touched the wall and sent a muffle spell across the room before opening the top drawer. Inside, he found a thick folder and pulled it out. The file contained several official documents—a marriage license, birth certificates, death certificates, and passports. He lay them on the desk. "They look real," he commented, snapping pictures before moving to the next document.

Shiff skimmed bills, taking pictures and making notes on what and where the King-Solomons spent their money. "I found pay stubs from a company called Antique Symposium," he said.

"Never heard of it. Anything for him?"

"Nothing yet."

"Well, well," Brite said a moment later and showed Shiff death certificates for Anne Elizabeth Pearce, Samantha Emily Pearce, and Jason Pearce. Brite took more pictures.

"You think she told her husband her first family died?" Shiff asked.

"You'd think he'd know these were fake if he's part of the Fraternitatem," Brite said.

"It's a lot of work to keep up appearances. Their bills are pretty average." Shiff returned the items to the desk and took the next drawer of the filing cabinet.

Brite finished sifting through the documents and placed them back in the drawer, continuing his perusal of the contents.

"Huh?" Shiff said as he pulled out a large bound document. "The will and testament of Gloriana Worthington." Shiff shuffled through the document. "Annie's grandmother's will. In the event of Emily's death, Annie and Samantha stand to receive quite a lot of money." Shiff snapped pictures of several sheets of the will before texting Bucky asking him to search for a full copy of it.

"The only family Annie ever talks about is the one she created after her parents died," Brite said.

"I can't imagine what she's going through right now." Shiff finished taking pictures and put the will back in its rightful place. "I think we have enough to prove it's her. Let's plan on coming back when they're not home."

After replacing what they touched, they snuck back down the hallway and back outside, teleporting home.

⁂

Annie trekked through the water, her arms outstretched, searching for the unmistakable chill that always radiated off of magical portals. Behind her, Starla grumbled as her pants grew wet from the stinky swamp. Though she shortened the height of her heels, they kept sticking in the mud. Spencer held up the rear, assisting Starla in between scanning the edge of the swamp for any company.

"Here it is," Annie said.

"Demons are getting more devious," Spencer commented.

For this entrance, he shoved his own cursed athame into the portal, immediately opening it. A heavy, tornado-like wind whirled at them, and lightning struck the water. Starla jumped out of the way as thunder boomed. She glanced inside the portal, a look of fear on her face.

"You okay?" Annie asked. She bit her tongue to keep from laughing, though she realized her first experience in the market had been a bit daunting as well.

"Yeah. I've never been to the market, let alone seen a portal."

Annie smiled and said, "See you inside."

Spencer joined Annie in the market, leaving one foot in the swamp and the other on the silky dirt of the market. The portal swirled and hummed against his leg, pushing on him as they waited for Starla to jump through. "Now. It's getting stronger," Spencer shouted as the lightning lit up consecutively, sending booms reverberating across the water.

Starla had started six months before the fall of the black market and hadn't had the opportunity to see what a large operation the market could be or the make up of the portals. She swallowed hard and stepped through; the portal closed when she was securely entered. She glanced behind herself when she entered and saw only the back wall of the market. She glanced across the market, her eyes widening in a mixture of anxiety, fear, and awe. While merchants and customers bought and sold items, a woman led a small dragon by a heavy, iron leash strapped around the dragon's neck.

"I've never been to the market," Starla admitted.

"The timing was bad. Sorry about that. You should have been trained in the market when you started. So look at this as your on-the-job training," Annie said. "Just remember, if this new athame works, this will be nothing compared to the real market. Keep your eyes open and listen." She led them across the five aisles to the last row, where Joseph's booth was located. He smiled when he saw her.

"Annie Pearce. You're back," he said.

She handed him a note and headed behind the storage shed.

"There's not much to this portal," Starla commented.

Spencer stood guard as Annie summoned her cursed athame. "See these here?" She showed Starla the four glyphs that formed a large square.

"It's in there? I don't feel anything," Starla said as she touched the wall.

"It's somewhere here." Annie estimated the center of that supposed square. She was about to place the tip of her knife to the center when she spied a small glyph near her proposed location and moved in for a closer look. Summoning a magnifying glass, Annie was able to ascertain she was looking at another Solomon's knot, small and perfectly centered.

"Damn," she said.

"Found something?" Spencer asked.

She touched the knot with the tip of her knife. As the poison touched the Solomon's knot, energy burst forth. Annie's arms tingled and shook, and that unmistakable portal chill radiated outwards as the portal materialized. Annie glanced inside; the market, much like the original one, stood before them.

There was no wind, no lightning, no thunder, as the portal revealed a five-foot-high entrance to the main market. Annie glanced at Spencer. "Look what we found," she said proudly as Joseph joined them.

"Yes, you did," he said.

Annie watched the market unfold before her. A dragon limped across the silky dirt, kicking up dust, and two elves deposited full baskets in the booth nearest them. The same familiar haze hung above this market. She could feel it seeping into her hair and clothing.

Annie grinned as she stepped inside.

"Smells the same," Spencer said as the scent of wet fur and burnt flesh filled his nostrils. He stepped to the side, allowing Joseph and Starla to enter.

A loud din enveloped them as they submersed themselves into the life of the market. Angry screeches filled the air as a booth owner argued a point. The air crackled with jinxes flying through the air, and fire rumbled with the creation of a fireball.

"Just like home," Annie said, almost giddy at their discovery.

"Better start blending," Spencer said. They split in pairs. Starla joined Spencer in taking the left as Annie and Joseph headed to the right.

"I always knew you'd find it," Joseph said as they followed the horde along the outside aisle.

"You have way too much faith in me, I think." Annie offered a smile as they took in the familiar scents and sounds of the black market. While this one was smaller than the original, it was so similar. Annie soon recognized several merchants.

I wonder...

Booths were filled with potion ingredients, creature parts, dragon eggs, and cauldrons. Annie stopped in the middle of the aisle after spying Gibbs's informant, a man by the name of Arrowhead. Not wanting to draw attention to themselves or to him, she and Joseph strolled slowly to his booth where she searched the items on the table.

She knew he would know who she was, so she waited patiently for him to assist his current customer. When he was finished, he strolled to her. Annie tossed five gold avrum coins on the table. The coins were ancient forms of payment for wizards; they weren't often used anymore, but they were still highly prized, especially at market.

Arrowhead scooped up the five coins and pocketed them in his upper breast pocket. "Are you looking for anything in particular?"

"Has the Fraternitatem of Solomon been here?" Annie asked softly.

Arrowhead's expression remained stony as he held out his hand. She placed six more coins in his palm.

"They come. I would prefer the return of the djinn," he said, referring to the being who tried to control the market prior to its collapse.

Annie pulled out ten additional coins and slid them to him. "Do they control it now?" she asked.

"No. But they're making a move." Arrowhead pocketed his new stash of gold coins. He glanced around the aisle, but anyone doing business was preoccupied with their own actions. He held up his finger and asked her to wait. Annie texted Spencer to let him know.

"They're getting a foothold," Joseph commented.

"Yes, they are," Annie agreed.

Arrowhead returned with a pouch, a stem from a poisonous foxglove plant poking out. "For you when you return home," he said and bowed once. When he looked up, Spencer and Starla were there. "I suspect your visit today will be short," Arrowhead said as he re-entered his booth.

Annie showed Spencer the bag.

"Now we know," Spencer said and led them from the market.

"What was that?" Starla asked as they exited the main market and stepped into the smaller one.

"Not now," Spencer said. He walked them to the portal that would lead them back to the swamp.

"Are you staying?" Annie asked Joseph.

Joseph shook his head, looked around the market one last time, and jumped through the portal, landing in the Louisiana swamp.

⟡

Joseph had never been to the U.S. Wizard Hall. When Annie landed him in the courtyard, his eyes grew wide with curiosity, he offered a hearty, deep laugh. "Well, look at the Americans," he said.

"We have a hotel at that far corner. You can stay there if you wish. We just want to see what Arrowhead left for us and then we'll head home. I've already let the team know we found the market," Annie said.

"That would be good, Annie Pearce. I am so enjoying this," Joseph said.

"It's a foxglove leaf. Why?" Starla asked, eyeing the pouch. Spencer glanced at her before looking inside the pouch. He pulled out a scroll and unrolled it.

The Fraternitatem of Solomon has a strong foothold in the market, and they are looking to control all magical trade.

Beware of Melichi, the leader of the Fraternitatem of Solomon. He has inquired several times about the Wizard Guard, specifically about Annie Pearce. They are coming for her and for her power.

I will be at the Snake Head Letters tomorrow at midnight. Meet me there.

A

"Stay vigilant. You want me to teleport you home?" Spencer asked.

"No. Go home. I'll be fine."

"Tomorrow, then," Spencer said as he gave her a goodbye hug. Air rushed into the space he vacated as he teleported away.

"Can I help? I'd like to do more," Starla said.

"You can come and work out of the main office any time," Annie told her.

"Tomorrow." Starla nodded and teleported home.

Annie and Joseph walked to the corner of Wizard Hall, where the all-wizard hotel had been established. They stopped just outside the front door.

"I had just set up my booth when you happened to find me," Joseph admitted.

"It was lucky I found that market," Annie said. The large courtyard was empty at this time in the morning. She watched the moon as it slowly traversed one end of the space to the other.

She leaned against a brick wall that lined the walkway into the hotel.

"How did you find this particular market?" Joseph inquired.

Annie glanced at the jovial man and smiled. "It's a mystery to me. My very good friend had a contact who told him to try there. I happened to meet the vampire Sturtagaard there that first night. And he said the portal was there."

"That's some coincidence," Joseph remarked.

"As I don't believe in coincidence, I'm guessing the Sturtagaard put someone on Robin Price and knew we'd be there. It's the kind of thing that asshole would do," Annie explained.

"I have heard about that vampire. I thought you'd have staked him by now."

"I thought I would have too. But as he always does, he dangled information in front of me. He knows I'm coming back for information on the other portals to the market."

"Don't let him influence your decisions. He's not worth your time. Though I'm not surprised he set you up to find the market. From what I've learned, he's the reason the Fraternitatem is after you." Joseph was no longer jovial. His demeanor was of protector and friend.

"You and everyone else are right. But for now, I need to concentrate on this. Anyway, I should get home. Have a good night."

Joseph laughed. "I shall, Annie Pearce. See you in the morning. This is amazing," he continued to chuckle as he entered the hotel.

Smiling lightly, Annie turned and looked inside the courtyard before teleporting herself home.

CHAPTER 12

CHAM SLEPT PEACEFULLY as Annie stripped off her clothes and entered the hot shower, washing off swamp and dragon dung. Even detangling her mess of hair, she couldn't stop smiling, knowing she had just discovered the main market.

Only because Sturtagaard helped.

She grimaced, not at the realization that he helped, but rather at the notion that he had tampered with her life and set her on the course when it was convenient for him.

That damn vampire!

While it irritated her, even angered her, she still felt no need to rush to his lair and stake him. The more entrenched she became in finding her mother, the less she cared about Sturtagaard. She preferred to think about what it would mean once Shiff and Brite proved that Emily lived near Samantha.

Beyond the bathroom door a jar or glass crashed. Annie jumped as the bathroom door squeaked open.

"You found the market!" Cham said as he sat down on the toilet.

"Yeah. The potion worked well. What crashed?" she asked.

"Zola. Are you almost done? Shiff and Brite are here," Cham said.

"I'm almost done." She rushed to rinse her hair and squeeze water from her thick tresses. She shut off the water and grabbed the towel Cham handed her.

"Okay. What's up?" she asked when she stepped from the shower.

"They have some things they want to show you."

Annie glanced at him quickly and threw on a T-shirt and shorts, leading them downstairs.

"Hey, Zola." Her Aloja fairy held a tray with a sandwich and drink. Behind Zola, Jason leaned against the counter. "Okay, this can't be good," Annie groused as she saw the folder on the table between Shiff and Brite.

"Sorry, Annie. We…" Brite glanced at Shiff. "We don't think this needs to be broadcast to the rest of the guard, but you should know now." Brite slid the folder to her when she sat down.

"First, I'm going to say, they haven't protected the house in any way. Almost like they're baiting you," Shiff advised.

Brite pushed the folder to her. "We can confirm Emily, Levi, and Shiloh live there."

Annie glanced at Cham before opening the folder. She found a copy of the marriage license, Shiloh's birth certificate, her grandmother's will, death certificates for her, Samantha, and Jason. Annie shuddered. Lastly, she found the photo of herself with Samantha and Jason. She showed Cham.

"We figure the picture of you and Samantha is either a painful reminder of what she lost or a reminder of what she had to do," Brite said. Annie glanced at him. She could read the sadness and worry in his face.

Annie continued through the pile and picked up several pages of her grandmother's will. "Grandma Gloriana is still alive. I have someone watching her house in case Emily tries to reach her." She began to read the copy of the pages.

"Did she come to my funeral?" Jason asked.

Annie looked at him. "If she did, I wouldn't have known her. No one that looked like Mom came up to Sami or me."

Annie returned to the pages. Her jaw flew open. "There's a crap load of money for Sami and me since Mom died."

Jason sat beside Annie and pulled the will from her. "I expected the girls would have inherited a large sum, when they turned twenty-five. Sami should have gotten hers last year."

"Mom has a six-million-dollar trust fund she's entitled to now." She glanced at Jason. "That would buy the Fraternitatem a lot of weapons, people, things."

"Gloriana could be in danger," Jason said.

"Good thing Milo and Lial will be watching the house," Cham said.

"Milo?" Shiff asked.

"He wants to protect Annie," Brite commented. He and Annie exchanged glances, sharing memories and emotions. Their silent exchange wasn't lost on Shiff or Cham.

"Michael and I will continue watching Emily's house. We'll follow the family as well. We could use an additional team though," Shiff said.

"We're limiting access to information about Emily. I'll vet another team and work out a schedule," Cham said. When they were finished, Brite and Shiff stood up to leave. Brite squeezed Annie's shoulder before they left.

"Mind telling me why we didn't have a relationship with Grandma Gloriana growing up?" Annie asked her father.

He ran his hand across his two-day beard.

His hair is growing!

Though he was a ghost and shouldn't have been able to physically change, he was. It was unnerving to watch his beard develop.

"From what your mom told me, they didn't get along. Emily refused to see her mother, and when she died, Gloriana blamed me for Emily's death. I wouldn't let her toxicity affect my girls. She stopped trying to see you after a while. I did feel guilty and sent her pictures and notes about you, but she never came back." Jason sighed.

Annie lay her head in her hands. She rubbed her cheeks. "That's all fine and good. If Mom knows what's in the will"—she pointed to the picture— "she might come back for her money. It looks like it would have come to her when she was thirty-five."

"I think I'll put a more detailed protection team on Gloriana. I'm starting to think the money could be an issue," Cham said.

Annie yawned deeply and glanced at the clock on the wall; it was 1:30 a.m. "Okay. You protect my grandmother. I'm going to spend tomorrow chasing down Sturtagaard. I have questions for him." She took a bite of the sandwich Zola had made for her.

"It's almost over," Jason said.

Annie nodded. She knew once it was, he would be gone, and either she or Emily would be dead.

CHAPTER 13

ANNIE GLANCED AT her phone as she walked to the hotel where Joseph was staying. When she arrived, he was sitting on the patio, sipping tea and enjoying the *American Sphinx*, the American wizard newspaper, as he waited for her. He offered a wide, infectious smile that matched his enthusiasm for the job when she entered the small patio.

"Annie Pearce!" Joseph's voice boomed as he pulled a chair out for her.

"Enjoyed your evening?" she asked with a smile.

He chuckled loudly. "I did. That is a wonderful hotel. Bagel?"

Annie shook her head and chuckled. "I just called in to security and they vetted you. So if you're interested, I can take you in to the hall."

Joseph nodded emphatically, paid his bill, took a final sip of tea, and tucked a bagel into his jacket pocket as he followed Annie across the court-yard. Joseph took it all in as they passed the picnic tables, some filled with employees drinking coffee or reading their phones or books.

"Can I ask how you came to pick that market to set up shop in?" Annie asked. While she didn't believe in coincidences, she had a sinking feeling that all the pieces were connected. There were too many to ignore.

"We had several contacts who offered leads. This particular market had a steady stream of foot traffic and we believed we could glean much information if I was set up there. I wasn't aware of the portal, however," he admitted.

"I haven't had the opportunity to investigate many markets, but it was by far the largest I had seen."

"You think there's more to it?" Joseph asked as Annie led him inside the employee entrance.

"Hi, Lorena," Annie said, pausing her conversation with Joseph. "I have a visitor from the South African Wizard Guard."

Lorena read the badge and reviewed his credentials. "No problem. I contacted South Africa after you called. They verified." After Lorena issued the visitor's pass, Annie cast her spell into the lock and led Joseph into the back hallway.

"To answer your question, yes, I think we are purposely being directed to the market. Why? I can't say." Annie had no reason to doubt that Sturtagaard was directing her to the market, but she didn't know how Joseph fit into that.

"Your vampire led you there and your friend's contact led him there. I was led there. Yes, that is disconcerting. I don't see how it helps the Fraternitatem though."

"You mind telling me who led you to that market?"

Joseph entered the elevator after Annie. She pushed the fifth-floor button. "You're asking for a contact," Joseph stated.

"Yes, I am." She leaned against the wall.

"Remember, I was a merchant at the market before it crashed. I sought out many of my contacts after the market's fall. While I was being trained as a wizard guard, my manager felt I was the right man to be useful back in this market."

"You're reluctant to give up the name."

He nodded as the elevator doors slid open. Upon seeing the fifth floor, Joseph's eyes bulged. The fifth floor buzzed and hummed as machines blinked and purred, and a thick din of voices hovered over the many departments on this floor.

He followed Annie through the maze of cubicles. "Here's my space," she said as she sat in her chair.

"This is amazing." He chuckled as he sat across from her.

"Actually, your Wizard Guard is doing the right thing, keeping one of you inside the market to track what's happening."

Joseph leaned against the back of the chair. His eyes darted across her small cubicle, taking in her artifacts, the books, the pictures on her back credenza.

"His name was Levi Chasen."

Levi?

Annie visibly shuddered at the name. She thought to tell him of her family situation, but she was holding the information close to her. Though the Wizard Guard security team had vetted him, it wasn't enough for her to be total open. "Thanks. I promise to keep it safe."

"What's in that name? I saw you react to it."

Annie leaned against her desk. "We've come across another Levi in our search for info about the Fraternitatem. It makes me wonder. When do you need to get back to the market?"

Joseph looked at his watch. "I need to check in at the office in about thirty minutes. I'll take my portal to the market a little after that." He returned to glancing across her cubicle.

Annie texted Bucky the name, *Levi Chasen*, and summoned the growing case file, leaving it on her desk. "I'll start pulling together everything we have and sending the findings to the other guard units. What to look for and how to get into the market," she said.

"So what's next for you?" Joseph asked.

"We'll be meeting here to discuss the next steps and update everyone on what we've found so far."

"It is so very good to be working so closely with the Americans. You have an impressive wizard hall and wizard guard." He nodded lightly.

"Thanks. It's nice to know we have friends elsewhere." She glanced at the clock on her wall. "Would you like me to walk you out?" He glanced at the clock and nodded with a very big grin on his face.

⤸

Bucky Hart texted Annie as she saw Joseph off, so she took a detour to the basement department.

"Hey, Bucky." She sat in his open chair.

"Levi Chasen? Where did that come from?"

After Annie explained Joseph's contact and how he helped him set up in the new market, Bucky handed her a thick folder. She opened the front cover and her jaw opened in surprise. There were information sheets for Levi King-Solomon, Levi Solomon, Levi King, Levi Worchester, and Levi Chasen. Annie stared at the pictures of each alias and knew that regardless of how he tried to change his look, it was definitely the same man. While he could change his hair coloring or grow a mustache, his nose remained long and thin, his jaw tight and square.

The rap sheets for each alias included the same crimes: burglaries, bad checks, breaking and entering.

"He wasn't too creative with his names or his crimes, Was he?"

"It made it easier to connect him. This guy really helped set up Joseph in the market?"

"Joseph gave him up as a contact and alluded to the fact he had contacts from his time in the original market."

Annie tapped her fingers against the file. "Did you notice the name Levi Worchester?" It was the same last name of the man, Gladden Worchester, who had destroyed the original market with the help of the djinn.

"Yeah. I saw that. So I dug for birth certificates, death certificates, family connections, school records. I ruled out the two names that had known death certificates. I made the assumption that the marriage license would be relatively close to his correct age, birthdate, and location of birth. I cross-referenced that information to each birth certificate, and only one was actually a perfect match."

Annie shuffled through the papers until she found Levi Worchester's birth certificate, college diploma, and family tree. She followed the line upwards; he was a younger cousin of Gladden Worchester. "We never understood how a low-level thug like Gladden Worchester ran the market. Now it's his cousin who married my mother!" Her voice was louder than expected.

Bucky placed his hand on his cubicle wall and chanted a muffle spell over his desk. "Do you want me to call Cham? Spencer? Ryan?" he asked.

Annie stood and paced a small path across his crowded cubicle. "No. I'll be fine. Maybe." She stopped and leaned against the wall. "They've been waiting for my powers to come in for centuries. They must have started planning when I was born, not knowing exactly when the powers would come. Could they have set Gladden up in the market? I feel like a chess piece in their game." She sat back down.

"Levi and Gladden are definitely related. And they are both tied to the market. Yes, the Fraternitatem could have set him up there. He also screwed it up, but that bodes well for the Fraternitatem," Bucky said.

"So, what do I do with this information?"

Bucky shrugged. "I'm sorry, Annie. I just don't know what it means."

෯

Jason borrowed Gibbs's cubical, affording himself some privacy. Annie shuddered as she entered and dropped the box, containing Jason's last case file, on the desk, startling him from his reading.

"Hi, sweetie. What's up?"

She opened the lid and pulled out the prophecy, rolling the scroll toward him. "Did you ever wonder who told the Fraternitatem about the prophecy?"

Jason took the prophecy with trembling hands. "No. I think I was too worried about you to think about that." He opened the scroll and read the prophecy. From the look on his face, Annie could tell he was remembering the events leading to his death, how Melichi told him Annie was in danger. He looked at his youngest daughter. "Who told them?"

"You believed a man who kidnapped your wife at face value when he said that there was a prophecy. And you believed the prophecy?"

"Yes! I was scared. They had powers I couldn't control. When I saw your mom, I believed they were going to come after you. Who told them?"

"Sturtagaard. Sturtagaard put them on this. He bargained for his life by giving me to them."

Jason's squeezed his fists together, exposing white knuckles of tight skin. His jaw tightened. "Why is he still alive?" he asked.

"Because I'm past the point of caring about him. Though he seemed resigned to that fact and is ready to be dead. I think keeping him alive is bothering him and that makes me happy," Annie said.

"That could be worth it. How do you suppose we find peace?" Jason asked.

"Stop the Fraternitatem so they can't manipulate us anymore."

"And so we shall," Jason said with a smile.

∽

In successive moments, Annie received a text message and a phone call. The call she answered right away, seeing that it was from Manny at the security office at the employee entrance.

"There's a Fabian Arnault here to see you," Manny said.

"You're kidding. Really?" Annie asked. "I'll be right down." As she headed to the front door, Annie read the text message she had received, from Jack Ramsey.

Tomorrow at 10 a.m.

She responded with a "yes" as she reached the first floor.

Fabien Arnault had been fired as the department manager of the French Wizard Guard when it was discovered that his guard, Marielle Beauchamp, used the vampire Princess Amelie to kill members of her own family for financial gain. But it was only part of the problem; the French Wizard Guard had utilized department resources to conduct memory modification spells on the French wizard population to hide what she was doing.

Annie hadn't seen the disgraced department manager in months and was surprised that he was visiting. When she arrived at the security room, she saw him waiting for her, reading his phone.

"Fabien?" Annie said as she extended a hand. "How are you?" She took note of his healthy tan and sun-bleached hair. He appeared healthy, muscular, and less grumpy as he took her hand and smiled.

"I am well. My suspension was actually a good thing. I'm so glad you could see me on such short notice."

"Not a problem." Annie waited as Lorena finished with his credentials and handed over a visitor's pass. After they gained entrance to the hall, Annie led him to the fifth floor.

Cham glanced with curiosity as Annie led Fabien to her cubicle. "Not sure why," Annie said to Cham under her breath as she followed him inside. "What can we do for you today?" she asked Fabien once they were seated. Cham joined them and sat beside Fabien, who nodded quickly.

"Well. I have been working… freelance." He looked at his manicured hands and glanced back up at Annie and then Cham. "I'm aware all of the Wizard Guard units are on a wild goose chase searching for the black market."

Annie and Cham exchanged glances.

"We're surprised to see you. Is there something you need?" Cham asked.

"I'm here to offer my services and to pass on some information." He pulled a scroll from his pocket. "I happened upon the coordinates to a portal in Greece. It didn't lead me to the main market, but this market was... close. There were whisperings amongst the merchants about a portal to the main market somewhere in that smaller market. I unfortunately have a lack of access to resources, records, notes, or correspondences between the wizard guards. But I do have this." Fabien handed the scroll to Cham.

"As you're still suspended, we're not able to hire you as a wizard guard," Cham said.

"No, you can't. But you can hire me as a contractor. I'd really like to be a part of it. I want to make up for my past mistakes," Fabien said.

"How much do you know?" Annie asked.

Fabien adjusted himself in the chair. "I know the Fraternitatem is making a play for the market and to do that they need whatever power it is that you have right now. The Fraternitatem is looking for you. They have contacts in all of the markets and I would think even here." He held his arms out as if to prove his point.

Again, Annie and Cham looked at each other anxiously.

"And how do you suppose we determine you're trustworthy and not working for the Fraternitatem?" Cham asked.

Fabien laughed and took out another scroll, handing it to Cham. Noting the wax seal with an arrowhead at the center, he read it and passed it to Annie.

Cham,

Fabien Arnault has been assisting in the market to ward off the Fraternitatem. He has been vetted.

A

Annie stared at the broken seal and said, "You know Arrowhead?"
Fabien nodded.

"I hesitate to trust you based on the past. This seal is his, but still, I'm not sure if it's legitimate," Annie said.

"Arrowhead said you would say that." He pulled out a gold avrum from his pocket and tossed it on her desk.

Annie picked it up and held it in her palm.

"You know what that means?" Cham asked.

"Yes. Do you know what it means?" she asked Fabien.

"You paid him twenty-one of those last night in the market."

Annie nodded. Cham motioned for her to show Fabien the files.

"Arrowhead obviously trusts you. But just know, we can give only give you information on the markets. Beyond that—" Annie began.

Fabien held up his hand. "No need to explain. I accept that. Just market information."

Annie handed him the photo of the wall of glyphs with the pattern highlighted. "Have you seen this?"

Fabien reviewed the picture and smiled. "I have seen many glyphs like this. They are scattered across each market I've been inside. I wondered what they had to do with the market, if anything." He continued to stare at the picture. "So, am I correct that the portal falls in between the four glyphs you have marked?"

Annie nodded. "This particular wall has the portal to the main market." She explained what they had learned in the last week, how she had found the portal, what the square might mean, and their hypothesis that there were three more portals out there.

"The four corners of Earth. Huh." Fabien took out a well-worn world map and spread it across Annie's desk. He divided the map like Lial had done and looked at the four quadrants. "You said Louisiana?" Annie nodded and pointed to the location on his map. "If that's the case, you expect that there are three more portals out there."

"That is what we expect. One in each quadrant," she answered. She passed him a copy of the potion directions for entering the market. "Use this to curse an athame."

Fabien glanced at the recipe and grimaced. "You've found much. I'm impressed. This Wizard Guard is truly productive," he said. He pointed to an area in Greece. "There is a market here. Most of the perimeter wall has a glyph here and there. But there's one wall that looks much like this. I wonder if it, too, has the portal."

Fabien pulled out a picture of the wall and showed Annie and Cham. She explained how they came up with the pattern and began marking the page like they had in the market. With each pass, she showed Fabien. After searching specific pictures, they came up with no square pattern. She showed them the picture of her wall again.

"If you find the square pattern, there will be a mark at the direct center of the proposed square. Place the tip of the cursed athame against the picture and the black market portal will open." Annie offered a smile.

"That is so much work to create the black market and hide it. There is much to do," Fabien said.

"Welcome aboard," Cham said.

Near the end of the business day, Annie had been all over Wizard Hall, meeting with just about everyone it seemed. She had more questions than she had answers and found herself exhausted as she doodled on a notepad and waited for Cham in the conference room.

"Am I late for a meeting?" Starla asked as she glanced inside the conference room.

Annie looked around at the others, who were all preoccupied with their phones or notes.

"No. If you didn't get an email, you're not on this case. Sorry," Annie said. Starla frowned as she debated her next move and made room for Cham to enter.

"Hi, Starla. Thanks again for coming to the main office today. But this is a need-to-know only meeting." He smiled as he closed the door on the young wizard guard and sat, looking occasionally at the window in the door to make sure she had left. "Sorry for the late hour. I just wanted to touch base with everyone." He passed out a thin packet. "Now that we have a wealth of names for Levi and Emily, we've managed to find credit card info, mortgage info, the kid's school records. This should help Shiff and Brite as they track their movements. Anything new?"

"The kid walks from the house to the middle school every day for the summer term. We'll review his school records, but he's there all morning and is home by eleven forty-five. We've seen no friends; he hangs out by himself most of the day. He mostly stays on the main road, entering some of the convenience stores but nothing suspicious. Levi, we've noticed, teleports from the roof every day at seven thirty in the morning and returns home at five forty. The family was home when we went in at midnight. We managed to find an unused bedroom with a filing cabinet. We'd like to go back when everyone's out so we can dig a little deeper and get something personal of his to use to scry for him," Shiff said.

As the report was given, Annie observed her father. He appeared upset by the update on his wife and her new family. Annie reached for him and held his hand.

"Lastly, Emily. When we were at the house, we found pay stubs from a company called Antique Symposium. As luck would have it, that's where we followed her after the kid left for school. Bucky's searching for company records, incorporation info, and tax returns. So far, nothing in the States," Brite finished and handed Annie their report.

"I'm still working out a second team for you. But this seems to prove it's her," Cham said and looked at Annie.

"I'm meeting with Arrowhead tonight at midnight, and I'm meeting with Rathbone tomorrow. Jack's arranged it," Annie said.

"Don't make a deal with that ass," Milo said.

"I have no control of it. Ryan is going with, in case there's a problem." Annie said.

Milo shrugged. "I've walked Gloriana's neighborhood with Lial. There are several great stakeout locations, so we can watch her without being noticed. If it's okay with Annie and Jason, I'd like to have her cars tracked and add some cameras in and around the house. Graham and the VAU can handle that. I want to make sure Emily can't get to her, or if she did, we can track Gloriana to her," Milo said.

Milo and Cham looked at Annie and Jason for approval. "You don't need my permission," Annie said.

"Mine either," Jason groused.

"I know this is hard for both of you. We just want to make it less difficult," Lial said. He added, "I'll be walking the perimeter tonight."

Cham fumbled with his list of wizard guards. "I was wondering if you knew Isaak and Eddy well enough to trust them with your grandmother. I'd like to put together additional teams so Milo and Lial aren't solely responsible."

Annie hadn't worked much with the two men but did work on two connected cases a few years ago. "I worked with them a few times. I'd say they can be trusted," she said.

"Okay. I'll talk to them. It's getting late; is there anything else?" Cham asked and looked around the table.

"You've kept me out of the mess working on additional cases, but my load just got lighter. Let me take one of the shifts at Emily's house," Spencer spoke up.

"You sure? You've been taking the extra cases so we could work this," Cham asked.

"Yes. I'd rather you put the younger guards on these extra cases and let me work with my partner. Besides, there are a lot fewer vampire and demon cases due to the Fraternitatem. I think the magical world is anxious."

"That's not filling me with confidence," Cham said. "Yeah. You work out the schedule with Shiff and Brite. Just let me know your hours worked. Anything else?"

No one had any further comments, so the meeting was concluded. Annie and Cham stayed back.

"You okay?" he asked.

"One year, five major cases all revolving around my dad's death in some manner. No, I'm really not," Annie said.

"I noticed the theme," Cham said.

"Whatever happened to a vampire kill, an evil wizard trying to take over the wizard council, or a wayward demon just out there?" she chuckled softly.

"Those were the days." Cham held Annie's left hand; her engagement ring sparkled against her jeans. "When we win this one, we'll plan a big wedding, celebrate for days, and go on a very long, very romantic honeymoon." He kissed her hand.

"You are a very good man to be hanging in here, with all this." She leaned back in the chair and looked up at the ceiling.

"I love the most amazing woman in the world. I'll take you however you are or wherever you are. I got your back," he said as he playfully punched her arm.

She rolled her eyes. "Check on Samantha tonight. I need sleep if I'm to make my meeting with Arrowhead tonight."

"I'll go to Mom and Dad's. You take a nap before you go tonight. I want a clear picture of this group and then hit them hard. We shouldn't have let them go." Cham admitted.

Annie sat up. "I need to let Ryan know about tomorrow. I'll catch you later?"

Even though they were still in the middle of the conference room, Cham kissed her. "I love you," he whispered and watched her head out.

᷍

Annie smiled at Megan Livery, Ryan Connelly's secretary. "Hi, Megan. How's things?" Annie asked casually. She knew it could be a wasted trip. It was never a good idea to come unannounced.

"Hi, Annie, I'm good. Two visits in two days. Must be busy in the Wizard Guard." Megan had worked for Ryan for the last five years and was as accommodating as any situation allowed.

"Yeah, it is. Is he available?" Annie asked.

"Actually, he's in. Let me see if he can see you," Megan smiled, knocked once and entered. When she returned, she held the door open. Annie stepped through and found Ryan reading documents in a folder, his reading glasses hanging at the end of his nose. As she closed the door, he looked up and smiled.

"Have a seat, Annie." He stood, met her at the reception chairs, and sat beside her. "Milo told me about meeting Rathbone. I've cleared my schedule." He took her hand. "You need to see Samantha. She's—"

"Angry, pissed, furious." Annie finished.

"Confused. Mostly worried."

"She blames me," Annie said.

Ryan shook his head. "No. She doesn't. She feels about what Marina feels when she believes her son is in danger. Sami's worried. Her mom and dad are back from the grave. It's unsettling."

"No kidding," Annie murmured.

"Annie, don't be so hard on her. In the last year, she's visited you in a hospital on multiple occasions while you were seriously injured. She watched you fall apart from the stress of Amelie and the black market, and she waited for you to come back from the past. You're all each other has."

Annie laughed. "Not all that I have. I have you, Kathy, Cham, friends. We just look at it differently."

"Go see her," Ryan said.

"I will tomorrow. I have to meet a contact at the Snake Head Letters at midnight. I'd like to take a nap before I go. Still working the market issue," Annie said.

"What time are we leaving tomorrow?" he asked.

"10:00 a.m."

"Go home and call your sister," Ryan said. Annie grimaced and left him alone to his work.

CHAPTER 14

ANNIE FINALLY SHUT down her computer, packed her belongings, and headed down the stairs. She pushed out the doors and walked along the back corridor to the main passage to the employee entrance with her head down. She didn't see who she bumped into until she looked up at Samantha.

"Hi," she said.

"Hi." Samantha dug into her bag.

"How's Marina and Don?" Annie asked.

"I feel safe, if that means anything." Samantha sounded terse, bitter.

Annie motioned for them to begin walking. Reluctantly, Samantha joined her.

"I was going to come up tomorrow. I have a… thing tonight," Annie tried to explain.

"Suit yourself," Samantha said as they exited the employee entrance. "Come, don't come, whatever." She turned to teleport.

Annie grabbed her arm and held tightly. "Stop being mad at me because you think this is my fault. I didn't ask for this. Just as much as you want me to fawn over you, I need you to let me finish this." She released Samantha and teleported before her sister could respond.

When she landed on her back porch, she nearly slipped and fell, her thoughts preoccupied with Samantha, her mom, her dad. She grabbed the handle of the door and held herself up.

She couldn't help but notice a partially hidden envelope behind a flowerpot. She summoned a latex glove and grabbed the letter, which was addressed to her.

Annie carried the yellow envelope inside and opened it.

The handwriting was familiar to her; she had seen it before but didn't know where. She read the letter.

Annie,

You have been a busy, busy girl. As you stumble through your cases, it has become clear to all that you are incapable of investigating them and putting an end to evil. You messed up with the black market. You were unaware of how it changed and would be crashing down around you. You were careless when investigating Princess Amelie's death. Had you discovered she had been turned, you could have prevented the multitude of deaths that followed. You, Anne Elizabeth Pearce, have been nothing. Nothing. You have screwed up everything you have ever attempted, and you must be stopped before you bring shame and destruction to the world.

I am coming.

EKS

Annie glanced through the kitchen window, past the small yard that had once been her safe playground, where she used to swing on the swing set or dig in the sandbox or eat picnic lunches on a blanket in the grass with her mother. What she remembered most was the joy of chasing bill-dads in the garden, listening to the Cubs games on the radio as she read in the hammock, or practicing tae kwon do stances before testing. It had consistently remained a safe, loving place, but as she stared out of the window now, she felt exposed and vulnerable. She felt like she should be angry, furious, upset, even shaking, but she wasn't. Instead she felt fueled and passionate about going after the Fraternitatem. She left the note on the counter.

"Are you okay?"

Annie swirled around to see Zola standing in her kitchen. The Aloja fairy moved softly, as if she floated on air.

"Mommy left me a love letter." Annie pointed to the note. Zola read it quickly and balled it into a garbage.

"She wants to unnerve you. Don't let her." Zola opened the refrigerator and pulled out a casserole, putting it in the oven. "Call Samantha," she said.

Annie took out her phone. "On it." She snuggled on her sofa with the crinkled note and called Samantha, who was temporarily living with her in-laws, Cham and John's parents, at their farm in Northern Wisconsin.

"What?" Samantha said into the phone. Pots clanked on the other end.

"Would you be more cordial if I come up there?" Annie asked.

"This sucks," Samantha groused.

"Mom left me a note behind the flowerpot on the back porch. She told me that Princess Amelie was my fault, the market was my fault, and that I am responsible for all of the deaths that have occurred because of that," Annie said.

"I'm so sorry," Samantha said. "I'm taking it out on you and you're the one she's after for real." Samantha cried, hiccoughed, and blew her nose. "I'm sorry," she whispered.

"Don't. Just don't. I can't do this. Not now. I have to take a nap. I have to go out at midnight. Just no. Not now," Annie begged.

"Just do what you need to do and please be careful."

Annie held her phone in her hand long after hanging up with her sister. She fell into a fitful sleep.

⊷

The spicy scent of lasagna woke Annie.

"Baby." Cham kissed her forehead, giving her time to gain her bearings and become fully wake. He was eating his portion of dinner, his feet up on the ottoman, the television playing the Witch News Network, with Braxton Bourne giving the full day's news, both magical and nonmagical.

Before she could ask, Zola handed her a plate. As good as it smelled, Annie had no desire to eat and placed it down.

"Did you see what Emily left today?" Annie asked Cham.

"It isn't true. You know that, right?"

Annie shrugged. "She's been watching me. Not necessarily in person, but news. She must get the *American Sphinx* newspaper and WNN. She knows stuff. She knows how guilt ridden I've been over Amelie and Jordan and the market."

Cham held her face in his hands. "Listen to me. She has the backing of the Fraternitatem. They are evil and powerful and have the resources. She is egging you on to come to her. She is playing you, trying to weaken you. But I know you. You are brilliant, strong, capable, and not to blame." He leaned his forehead against hers and kissed her nose.

She glanced at the phone she still held in her hand and checked for messages and the time. She still had six hours. "My world is falling apart for real. Sami is a mess. All my feelings are churned up. It's like everything is now coming to a head," she said.

"It is," Jason said. Annie looked up to see her father standing at the entrance of the den with Emily's note in his hand. "The plan is to unnerve you. Throw you off your game."

Jason sat beside Annie and lay the uncrumpled the note in his lap. "It's her handwriting." He stared out the window, at nothing in particular. "They really did a number on her. She was a good mom once."

"I don't remember," Annie admitted.

Jason held out a VHS tape. "I'm not sure if it's a good idea to see the side of her you don't remember, but if you still have a VCR, it might would be worth it to look at this." He stood and left the note with Annie as he made his way out.

⌘

The only VCR Annie owned was in a storage unit in the basement. She pulled it out and dusted it off. After futzing with the cables, she and Cham finally hooked it to the basement television set and sat on Cham's old sofa. She took a bite of lasagna as the tape began to play.

It was what she remembered or thought she remembered. A young, redheaded mother placing her baby daughter in a stroller. Annie watched Emily lovingly hook her into the seat.

"I must have been about a year old here," Annie said.

Samantha, who was probably around three, rode a small tricycle, her small legs working hard to keep up. Emily laughed as they finally made it down the street and back to the house.

Pictures switched to a bubble bath with Annie in a toddler seat, Samantha beside her, helping Emily wash Annie and Annie pushing them away, using the washcloth to bathe herself.

"You were always independent," Cham noted.

"Some things don't change," Annie said.

There were family pictures, a soccer game for a three-year-old Annie, dance lessons for a five-year-old Samantha. The tape showed snippets of life, some of which Annie remembered, but most experiences were new and painful to watch. When it was over, Annie's food was cold, her stomach ached, and she needed to sleep.

"You okay?"

"I will be," Annie replied. She kissed him deeply before turning away for another small nap.

∽

Spencer stared into the window of the Snake Head Letters as Annie walked toward the store.

"Anything?" she asked as she stepped up a small stoop and jiggled the handle.

"Just the normal," Spencer said. They entered the aged store and walked across the linoleum, which was so old the underlayment was visible. They followed the only light emanating from the back corner, passing the cash register. Walking down the aisle, they eventually turned right and entered Mortimer's office. He sat behind his rickety desk, with and Arrowhead sitting across from him on a metal chair in the depressing, dimly lit room.

With a swipe of his wrist, Mortimer locked the front door. "You're playing with fire. Again," he said to Annie.

She took a seat beside Arrowhead and put her feet on a pile of folders at the edge of the desk. "Not my fault I have a crazy-ass woman after me." She turned to Arrowhead and handed him the note from Fabien. "Is that you?"

Arrowhead handed it back. "Yes. He's not working for them." He summoned a notebook and handed it to Annie. "I come at great risk to myself and others. But that consists of names of those at market, plus maps of several other markets."

Annie opened the notebook and shared it with Spencer, pointing out Melichi's name and further down the pagethe listing of a man named George Worchester.

"Do you know where the other portals are?" Spencer asked.

"No. I don't. What I do know is, that Ezekiel was batshit crazy. Gladden Worchester was a puppet. The Fraternitatem… they are a new level of doom," Arrowhead said.

Hearing these words come from Arrowhead surprised Annie. To work in the market, a merchant dealt with the cursed and illegal. As such, they needed to be tough and not easily frightened. Before today, Arrowhead had fit that description. It was jarring to hear him sound this worried.

"Are you willing to work with us?" Spencer asked. As Gibbs's partner, Spencer had worked with the merchant for years and developed some trust.

"They wish for global power. Not just in the magical world but in the nonmagical one as well. They tricked you into believing your mother was dead and they killed your father. They are capable of much damage to both worlds. I would work with you to remove this dangerous and oppressive monster."

Annie weighed what he said and how he said it. *Fear must be spreading.*

"Annie, they extort money and they kill for very little. The Fraternitatem has established dominance. Even the last market wasn't this ruthless. I have difficulty making money because my customers, while they are not considered the kindest, are very loyal, and they are frightened. You know who those customers are."

While Annie hadn't worked with Arrowhead in the past, she knew him and was worried by his impression and reaction to the new market. "And you?" she asked Mortimer.

"Business is booming here because the market is different." He reached down on the floor and pulled up a jar filled with a yellowish jelly liquid. Inside, a small creature, with pointed ears and a tail. Annie and Spencer moved closer. It was a dead elf. Annie shuddered.

"They're trafficking in magical creatures, whole and parted out.

Poisons, cursed objects unlike what was there before. Those things were done... in extreme privacy in the past. Not like this," Arrowhead said.

Annie and Spencer exchanged concerned glances.

"If they harness her power, they control the world," Mortimer said, pointing to Annie.

Annie looked at her hands. Magic billowed into the office and her palms itched. "This is the power," she said. Mortimer and Arrowhead stared in awe.

"What can you do now that you didn't before?" Mortimer asked.

Annie shook her head. "In the past, I conjured a ghost and inadvertently turned him corporeal. Aside from that, my powers seem stronger, but nothing else."

"The power to bring back the dead is enough; don't you think?" Mortimer asked.

"But you don't need this power to do that. Necromancers have been able to do that through very specific spells. It doesn't seem like enough to kill me. What have you heard I can do?"

Mortimer glanced at Arrowhead and shook his head.

"There are rumors. Powers to control the elements," Arrowhead said.

"Water, earth, air, and fire? We can all do that to some degree with the proper training and spell work," Spencer said.

"Volcanoes, hurricanes, tornadoes, tsunamis, man. Big stuff. They're rumors though. I can't believe them coven members didn't tell you more," Mortimer growled.

"So you know nothing. No problem."

"Annie, it's all conjecture. What they know or where they got it from—who told them about the prophecy in the first place?"

Sturtagaard!

Annie sighed.

"We'll keep you posted, get you what you need," Arrowhead added.

Annie leaned against a crooked wall. "In the market accessed through the Louisiana swamp is a man named Joseph. You can pass him info and he can pass it to us," she said.

"I know the man. Tell him to expect items from me." Arrowhead joined Annie at the wall and took her hand. "Melichi has been asking about you. Gathering the smallest bits of news and information. They waited patiently for the power and now they're taking their time to get it from you."

"What do you think I should do?" Annie asked.

"Run and hide, girl. I've told you that already," Mortimer said, and yet he wasn't joking or jeering. Annie could sense the seriousness in his voice.

"I can't do that," Annie murmured.

Arrowhead, still holding Annie's hand, looked her the eyes. "Gibbs and I worked on opposite sides of magical law, a choice I made long ago. I chose to help in his quest for truth and justice and all that bullshit you guards believe in. Gibbs was a good man who cared deeply for you and for the wizard guard, and I will do what I can to help you."

"At a great risk to yourself," Annie said.

"All that I've learned, I have in that book. I will pass your man anything new. That I promise you."

Spencer took the book from Annie, shrunk it, and hid it away. He nodded once and held onto Annie's arm as they left the store. They found the teleportation area two doors away and hid themselves inside. Spencer said nothing as he teleported her home.

CHAPTER 15

WHILE ANNIE WAITED on her back porch for Ryan to arrive, she scanned the trees behind the alley for any signs of movement or voices. She was usually aware of her surroundings, but the Fraternitatem had made her hyperaware. Ryan landed and observed her watching the trees.

"What's out there?" he asked.

"I think someone's hiding in there." Annie pointed past the alley.

"If not her, one of the Fraternitatem, I suspect. Where are we meeting Jack?" he asked.

Wolfgange Rathbone was housed in the federal correctional facility in Terre Haute, Indiana, incarcerated for murdering Princess Amelie of Amborix. To get there, they would need to arrive to the prison by car, but Annie only wanted to drive part of the way. She hoped Jack wouldn't mind.

"I'll teleport you to the location. Jack will meet us," Annie said.

She closed the back door and locked it with a very strong spell. She expected the Fraternitatem had tried to get in, but as of yet, they hadn't succeeded. She glanced inside the trees, thought she saw an arm move, and shuddered. She reached around Ryan and teleported him out.

They landed in an abandoned parking lot scheduled for demolition. Annie walked to the entrance.

"You okay?" Ryan asked.

"Just tired. It's been a long year of chasing down my father's killer and way too many cases connected to it. I'm ready to be done." She stepped onto the sidewalk and checked her phone. They had five minutes.

"I was sent a copy of the note from your—from Emily," he said.

"It just strengthens my resolve to end this. Send my dad back to wherever it is he came from and get married. Get on with my life," she said.

"I think Jason's human," Ryan said.

Annie glanced at him and swallowed. "I didn't imagine the lines around his eyes, the gray at his temples, or his beard?" She glanced down the street, Ryan followed her gaze though he had no idea what car he was looking for.

"You didn't imagine it. I'm not sure why it's happening. Ghosts shouldn't be able to 'come alive.'"

"What do we do? He doesn't belong here."

"I don't know. I suppose we take that on when it's time. For now, I talked to the executive council. They've agreed to create a position they'll call Manager of Educational Liaison."

Annie smiled. "Good." There wasn't time for more, as Jack's car pulled up to the curb. She sat in the front seat, leaving Ryan to sit in back of the SUV.

"Nice car," Annie said.

"Better for traveling. So based on the time, I expect we're teleporting from somewhere," he said as he pulled from the curb.

"Yeah. Drive here and I'll teleport us to Indiana." She gave him a location and he headed toward the highway.

"What's the goal for today?" Jack asked.

Annie was searching her tote bag for items pertaining to the Fraternitatem. She glanced at Jack. "I need Rathbone to give me as much information about the Fraternitatem as possible. He killed my dad for them, so he should know something useful."

"Is he going to ask for something in return?" Jack inquired.

Ryan chuckled from the back seat. "Probably. I'm here for that."

"Follow along that way," Annie directed as Jack pulled into an industrial area. "There's a space through the trees. We'll take it from there."

Jack did as instructed, pulling into a hidden spot along the trees. He held on to the steering wheel with a tight grip. Annie glanced at Ryan, placed her hand on the console, and teleported them several hundred miles away.

While the process took less than a minute, it felt like hours as the world flew past them in multiple colors. When they landed beside another industrial complex in a thick swatch of trees, Jack was pale green and confused. He pushed open the car door and slipped out. He bent over and sucked in air, waiting for the dizziness and nausea to abate.

"I'll never get used to that," he said when he re-entered the car and glanced at Annie. Her eyes were closed; she had sweat along her forehead. "You okay?"

"Yeah. It's exhausting using so much magic. But I'll be fine." She offered a wan smile. "You would get used to it if you hung out with us more. You okay to drive?" Annie asked.

He nodded and started the car again.

"Take that road," Annie said, pointing.

He nodded but made no motion to move. He took several deep breaths before he was able to pull out and follow the road toward the highway.

"Why is that still so hard?" he asked.

"You have no magic. You're doing a great job dealing with it though," Ryan said.

Jack glanced quickly at his GPS, it was taking time to reload after the teleportation. When it finished, he found they were twenty minutes from the prison. "I checked. He hasn't been visited since he's been there. He's been well behaved, reads a lot," he said.

They continued in silence as Jack followed the signs to the federal prison.

He showed his FBI badge to the officers at the gate and they were waved inside. Jack drove until he found a convenient parking location where they exited and followed him into the building. They each showed their FBI badge and were asked to relinquish any guns. Jack signed them in.

"We're here to see Wolfgange Rathbone," he said.

The guards looked at each other before turning back to Jack. "We knew you were coming which is why we hadn't called. He was murdered in his cell last night," said an officer with a nametag identifying him as Justin Smith.

Annie felt her heart pound when she looked at Jack and Ryan.

"That's unfortunate as we're here on another case that he had information on. May we look at his cell and his things to see if it can help?" Jack asked.

"Yes. We were told you can have the time you need," Justin said.

They were led through the corridors, past the first security desk, and down a corridor of cells. The doors were thick metal with small, dense windows in the upper half of the cell door.

Rathbone's cell door was left ajar. Annie and Ryan glanced inside; the bed was covered in blood, and a handmade shank lay on the floor.

"It's been gone through with a team?" Annie asked.

"Yes. We left it for you to see," Justin said.

"Do you mind if we have some privacy?" Annie asked. "The case is restricted."

Justin nodded and left them to examine the room.

Annie saw the camera in the top corner of the small cell and discreetly shut it down before summing a crystal for Ryan. "I'll take pictures," she said.

Ryan traversed the small room capturing magical signatures as Annie took out her phone, snapping pictures of the bed and the blood pool, the knife on the floor, the blood spatter across the wall. When she finished, she donned rubber gloves and perused the books he had been able to keep in his cell, many of which were antique, dating back to the eighteenth and nineteenth centuries. There were books on philosophy, horticulture, the occult. She opened each, scanned the pages, and found several sticky notes in Rathbone's script. He seemed to have settled in the past year, according to several notes proclaiming his guilt and his wishes for things to have been different. She showed Jack.

"Sometimes they grow a conscience," Jack said as he read the notes.

"I wouldn't have expected it from Rathbone, though. He's without magic, living like a commoner," she joked.

"Is that what we are?" Jack asked.

"Not really." Annie picked up the final book, a new edition of Dante's *Inferno*. The front page had the world 'Fraternitatem' scribbled across the top. She shuffled through the pages. Some had letters circled or squares drawn around them.

"That mean anything?" Jack asked.

"The *Inferno*? Not sure." Annie shrunk the book and pocketed the tome.

Ryan tapped Annie's shoulder and showed her the crystal, which was now full of multiple magical signatures. She pocketed the crystal and texted Bucky asking for a list of prison employees.

"Damn, what a mess. The guy deserved life in prison. Not this," Annie said. She sidestepped the blood and pulled up the thin mattress. On the underside, she found a slit and dug inside, pulling out an envelope addressed to her.

Beyond the door, footsteps clacked against the cement floor. She pocketed the letter as a second security guard passed by. She glanced around the small cell; Rathbone had very little to remind him of better days. "He didn't keep much." Ryan finished a search of items on Rathbone's shelf and checked the toilet tank.

"Anything?" Jack asked.

"Nothing. Maybe he was repentant," Ryan surmised, but neither wizard guard believed that.

"If you're ready, we can leave," Ryan said. Annie nodded and discreetly reset the camera. Jack led them from the room to the security desk.

"I think we're good. We didn't see anything." They were buzzed through. "Let me know what turns up from the investigation," Jack said to the security guard.

They remained silent as they were escorted back outside. "Thanks for your time," Jack said. At the SUV, they slipped inside their seats. Jack pulled away. It was then that Annie finally felt comfortable.

Jack said, "Well?"

"There's magic inside the cell. We'll search for the signatures in our magical database and compare them to anyone who recently got a job at the prison," Ryan said.

"He wasn't killed with magic, was he?" Jack asked.

"I did not capture a kill spell. Without the body, we won't know for sure. I did find teleportation spells and what looks like a freeze spell of some kind. He was probably murdered with the shank," Ryan said.

Jack pulled out of the parking lot and followed the quiet, empty road to the highway. The car bounced and the engine hummed.

"I found a book with the word 'Fraternitatem 'on the front page. He left me this." Annie held out the letter.

"He must have known who it was and what was going to happen," Jack surmised.

Annie opened the envelope.

Annie Pearce,

I recognized him as soon as I saw him. Benjamin Baker. At least that is what I've known him to be called. You put me in here, and while I am sure you would do what you could to get me out of here and back to Tartarus Prison, it will be too late. They will kill me because they do not want me to talk. I have left you a book. Read it. It will help you stop them.

You were a worthy adversary.

Wolfgange Rathbone

⟡

Annie sat in her club chair across from her desk, placed her legs up and stared at the note from Rathbone. "I left you a book," he had written her. She assumed she pulled the correct book, as it was the only one with his handwriting in the margins.

I hope it's the right book.

She sighed, placed the note inside of the book, and opened it to the title page.

Inferno by Dante Alighieri.

She found his choice of books telling as she began skimming page one. He clearly wanted her to know something. Each time she found a letter circled, she noted it on a pad of paper. There had been no other notes in the margins, and after an hour, she found one word: September 1.

September 1?

It was a day known through the magical world: the Day of First Sun, the anniversary of the day the portal between the magical and nonmagical worlds was closed permanently. On that day, demons and magical creatures that were already on Earth were trapped there, and other demons and magical creatures wanting in were no longer able to enter. All wizards across the world knew that magic was the strongest on that day, when all magicals had a power boost. Annie shuddered.

"What are you trying to tell me?" she murmured.

Annie placed Rathbone's note in this spot. She would pick up the search later. In the meantime, she stood and stretched, put the book in her field pack, and headed out.

∽

Annie watched the traffic below Ryan's office.

"We assume they've been watching you for years. So why wouldn't they put someone in the prison to watch him?" Ryan said.

Annie leaned against the wall. Hundreds of people streamed out of the surrounding office buildings. None of them would ever know of the situation within these walls.

Wouldn't it be nice to be them?

She loved her life, her magic, knowing what creatures hid in the dark. But now, with the stress near its breaking point, with the strange magic coursing through her, she wondered what it would have been like had she not known, had she gone to college and done something else. She sighed.

"I asked Bucky to search for Benjamin Baker." She continued to watch people leave the building across the street.

The office door opened and footsteps shuffled against the short, weaved carpet. Milo, Cham, Spencer, Lial, Brite, and Shiff took a seat across from Ryan. They were closely followed by Eddy and Isaak; neither man had ever had occasion to be in the Grand Marksman's office and they shifted between looking at his office in awe and in terror of being there.

Annie sat beside Brite and gave a rundown of the events at the prison.

"It makes sense that they kept an eye on him," Cham said. "He must have known a lot of information. I'm sorry I hadn't thought to ask him what he knew beforehand."

"Rathbone let me know he knew Benjamin Baker, so we're starting there. If this Baker received orders to kill him, he either knew Jack was going to speak with Rathbone or someone told the Fraternitatem we were coming and had him offed, so to speak. Is there any other point in this process where we could have a mole, someone watching Annie at Wizard Hall?" Ryan asked.

"I didn't have time to fully vet Joseph Agrante from the market, though South Africa did verify him. Fabien Arnault was here, as were all the American wizard guards, plus I've been in contact with Mortimer and Arrowhead at the market. But I never told any of them what we were doing," Annie said.

Ryan, keeping things informal when he could, stood and leaned against his desk, crossing his arms. He looked at Annie briefly and said, "Let's look at this rationally. Mortimer and Arrowhead weren't here in the building, so rule them out for now. Everyone else on your list could have, at one time or another, placed a bug in your cubicle. I suggest you ask Graham to debug Annie's cubicle."

Annie tapped her fingers against Rathbone's tome.

"All the satellite offices have been in this week. It could be any of us," Eddy said.

"I chose the two of you for this because you've been here for over a year and your records are clean. Do I have a reason to question that?" Cham asked.

"No. Not with me, Cham," Eddy said.

"Nor I," Isaak answered next.

Milo said. "You need to think farther back. They've been watching Annie for years."

"Having said that, are you in cahoots with them?" Annie asked Milo.

He laughed. "No, but I'm glad you're not ruling anyone out. Gibbs was the only older member beside Ryan." He stared at the Grand Marksman.

"Really, no."

"The rest of the team from back then is no longer in the Guard. I haven't seen anyone come in. I've been here all week," Spencer said.

"It stays in this office. Do not discuss with anyone. I'm serious about that," Cham said. He typed on his phone. "I will handle the leak. Eddy and Isaak, you were at Gloriana's house today. Anything?"

"Nothing to report," Eddy said. "We'll go back and stay through midnight if that works for Milo and Lial." Both men nodded.

"I have something I need to take care of. I think we're done for now." Cham dismissed the meeting and watched until everyone left except for himself, Annie, and Ryan. He closed the door. "I'll have Bucky pull all Wizard Guard employee records for employees who have been hired in the last year, including their background checks. I want to make sure we didn't miss something glaring."

"Pay attention to Starla. She likes you," Annie said.

"I've noticed. She spent thirty minutes in my office trying to keep an inane conversation going." Cham grimaced. "It's a weird way to get rid of her competition."

"That's not funny," Ryan chastised.

"I don't think it is. What if it's someone we trust?" Cham asked.

"Keep it to the smaller group. Just be careful," Ryan said.

Annie landed behind a chimney on the roof top of Samantha and John's townhouse. She adjusted the placement of the table and chairs and patted down the cushions and pillows on the outdoor furniture. She leaned against the half wall at the edge of the rooftop and stared at the amazing cityscape before returning her attention to the courtyard below.

Townhouses wrapped around the courtyard, a lush, green lawn with six-foot-tall trees lining two sides. Even in the middle of the day, it was filled with young families, older couples, and teenagers. Children ran with wild abandon, families tossed balls back and forth, and people sat on blankets reading or eating, generally enjoying the beautiful summer afternoon.

As much as she tried to not look at the corner townhouse, Annie couldn't help but stare at it. It was the same as all of the others in this development, nothing exceptional about it except for the secret inside. She caught Brite's gaze. He nodded and returned to his hiding spot as they waited for the family to make an appearance.

Annie returned to viewing the courtyard and took notice of a young boy around twelve or thirteen walking along the sidewalk that trailed around the townhomes. There was nothing unusual about his backpack as he slung it over his shoulder or his colorful shorts and T-shirt. What made Annie stop and hold her breath was the shocking curly, red hair that fell into his eyes.

He's curly like me and Sami!

As she watched, Shiloh King-Solomon casually strolled home, pulled open the gate, and entered the house. Within minutes, he reemerged without his backpack and carrying a skateboard. He headed back toward the road where he stepped on the board and pumped his arms as he moved. Annie teleported behind the garage, hit the sidewalk, and followed the boy.

He maneuvered his skateboard through the human traffic along the sidewalk and stopped at a corner convenience store, just as Shiff and Brite had reported. Annie caught up, entered after him, and stopped along the first aisle. While she casually examined the junk food, she occasionally glanced up quickly, taking note where he was, and watched him pour himself a fountain drink. Annie picked up a box of crackers and read the ingredients list before looking up again. Shiloh was now at the donuts, choosing a chocolate-covered cake one. With his items, he patiently waited in line to pay for his snack and thanked the cashier when it was his turn. Annie noticed his thick accent.

He's definitely not from here.

After paying, he left the store and started up on his skateboard. Giving him a five-minute head start, Annie paid for several candy bars before exiting. Shiloh was already a block and a half from her. He appeared to be acting responsibly, looking both ways at the stop sign, picking up his skateboard as he crossed and started again, slowing down to pass a mother with a baby.

Clearly already acclimated to his life here, the boy found a spot in the courtyard against a thick tree in the center and pulled a book from his jacket. He found his page and began to read while enjoying his snack.

Annie strolled across the lawn to Samantha's house, entered the gate, and let herself into the foyer. She watched the boy for several minutes. He did nothing suspicious, just acting like a perfectly normal thirteen-year-old. She held her breath when Emily crossed the courtyard and met her son. Their mother knelt beside the boy and offered him a hug, Annie chuckled when Shiloh pulled away.

"Mom," he complained. Annie didn't need to hear what he said; she could read his lips.

Since she had grown up with her father, Kathy, and Ryan, this exchange seemed foreign to her. In a way, she envied her half-brother because of the time he had time with Emily.

But was it happy with the Fraternitatem?

More than envy, however, she felt anger at the Fraternitatem and hoped that was what would sustain her after she finally met her mother.

CHAPTER 16

ANNIE DROPPED HER bag on her desk. While she waited for her computer to load, she pulled out a picture of her and her mother taken about six months before Emily's recorded death. After seeing Emily with Shiloh the day before, Annie had spent the evening searching through her early baby pictures, looking for any sign of when things had changed for her mother. She stared at each picture with a magnifying glass, asking herself if Emily's smile had changed, if her eyes were growing wide with fear, if she was pulling away from the family.

Cham thought she was being sentimental or curious as Annie returned to her childhood and the memories she had long since forgotten. He didn't know she was searching for answers she really thought she wouldn't find. Annie placed this single picture against her desk lamp; it left her cold. There was something in Emily's smile, her eyes, and the way she turned from her daughter even though Annie was sitting in her lap.

Was that when they started to scare her?

Annie glanced one last time at the picture, before she pulled her first case file for the day. She was on a roll; the cases were simple and required little thought as to the next step. She made notes and worked her way through several, periodically staring at the picture of her mom. Emily's eyes expressed sadness, her smile was too wide, and she was turning from her daughter. Annie was sure she was hiding a secret.

After Annie cleared the pile and tucked it into the outbox, her phone buzzed. She jumped, stared at the screen, and headed to Bucky Hart.

"Hey, Bucky. Got something?" she asked once she got to his cubicle. He reorganized the information on his multiple screens as she sat beside him.

"Believe it or not, this one was easy," he said as he pulled out the new folder and handed it to her.

"Okay. Thrill me," she said.

"First, I compared the magic from Rathbone's cell to the database and didn't get a hit," he said.

"If they're Fraternitatem, I'm not surprised," Annie said as she followed along with his notes.

"I wasn't expecting it either. So after that, I dug into the employee records at the prison. Turnover at the prison is high, whether guards are rotating out and to other prisons in the system or leaving altogether. I did find two employees who were hired within months of Rathbone's incarceration. So, I started with them. They are David Stein and"—he glanced at his screen— "and Michael Mann. Their photos and employee records are in there."

As Annie stared at the two pictures, her mouth dropped open. David Stein had a thin face, a long, thin nose, and thin lips. His skin and blue eyes were pale, and his thick, curly hair was dark brown. Michael Mann had a thicker, fuller face, a wide nose, brown eyes, and curly hair. Annie summoned the folder Bucky had given her with all of Levi's aliases and found the picture she was looking for, placing it beside the man with the long, thin face. She took her time, comparing the eyes, the chin, the nose. "Uh. David Stein is Levi Worchester," she said.

"I would conclude that as well," Bucky agreed.

"Okay. Which one is going as Benjamin Baker?"

Bucky smiled and handed her Benjamin Baker's background check. "His hair color is slightly different and I think those are colored contacts. I had the software compare all of the facial features. They are definitely the same man."

Annie stared at the pictures of Levi, Benjamin, and David—all one face and yet different.

"The Fraternitatem worked hard to get a known criminal into the prison system as a guard. It's a lot to keep an eye Rathbone. Explains why he didn't contact anyone and had no visitors," Annie said.

"They could've stopped any letters or calls for sure. I'm surprised they didn't go through his stuff. They might have found your source," Bucky said.

"Maybe they didn't have time. I mean, we had a year to contact him and didn't. They probably just found out about it and acted quickly to stop it from happening," Annie suggested.

Bucky deleted and added items to his screens as he searched for additional data. "I sent the signatures to the Middle Eastern Wizard Guard, along with their names and all of the aliases I've found so far. I'm hoping they have a match in whatever database they use," Bucky advised.

"This should help them as much as it helps us. Thanks for finding this so quickly." Annie stared at the picture of her stepfather and cringed.

Bucky placed a muzzle spell on his cubicle. When they were secure, he bent over and sent a spell into his bottom drawer, releasing the lock. The drawer popped open; he pulled out a thick folder and handed it to Annie.

"The background checks we have on file?" Annie asked as she felt the heft of the paperwork.

"We did a thorough check on everyone. Though without context, we can miss something. Everything seemed normal, even with this case. Except one seemed odd, under the circumstances."

The employee record was on top, the information highlighted in yellow. Annie noted it was from Starla Lakin's bank statements. "She was paid $5,000 twice in the two months prior to starting here. What did she do before getting this job?" Annie perused her resume.

"Retail, if you believe her resume. We could have assumed it was a bonus," Bucky said.

"On the surface, it still looks like it. Anything odd in her employee record?"

"I don't have access once they're vetted and hired. Cham can tell you that. I was able to pull the deposited check. And it's not a bonus from a retailer."

Annie shuffled through the papers. The check was written by Antique Symposium. "Huh," she said.

"Quite the coincidence, don't you think?" Bucky asked.

"Emily's pay stub is from there as well."

"I finally did find something on the company. It originally incorporated in the U.S. in 1970. It was moved to Israel in 1982, and the president since 1970 is Michael Milner." Bucky pulled out a picture of Michael, which looked like it had been printed from the company website.

"What does the company do? What do they sell? How much do they make each year? Are there employee records?" Annie asked.

Bucky shook his head. "I can't find anything. I'm still looking though."

Annie blew stale air from her lungs. "Fake company, probably. Besides that conundrum, anyone else seem suspicious?"

"No. I looked at the three wizard guards that started in the last year. Nothing in the timeline, nothing odd. I can expand the search on the off chance and older member of the guard is involved."

Annie summoned a list of employees from the time of her mom's death and handed it to him. "This is from the lab. Can you pull these records? We're curious if the Fraternitatem infiltrated the lab."

Bucky glanced at the list. "1999?"

Annie nodded. "Someone tampered with the body. If anything seems unusual, let me know. I'll let Cham know."

Bucky nodded and watched Annie leave for the fifth floor.

As Annie approached Cham's cubicle, she could hear a familiar female voice. Though Cham couldn't seem less interested in what Starla was saying, Annie wasn't sure if she should be incensed or chuckle as Starla openly flirted with her fiancé.

She took a deep breath. Rather than alerting Starla she was there, she entered the cubicle and sat beside her in the empty chair.

"I—Annie, I thought you were out in the field," Starla said sheepishly.

"I'm sure you did. But I'm not. I expect you'll be less obvious next time you flirt with my fiancé," Annie said with a smirk.

"I'm not..." Starla picked up her folder and exited without saying goodbye.

Cham turned and placed a hand on his wall casting a muffle spell. "Sorry," he said sheepishly.

"Did you encourage her, flirt back, or offer to promote her for sex?" Annie asked.

Cham laughed. "Do you need me to answer that?"

"It's annoying," Annie said.

"I interviewed her with Milo and she barely looked me in the eye. I've seen her a handful of times when I've been to the satellite offices. Nothing. It's a little obvious, and I apologize. I did tell her to knock it off. It's inappropriate on so many levels," Cham said.

"She's angling for information?"

"I think she thinks she's clever in how she's trying to find out more about the need-to-know case. I think her goal is to butter me up first. I'm half tempted to give false info and see what happens."

Annie dropped the file on the desk and explained who the prison guards watching Rathbone were and which one was her stepfather.

"So Bucky found Levi King-Solomon. At least we're closing in on them. Anything about the background checks?"

"Do you remember your little friend received two payments for five thousand dollars, months before coming aboard?"

Cham nodded. "She was in retail. We figured it was a bonus. We didn't push. It's not a bonus, I take it?"

"The check came from Antique Symposium."

Cham looked at her, his mouth open in surprise. "I'm not sure what to say to that."

"She was placed here as a mole, though why a satellite office? Not to mention, it bothers me that I misjudged her so badly."

"There's only so much we can do in the background check without context. She's due for her wizard guard test. I can only hold that off for so long," Cham said.

"I never suspected anything, though I only trained her for about two hours in potions. She mentioned retail jobs in passing, but she really understood potions," Annie said.

"That isn't odd. Other guards come to us the same way. They have a job outside the Hall, and later decide to try it here. Not many go that route, but it happens," Cham said.

"I wouldn't fire her yet," Annie said.

"I can easily string her along. She started when, a year ago?"

Annie nodded.

"Around the same time as the prison guards went to work at the prison."

"The Fraternitatem hid all of this well for a year, but the cards are falling fast now that we know," Annie surmised.

"Once we found the prophecy and you received your powers, we had something to look for," Cham said. "Who else is out there that we should be watching? I mean, we have two teams on your grandmother. Rathbone is dead. Who else would the Fraternitatem go after?"

Annie ran through the players in the black market debacle and bit her lip. "Even though Gladden Worchester is dead, it appears his cousin is part of the Fraternitatem. We should separate him from them. Maybe Arden Blakely? Even with a memory modification, she could be in trouble."

Cham took notes on a pad. "I'll pay her and Ariana a visit. It might be worth it to bring them in and keep them safe. Anyone else we should worry about?"

"The only other person that might be a threat to them is Mortimer. He's making out like a bandit because wizards are afraid to go back to the market. He knows something but won't tell me what. I'm surprised he hasn't run yet."

"The Fraternitatem is probably watching both of them. I know we want to keep this close to the vest on the off chance we have a mole. But we'd need more teams. I suppose I can tell them just enough to not arouse suspicion. But I'd have to give them some reason," Cham said. He made additional notes. "Any other surprises?"

"Nope. If I were you, I'd fetch Arden and Ariana and bring them to Tartarus where they'll be safe. Mortimer will take care of himself. And either let Starla flirt with you and give her false info or assign her somewhere out of the offices," Annie said.

"You're not jealous, are you?" Cham asked with all seriousness.

"Jealous? No. Irritated, yes. It's pretty gutsy to flirt with the boss at work while his fiancée works across the aisle."

Cham grimaced. "Sorry. It's uncomfortable for me too."

Annie frowned. "I'm going to get back to what I was doing, if you don't need anything else."

᪣

The portal spun with colors of pink, blue, and yellow. It made Annie dizzy. As she looked inside the lights, air blew around her hair. She ignored it and watched her younger self with Emily.

Annie vaguely remembered the red-and-white checked pedal pushers her mother yanked up her lean legs. She also had a far-away memory of the white shirt and her insistence that she could put it on herself, "I do it, Mommy."

As she watched her tired, fussy younger self push Emily away and pull the shirt over her short curls, she felt an ache in her stomach.

A frustrated Emily pulled Annie onto her lap and gathered her short, curly hair into two ponytails. They sprang out from each side of her head. The toddler Annie squirmed until she reached the ground. Emily sighed as Annie escaped her grasp and ran for her toys in the den.

Annie watched through the portal, her past that she couldn't remember. She reached out to touch the memory, to burn it in her head so she could recall it if needed. Emily turned toward the portal, catching Annie's gaze. "You're not her anymore," Emily said.

"Neither are you," Annie replied.

Annie woke and glanced at her phone; it was 2:00 a.m. Even after making love to Cham, she found herself restless, unable to relinquish thoughts of her mother mothering a son.

Why not me?

She snuck out of bed, leaving Cham in a blissful sleep and headed to the den. She left the television on low and leaned against the back of the sofa, her baby book open to a time she couldn't remember.

When she heard footsteps against the wood floor, she thought Cham was coming to find her but when she looked up, she matched Jason's gaze.

"Hi," he said and sat beside her, glancing at the book. "You saw Emily today."

Annie wiped her tears and took a sip of tea. "Yeah."

Jason took her hand and looked at her engagement ring. In a perfect world he'd still be alive, this would be his house, Annie would be blissfully chasing demons and vampires, and when she returned home at the end of the day, she'd put her work away and live her life.

"The ring is beautiful," Jason said.

Annie pulled her hand away and tucked it under her arm as she sulked. "Cham knows me better than anyone. He knew what I'd like."

"You're peeling away the layers of their plan. You're learning about your enemy. It's all useful," Jason said.

"I know it takes time, right?" Annie chuckled. "I'm sorry. I've been horrible to you since you've been back. It's my fault you're here."

"Don't apologize for asking for help." Jason stared at the television screen.

Annie dropped her baby book. "I feel a little nauseated." She held up her hand. The fine white mist billowed from her palms, faster than it had before. She scratched her arm as the magic flowed faster. Annie stood but stumbled from dizziness. Jason held her arm to keep her steady.

"Magic overload and stress, I think," Jason said.

She faltered against her father. He held her against him. "I don't feel so good," Annie said as she passed out.

※

Annie shivered under thin blankets. Her eyes flew open and darted around her as she tried to place her location. A warm blanket was placed over her chilled body; a woman in scrubs smiled at her.

"You're awake. That's good," she said.

"How did I get here?" Annie's throat was raw. Her jaw itched as she tried to speak. The nurse took her pulse. "Your fiancé and father brought you here. They're outside now with the others."

Annie glanced at the nurse's name tag. "Thanks Susan." She cleared her throat—her mouth was so dry. Susan poured a glass of water and helped Annie to sit.

"Here. Drink this," Susan said.

"What time is it?" Annie handed back the plastic cup.

"It's four in the morning."

Annie lay against the raised bed as Susan tucked the blanket around her. She closed her eyes.

"I'll let them know you're awake. They're waiting for you in the waiting room."

Annie listened to Susan's shoes squeak on the linoleum floor as the nurse left the room. She opened her eyes again when she heard voices and footsteps entering the room as Cham raced for the bed.

"Damn, you scared me." He held her chilled hand.

"So naturally you take me to the hospital," Annie said. Kathy, Ryan, Jason, and Samantha filed in the room. Annie sighed. "Haven't we done this already? Go home and get some sleep."

"We were worried." Kathy touched Annie's shoulder and sat beside her.

"This is nuts. Everyone, go home." Annie yawned, suddenly exhausted.

"We just wanted to make sure you were okay," Jason said.

Annie stared at Samantha. Her lips were pursed and she couldn't meet her sister's gaze, but when Annie reached for her, Samantha held her hand and squeezed.

I'm so sorry, Annie thought. Samantha glanced at her confused for a moment and released Annie's hand.

"I appreciate you running all the way here, but I'm tired. As much as I'd like to go home, I'm sure I'm stuck here for a while. You go," Annie said. They glanced at each other, lips tight and eyes crinkled in worry.

"Tomorrow," Jason said.

Reluctantly, they kissed her goodnight and filed out.

"Go home," Annie said to Cham.

"I'm staying."

Knowing she couldn't fight it, she curled under the blankets and let sleep overtake her.

CHAPTER 17

ANNIE STARED AT the townhouse. Her gaze followed the front of the house and stopped at the front bedroom window. It was black and empty; if Emily was home, she wasn't watching. Annie opened the latch on the front gate and stepped into the small yard, then let herself inside.

As she climbed the stairs, she heard laughter, light and free. She moved toward it, her curiosity growing—she wanted to laugh like that. Shiloh sat at the counter, showing Emily something from a book. She chuckled, fluffed his hair, and returned to preparing dinner. Annie's skin itched from the stress and resurging anger the scene caused her.

It should have been me.

Annie took cautious steps into the kitchen as if she had to hide herself, even though she wasn't really there. Her presence went unnoticed as her mother seasoned the chicken and popped it into the oven. Emily pulled lettuce from the refrigerator, carefully pulled it apart, washed each leaf, and paused when Shiloh showed her another comic book; they both laughed.

Seeing Emily like this challenged Annie's belief that the Fraternitatem had severely brainwashed her and removed her humanity as they fashioned her into a killer. In this moment, Emily was a tender, caring, supportive mother. For the first time in twenty years, Annie missed her mom. It felt so overwhelming, she strode to the kitchen as if to join them, even if they couldn't see her standing there.

It was the closest Annie had been to her mother in twenty years. Emily's familiar scent was fruity and sweet; the same scent Annie wore.

She took a deep breath. As if on its own, her hand reached out and touched Emily on the shoulder. Though her mother shouldn't have been able to feel her, Emily glanced to the side, but by then Annie was gone.

Annie groaned as she woke up. Pulled from the dream, she felt jealousy. *I don't like that feeling.*

"You okay?" Cham asked from the chair beside her bed where he had been sleeping. He stretched it to release the tension and kinks.

"Weird dream." She yawned and stretched. "Can we see if I can get released? I feel fine." Annie picked up her hand, shook it out, and watched the magic flow from her palm.

Cham left and quickly returned with Dr. Christine. "I hear you're anxious to leave," she said as she read Annie's chart.

"Yes. I can't do anything here."

"The extra magic raises your blood pressure and causes the dizziness. I'm worried about you having a stroke," Dr. Christine said. She wrapped Annie's arm in a blood pressure cuff and began to pump.

When she read Annie's vitals, she said, "Your blood pressure is fine today. Have we figured out how to get rid of this magic?" She looked directly at Cham.

"No," Cham said.

"Binding it nearly killed you," Dr. Christine warned Annie.

"I'm fine. I feel great."

Dr. Christine made notes in Annie's chart. "I'll conditionally release you. But I worry about the consequences if you're not careful."

∽

Annie curled up on her sofa with a blanket wrapped around herself. The television was on in the background, but she didn't completely watch. She picked up her phone, glanced at it, and then tossed it beside her.

Kathy walked into the room. "You should have stayed," she said as she sat beside Annie. "You can stroke out."

Annie closed her eyes. "I'm fine." She knew she wasn't. The magic that didn't belong to her could kill her if they didn't find a way to remove it.

"Annie," Kathy began.

"I astral projected last night," Annie said.

Kathy held her breath for a moment before blowing out the stale air. "Where did you go?"

"Emily's townhouse. I watched her and her son. I touched her and she felt it." Annie said. She watched Kathy's reaction.

Kathy hid behind a smile. "It's understandable that you want to find out about her. She is your mom."

"You were more a mom to me than she ever was."

"Sweetie. I know you love me. Wanting to find out about her doesn't change that," Kathy said.

Jason entered the den, returning home from investigating several leads in South America. He glanced at Annie.

"Find anything?" Annie asked. She rolled to her side.

"How are you feeling?" He sat beside her.

"She astral projected last night," Kathy said.

Jason looked at her with wide eyes. "Where did you go?"

"To see Mom," Annie said and yawned.

"You can astral project and turn a ghost corporeal. It's rare to have one of those psychic abilities; you seem to have two," Jason said, worried. While it was widely accepted that some magical beings possessed extraordinary abilities; Annie was showing signs of two gifts.

"Did you find anything in the markets?" Annie asked, ignoring his concern.

"They were bigger than I expected, but I saw nothing in line with the portal markers you found." Jason patted her hand. "I think we should stop worrying so much about finding the other portals and concentrate our efforts on going after the Fraternitatem."

Annie closed her eyes again. "That sounds like a good course. Waiting for something to happen is hard."

"Enough. Your daughter can stroke out. No more working," Kathy said. "Shoo. Leave. Get back to Wizard Hall."

Jason chuckled and kissed Annie's forehead. "I'm going. I'll talk to Cham. He's at work?"

"Yeah. I made him go in. He'll be back after lunch, I think. There's so much stuff to do."

After saying goodbye, Annie sat up and looked around, searching for her field pack.

"You're not working now, are you?" Kathy asked.

"I have to," Annie said as she prepared for the rest of the day.

❧

Cham peered out from his hiding spot and scanned the street and nearby rooftops for possible hiding spots.

"If they're here, there's not much I can do about it," he murmured and stepped onto the sidewalk. He strolled at a leisurely pace, certain he was being watched.

The last time he was here, six months ago, he had been investigating the death of Benaiah, found outside the portal to the original black market.

So much has changed since then.

Cham stopped at Arden and Ariana's building and glanced across the street. Drapes in the upstairs window of the building fluttered. He turned back to the door and cast a spell to pop the lock and let himself inside.

His footsteps clicked against the green and white tile, and he felt the smooth coolness of the handrails as he took the stairs two at a time. At the front door of Arden Blakely's condo, he knocked with some urgency.

Ariana opened the door, her jaw tight. "Go away!" she snapped. She began to slam the door, but Cham stuck his foot inside and pushed his way inside.

"I thought we were done with you!" she shouted and looked toward the bedroom hallway.

"The Fraternitatem is back," Cham said. He closed the front door, locked the dead bolt, and slid the chain closed. He ran to the front window and peered through the drapes. The street was clear.

Ariana shook as she reluctantly led Cham to the front room. Six months ago, the room had been dark and cave like, filled with artifacts, maps, and books. Since then, someone had removed most of the items and organized the rest and generally opened up the apartment to space and light.

"What do they want?" Ariana sat across from him in a weathered leather chair. Her back was straigh, and she balled her hands into tight fists.

"Annie received a magical power. It's... really, really dangerous," Cham began.

"Can they get at the power?" Ariana asked.

Cham nodded. "After they kill her."

Ariana squeezed her fists tighter.

"The Fraternitatem's been watching Annie her entire life. They are surveilling anyone with direct knowledge of them. One such person was killed while in prison."

Ariana's hands shook. She glanced toward the hallway that led to the bedroom. They had agreed to modify Arden's memory so she would forget about magic, the Fraternitatem, and the Wizard Guard. She was left only with the memories of her long career, all of her accomplishments, and her love for Ariana.

"They're going to kill her," Ariana said.

Cham nodded.

"Why are you doing this? Why can't you just leave us alone?" Ariana cried out. "She's doing well. She doesn't have vague nightmares; she doesn't need her meds anymore." Down the hallway, Arden moved about in a second bedroom. "We turned the guest room into an office," Ariana said. "She's researching."

Horns blared from the street outside. Cham glanced to the front window and ran for it, peering behind the curtains. A man dressed in jeans and a hoodie approached the building from the sidewalk, his gaze on the upper window, Cham ducked out of view.

"I'm sorry. There's not enough time to explain. Even if they know we performed the memory modification spell, it won't be enough to protect her. She's still a liability to them." The man below stood on the sidewalk outside the building. He glanced down both sides of the street and then back up to the apartment. Cham stepped away from the window and walked to the front door.

Ariana closed her eyes. Tears streaked her cheeks. She wiped them with the back of her hand. "Do we have to do the spell? I'd rather her not remember."

"We can discuss this when we have you safe. Tell her there's a problem and we're leaving. Go pack something now," Cham said.

"What do I tell her?" Ariana asked.

"A gas leak might work. Though I'm teleporting you out of here, so she'll figure it out soon enough," Cham said. He watched the hallway through the peep hole.

"I guess the truth will be the best." Ariana left to get Arden.

"Why? Where are we going? I don't want to leave!" Arden Blakely shouted as Ariana spoke softly to her. She looked at Cham with confusion and fear. The sound of shattering glass came from below them.

"What was that?" Arden asked.

"Listen, Dr. Blakely, someone is coming here for you. You won't remember it, but we need to go," Cham said. "Go pack!" he shouted to Ariana, who ran to the bedrooms.

Cham reached for the archaeologist and held her wrist tightly as he placed his other hand on her forehead, an open vial inside his palm. When he finished reciting the spell, a fine mist billowed out and covered Arden's head. She shook, and then her head titled backward and forward as the memories poured back into her brain. She screamed and slid to her knees.

"What... did you... do to me?" Arden's skin was pale and she struggled to breathe, appearing to be holding back vomit.

"I'm sorry. But someone just broke in to kill you. We need to go, now!" Cham looked at the front door. "Is there a way out of here to the roof?"

"No."

Cham spied the kitchen window and flicked his wrist, opening it. Ariana returned with two bags as the front door handle rattled.

"Tell me what's going on? I demand to know!" Arden shouted.

"I will, I promise, but we need to get out of here. Now!" With that, Cham shrunk the bags, took hold of Dr. Arden and Ariana, and teleported them away.

⚖

Annie felt better and therefore felt trapped inside the house. She hadn't intended on leaving but found the pull too great. From her back porch, she glanced inside the trees and teleported herself away; the last thing she thought she saw was a tree as it swayed.

She thought the neighborhood would be a foreign location until she landed behind a shed. She stepped onto the sidewalk and walked to a house that on first glance seemed more familiar than she expected.

The white stucco house gleamed in the sunlight. A large two-sided staircase wound upwards to the double front doors. She knew her grandmother lived there, and while Annie had no memory of this mansion or her grandmother, she couldn't help but think she had been here before.

I wonder what it was like for Mom.

She spied Eddy and Isaak walking the neighborhood and strolled toward them, catching their gaze. Rather than meeting them, she stopped at a park a block away and took a seat across from an ornate water fountain. Both Eddy and Isaak walked to the park, taking a seat near her.

"We've walked the neighborhood and watched the house. Emily hasn't been here," Eddy said. He continued to watch the house and the street from his position on the bench.

"How are you feeling? I thought you were at home?" Isaak asked. He leaned against a lamp post, keeping his eye on the mansion.

"I feel fine," Annie said. She didn't really; the magic raced through her and she knew she'd have to expend some soon. "Anyone else live here?" she asked.

Eddy produced a folder labeled "Gloriana Worthington" and handed it to her. The first page was a picture of Gloriana. Annie recognized the face, Emily's face, her face—clearly, she was related to the women. They should have been her support system, her family, and yet, she didn't know them. Annie turned the page and saw a picture of three people she didn't know. She read the descriptions: "Melissa Worthington, Brandon Worthington, Abigail Worthington." She knew the name Brandon, Emily's brother.

The others must be her cousins. Cousins.

"We're guessing they were having lunch. They were here for a few hours and left," Eddy said. He glanced back at Isaak, who was still intently observing the house.

"You see something out there?" Annie looked out into the yard but saw nothing.

"I thought I did. I'll keep close to the mansion today and have Graham sweep the yard tonight," Isaak said.

"Are you okay, Annie? You seem a little low, tired maybe," Eddy said.

Annie stared at the house where her grandmother lived, where her mother had grown up. It could be hers for the taking: a family, the money, all the pieces coming together. All she had to do was ring the doorbell.

But do I want the life Emily left?

Annie knew something must have happened to make Emily leave home for an older man, one who was magical. Emily had given up everything for him and for Annie and Samantha. She had left it all. Annie sighed and handed the folder back to Eddy.

"Is there anything else we can do for you?" Eddy asked.

"No. Just keep Emily away from them. I'm not sure her return will be the best thing." Annie tried to smile, but dizziness was slowly creeping up on her. "I'm going to go. I'm starting to feel a little weird."

She hid herself behind a tree and watched Eddy and Isaak return to their watch on the mansion.

⤸

Cham felt a burning sensation in his leg as he landed in the teleportation area on the island that housed Tartarus Prison. He remembered a flash of a spell as the front door was blown open. He hobbled as he waited for Arden and Ariana to catch their breaths.

Arden stumbled to the picnic table and sat down. Her restored memories seemed to have overwhelmed her, and with that, came the knowledge of what she had lost. Between that and the teleporting, she was nauseated and confused. While Arden bent at the waist and sucked down air, Ariana shook, ran for the tall grasses, and vomited.

"I know this is a shock and confusing," Cham said. "But we're not there yet. We need to leave now before the Fraternitatem finds you."

Arden looked at him. "I remember them. Why?"

"I'll explain everything. But right now, we need to go," Cham said.

"Where?"

"The prison is the safest. You'll be fed and relatively comfortable. I can promise you that. And we're hoping you can help us stop the Fraternitatem. They're coming for Annie and they won't stop until they have her."

Arden shook her head.

Cham helped her up. "We're going to the prison and then we'll talk. Or you can go home and fend for yourself."

Ariana and Arden reluctantly followed Cham along the path the prison. The warm sun beat down on them as their steps kicked up dust from the roadway. Above them, birds squawked loudly as they cooled off in the trees.

Arden and Ariana looked as though they had been traveling for days, lost and confused and sweaty.

When the prison loomed in front of them, Cham picked up the pace, his senses tingling. As they neared, the metal gates swung open, revealing a giant waiting for them at the entrance. Ariana stopped and gaped, but Arden seemed unaffected by the creature and continued. After they entered, the giant slammed the door shut and watched along the trail for the Fraternitatem to see if they had traced the archaeologist there.

They walked up to the security desk where the day officer, Beverly, greeted them. "Hi, Cham. Glad you got here safely. We've got cameras across the island and have been watching for signs of anyone. The giants will be walking the lane. So far, we're clear," she said.

Cham glanced at the pictures that rotated between several locations. "If anything changes, let me know. I'm going to get them settled." Beverly nodded and let Cham through. Ariana and Arden exchanged frightful glances and followed cautiously.

The room had been designed as a small studio apartment with a small kitchen, private bathroom, a Murphy bed, and a living room with a sofa, table, television, and storage armoire.

The walls were painted, the floor covered in rugs. The room had previously been used as a conference room; Cham was impressed by the Tartarus guards' diligence in preparing a room so quickly.

"Okay. You can use the storage," he told the two women. "We have food for you. Have a seat and get comfortable."

He turned to the prison guard waiting at the door and ordered some food to be brought in. When he finished, he pulled a chair to the sofa.

"If I had more time, I would have fully explained what we did to you in March. I apologize for the decision we made that affected your life, but we were hoping that if we erased those memories, you could live the rest of your life in peace," he said apologetically, fiddling with his hands.

Arden jumped up and pointed to him. "You removed my memories to suit your own needs. How dare you!" she shouted. She was feisty and aware, unlike what she had been when he first met her. Back then, the former archaeologist was anxious, scared, heavily drugged, and docile. He assumed whatever drugs she had been given had kept her compliant. This wasn't the woman before him today.

"You're right. We made a decision based on your knowledge of the magical world. You knew our secrets and we couldn't afford to let them out. I think you'll soon remember that as an assassin for the Fraternitatem, you came to my home to kill me," Cham said.

Arden took in a breath. The memories must have been coming so quickly she didn't have time to sort through them. She blushed at Cham's reminder of her going to his house with a gun.

"I was doing what I was trained to do," she murmured.

"Yeah. You were. We could have imprisoned you instead. We chose to modify your memories and let you live your life."

"So you put me in prison without my knowing." Arden glanced at Ariana. "I'm sorry I tried to kill you."

"We understand what the Fraternitatem did to you. It wasn't your choice. But you have a choice now. The Fraternitatem killed Wolfgange Rathbone in prison because we were going to talk to him. They will kill you if you choose to return home," Cham said, nearly begging. "We can keep you safe, but we need info on them. They're about to control a new black market and they're after Annie. We can't have either of those things happening."

Arden took a seat beside Ariana on the sofa. "My memories are still fuzzy," Arden said.

"We'll give you some time. We just don't have much of it left."

Food was brought in by two of the many elves that worked in the prison, Bitherby and Willie. Ariana's eyes widened with surprise. If Arden was also surprised, she didn't let it show.

"Hi, Bitherby," Cham said.

"Where's Miss Annie?" the elf asked, confused.

"She's recuperating from an injury. I'll tell her you asked about her," Cham said.

Bitherby glanced at their guests, who looked at him. He returned his gaze to Cham before he and Willie bowed slightly and left.

"How long do we have to stay here?' Ariana asked as she picked up the first sandwich.

"Not long. We need to place protection around your home. If it's okay with you, we'd like to go through your apartment search for any listening devices or magic that shouldn't be there," Cham said.

"When the memories become clear, I'll tell you what you want but the what I know is outdated; I haven't been to the Cave of Ages in years," Arden finally said. "I'm not sure if any of the information is still available. Someone cleared out the apartment." She glanced at Ariana.

"I have the information. I thought it might be needed in future. I'll tell you where it is," Ariana said.

"Thanks. I promise you're safe and you'll get out of here soon." But Cham was really trying to convince himself and it didn't ease the churning in his stomach.

⟡

Samantha paced the large living room at Cham and John's parent's house. Marina, Don and John sat patiently as Samantha processed what Annie said. "You're nuts. You can't go to her! She's here to kill you."

Annie leaned against the wall, her arms crossed against her chest. "So you want me to wait for her to nab me?"

Marina muttered to herself.

"No, I want you to run away until the Wizard Guard has enough evidence to bring her in."

Annie flicked her wrist, moved her hand around, and let the magic billow from her palm. To amuse herself, she directed the golden mist toward Samantha and wrapped it around her legs and up her torso.

"What are you doing?" Samantha shouted as she swatted the magic away.

Annie dropped her hold on the magic. It dissipated into the air. She walked to her sister and placed her arms around her. "I have the power of astral projection. I went to Mom. She felt me," Annie said.

"You can't go," Samantha said.

Annie walked away and stared out the sliding glass door. Cham landed in the back yard and walked up to her.

"Hey." He kissed her quickly and entered the house.

"Arden's settled?" Annie asked. She continued to glance out the window into the large yard, past the wood pile. She followed the fence that weaved in and out of the trees.

"I went to the mansion to see Eddy and Isaak. Emily hasn't been there. The next team will keep watch."

"You're supposed to be resting," Samantha said.

"I'm supposed to, I'm supposed to nothing," Annie groused. She crossed the room and sat on the far end of the couch away from everyone else. She looked at Samantha. "We have a grandmother, two cousins named Abigail and Melissa, and an uncle named Brandon if you care."

Samantha clenched her fists. John held her arm. "I want to come with you when you meet her," Samantha said.

"I'll remember that," Annie said.

"Are you still going to talk to Emily?"

Annie looked at Cham. He nodded. "We have a plan," Annie said. "I'd rather put her off of her game than let her control the situation. In the end, we can modify her memories and let her live with Shiloh in peace."

"That's mighty nice of you after what she did to us!" Samantha snapped. John moved in and placed a hand on her shoulder.

"I don't care why she left. All I care about is the fact she's living in your neighborhood and has eyes on you. I don't want her using you to get to me. You stay up here and keep safe," Annie said.

"I'd still want to see her," Samantha admitted.

Annie turned. "I'm not sure that's a good idea. You're emotionally invested in a way I'm not."

"She's my mom. I want to know why she left."

"No! Not if they're bringing in the people who are going after you and Annie," John said.

"When we're done, I promise, you can see her, before we send her away," Annie said. "In the meantime, John's right. You stay away." She leaned against the sofa and closed her eyes. The itching reached her head, her neck, her ears. She scratched at her neck, leaving behind red marks.

"Is this going to work?" Samantha scooted to Annie and removed her hand from her neck.

"I hope it does." Annie took a deep breath.

Cham's mom Marina had never liked his career choice and had been very vocal about when he first became a wizard guard. The enormity of this case left her pale and scared. "I hate what this job has made you do in the last year," she said to Annie. "But what I do know is, you can't run from this. Annie, I worry about you and Bobby all the time. But I also know you're very good at what you do. I agree. You need to strike them first."

They all turned toward her, surprised by her pronouncement. Marina walked to Annie. "It was a great gift to receive you as a daughter. I want you to end this the way you know how. No holds barred. Kill her if you have to. You are the best thing that ever happened to my son and I want to see you get married." Marina, at four foot eleven, was shorter than Annie by three inches yet was still mighty and a bit scary at times. She hugged Annie tightly. "I love you."

When they separated, Annie touched Marina's shoulder and stood beside Samantha. "We're taking them out before they get me. I promise I'll keep you posted." She gave Samantha a hug. Cham held her tightly as he teleported her home.

CHAPTER 18

CHAM DIDN'T SUBSCRIBE to coincidence and believed that people, places, and things didn't just happen. Usually someone was controlling the situation. He did believe, however, in his gut and honoring that feeling that something was up. He stood in the conference room doorway and stared into the floor that housed the Wizard Guard department. It was his to lead, an honor he didn't take lightly, and he was grateful the Wizard Council trusted him so early in his career.

The feeling in his gut was strong, and though the guards in the Hall worked diligently on their caseloads, he knew.

Someone here is working for them.

He sighed as he closed and locked the conference room door. He pushed aside his guilt about no longer being transparent—Annie's safety was the upmost importance. At least that's what he told himself before taking a seat at the table.

He fiddled with his fingers as he glanced at the faces of the guards he chose to trust. "I just wanted to give some updates," he began. "Make sure we all know what's going on. First, I was able to bring Dr. Arden Blakely and her partner Ariana to Tartarus Prison. They're safe and Dr. Blakely is willing to assist." His hand rested on the file with several lists. Some included names of people who once worked for the Wizard Hall lab when Annie's mom was brought in after her death; others listed names of those working in the Wizard Guard now, their original background checks reprinted and re-verified. It pained him to think that they might have missed something, that there might be a mole in the department.

He clenched his fists. "We managed to get to Dr. Blakely before the Fraternitatem. They know we have one of their own and expect they'll be changing their tactics. Having said that, we think it's time to bring in Annie's mom and half-brother." He nodded to Brite and Shiff, who still led the surveillance on them.

"Shiloh King-Solomon leaves for summer school at 7:30 a.m. every day. About fifteen minutes later, Emily leaves and walks to this building here." Brite pointed to the map. "The building is owned by a company called Antique Symposium."

Annie held her breath as she turned the map toward her. She touched the street, reviewed the buildings, and noted a narrow alley between Antique Symposium and the building beside it. "This is promising," she said. "I think Dad and I can hide here. We'll nab her and teleport her to the safe house in Evanston before she gets in to work." The safe house had been a dilapidated house where Annie had found a regenerating demon clawing at the wall, searching for an ancient talisman hidden between the studs. It had been owned by Gila Donaldson, a descendant of the original coven, and used in a plot to send Annie to the past. When Annie returned, there had been several heated discussions amongst the Donaldson family and the Wizard Guard, before the Guard finally purchased the house from her. With much magical help, the house had been rehabilitated into a safe house.

Reluctantly, Cham nodded in agreement. "Is the place warded? As soon as Emily fails to show for work or whatever it is she does there, they'll know we have her. I'm guessing the Fraternitatem tracks her and the boy. I don't want them to find the safe house."

"It's cloaked with multiple spells and we have magical wards around the property. I can go back and increase the magic," Spencer said.

Cham nodded.

"We'll text Annie when Emily leaves the house," Brite said.

"And when does Shiloh leave school?" Annie asked.

"He's done at eleven thirty. It takes him about fifteen minutes to get back home from the middle school. As you've already said, when Emily doesn't show, they'll know something's up. I suggest we intercept him at the school," Shiff said.

"Unless I call her in sick," Annie suggested.

Cham hesitated as he thought of the risk. "Do we have a phone number for Antique Symposium? How likely do you think they'll believe you're her?" He sighed. "No. I don't want the Fraternitatem to guess it's you." He leaned on the table and placed his face in his hands as he thought through the plan. "Okay. This is where timing is going to be a problem. Let's assume they'll know immediately something is up when she doesn't come to work. I worry we'll have an issue at the school. We're talking children."

"He's taking math with Mr. Prince, in classroom 513. We can send a freeze spell as the last bell rings and nab him inside, then send a second team around eleven to look for suspicious lingering by the Fraternitatem," Brite said.

"Lial and I will go," Milo said quickly.

"Fine," Cham was curt as he studied the map. "Do not share this meeting with anyone else. I expect if we do, the Fraternitatem will find out before we can intercept Emily and Shiloh."

Cham stared at his guards assembled and assessed their reaction to his proclamation.

"This is the second hint at a mole. Care to share?" Shiff asked.

"No." Cham grabbed the folder of names and placed it on his lap. "Once we get a hold of Emily and Shiloh, we expect there might be an issue with Annie's grandmother. That leaves you, Eddy and Isaak, to be very careful. We're still concerned Emily might return for the money," Cham said.

"We're on it," both men said in unison.

"Well, then, I think we have our assignments."

Annie curled in the club chair of her den and picked up where she had left off on Rathbone's copy of Dante's *Inferno*. He most definitely wanted her to know something, and yet he had hidden his markings carefully. She stared at her notes.

September 1

1. Day portal was closed
2. Located northern Chicago
3. Demons????

She scanned the pages of his book. Every time she found a letter Rathbone had circled or marked in any way, she marked it down in her notes. First, she found "September 1." After thirty minutes and ten additional pages she now had two more letters: *SN*.

While Annie's brain went to one location in particular, she refused to give in to her assumptions and glanced out the window overlooking her back yard. As in recent weeks, her eyes trailed off toward the trees and stared inside at the full, green foliage. What was once a happy place where she spent most of her summer vacation exploring now left her feeling cold. On several occasions, her eyes tricked her; she thought she saw movement in the branches.

She marked her spot in the book and stared back into the trees, blinking several times.

It's just dark.

But the sun shone between the houses, and this time, she thought she saw a twinkle against the tree.

"Whatcha doing?" Cham asked. He tossed his folder on the ottoman and stared into the backyard. "You think they're out there?"

"I thought I saw movement. Now I think I saw something shiny."

"Well, good news at least. Bucky has the list from Perkins. He's searching the names against known criminals. Hopefully, we'll find out who was here when your mom died." Cham picked up her notes. "September 1?"

Annie pointed to the book. "Rathbone left me that. I think he's trying to tell me something." She returned her gaze to the trees. "There's something out there." She opened the sliding door and stepped on the deck.

The light had lowered as evening fell and dark shadows were growing across her yard.

Cham summoned a flashlight. "Come on. Let's see what they've been up to."

Annie walked closely and held his hand as they stepped into the trees. He scanned the branches and trunk, looked carefully at the bark and leaves, and turned his attention to the ground. Just inside the tree line, fresh footsteps littered the mud. Annie kicked at the base of a tree, moving away the foliage. She knelt down and dug away in the dirt.

"Find something?"

Annie unearthed a crystal and continued to dig until she loosened it. She cleaned it off and stared inside. "I saw something shiny a little higher up." She waved her palm across the rock. As if she held a video camera, scenes appeared above the crystal. "What the hell?"

Cham watched Annie's look of horror and turned to the early scene from her life as it played out before her. A three-year-old Annie ran across the backyard with Samantha following and Emily and Jason looking on. The scene changed, showing Annie in the back yard swinging on the swing set with Janie beside her.

"No," Annie murmured. She waved her palm across the rock again and more flashes of her life appeared before her. She and Jason, Annie and her mother, her fourth birthday party—Emily had been dead for six months at that point. Annie felt violated as she watched her life play out before her eyes.

"We knew they were watching you, but this is invasive and beyond what I expected," Cham said. He scanned the trees again and caught a flicker of light just above him. He raised his palm and summoned a crystal that had been embedded in bark where the branch sprouted from the trunk. The tree had grown around the rock, so he added more magic until it hovered above his palm. He waved his hand across the smooth stone and watched as more of Annie's life whirled in front of him. "This is the night I told you I loved you." He showed her the magical recording as it hovered above the rock.

"I can't—" Annie lost her hold on the rock. It slipped into the foliage as she ran across the alley, through her yard, and into her house. Once it was a safe haven, a respite from her work and now...

Cham grabbed the crystals and ran after. Annie struggled to breathe as she realized the enormity of what the Fraternitatem had done. He wrapped his arms around her and she squeaked softly until the tears fell uncontrollably.

Jason appeared, his expression grim as he watched his daughter.

"We know how they've been watching her." Cham handed him the crystals.

Jason watched. His expression never changed as he flicked his wrist, rewatching each moment of Annie's timeline, of his own past, as though it were a train wreck he couldn't look away from. "How many are out there?" he finally asked.

"We found two." Cham typed on his cell phone. "I just texted Graham. He'll come and find the rest. I've asked him to destroy them all."

"I don't know what to say to you, Annie. Somehow, I screwed up. I should have seen this. When I found out about the prophecy, I should have done more to figure it out."

Annie wiped her eyes. "Sturtagaard did this. The coven did this." She grabbed the crystals from her father and placed it on her counter. She summoned a hammer and bashed the crystal several times; pieces flew across the kitchen and left a crack against the counter.

"Feel better?" Jason asked.

"A little," Annie said as she turned toward the window. She saw Graham and his small team already searching for the story of her life.

"I'm sorry," Jason said. Several hours had passed since Graham and his team called off the search for the evening. They'd return in the morning and continue searching for additional crystals. Annie left Cham lying in bed where neither of them could sleep, and decided to return to Rathbone's book. At two in the morning she found herself up to four letters, *SNAK*, leaving her with a bad feeling in her gut.

She glanced at her father. "It's not your fault. This is squarely on Sturtagaard. He gave me up." Annie returned to the book and found the letter "e." She grimaced.

"What did you find?" Jason sat beside her and looked at her notes as she added the next letter. "Snake? Does he mean the Snake Head Letters?"

Annie shrugged. "That's where my brain went, though I'm not ready to assume anything." She sighed and placed her work to the side. "It's not your fault."

"Really? I should have stopped what I was doing, got the hell out of there, and looked for that prophecy. Had I done that, I could have given you what you needed." Jason ran his hand across the stubble on his chin.

"They still would have killed you. You knew Mom was alive."

She glanced toward the den, at the window that overlooked the yard and the forest. It was dark now, so she assumed Emily or whoever was watching was now gone. She turned back to Jason. "So, why are you awake?"

"Tomorrow."

"Me too."

Jason pulled hair from her face. "We need to get some sleep. Tomorrow is gonna be a rough one."

CHAPTER 19

MORNING CAME QUICKLY. Just after sunrise, Annie, Jason, and Cham roamed the house, lost in their own thoughts, readying themselves for the day.

Annie checked her phone and glanced at Cham before kissing him goodbye.

"Be careful," he said.

"I'll see you soon." Annie waved as she and Jason teleported to the alley.

The narrow alley protected them from view, dark as it was between two recently renovated buildings. Annie traversed the length, searching for cameras or recording equipment. She noted two metal doors, one in each building, and opened several garbage cans neatly lining both outside walls.

She glanced up. Neither building had windows to the alley. Walking to the sidewalk, she peered along the road.

"Anything?" Jason asked, amused by his daughter's thoroughness.

"No. It's quiet here." She glanced up again. The building that housed Antique Symposium was three stories. The windows on the front of the building overlooked the empty street below. "I think we're okay here," she said as she slipped back inside the alley. She remained cautious, still reeling from the night before.

All of those crystals!

The Vampire Attack Unit had returned to the forest, where they had discovered twenty-five crystals spanning her entire life. Graham sent her the video of him and the team burning them all to ash. Knowing they were gone didn't reduce Annie's feeling of being violated. She paced beside the brick wall and glanced at her phone.

"Are you going to be okay?" Jason asked, worried for his daughter.

"Twenty-five crystals." Annie kicked at the brick wall, turned, and leaned against it, resting her head.

"We figured they were watching you for years. How do you think they were doing it?" Jason asked.

"Not recording every bloody moment!" Annie whispered. She glanced at her phone,

Ten minutes!

"They'll text when she leaves," Jason said. He leaned against the opposite brick wall. "Can you do this?"

I'm fine, Annie thought.

Jason glanced at her. "What?"

"I hadn't said anything yet. I'm fine, though." Annie grumbled and watched her phone.

"I thought I heard your voice." Jason frowned.

Annie looked at him. Her phone buzzed with a text from Brite: *She just left.*

⸙

Samantha looked out the sliding glass window into Don and Marina's large back yard. The acre clearing was surrounded by a perimeter of thick trees with a magical protection spell that kept out the evil things that went bump in the night. While they had never had a vampire, werewolf, or demon attack the property, the spell didn't keep out the billdads, magical elves, and magical, poisonous snakes. Samantha watched one such snake slither across the grass and make its way back into the wood pile.

It wasn't much of a distraction like she had hoped. Today, the safety of this place couldn't help her feel any less vulnerable than she did, not when she knew she'd be seeing her mother for the first time in twenty years.

I'm fine.

Samantha jumped when she heard Annie's voice and turned back into the living room. It wasn't the first time Annie's voice rang in her head, though the first time it happened, Samantha swore she imagined it. Today, it sounded as though Annie's voice came from beside her.

"Just nerves," Samantha murmured to herself and looked back into the clearing. Wind began to blow across the trees creating a dull roar of white noise. She shuddered thinking of the moment she'd first see her mom again.

What will I say?

Her stomach churned. She thought she might stay home instead. But the curiosity was too strong and she had to know. Samantha glanced at her phone, exited the house, and teleported to the safe house to wait for Emily.

∽

Cham walked along the sidewalk to the Wizard Guard safe house, one of two in Chicago, and one of six across the United States. He stared at the newly restored house, its fresh, white paint, the new porch, the newly planted bushes. Even the sidewalk had been fixed and was nearly smooth except for the wards drawn into the cement, hidden along the sides.

It's amazing what magic can do, but the magic won't be enough.

The magic buzzed against his skin as he stepped onto the porch. He hoped whatever tracking the Fraternitatem used to keep tabs on Emily and Shiloh would be well hidden once they arrived at the property.

He glanced at his phone before inserting his finger inside the blood lock, springing the door open. Safely inside, Cham locked the door and stood at the bay window, observing the neighborhood.

The house was located at the end of the street, with a pocket of trees to the south where Annie had taken the portal to the past. He glanced at the path coming from the trees; Samantha made her way from the trail.

I wish she had stayed home.

He sighed and opened the door. Samantha glared at him as she walked around him and placed herself on the sofa with a clear view of the door.

"She's my mom too," Samantha said as she crossed her arms against her chest.

Cham glanced down the street, the neighbors were gone or hadn't left their homes yet. He closed the door and looked at his sister-in-law. "I'd rather you waited until we got her to the prison. This could go badly."

"I just… I just want to see her," Samantha said. She crossed her legs, bouncing her top one with nervous energy.

"Just stay out of the way. If you get hurt, John will kill me," Cham said. He glanced at his phone as the minutes ticked by, beginning to regret agreeing to the plan.

⁓

Emily left the house at 7:44 a.m.; the gate swung closed behind her. She walked with a spring in her step, looking like she didn't have a care in the world. While she did glance at Samantha's townhouse as she passed, nothing in her demeanor implied that she knew who lived there or even cared. Brite watched as she turned the corner for work, sent his text, and teleported behind a thick, cluster of bushes.

He continued observing her, watched as her hips sashayed widely, making her skirt swing out on both sides. He wondered for a moment if she knew she was being followed, if she had been taught these exaggerated moves as though that would turn her pursuer away. But then, there was something so innocent in the way she moved, he thought, watching her pay for a newspaper at the local stand. Most people being followed would glance backwards maybe once and wouldn't stop until they reached their destination.

Emily seemingly looked as though she had no idea her life was soon about to change. Brite continued to watch her stroll along the sidewalk. When she turned toward Antique Symposium, Brite texted the team and returned to Emily's rooftop.

⁓

Shiff looked at his phone to note the time: 8:17 a.m. When he glanced back up, Emily had turned down the street and was a block and a half from Antique Symposium. Emily passed the alley, unaware that her youngest daughter lay in wait. She stopped at the front door, reached inside her backpack and pulled out her key card. She was so preoccupied; she didn't see the man leaning against the streetlamp.

Jason turned and called her name. "Emily." Emily froze at the sound of his familiar voice. Jason pulled off his cap.

"What are… You're dead." Emily stepped backward to create distance between her and Jason.

"So were you," he said and walked toward her. Emily stumbled back and fell against a warm body. She turned in fear.

"Hi, Mom," Annie said as she pulled her mother into the alley.

∽

From the moment Annie lay hands on Emily, her mother kicked out, waved her arms, and pushed against her. She wrapped her arms tightly around Emily and teleported them to the safe house. Emily, knowing she was being taken, fought against it even as the light and space swirled around her.

They landed on the back porch of the safe house.

"Let go of me! Let go of me!" Emily shouted as she began to run off. She ran into Jason as he landed and both fell into the newly planted sod.

"Stop. Emily, stop," Annie said as she reached for her. Exhausted from the teleport, she whipped her hands over her mother and reached out to catch her as she fell. "Awesome," Annie said as she and Jason pulled her up and walked her to the back door.

"What did you think she was going to do?" Jason asked.

"I was hoping she'd be too surprised to do anything." Annie waved her hand across the back door and led them inside.

"What the hell?" Cham asked. Samantha turned to see her mother's limp body being carried inside.

"We should have done this to get her here. She kicked the crap out of me through the teleport."

Jason lay his wife on the sofa.

"What happened?" Samantha asked.

"Didn't want to come," Annie said. She glanced at her father, her mother, and Samantha. Samantha sat across from them, her mouth agape. "Okay. We have to get a grip. I'm going to wake her. You okay, Sami?"

Samantha nodded. Annie waved her palm and Emily woke. Her eyes darted from Annie to Jason and found Samantha.

Emily quickly sat. She scanned the room, clearly searching for an exit. When she saw the front door, she jumped up and lunged for it, jiggling the handle. When it wouldn't turn, she attempted the lock, but it, too, wouldn't budge.

"Let me out of here!" Emily shouted as she banged on the door.

"Emily. Stop." Annie grabbed her hands and held them firmly. "No one can hear you. You need to calm yourself so we can explain."

Emily pulled her hands from Annie and feverishly pulled on the handle. "When I don't show up, they'll get my son!" she screeched. She pounded the wood door. Annie reached for her mother, but Emily pulled her arm away from Annie.

"Mom. Please come in and let us explain." Annie firmly grabbed Emily's wrist, keeping her gaze on her mother.

"Annie?" Emily asked, recognition seeming to hit her eyes for the first time.

"Hi, Mom. Come with me." Annie gently directed her mother to the living room, walking over the newly installed hardwood floor that covered the entire house.

Emily scanned the front room. The newly painted walls reflected the front window light, and the furniture was comfortable and soft. Cham smiled and motioned for her to sit on one of two sofas. She met Jason's gaze and momentarily froze from fear.

"I need to leave. If I don't show up they'll—" She began to shake.

"Emily." Annie took her shoulders firmly. "We know the Fraternitatem will figure out you're missing. We have someone watching Shiloh. He's safe and he'll be with you soon. Come sit." Emily refused and kept a firm hand on her shoulder bag, tears in her eyes. She kept them to the floor, avoiding Jason's sad eyes.

"Mom." Emily shuddered at the new voice and looked at Samantha sitting on the sofa.

Samantha, who had always been attached to the memory of her mother, cried as she watched Emily falter. She patted the sofa. Reluctantly, Emily sat beside her oldest daughter.

"Sami. My Sami." Emily wrapped her arms around Samantha. Her shoulders heaved as she clung to her daughter.

Samantha, still so emotionally unprepared to see her mother, stared at Annie, tears streaming down her face. She held her mother and patted her back. "It's okay, Mom. It'll be okay."

Emily pulled away. "I need to get my boy. Shiloh. They'll get him." She took a shallow, panicked breath. "I need my son."

"The Wizard Guard will protect him. There's someone at school to fetch him and bring him here. I promise," Samantha said.

This is not what I expected.

Annie heard Samantha's voice in her head as if she were speaking out loud. But Annie knew Samantha's lips hadn't moved. She stared at her. *What?* thought Annie.

"This isn't how it was supposed to go. He'll be so angry," Emily looked at her hands in her lap. She shuddered, and tears fell to her pant leg.

Samantha and Annie exchanged glances.

"Emily," Annie began. "I don't know what the Fraternitatem promised you, but I expect they'll kill you once you kill me or deliver me to them or whatever it was you're supposed to do. Your son will be safer with us."

"Son..." she murmured. "I need to go. PLEASE!"

"Mom! Stop! There's a muffle spell around the house, so no one can hear you. Shiloh needs you to focus. Now. Or you'll lose him," Annie said.

Emily's eyes darted from Samantha to Annie and back to Samantha. "I need to get home," she said, fearful. "They'll take my Shiloh!"

"Mom, he's fine," Samantha said.

Emily's hand shook and her body quivered as she continued to cry. "They promised they'd leave you alone if I did what they asked. They promised to leave Shiloh alone. I need to go."

"Emily... Mom." Annie touched her mother's cheek, her hair, her shoulder. To Annie, her own attempts at comfort felt fake as her own anger boiled at the surface. She found it difficult to care about what her mother wanted.

The boy is another story.

Emily kept crying. "I can't lose him too."

Annie glanced at Cham. He left the room to make a phone call.

Jason sat back, pain showing across his face, and observed his daughters as they attempted to comfort the mother they hadn't seen in twenty years. The moment wasn't special or loving; it felt stifled, suffocating. Annie's newfound grief was strangling her.

Jason glanced at Cham as he returned. "Shiff and Brite are stationed at Shiloh's school. They'll bring him here as soon as they can get him."

"What will you tell him?" Emily asked when she pulled away from Annie.

"It's better you don't know." Cham sat beside Jason.

Emily wiped her tears away and looked at Jason. Annie read the pain on his face. It was the same pain he had lived with when Emily died.

"How did you... when?" Emily asked.

"I'm a corporeal ghost. Thanks to Annie, I'm here to protect my girls." *But you're not a ghost anymore.*

Samantha glanced at Annie quickly but returned their attention to Emily who looked like she was still trying to process what was happening.

Annie's stomach roiled. Her head ached with tension.

This is harder than I expected.

Samantha glanced at Annie.

Annie saw her confused expression and mouthed, "*What?*"

Emily held her hands in tight balls. "They kidnapped me. I waited for you and you didn't come!" she screamed at Jason. "You didn't come," she murmured more softly.

"When I came home, your dead body was sprawled on the floor," Jason said. "The girls were asleep in their rooms. Zola was missing."

Annie had read Jason's case file so many times she'd lost count. Emily's revelation shocked her; it wasn't what her father had recorded.

"All that stuff in the notes. The reasons you gave Dad eight years ago were lies. They didn't tell you I was to receive powers? You didn't trade your life for mine?" Annie asked cautiously.

She had no doubt the Fraternitatem had brainwashed Emily and what she was told made no difference. If Annie had to believe one of her parents, she would always choose her father, even if what he was told came from the Fraternitatem. As she looked from her father to her mother to Samantha, her stomach churned with the anxiety and stress their reunion brought. It wasn't happy; it wasn't meant to be.

Annie turned away from her father. The ache in his eyes was much too hard for her to process. She turned to her mother instead. Her curiosity was so much greater than her desire to run from the tension.

Emily looked like she was feeling the stress too. She ran her hands through her hair, turned to Annie, and pursed her lips. "You have to understand. The Fraternitatem, when they want something, can be very forceful. They threatened Shiloh." She closed her eyes and murmured something under her breath.

"Shiloh will be here soon," Annie promised.

Emily nodded. "I'm sorry, Annie. I'm so sorry, but they were so convincing, claiming the only way I could save you was to come with them. I was so scared." Her eyes were we, and her lips quivered. "I still loved you." She looked at Jason, as tears ran down both their cheeks. "I didn't— I couldn't marry. Not until you died. I saw your body." She hit her fists against her thighs. "I didn't want to. But Levi, he… When Shiloh was born, they had a new way to keep me there. They threatened to take him from me if I left." She slapped her thighs repetitively and began to rock herself.

"In the note you left for me, you mentioned that I was evil. You were coming to stop me," Annie said.

"I don't know. I don't know." Emily's hands flew to her ears as she rocked harder. She slapped her head.

Annie grabbed her mother's hands and held them firmly. "Cham, grab a crystal, please."

Cham obliged and held the crystal over Emily; the rock lit up white, black, and dark purple.

"There are a lot of jinxes and spells. I wonder if that's how they're controlling her. I'd feel better if Dr. Christine examined her," Cham said. "Emily, we're going to get you help." He left to call the doctor.

"Mom! Look at me." Annie held Emily's face in her hands. "Did they force Levi on you?"

Emily looked at her with a blank stare. Annie was suddenly reminded of Dr. Arden Blakely, who had similarly been drugged and controlled by the Fraternitatem.

Annie had always been conflicted where her mother was concerned. Because she didn't remember her, she felt no particular pull toward her.

When she thought of a mother, it was always Kathy. When she learned that her mother was still alive, she had become angry, partially at Sturtagaard, partially at the Fraternitatem. But most of all, she was angry with Emily, who Annie felt was naïve and stupid for leaving her young children. But finally, having Emily here with her, she was conflicted, torn between resisting a mother who was brainwashed to kill her and understanding how proficiently the Fraternitatem had worked to make Emily this way.

She held her mother's hand. It was just like hers. Her lips, her eyes, her nose—they were all Annie's, all Samantha's. Annie's conflicted feelings grew deeper; maybe that was the plan. That anxiety caused the magic to flow faster under her skin. She scratched at her belly, her arms, her legs as the itching deepened.

"Dr. Christine is on the way," Cham said.

"Emily's just like Arden," Annie said.

Cham nodded and read the message that beeped on his phone. "Shiloh's on his way now."

Annie released Emily's hold on her purse and glanced inside. She found four prescription drug bottles inside.

The doorbell rang. Cham held his hand in front of him as he checked through the peep hole. Dr. Christine Andrews stood on the porch and scanned the neighborhood.

"Thanks for coming. Come in." Cham glanced down the street as Christine crossed the room and read the magic in Cham's crystal. "They've got her hexed. Several of them."

Christine knelt beside Emily. "Hi, Emily. My name is Dr. Christine Andrews. You can call me Dr. Christine. How are you feeling?"

"I'm worried about my son. I'd like to go home," she said.

Christine held her hand. "Something's been done to you. There's magic attached to you that doesn't belong."

Emily nodded. "They give me medicine to help." Annie handed Christine the bottles of pills.

"They give her orphenadrine to create visions and cause agitation, and then Valium to counteract that. These doses seem off. It explains how they brainwash their marks so easily," Christine said, pocketing the drugs. "Good call on the drugs. We need to dry her out; she seems a bit high.

I can give her something to help her sleep but that leaves her docile and easy to control."

"Not much better than what they did to her." Annie turned back to her mother. Samantha was doing her best to keep Emily calm, but to Annie, it appeared that Emily seemed more confused the longer she was with her family.

"Shiloh is on his way here. We can move her upstairs," Annie said.

Dr. Christine nodded. "I'm going to take you upstairs, Emily. I want to examine you and make sure you're okay." She gently led her upstairs.

"Arden got very confused the same way Mom did," Annie said again once Dr. Christine and Emily were out of the room. "It's like they're conditioned to be that way if they're separated from someone or off their meds or something weird." She glanced at the stairs.

The kitchen door opened and then slammed shut as footsteps entered the house. Cham approached with his palms up and met Shiff and Brite, who were carrying a sleeping thirteen-year-old boy. He looked at Emily's youngest child, at his shocking red hair, at the lips and nose the shape of Annie's and Samantha's.

"Whoa," Cham said as they carried him in. "Put him in the smaller room upstairs. Dr. Christine is examining Emily in the front bedroom."

They carried him past Jason, who looked on in curiosity.

"You okay?" Annie asked her father.

"Are you?"

Annie, Samantha, and Jason sat on the sofa together, his arm around both of them. They both put their heads on his shoulder and leaned against him. "I can only imagine what this is doing do both of you," Jason said.

"It's confusing," Samantha admitted.

"It makes me angry," Annie said. She closed her eyes and blocked out the light, listening to the work happening upstairs.

"Why do I hear Annie's thoughts?" Samantha asked.

Annie pulled away from Jason. "What?" she asked.

"I've heard some of your thoughts. Nothing explicit. Just that this is harder than you thought. I heard you when I was at the farm before I came here and a few times before that."

Annie pulled away from Jason. "That's a little disconcerting that you can hear me think."

"It's not that. Just a few simple thoughts. Sorry. You must think I'm nuts."

Annie smiled at her sister. "Yes, I do, but not because of that. To be honest with you, I thought I heard your voice saying something to Mom."

It must be the stress.

"It could be the stress," Samantha agreed, though Annie hadn't said anything out loud. "But then we're both a little nutty."

"You're telepathic? Since when?" Annie asked incredulously. Jason and Cham glanced curiously at the two of them.

"It just started a few days ago. But it's only your voice I can hear."

Jason frowned. "Sami. What am I thinking?"

Samantha looked at him, closed her eyes, and concentrated on Jason. She opened her eyes and shook her head. "I usually hear Annie's voice when I'm not trying. I didn't hear anything."

"You thought 'I'm sorry,'" Annie said.

Jason nodded. "I don't think it's Sami with the power. I think it's Annie."

Annie shook her head. "I've only heard Sami once and now you."

"It's a very rare power and it's new. You're probably tossing your thoughts her way because you're sisters." Jason looked at his daughter. "The fact that you're showing signs of telepathy is scary and makes it even more urgent to stop them."

Cham put his arm around Annie. "Turning ghosts corporeal, astral projection, and telekinesis. That's a triple threat. The itching's got to be tormenting."

"I feel like I'm on fire," Annie said as Dr. Christine came down the stairs.

"I gave her something to help with the agitation," Dr. Christine said. "I see her son is here. I'm going to examine him while he's asleep. Is there anything else you want me to do when I'm done?"

Annie glanced at Cham. "We need to get them out of here before the Fraternitatem can find them. Can you let Tartarus know about their conditions? The prison knows they're coming in."

Christine nodded. "I'll go check out her son and come back down."

"That's two." Cham sat across from Annie.

"Shiff and Brite went back to the townhouse to wait for Levi. He'll know they're gone, either now or as soon as he gets home. What do you think about Starla?" Annie asked.

"Bucky's on it. We just need enough to prove she's working for them. He's also trying to determine what Antique Symposium is. I'm not sure that's enough to prove she's in on it." Cham ran his hands through his thick curls. "He also ran a list of all employees who worked in the Wizard Hall lab when Emily was processed in the morgue and is searching for anyone with a history in the Middle East or the black market. He'll compare that list to any known names we have."

"And?"

"Nothing yet. We might not know who helped the Fraternitatem in the morgue."

"Was that too easy?" Annie asked.

A loud rumbling sound roared down the street, they felt its vibrations against the floor.

"What is that?" Cham asked. They ran for the front window and saw a large truck rolling toward the house.

"You jinxed it," Cham said as Dr. Christine came downstairs again.

"We have a problem," the doctor said.

The truck picked up speed.

"So do we. We need to go," Cham advised. "Sami, leave. Jason, help me get them to the prison. We'll discuss your problem later."

As the truck roared closer, Cham and Jason ran for Emily and Shiloh. The walls began to shake.

Annie grabbed Samantha and Christine, and ran toward the back door. Annie embraced Samantha and teleported her away, quickly followed by Dr. Christine.

Cham threw Shiloh over his shoulder and opened the back-bedroom window. Jason held his former wife and ran to the back room as the house began to move. They both teleported from the house as the semi-truck rammed the front bay window, knocking the house to the ground.

CHAPTER 19

WHEN ANNIE LANDED, she surveyed the landscape surrounding the teleportation clearing. When she heard the air being pushed out by Dr. Christine's arrival, she turned. "We thought they might be tracked. Our protection spells weren't enough."

"How long do you think we have?"

Annie glanced at her phone. "Ten or fifteen minutes." As she walked along the perimeter of the teleportation area, she scanned for magic and added additional magic to the protection spell. The magic flowed from her palms, leaving a trail behind her. It rose upwards, shimmering in the sunlight. When Annie finished, she returned to Dr. Christine. "Go. Get ready for them."

"You okay? That's a lot of magical release."

"Go. Worry later." Dr. Christine nodded and ran through the clearing to the path leading the prison.

The air popped as Jason landed with Emily. Cham was seconds later with Shiloh lying in his arms. They spotted Annie and ran toward her.

"Go! I'll wait for anyone else." Annie shouted.

Cham nodded and reluctantly left her behind as he and Jason lunged for the path leading to the prison.

As their footsteps became softer, Annie relaxed only slightly as she continued to focus on the sound of air popping and being replaced by humans. She held her palms up as the first body landed. A tall, lean man glanced across the landscape and turned quickly, as if he didn't know where he was landing. He craned his neck to look around a large evergreen tree.

"Hey, idiot!" Annie shouted as she shot off a jinx, rendering him frozen. He stood like a statue in the center of the clearing, his eyes darting from her to the other side of the clearing and back again.

A second man appeared in the clearing. He was short and stocky with no neck and closely buzzed hair. He gritted his teeth when he saw her standing at the clearing exit. When Annie cast a jinx, he lunged away from the magic so that it flew past him and hit a tree.

A nervous energy flowed from Annie's palms as she cast another jinx, this time hitting his shoulder. He was a solidly built man and easily resisted her spells. Not knowing who she was, he smiled and ran for her. Annie continued to cast successive spells; the magic poured from her palms, draining her energy. She backed away from him as he jumped her and knocked her backward. She cast another spell; he flew from her and landed in the tall grasses.

Sore from her collision with the ground, Annie rolled over and gingerly pulled herself up. She crept toward the man lying unconscious, felt his pulse, and checked his eyes. Determining he was out cold, she bent to tie his hands together. Before she could, he reached for her and flipped her over. She landed face down.

"Damn it," she muttered. He pulled her arms behind her. "Ahhh!" Annie cried as he pulled up, lifting her from the ground. She closed her eyes, sure she had more power in her pinky finger than he had in his whole body. Though she couldn't twist her wrists to cast her spell, she could feel her magic flying from her palms, seeking out her target. Magic wrapped around the man.

"What the hell is that?"

The magic covered his hands and arms, moved up his torso, and encased his head. He dropped Annie to swat the magic away. "Ooof," she said as she landed on the ground.

He continued to swat at the magic that followed him. His counterpart, still frozen at the center of the clearing, watched him as he ran from the magic that continued to swarm him.

Annie rolled over. Her arms felt heavy and limp. She raised them carefully and aimed the spell, but the magic appeared to act on its own, streaming from her palms until it found the Fraternitatem member.

The magic exploded when it touched him. He flew backwards and smashed to the ground. Cautiously, Annie walked to him, kicking the bottom of his boot. He made no move to reach her. She knelt beside him and felt for a pulse. He was completely unconscious.

Annie sighed as she summoned magical rope and bound his hands together. She watched the magic as it billowed in the light. She tugged at the knot for good measure; the rope was the strongest she had ever created.

She returned to the second man, who was still frozen, his eyes moving on their own. Annie tied his arms. When she finished, Cham appeared in the clearing.

"What the hell happened?" he asked as he saw the two frozen men.

"This guy was easy, but his bud over there lunged at me."

"At least they only sent two." Cham bent and pulled up the unconscious man, floating him in the air beside him. He directed the body toward the pathway; Annie followed, floating the other man, who was watching in horror as he was being moved to prison.

"Everyone settled?" Annie asked.

"They're still asleep, so I expect it will be a shock when they wake. I did see what Dr. Christine found. I'm not sure what to make of it."

Annie glanced back to make sure they were the only ones on the lane. "What was it?"

"Not sure." They reached the gates to Tartarus Prison. Waiting for them was one of the many giants that roamed the island and worked at the prison. He nodded when he saw them and let them inside.

Beverly, who was at the front desk again, glanced at the men floating in the air. "I sent Cham when I saw them show up. You okay, Annie?"

Annie nodded sheepishly as the giant pulled each man over a shoulder and walked them to the wizard prison cells. Annie shot a spell through the lock and was admitted inside.

"Dr. Christine is still waiting for you," Beverly told her.

෴

"You look like hell," Dr. Christine said when Annie entered the small apartment that had been set up for Emily and Shiloh. They both lay sleeping on twin beds against the far wall. Annie sat on the open sofa.

"A minor fight." Annie leaned against the back. "Cham said you found something."

Christine held the crystal for Annie.

Annie stared inside the transparent rock and squinted as she read the magic. "What the hell is that?" she whispered. She was unsure of the magical readings and could only make out a jumble of colors surrounding a dark spot.

"Whatever it is, it doesn't belong to him," Cham said.

Christine nodded. "I read so much magic on him, you'll have to sort through it all to determine exactly what was done to him."

Annie glanced at Shiloh stirring on the bed. Absently, she scratched her abdomen.

Christine lifted Annie's shirt, and stared in awe at the broken skin. "It obviously still itches. I think I'd like you on antibiotics, so the wounds don't infect."

Annie pulled down her shirt. "I'm fine. It only itches when I'm stressed. So guess what…" Annie leaned against the sofa back. "So how do we get that magic out of him?"

"Until we know what it is, there's not much I can do for him. I suggest the Wizard Guard get on in and figure out what we're looking at," Christine said. She turned to Cham. "I'll document all the medical issues for Emily and Shiloh. We know they kidnapped a wizard guard's wife, held her against her will, drugged her, and brainwashed her. That will be enough to go after the Fraternitatem."

"Plus the two guys Annie took down and Levi." Cham grimaced.

"It's almost over," Dr. Christine said.

"The worse hasn't happened yet, I'm afraid," Cham warned.

Annie looked at both of them. Her stomach roiled.

᠅

Jason leaned against the doorway, his arms crossed against his chest. He absently rubbed the stubble on his chin as he watched them. "He's small for his age."

Annie wrapped her arms around her father, hugged him at his waist. He had gained weight since she'd brought him back. She knew what that meant for his ghostly status and didn't care. She lay her head against him, feeling his warmth.

"You okay?" Annie asked.

"I'm not trying to be flippant," Jason said.

Annie pulled away and stared inside the makeshift apartment. "I never said you were." Shiloh began to stir in his sleep; a soft moan escaped his lips.

"None of this matters once I'm gone."

Annie thought she ought to say something to him, to tell her father she knew he was no longer a ghost. She saw it in the gray hair on his temples, the weight he was putting on, the new wrinkles. But she didn't, concerned it might make him reckless in his attempt to keep her safe.

She watched over her mother and brother with a heavy heart.

Annie? Annie, can you hear me?

Annie was startled by the sound of Samantha's voice and turned toward the hallway; Samantha wasn't there.

I hear you, Annie thought. She held her breath and closed her eyes.

"Are you okay?" Jason asked.

Annie nodded quickly.

I can't bear to see her again. Samantha's voice was strong in Annie's head.

Annie opened her eyes and observed her mother sleeping fitfully on the cot.

It's okay. You can come when you're ready. You don't even have to come at all.

"You should go, Dad," she said aloud. "I can't imagine your presence will help."

"You're probably right." He kissed Annie on the forehead, touched her shoulder and walked from the apartment down the hall. Annie watched him; he walked with a slight limp, a result of a work injury he received early in his career.

I forgot he limped.

When Jason turned toward the front entrance, Annie entered the apartment, grabbed a metal chair, and sat beside Shiloh. Her curiosity was strong, and yet watching him broke her heart. Had Sturtagaard not given her up to the Fraternitatem, Shiloh wouldn't have been born. Since he had, there was so much that kept the siblings apart.

So much evil.

Annie rested her elbows on her thighs and her chin in her hands to keep from fidgeting. Suddenly, Shiloh's eyes popped open. They were so much like her own, and they darted back and forth as the memories returned, and he attempted to make sense of where he was. He settled his gaze on Annie, a face so familiar, and yet he had no idea why. Frightened, he scampered backwards on the bed, away from her.

"It's okay, Shiloh. You're safe here," Annie said.

"Where's Mom?" he asked. His voice was soft and weak. Annie pointed to the bed beside his. Shiloh stared at his mother, vulnerable beside him. "What's wrong with her?"

"She's been through a lot. I'm sure you have too." Annie looked at her mom. "She just needs to rest." She smiled at him. It felt fake on her lips.

Shiloh stared at Annie carefully. "You look familiar," he said.

"I'm Annie."

He shuddered at her name. "I've heard of you. How do you know my mom?"

Annie frowned. *I don't really,* she thought. "I knew her a long time ago. I haven't seen her in a while."

Annie dug inside the drawer on the bedside table and pulled out several comic books, handing them to Shiloh. "We had these lying around. If you're interested."

Shiloh glanced at the covers, which featured Captain America, Spider Man, the Avengers. He reached for them. "Thanks." He glanced at her cautiously before leaning against the wall and reading.

Annie shifted to Emily's bed. She had been given a powerful sleeping pill to help her rest, yet she still slept fitfully, her arms and legs jerking. Annie touched her arm and Emily calmed for a moment.

"Uncle Melichi warned me about you. He said I shouldn't trust you," Shiloh said in a matter-of-fact tone.

Annie glanced at her half-brother. He seemed to stiffen. His eyes grew black; his demeanor, fearless. Annie's stomach felt queasy.

"I've only met your 'uncle' once, when I returned something that belonged to him." Annie returned to Shiloh's bed. "I'm not sure why he wouldn't trust me. I'm actually kind of nice." Annie smiled at him. "I can get you some food if you're hungry."

Shiloh nodded. "Do you have chips?" Annie turned to the cupboard in the room and perused the snacks, pulling down a bag of chips and offering them to Shiloh.

"Uncle Melichi say anything else about me?" She returned to the metal chair, keeping her distance from him.

"He said a lot of people died because you let a vampire loose. Did you really do that?" Shiloh looked at her expectantly, as if he wanted his uncle to be lying.

Annie took a deep breath and held it before releasing it, as if that could cleanse away the guilt she still felt. She knew she wasn't responsible, but sometimes she felt as though everything had been her fault. "No, I didn't. I have a dangerous job and sometimes people get hurt. But the stuff Uncle Melichi's talking about was a series of events created by other people. It was the entire magical community, not just me alone. We saved a lot of people."

Shiloh thought about what she said and dug into the potato chips. Crumbs fell against his shirt and on the bed. He glanced up at her, his face wide with realization. "You're Mom's daughter?"

They told him a lot!

"Yes. Emily's my mom too." She refrained from wiping the crumbs from the bed. He took another handful of chips. Annie held her palm out and summoned a can of pop from the mini fridge. "Here."

Shiloh popped the lid and took a large draw. When he finished, he burped loudly. "Excuse me," he said.

Annie chuckled. "Do you need anything else?" She turned and looked at Emily, who was stirring, finally coming out of the sleeping draught.

"When will it be lunch?"

"Soon. Mom's finally waking. I'll get something for you to eat."

"You're really Annie?" Shiloh relaxed and scooted to the edge of the bed. Annie observed him carefully, unsure if she could trust the young boy, afraid the Fraternitatem might have plans for him. She jumped up when his eyes flashed orange. "Melichi said it would be easy to get to you," Shiloh said in a voice several octaves lower. While his smile was familiar, it lost its warmth. Annie shuddered.

"How's that?" Annie asked. It felt as though she were now speaking to another person.

"Melichi said you would come after us. He said we should just let it happen and we'd have you where we wanted you," he said confidently. The quick change in Shiloh's manner frightened Annie. She wondered if he had been brainwashed, too. She waved her palm across his head, freezing him. His body stiffened with a smile plastered to his face like a puppet. Annie observed his motionless body. She blinked and searched his face.

He's still breathing! Is he possessed? Is that's what inside of him?

Her eyes widened.

"That's creepy," Cham said as he entered the apartment.

"Yeah, it is. He's good, but I'm better," Annie commented. "I can see you breathing," she told Shiloh. "Did they give you an amulet to protect you from magic?"

"You're really good, too," Shiloh said.

Annie shuddered. "They're tracking you with the amulet then?" she asked.

He smiled broadly. "Yep."

Annie thought carefully before she moved to the bed and sat beside him. "That explains how they tracked you to the safe house."

"You're not afraid of me," Shiloh said.

His statement made her chuckle. "Why should I be. You're what, thirteen? I have power you can only imagine. Besides, you're not the one who's going to kill me. That'll be who, Melichi, maybe?" Annie said.

Shiloh smiled again. His calm and confident demeanor unnerved her. She believed he had been groomed for this; he was convinced she was evil.

Annie reached for the amulet hanging from his neck. Shiloh looked on in horror and grabbed her hand, trying to release her hold on the chain. But Annie was stronger. Her fingers gripped the necklace as he kicked out at her. She pulled away and stared at the charm dangling from the chain; it was the six-pointed star, surrounded by four dots, forming a square.

Shiloh no longer appeared confident. As he watched Annie summon a fireball, his mouth opened. The fire floated above her palm and she dropped the amulet into the flames. As it melted away the metal, it consumed the magic inside.

"No!" Shiloh shrieked.

Annie caught his glare. As the magic diminished, his eyes grew dimmer. When there was nothing left of the amulet, Shiloh slumped against the wall, tears in his eyes, his hands shaking.

Emily murmured softly as the sleeping draught finally wore off. "Where am I?"

"You're safe, Emily. The Fraternitatem can't reach you here," Annie said.

Shiloh grimaced. "Do you know what you did? Dad will kill her if we don't go back home." He could barely speak.

"Shiloh, love?" Emily turned. She smiled and reached out for her son.

"Mom." He slipped from his bed and sat beside her.

"I've been so worried. Are you okay?" She rolled to her side, still weak. Shiloh let her take hold of him. He lay beside her in a safe and warm embrace.

Annie turned away to look for food, a heaviness filling her heart.

CHAPTER 20

SHIFF AND BRITE teleported to the roof of the King-Solomon townhouse. "We have four hours," Shiff said as they entered through the roof door.

"That should give us time to find any Fraternitatem plans or rosters or maps," Brite said as they entered Shiloh's bedroom.

Brite looked under the bed and felt for holes in the mattress while Shiff began to look through his desk.

"Huh?" Brite said as he pulled out a thick envelope. Brite opened it and looked inside. The pile included a thick notebook and several folded maps. "Looks like we have..." he trailed off as he opened the notebook. It was listed with names, dates, and locations. He unfolded the first map, which showed the cliff that housed the Cave of Ages.

"Anything useful?" Shiff asked as he closed the first drawer and opened the second, moving around baseball cards, bits of paper, packs of gum, and candy wrappers.

"Not sure. It could be outdated or it could be fake to throw us off." Brite put the items back in the envelope and dug through the laundry basket.

Shiff closed the last drawer. "He appears to be a stereotypical boy," he said. He found an overnight bag in the closet and tossed it on the bed, returning to the dresser drawers to pull items for the boy.

They slipped inside Emily and Levi's bedroom, a bare room with white walls, basic beige curtains on the windows and the floor, and a simple white bedspread.

"No romance here," Shiff said as he stared at his partner.

Brite felt his stare and returned his gaze. "How did they get her to marry him?" he finally wondered aloud as they repeated their process, examining under the bed, through the drawers, and in the walk-in closet.

Shiff felt his way between the mattresses and finally found a journal on Levi's side. He opened the book and perused the notes.

"What did you find?" Brite asked.

Shiff held up the book. "It's notes on their surveillance. They've watched Annie, Samantha, Dr. Blakely, and get this: they've been watching the Snake Head Letters."

"That makes sense. Mortimer knows people and things. They probably want to know who's coming and going, or maybe they're waiting for Annie," Brite said.

Shiff shook his head. "No. They have the store name circled. Notes like 'magical energy,' 'a magical vortex of some kind.' Question mark, question mark." Shiff showed him the book. Brite continued to peruse the pages.

"They also think there's a source of magical energy in Chicago. They're trying to tap into it to help them with the market. It looks like they're mapping magical hot spots," Brite said.

"Can they tap into the magic to gain power?"

"With black magic they just might." Brite put the book inside an envelope as they moved to the closet. They searched under sweaters, in drawers, behind shoes, and between the clothes on hangers.

Brite stepped to his left. The floor felt spongy and crackled. He knelt at sound and found the edge of the carpet and pulled up. Below was a hole in the wood, so he pulled that up and looked inside. "They've got a lot of hiding spots," he commented.

Brite dug inside the hole and discovered that Levi and Emily had hidden potions, amulets and two athames there. Shiff held his crystal inside and ran it over the items. His crystal glowed a black light.

"We'll have to send the VAU in after we get Levi and have them scan for additional hiding spots," Shiff said as he pulled the items from the floor and put them inside his field pack. "We have three hours."

They reentered the bedroom and took one last look for anything that seemed out of place or odd. The dresser held several family pictures; Brite found one of Shiloh with Emily when he was a toddler.

"Shiloh looks like Annie," he noted. "I think I'll pack a bag for Emily." He found a bag and took what he could without invading her privacy. When he was finished, they made their way down the stairs.

"They weren't meant to live here for any length of time," Shiff said.

They closed the door, made their way down the staircase, and entered the living room, repeating their search procedures inside drawers and baskets and behind pictures.

Shiff pulled away the picture above fireplace. "Here's the actual safe," he said. He whipped up his magic, spinning the lock until the door sprung open. "Jackpot!" The safe contained several bottles of prescribed medicines for Emily and Shiloh. "They were both drugged," Shiff said.

Shiff dug inside the safe, finding several envelopes and opened the first. "Passports, marriage licenses, driver's licenses, bank accounts. Different last names, same first names. Looks like the cache of fake IDs."

Shiff placed the documents back in their envelopes and stuffed all of their finds in their field packs as they waited for Levi to return.

◈

Levi closed the front door and dropped his keys on the glass-top table, placed against the wall. He ran up the stairs, unaware Emily and Shiloh had been taken into protective custody, away from him and the Fraternitatem.

He was still working at the prison; his job hadn't ended with the death of inmate 9100083, Wolfgange Rathbone. He still had to maintain appearances, still had to clean up the magical mess to ensure his death wouldn't lead the Wizard Guard to the Fraternitatem.

It had been easy for Levi King-Solomon to get a job at the prison. His magically created documents were flawless; his fake resume and the magical spells on his contacts allowed him to get the cushy job and therefore watch over the man who could upset all of their carefully laid plans. Levi had watched the prisoner visitation requests, listened in on any phone calls to Rathbone, and searched carefully for any mail. In the year since Rathbone had been incarcerated, the prisoner received no calls, no mail, and no visitors. Levi was surprised it had taken the bitch daughter, Annie Pearce, such a long time to make contact with Rathbone. How she didn't know the Fraternitatem would be back made her seem even more stupid than he originally thought.

For the first time all day, he finally checked his phone. He grimaced as he finally realized that Emily had never made it to Antique Symposium that da, and Shiloh had never made it home.

He glanced up. A man he had never seen before stood in his front room. "Who are you?" Levi barked. He didn't see what hit him from behind as he was knocked unconscious with a magical hex.

"Seriously, why did they make this so easy?" Brite asked. He knelt down and checked Levi's pulse.

"Don't know. Let's get him back. We can ask him later," Shiff said. He pulled Levi up and threw him over the shoulder as he followed his partner to the roof to teleport away.

With the added security around the prison island, the trip to Tartarus was uneventful. When they entered through the reception area, Shiff and Brite were directed to the wizard wing, where Shiff unceremoniously dumped Levi on the cot in the maximum-security wizard cell.

"I'll stay," Brite said as he set up a metal chair in the hallway.

"You don't have to save Annie all by yourself. You know that, right?" Shiff asked.

Brite stared at him. "I know. I'll do what I can to help though." He slid the cell bars shut, locking Levi inside.

Brite pulled out Levi's notebook and stared at the pages, but he couldn't stay focused. He glanced at Levi over the top of the book and watched as he stirred on the cot.

One spell and it would be over.

He refrained from attacking Levi and stared with contempt when the man groaned to wakefulness.

"That took a while," Shiff said.

"Good spell," Brite said.

"Where am I?" Levi demanded to know.

"As an agent for the Fraternitatem of Solomon, you are being held in contempt of an agreement made with the U.S. Wizard Council. We have a few questions for you," Brite said.

Between the strong magic and the restraints, Levi staggered up and made his way to the cell bars. "I don't know who or what this Fraternitatem is. I demand to speak to a lawyer."

Brite raised his eyebrows. "Then a lawyer shall be provided." He wasn't in a hurry to oblige and thought it would be prudent to make Levi sweat for the moment.

Brite cast a spell at the door. It flew opened and crashed into the wall; the sound reverberated against the stone. The security guard outside glanced down the hall with a confused expression on his face.

"Mr. King-Solomon requested a lawyer," Brite said. "Can you call John Chamsky? If you can't find him, try his wife, Samantha Pearce Chamsky."

The security guard's confused look deepened, John Chamsky's specialty wasn't criminal law; another lawyer would have to be called. But the mention of Samantha made Levi squirm and that pleased Brite.

Shiff and Brite sat outside the cell, their feet on the bars, as the security guard took the clues and called for a lawyer. Shiff glanced down the hallway impatiently and Brite glared at Levi with a smug expression.

"Why am I here?" Levi grunted.

"You know why. I suggest you wait for your lawyer. He should be here soon," Shiff said.

Levi's hands had been tied behind his back, his palms facing together, rendering him incapable of shooting off a spell. "I already told you. I don't know this Fraternitatem!" he said as he fought against the strong rope.

Instead of responding, Shiff read something on his phone while Brite split his attention between the end of the hallway and Levi. When John Chamsky eventually entered the cell block, he brought with him an actual criminal lawyer, Annie's best friend, Janie. They strolled down the hallway and stopped at the cell bars.

"So that's him?" John asked.

"That's him." Brite handed them the case file including all of the aliases attached to Levi. John and Janie shared a look into the folder.

"Okay, Levi King-Solomon—or, as I see here, Levi Worchester. I assume they explained why you're here?" John asked Levi, who jumped at the mention of his legal name.

"No, they didn't," Levi growled.

"He lawyered up after telling him we had questions for him concerning the Fraternitatem of Solomon. He got as far as denying he knows who they are," Shiff said.

Brite turned on his crystal and held it for John. "We need to rule him out as a suspect in the murder of Wolfgange Rathbone. As it turns out, he is working as a prison guard by the name of David Stein."

"Open the cell for me, please," John said.

Brite obliged and slid the door open for John and Janie. Brite and Shiff stood with their palms up, ready for Levi should he try to run. John undid the rope and pulled Levi's hand out. Levi, realizing what was happening, pulled against John's grip.

"Levi. I suggest you cast a spell into this crystal. If you do not know who the Fraternitatem of Solomon is, then your magical signature won't be tied to any crime tied to them," Janie said smoothly. She held the crystal for him.

Levi glanced at John. "You're my lawyer. You're supposed to be here for me," Levi said.

"Actually, I am part of the criminal defense legal team that will represent you." Janie said. She was the on-call lawyer for the day, and while she was well familiar with the case through Annie, her involvement would be limited to taking Levi's statement and magic signature to return to the criminal defense team. There was just too much of a conflict for her to do any more than that.

"I don't want you. I want him!" Levi continued to pull against John's grip.

Janie touched Levi's wrist without anger or judgement. He glanced at her.

"Cast a spell into this crystal, now," she said. "They have a lot of evidence against you, so I suggest you start cooperating or nothing the team does will make a difference."

Janie held the crystal for him. Reluctantly, Levi shot a spell into the rock. When it glowed, Janie tossed it to Shiff while Brite and John retied Levi's hands behind his back.

"I need the report ASAP," Janie said.

Shiff saluted her and ran the magical trace to the prison lab. Levi watched Shiff leave and glanced at both lawyers. Though it was cool in the cell, he began to sweat and shake as he shifted his weight between his feet.

"What can you tell us about the Fraternitatem of Solomon?" Janie asked, turning on her recording device and pulling out pencil and paper to take notes.

Levi sat on the cot and slumped. "I work for the Fraternitatem of Solomon. We are an ancient organization that protects the treasure of King Solomon. We seek out items that are stolen from the treasure or haven't been discovered yet. Our mission is to protect the world from magicals who attempt to use those items for their own purposes."

Brite read the recent lab results on his phone; only two fingerprints were found on the prescription bottles. He glanced up at Levi. "Did you administer the drugs to your wife, Emily King-Solomon, and son, Shiloh King-Solomon?" he asked.

"Yes. She gets confused and forgets them. I help her." He looked at the lawyers. "I love my wife."

Brite knew what the drugs were used for, how the Fraternitatem of Solomon had used them to control Emily. He heard the chill in Levi's voice as he proclaimed his love for Emily. Brite could feel his lies and shuddered.

"So, Melichi isn't coming to kill Annie Pearce, your wife's daughter from her first marriage? They're not going to take her power and control the market?" Brite retorted. John and Janie were surprised by his question, and Janie continued to write.

"I don't know what you're talking about!" Levi said. "That's not the Fraternitatem's mission."

"So you, Emily, and Shiloh aren't here to spy on Annie Pearce and gain her trust?"

Levi looked down on the floor and took several deep breaths as if clearing out his emotions.

"When and where are they going to take Annie?" Brite asked.

Levi looked up. "I don't know what you're talking about." His voice was calm, but his muscles tensed.

Brite dragged the metal chair across the stone floor and sat across from Levi. "I happen to know a few things. First, I know that you are David Stein, Levi Worchester, Benjamin Baker, and a host of other aliases. Any idea what they will do to you when this is over?"

Levi burst out in laughter. "I'm a powerful member of the Fraternitatem. They won't do anything to me."

"What about Emily and Shiloh? You really don't think the Fraternitatem will keep them alive, do you?" Shiff said, matching his glare.

Levi didn't answer. He crossed his legs and stared at Brite, looking unconcerned. His demeanor irritated Brite; there was nothing he could do to Levi without it causing problems for the Wizard Guard's case. He balled his hands into tight fists.

"They must have offered you quite a lot to marry someone you didn't love. And all for what?" Brite asked as he marched away.

∽

When the door at the end of the cell block slammed shut, Janie looked at Levi.

"You're supposed to protect my interests," Levi growled at her.

Always professional, Janie occupied the seat left by Brite and stared at Levi.

"This is the deal," she began. "The Fraternitatem made a magical agreement with the Wizard Guard. They are required to stay out of the United States. You admitted you work for the Fraternitatem of Solomon. That breaks a magically binding agreement."

Levi glared at her. "I don't want a woman lawyer," he groused.

"And I will write that in my notes on this interrogation. Unfortunately, we have no way of defending you against that agreement," Janie advised. She looked up at the sound of footsteps in the hallway. A moment later, Shiff walked in with a folder, which he handed to Janie. She took a quick read of the lab results and passed them to John.

"It looks like they can place you in Wolfgange Rathbone's cell the night he died," she told Levi. "That leaves you two options. One, you plead guilty to all of the charges and remain in Tartarus prison for the rest of your life, and you will tell us everything you know about the Fraternitatem. Two, the Wizard Guard will give the nonmagical FBI all of the evidence that you killed Rathbone, your powers will be bound, and you will go to a nonmagical prison."

"That's not fair!" Levi shouted.

"It's not fair that my mother-in-law was kidnapped twenty years ago and brought back here to kill her daughter. It's not fair that Emily's been drugged for years and it's not fair that my sister-in-law is on the block to be murdered. All in all, your little predicament is on you. I'm only here to rattle your cage. But Janie and the team will defend you in a joint magical tribunal between the U.S. Wizard Council and the International Wizard Tribunal. Either way, they've got you. You're screwed." John glared at him as he turned and left Levi to stew in the evidence against him.

CHAPTER 21

"HI, BEVERLY." CHAM cast his spell into the security lock at Tartarus and was buzzed through. "How are Arden and Ariana doing?" He pointed toward their makeshift apartment.

"The best they can under the circumstances. Trying to keep them comfortable, you know. There are chairs in the courtyard. It's not much." She smiled.

Cham laughed. "Thanks for keeping them safe. I appreciate the efforts." He pushed through the gate.

"Just to let you know, when Graham went to get their things, the house was torn apart," Beverly said.

"Thanks. We'll take care of it." Cham nodded and walked the short distance to the apartment. Rather than rushing inside, he observed them through the side window. Ariana was watching something on the television that appeared to be a documentary. She was curled inside a heavy blanket; the prison wasn't known for its warmth. He found Arden at a table, surrounded by books, maps, and scrolls. She was writing copious notes in one of the books and looked up with a smile when Cham entered.

"Your man, Graham, is very sweet. He brought my things from home," Arden said. She returned to her notes.

Cham sat at the table with her. "How are you feeling?"

"She's been great without all the drugs," Ariana said. She joined them at the table, still wearing the blanket.

"Is that true?" Cham asked.

"Yes. I feel alive and well. I have you to thank for that." Arden Blakely offered a genuine smile and took his hand. "The good news: Graham found most of what I wanted from the apartment. There are maps, names, locations of safe houses, and locations of members in nonmagical locations across the world."

Cham glanced at the things she surrounded herself with. "Where did you keep all of this? The Fraternitatem went through your house after we left."

"Floorboards. Secret compartments in the walls. In the ceiling."

"You knew someone would need this someday," Cham said.

Arden, still holding Cham's hand, squeezed it lightly. "Unfortunately, I know nothing of the plan for the black market or what they're planning for Annie. You're on your own there." She smiled again, and stood and walked to the large suitcase on the counter. She dragged it to Cham and laid it on the table. He opened the lid.

"There was a time when I was an important member of the Fraternitatem. I knew many people and many secrets. But I knew they were going to release me and I needed insurance." Arden touched the pile in the suitcase.

Cham pulled up the first notebook, perused a few pages, and placed it back inside.

"Most of the data is older," Arden continued. "I hope you can make use of it. They took almost forty years of my life and I'd really like to be free. I'm here for you and your team. Whatever you need."

Ariana reached for Arden's hand and held it, all the while smiling lovingly at the woman she had regained.

"We talked about it after you brought us here. I convinced Arden it was the only way to truly be free. No offense, but I don't want to live in this prison forever."

Cham chuckled. "Fair enough. Anything I should know before I dig into this?"

"They use black magic as if it's nothing, but you probably know that already," Arden said. "What you really need to know is there's a back entrance to the Cave of Ages. It's on one of the maps." She shuffled several maps until she found the one she wanted. "Here. Right here. It leads through the mountain. There are rooms off of both sides of the passageways."

"This is amazing. This could mean the difference of losing and winning." He glanced at her. "Even if it's older, this will help us trace crimes back years. At least forty years. Thank you." He closed up the suitcase. "Is there anything else you know or is there anything else I can get for you?"

"I knew Emily well. Her purpose in the Fraternitatem was to get to her daughter. I know she was brainwashed like me. We all were. It's how they controlled us. Is her son here? I worry about the boy. He was brainwashed, I'm sure."

"He and Emily are here in the prison. They're in another apartment on the other side of this floor. Did you know Levi?"

Arden grimaced. "I did. I don't like him. I think he was hurting them. I never understood why she took up with him. He was mean. Emily's safe?"

"Yeah. She's safe and we're weaning her off of the drugs."

"Good. She was sweet. Having the baby was helpful for her emotional well-being. It gave her purpose after losing her girls." Arden continued to write in the notebook.

"What are you writing?" Cham asked.

"Names, dates, stories. I fear I killed a lot of people for them." Arden sighed. "If you have questions about the Fraternitatem, let me know."

"Is there a council of higher-ups? Rulers or leaders?" Cham asked.

Arden smiled and chuckled lightly. "There was Melichi. Benaiah until he died. Simon. Levi, until he was demoted. Mostly now it's Melichi. At least the last time I was there. It's been a while since I was part of the group. You understand that?"

"Yes. I do. How old is this information?"

"About ten years old. Just remember, though: once a Fraternitatem of Solomon member, always a member."

Cham understood that. It was the same in the Wizard Guard.

❧

Annie landed on her back porch and entered her house through her hallway as the front door bell rang. The magical protection around the property was designed to protect her from evil magic of demons, wizards, and vampires. Over the last year, the spells had been attacked and upgraded, restricting additional people. Annie felt safe most of the time—except for now. It was nine in the evening and anyone she wanted in her house would have been able to pass through the spells. This surprise visitor alarmed her.

She peered through the peephole. The woman she saw was short like her, with wavy gray hair, cut in a short bob. Her face was Annie's, the same face as Emily and Samantha. The older woman stood beside a man in a black suit and tie, his hair combed in a straight, conservative style. He carried a briefcase.

That can't be!

Annie placed a simple spell around the door jamb and turned on the porch light. She took a deep breath, nervous by this impending conversation with a woman she didn't remember and couldn't ever recall seeing in a photo. Curiously, she opened the door.

"It's awfully late for a marketing call," Annie said with some levity.

"I apologize for the lateness of my visit, but I fear if I didn't come here straightaway, there would be dire consequences. May I ask if you're Anne Elizabeth Pearce or Samantha Emily Pearce?" the woman asked.

Annie couldn't get over her grandmother standing on her front porch. "You're Gloriana Worthington."

"You know who I am. I must admit I'm surprised, especially after the way your father treated me when my daughter died," Gloriana spat.

Annie held the edge of the door. She had never known why she and Samantha had no relationship with their grandparents, aunts, or uncles. It had never occurred to her to ask and Jason had never offered an explanation. Being harassed by this stranger who looked just like her made her protective of her father, regardless of how stupid his reasons might have been.

"Ground rule: I don't want to know nor do I care why Jason did what he did. You obviously have something to say to us, and I admit I'm confused why it took you eight years after he died to come and say it. But since you're here, I'll let you have your say and then I want you to leave," Annie said.

Rather than seeming offended by Annie's words, Gloriana smiled. "You are feisty."

Annie moved aside and motioned the pair inside.

Gloriana glanced around the small, cozy front room. She stopped at the few pictures on the fireplace mantle and looked at the picture of Annie, Cham, Dave, and Janie, then at the wedding picture of Samantha and John. The only family picture Annie had of her and her parents was from when she was three years old. Gloriana lovingly touched the frames and picked up the family picture. After wiping a small tear, she placed it back.

"Based on the wedding picture that's not you, I'm guessing you're Anne," she said.

"Annie. Please have a seat." Annie switched on a table lamp, uncertain how much her grandmother and this man knew of the magic.

She scratched at her arm nervously as she sat on the ottoman across from them.

"When your father died, I was advised to not try and win custody. Your magical lawyers told me I wouldn't be able to handle the magical children and that Samantha was almost old enough to retain custody of you. I regret that I didn't try to have a relationship, though." Gloriana tightly clutched her small purse.

Annie glanced at the man beside her grandmother and back to Gloriana. "You and your lawyer know of magic?"

Gloriana nodded. "I always knew. Since your mother told me. I felt I needed to be truthful with him when he asked why I didn't have custody of my granddaughters. Is that okay?"

Annie shook her head. "Sorry, it's really not. Though I expect that you won't breathe a word of this to anyone," she said to the lawyer.

"I will not. It was explained to me that should I reveal this family secret; I will not have my career to look forward to anymore." He pulled on his tie and avoided looking at his client.

"I hope you can refrain from spilling the beans. In the meantime," she said, turning back to Gloriana, "I'm sorry Dad kept you from us. I know he made lots of mistakes. I won't apologize for him, but I don't remember seeing any pictures of you and Mom. So I'm guessing there wasn't a good relationship?"

Gloriana nodded. "Most of the painful memories revolved around their relationship. But as you said, nothing about your father, so I'll get to the point. I've been noticing several strange men and women walking past my house. I feel as though it could be explained by you."

She's all business.

"I'm surprised they were so obvious. But, yes. We are protecting you from magic. We fear you might be in danger," Annie said.

"From what and why now?" Gloriana asked.

Since both her grandmother and the lawyer were familiar with magic, Annie didn't bother standing up and instead summoned her father's missing file. She took out the first picture of Emily.

"I found this three-months ago. My dad was killed because he found Emily alive." Annie handed the picture to Gloriana. "The picture was taken almost nine years ago."

Gloriana's hand flew to her heart. She let out a small chirp. "Oh my. She never died." She shuddered, the picture slipping from her shaking hands.

Annie reached out and held her grandmother's hands. "We don't know how it was done. How we had her body even though it really wasn't her. She's alive and she's under protective custody now. We were afraid she would come after you or that the group who kidnapped her might." Annie picked up the picture and put it away.

"I... why?" Gloriana held her hands across her mouth as if she might be holding in vomit.

"There's a group of people, dangerous people, who kidnapped her. And while she was with them, they brainwashed her into believing I was evil and destructive and that I need to be stopped. They sent her to kill me."

Gloriana stopped quivering and burst out laughing. "That's... that is the biggest bunch of bullshit I've ever heard." She sat up straighter.

"Sorry, but this group felt it would be easier to get to me if it they sent my mother. We still think Emily might come for you." Annie ignored her grandmother's disbelief.

"You're not joking," Gloriana stated. Annie shook her head. "Well, still, how can this be? How can they just kidnap my daughter, keep her from her children, and use her to kill one of them? That's... I knew this life was bad for her. I begged her not to marry Jason. When she told me he was a wizard, that magic was real, I thought he was going to be the death of her. I was nearly correct!"

Gloriana stood and paced across the front room, turning at the dining area and walking to the den. Her high heels clicked against the wood floor. Annie glanced at the lawyer, who was still playing with his tie.

When Gloriana returned, she picked up the picture of Annie and Cham. "Is he your boyfriend?" she asked.

"His name is Bobby Chamsky. He and Samantha's husband John are brothers," Annie said.

"Oh. They're magical too?" Gloriana put down the picture and took up the one of the Pearce family. She touched Emily's face.

"Yes. Bobby and I are engaged."

"Congratulations. I suppose it will be another event for me to miss." Gloriana dabbed her eyes with a handkerchief. "I'm sorry. I would have liked very much to see you grow up. You're a beautiful girl, as is Samantha. I'm sorry I missed so much."

"I'm also brilliant and strong."

Gloriana laughed. "And mouthy like your mother."

Annie walked to her and took her hands again. "I don't know what caused the riff. We weren't told. There is time. But for now, you have to understand. I work as a wizard guard—" Annie stopped when her grandmother looked upon her with a look of horror.

"How could he allow you to take up that career?" she murmured.

"Cham is the Wizard Guard department manager. We know what we're doing and we know that you need to be kept safe. I can do that, but for now, you need to state your business and go back home." Annie pointed to the man in the suit.

"That's Sawyer Brown, my lawyer. I was going to have him give you and Samantha your inheritance. It'll have to wait, seeing as my daughter is still alive."

CHAPTER 22

ANNIE SAT WITH Rathbone's copy of the *Inferno* open in her lap; she had gotten as far as finding the letters *SNAKE H*. She was fairly certain the letters would spell "Snake Head Letters," though she had no idea why Rathbone would lead her there on September 1. She pushed the book away and stared into the trees. Kidnapping her own mother had left her restless and anxious.

"You saw Emily today?" Zola put her arm around her charge; Annie leaned against her.

"Yeah. She was happy to see Sami."

"She thinks you're evil. Give her time."

Annie chuckled and summoned a map of Illinois.

"What are you doing?" Zola asked.

Annie set the map on the table and sat down. "I need to keep myself busy. The itching is getting worse. My skin is burning with pain." She wrapped her scrying necklace around her hand and let it hang above the map.

Zola wiped away the tears as they slid down Annie's cheeks. "None of this can be easy. You should sleep. I'll make a strong potion so you can't feel the itching." She placed a cool hand on Annie's warm one.

"As pleasurable as that sounds, I need to do this."

Annie let the crystal swing from Chicago to southern Illinois in large swift circles. It landed in the middle of farmland in central Illinois.

Annie scried a second time for Sturtagaard, to ensure his location was correct. It wasn't long ago that his preferred hiding location was an abandoned building in the city, close to a good selection of victims. She wasn't expecting to find him in an empty barn in the country.

"You're not going after the vampire, are you?" Zola asked.

Annie dropped the fabric, which had been ripped from one of his items of clothing. "Good guess," she said as she wrapped up her map and crystal. "Yes. I need something from him."

"Don't let him get to you. You look ill."

Annie kissed her friend. "I need to go. I'll be fine." Zola squeezed Annie's hand before Annie pulled away and teleported to the vampire.

She gave up believing stealth was key to sneaking up on him; Sturtagaard knew her scent and would smell her before he saw her. Unafraid of him and knowing he was unafraid of her, she landed beside the barn and surveyed the landscape as she walked around the perimeter of the building. She found a small door and let herself in.

While it and the land appeared abandoned, the barn was still fully stacked with boxes, farm implements, and, surprisingly, a car. Sturtagaard had cleared a small patch of floor and "decorated" it with a sofa, a refrigerator that buzzed, and a bookshelf. She hadn't realized until this moment that he was a reader.

"You didn't make it difficult to find you," she said as she squeezed herself between a pile of boxes and the car, rubbing against years of dirt.

A low light was cast from a small lantern beside the sofa. The vampire glanced up and matched Annie's gaze. He said nothing.

She pulled up a crate and sat across from him. "Something's been bothering me since I found you in Louisiana."

"Yeah, what's that?" He placed a book of Shakespeare sonnets on the table and looked at her. For a short moment, Annie could see the human face she had left in the past.

"How coincidental it was that you were at the same portal at the same time as me," Annie said.

"Interesting. No stake?" Sturtagaard jeered, but Annie saw something different in his face, in his eyes. He looked as though he had no more fight left.

"I'm fairly certain I could, with a flick of my wrist, cut your head off. It's a lot cleaner and a lot less work," Annie retorted.

"Fair enough. So, that was the question. What do you think the answer is? Because I've known you for a long time, girl. I'm pretty sure you already know."

"The name is Annie. Anne, if you'd like to keep it all business." Annie summoned a stake to appease him. It was so sharp at its point; she could easily push through a breastbone and pierce a heart. His heart, to be precise. "Robin Price has a contact who occasionally passes on information and I'm fairly certain you told that contact to tell Robin."

She watched Sturtagaard closely. He made no expression of agreement or acknowledgement.

"Am I close?" she asked. She hated when he played games.

"I'll miss doing your job," he said. It was the first time he acknowledged his impending death. She almost felt sorry for him and then she didn't.

"How did you know about the market?" Annie asked.

"I've been alive for many generations. I have contacts," he said and winked.

Annie's stomach roiled at his levity. "Do you know where the other three portals are?" she asked.

Sturtagaard raised an eyebrow. "And how do you figure there are only four portals?"

Annie stood at the bookshelf, reading the titles of his library—Shakespeare, Milton, Chaucer—impressed by his selection. "Four quadrants that represent the four corners of Earth. We expect they'll be a portal in each hemisphere, north and south. It's a shame when I have to do your job," she said.

She pulled down *The Legend of Sleepy Hollow*. It was a first edition and yet it looked pristine, as if it had never been used. "Where do you keep all of your personal items? I don't remember this at the warehouse."

"I have secrets that are none of your business."

"Whatever. Ask your contact if he knows anything about the other three portals." She looked at the vampire, sitting there, an old man in a young man's body. He was filled with so much wisdom and so much evil, and yet he holstered his anger. She tossed the stake and let it slap against her palm.

He jumped slightly. "Gir—Annie, that's still not funny."

Annie smiled. "Yeah. It kinda is," she said as she placed his book back. Still, she didn't leave.

"What now, Annie?"

"What do you know about my powers?"

Sturtagaard smiled to himself like he was remembering a funny joke.

"You do know something."

"Oh, girl. The things you don't know. What will you do without me?" He walked to his small kitchenette and pulled out a pouch of blood. She watched with disgust as he microwaved the entire package.

"What do you know about the powers?"

He turned and faced her, still holding the now-heated blood packet. "I know you turned your father into a corporeal ghost in the past. That's what I told the Fraternitatem."

Annie frowned. "And that was enough for them to wait centuries to kill me?"

Sturtagaard laughed deeply. "I lied to them girl. I. LIED! I'm a vampire. It's what we do."

Annie flipped the stake; Sturtagaard jumped. "What did you tell them?"

"I told them you could control the elements: water, fire, earth, and wind. You know, tornadoes, hurricanes…"

"Volcanoes and earthquakes. Yeah, I've heard that recently. In otherwords, you're just an ass and know nothing." She crossed her arms against her chest and glared at him.

"Why are you so surprised, girl? I lied to them and told them all that junk. But you can turn a ghost corporeal. Have you done anything else odd?"

Annie looked at him. "I have, but I'm not telling you. As you say, you're a vampire and you lie. Just for the record, you really are an ass." She tossed him the stake and left him alone, curious as to what other powers she might now possess.

❧

"Sturtagaard knows his time is almost up," Annie remarked as she climbed into bed.

"You saw him tonight?" Cham asked as he changed his clothes.

"I was curious about something and he basically corroborated it. I won't miss him." She pulled the blankets up around her to remove the chill. "Are Arden and Ariana adjusting okay?"

Cham glanced at her as he took off his watch and lay it on the dresser. "Now that she's not being drugged and has her memory back, she's a whole new person. She actually had a bunch of stuff for us. Names, places, a hidden entrance into the Cave of Ages."

Annie raised her eyebrows. "That could change everything. I'm glad she's willing to share." She lay her head on her hand as she reclined on her side. "I also saw someone else tonight."

"You had a busy night. Who else?" He climbed in beside her. She shivered against his chilly skin.

"My grandmother showed up at the door."

He matched her position and looked into her eyes. "Really? She saw the protection detail around the house?"

Annie nodded.

"You sure it was her?" Cham touched her hair that hung across her chest.

"Looked like Mom and me, just with white hair," Annie said. "I didn't use a crystal to be sure, but... she looked like me."

"Hmmm. So, what did Grandma want?"

"After seeing the protection detail, I guess she decided it was time to give us our inheritance."

"It belongs to Emily."

"I told her Emily was alive. Surprisingly, she took it well. I explained how we thought she might be in danger. Especially if Emily wants the money." Annie closed her eyes as Cham touched her head, her cheek. "Gloriana wants to come to the wedding."

"She's missed out on a lot, for whatever reason."

Annie rolled to her back and stared at the ceiling. A crack was growing at the center. "Sturtagaard didn't know about the four corners of Earth in relation to the portals. I told him he should ask his contact for the other portals." She yawned. The late night was getting to her. Cham lay beside her, pulled her into him, and held her. "He also lied to the Fraternitatem about my powers. He doesn't know what they do."

Cham chuckled into her hair. "It's almost over," he whispered. She kissed him gently and let the sleep come and take her away.

CHAPTER 23

FROM THE FIFTH-FLOOR conference room, Annie overlooked the busy street. Traffic started and stopped, and a steady stream of people entered and exited the surrounding buildings. As it was a warm summer day, several tour buses zoomed down the street.

The magic flowed strongly through her this morning. She leaned against the cool glass for some relief. For a short moment, the coolness eased the itching across her forehead. She refrained from scratching the rest of her body until she couldn't stand it anymore. Her arms and legs were red and patchy, stinging when she touched them.

"Hi."

Annie turned. Ryan stood at the entrance. "What are you doing in here?" he asked, taking a seat beside the window.

"Itchy. I needed a break," she said.

Ryan could see the red patches she no longer hid. "Everything else okay?" he asked.

"Yeah. Is that why you're here?" She pulled at her legs, never taking her eyes from the street below.

"I wanted to make sure you're okay. It's been a lot this week."

"Now that the first-line spies are all locked away, we can concentrate on the rest of the plan." She absently scratched her thigh, which was so red it burned at her touch.

"Go home and take a potion for the itching. You're entitled," Ryan said.

Annie glanced at him and smiled. "Not yet." She returned to the window; the flow of the city seemed to calm her. She was safe here.

"Emily banned Gloriana from seeing you. Jason was just honoring that after she died," Ryan told her.

"It doesn't matter now." Annie scratched at her hands.

"No, I suppose it doesn't," Ryan said thoughtfully. "Go home and take care of yourself."

Annie moved her hand and watched the magic trail after it, shimmering and popping like bubbles.

"It's going to send you back to the hospital," Ryan said.

Annie looked at him and shook her head. "No. The magic builds up, the itching starts, and then I pass out. Unless I..." She held her hand in a fist and quickly released it, letting her fingers fly out. A burst of magic flew from her palm.

"You can release the magic buildup?"

Annie raised her eyebrows and smiled. "Everyone needs to stop under-estimating me. I'm kinda smart, you know." She clenched her hand into a tight fist again and released her fingers. Another burst of magic flowed from her palm.

"Sorry. You're no longer a kid." Ryan produced a rolled scroll, officially closed with the seal of the Grand Marksman, and passed it to Annie.

She looked at it and then at Ryan before peeling the seal from the parchment. It was a contract for Annie to take the position of Manager of the Educational Liaison Department.

"It's all set if this is what you want to do." Ryan smiled broadly.

"I'll miss the Wizard Guard. I was born to do that," she said as she looked at the contract.

"Bigger salary as a department manager. More money as a teacher. You'll be safe," Ryan said.

Annie sighed and sat at the table, signing her future into being. She always knew this day would someday come. She always knew she'd do some-thing different when she had children; she never wanted to risk leaving her kids without parents. She held her breath as she signed her name and blew on the ink to dry the parchment. She passed it back to Ryan; the magic trailed behind her hand when she moved.

"It looks like the magic's building again," Ryan noted.

Annie looked at her hand, formed a figure eight by swishing her hand in a quick motion, then shook it quickly. "I'm heading to the gym. I need to expel this energy. I think it time to bring in the Middle Eastern group. A plan needs to be created." Annie gave Ryan a hug and headed to the basement.

◈

Target hung from the ceiling like piñatas. Body forms stood in a haphazard pattern across the gym floor, waiting for an attacker. Annie walked the obstacle course of sorts, whipped out her palm, and cast a spell, exploding the first dummy. Fuzz and fabric flew all over. Her itching decreased.

Annie prowled as if she were stalking a magical creature. She turned and shot another spell, concentrating on the practice dummy's head only. It blew apart with such force, fuzz landed on the ceiling beams, twenty feet up. Annie smiled and watched golden bubbles of magic billow from her palms, float upward, and pop.

She cast a spell upwards at the ceiling target. The cartoon character blew apart and paper in multiple streams of color rained down, covering her. Annie left behind a scorch mark across the ceiling.

"Whoops," she said as she shot successive spells upward, knocking out the remaining five targets.

"You were right. This could be an effective training method," a voice said.

Annie walked out from the group of practice dummies. Perkins Abernathy stood beside the headless dummy.

She summoned an ash stake and plunged it into the dummy beside her. "I have ideas," Annie said. "What's up?" At the window separating the gym from the morgue, Annie saw a familiar face staring back at her.

"Fabien Arnault is waiting for you. Are you ready or still letting off energy?" Perkins asked.

Annie glanced at her hand, magic still billowed. She glanced back at the window and waved Fabien inside. "A little more magic, I think," she said.

Fabien entered the lab; he and Perkins watched Annie strike several more dummies, blowing more cotton and fabric across the gym.

"Hi, Fabien. Sorry about that. Just burning off the magic," Annie said. She enjoyed this new Fabien. He seemed relaxed, dressed in jeans and a collared shirt. The only difference she could discern quickly was that he now had a large scar across his chin.

"I see. It's pretty impressive," he said.

Annie cast another spell, blowing apart the farthest practice dummy. With the itching decreased, she finally felt relief. "Sorry. This magic is very difficult to deal with sometimes," she admitted.

"No problem. Just here with an update," Fabien said.

"Great. Give me a sec to clean up my mess and I'll walk you up." With both palms out, Annie waved the debris to the side.

"Leave it, Annie," Perkins shouted out.

"You sure?" He nodded and Annie led Fabien out of the gym.

∽

"It's an impressive Wizard Hall," Fabien said as they entered the fifth floor. Annie took him straight to her desk and offered him a seat.

"You've been here before." She sat across from him and folded her hands on the desk.

"I know. It's just so clean and big, and you haven't been duped by one of your own," he said.

"You never know what goes on behind closed doors," she said, thinking of Antique Symposium's payment to Starla.

"I hope to find out what that means someday." He smiled and summoned his folder, passing it to Annie.

She stared at the pictures he had taken in the market in Greece. "Did you get in?" she asked.

"I did. Keep reviewing," he said.

Annie shuffled through the pictures. The glyphs were the same in the Greek market and they led to the main market. "I see you did." She put them back in his folder and passed it back. "That's encouraging. We have what we think is two left. We're starting to plan to take down the Fraternitatem."

"I'm here to help," Fabien said.

Annie frowned. "Do you think you could bring the French Wizard Guard on board?"

Fabien looked at her tired face. "The good news is; I have something to offer them. I think they will listen," he said.

"I'll leave that to you. If you need our help, though, we're here for it. I suspect we'll need all the teams we can get," Annie said.

"I realize I've made mistakes and abused my powers, but I really want to make the world a better place. That's why I joined the Wizard Guard in the first place," he said.

Annie glanced at him. She knew it was why he joined the Guard; most joined with hopes of changing the world. Sometimes good intentions led a person down the wrong path. She wondered if she could fully trust him. "Will you be going back to France now?" she asked.

"I'm still available to assist."

"Well. All the work is menial at this point. I know deciphering notes on the Fraternitatem and finding the remaining portals isn't all that exciting, but we need answers about the Cave of Ages," Annie said.

"Can I pull up a chair and dig in?"

Annie chuckled. "Follow me."

Fabien followed her to the conference room. He stopped at the door and held his breath. The last time he was there, the walls had been covered in crime scene photos and incriminating emails. He was being presented with charges against the French Wizard Guard and Marielle Beauchamp for attacking the Wizard Guard of the United States. He slowly let out stale air and entered the conference room. Along the far wall was a large map of the world. Red-tipped pins highlighted the location where a portal had been located. Purple pins represented the location of the portal to the main market. Annie added a purple pin to the market portal in southern France.

Fabien walked to the window and watched the traffic stop and start. "Today, I am enjoying my visit." He sat at the window seat and watched for a moment. When he turned to Annie, she was standing at the map. "There are a lot of false markets," Fabien said.

Annie nodded. "They went through a lot of work to hide the main market."

"It's not just hiding the market from you. They're hiding from all of the merchants. I wonder how they chose the merchants to keep at the main market."

Annie stared at the board. "The strongest, most powerful merchants with a lot of contacts, probably."

"Those they think they can trust," Fabien added.

"Arrowhead. The Fraternitatem doesn't know their merchants like they think they do."

"Do you really trust him?"

Annie grimaced. While she didn't know Arrowhead well, Gibbs trusted him, and for that, she did. "Actually, yeah I do." Annie sat at the table. "If you really want to help, you can come with me to see Sturtagaard. I asked him for help."

"And he'll give it to you?"

"He's trying to bargain for his life," Annie said.

❧

Sturtagaard was where Annie expected him to be: the barn in the middle of a cornfield in central Illinois. Annie and Fabien teleported behind a wagon and walked to the building where a low light emanated from a single window. She pointed to the barn. "He's lying low. Knows he'll be staked when this is over."

"I find it hard to believe that he's giving up so easily," Fabien commented.

"I expect a change of heart when the time comes. Until then, he seems resolved to his end," Annie said.

They entered the crowded barn and scooted between the car and a wall of boxes. Sturtagaard was in the same spot Annie had left him, on a corner of his sofa, reading a book.

"Talk to your contact?" Annie asked.

He pulled a folded piece of paper from a pocket in his shirt and handed it to her without looking. She opened the paper and read it in the low, dim light. "We know about this one," Annie said. She showed it to Fabien.

"Yeah. That's where I found it," Fabien said.

Sturtagaard looked at her and shrugged.

In the face of his docility, Annie refrained from yelling, screaming, or being an overall pain in the ass. Instead, she chose to sit beside him on the sofa and pull the book from his hand.

"Where are the other two?" she asked.

Sturtagaard looked upon her with disdain, as if she were bothering him. "That's the one he gave me." He pointed to the paper and glanced at Fabien. "No more Spencer, Cham, Gibbs?" His name made Annie squirm. "Oh, yes, Gibbs," he said, smirking.

"You're an ass." Annie stood up and glanced Fabien, an apologetic expression on her face.

"The Fraternitatem is after you," Sturtagaard said. He stood and touched Annie's cheek. The chill emanated off of his skin. She shuddered but kept her gaze on his. Behind her, Fabien flipped his stake in his hand. Sturtagaard jumped but retained eye contact.

"I wanted to kill you, before I turned," he said.

"What happened wasn't my fault."

"You are so beautiful and too smart for your own good. I could have done this for them so long ago. What's to stop me now? You're only one insignificant little girl." He pulled another sheet of paper from his back pocket and handed it to Annie.

"To you, maybe. The name is Anne Elizabeth Pearce. Don't forget it." She took his information and left the barn with Fabien close behind.

"He doesn't like you at all," Fabien said.

"The feeling is mutual." Annie glanced at the coordinates Sturtagaard gave her and placed her arms around Fabien as they teleported to the first portal in Louisiana.

❧

"Are you sure that's what it is?" Dr. Christine asked Graham Lightner. She stared at the crystal, the unknown magic waving about inside the rock.

"Yes. I took it to Perkins and to Mrs. Cuttlebrink. The Wizard Guard researcher, Emerson Donaldson, also looked into the magic. It's all in the report," Graham said.

Dr. Christine had collected the magic herself when she first examined the boy. No one at the time recognized what it was. Today, Graham had ascertained it was a dark evil magic inside of him.

"He's carrying someone else's soul?" she asked. "How did they do this and why would they do that to a thirteen-year-old boy?"

"How? We're not sure. What we do know is, you can read someone's magical energy. Most of us have one magical signature. This boy has a second magical signature. Annie will read the same way. We pulled the magic from the crystal, it acted…"

"It acted what?" Dr. Christine asked.

"It acted like a human. An angry, angry human."

"That's why you think it's an actual soul?"

Graham nodded.

"I've never seen this. Ever. And my specialty is magical dark arts medicine," she admitted.

"I've never seen it either. But then again, I didn't know anyone could receive additional magic, not their own, until it happened to Annie. I shouldn't be surprised to see this now."

"The magic is evil. That much we know. Since we're assuming we can't remove Annie's magic without killing her, should we assume the same with this magic?" Dr. Christine stared inside the crystal and frowned.

"Where's Annie's magic? Do you still have her crystal?"

Dr. Christine summoned the crystal she used on Annie when she returned from the past and handed it to Graham. He stared inside.

"It billows and flows like you'd expect magic to," he said. "Not like that angry, vibrating, human-like magic in his."

Christine stared inside the crystal again and compared the two foreign magics, her frown lines deepening as she thought about their immediate problem: how to remove the magic from Shiloh. "Why do you suppose they did it?"

"It's a lot easier to trust a boy who looks like that than any adult. Make him evil, and he can either kill or get her to leave with him," Graham said.

"That poor kid. What a life."

"Do you think we can exorcise it from him?"

"If we presume it's an unwanted soul and not magic, then yes, I can exorcise the presence," Dr. Christine said.

They glanced at each other with trepidation before entering Tartarus Prison. After casting spells inside the lock, they were taken to the prison hospital wing where Emily King-Solomon sat with her son.

"Hi, Emily. I hear he's suffering from a high fever," Dr. Christine said.

Shiloh was covered with ice packs; his skin was red and clammy. He slept fitfully. Dr. Christine checked his vitals and reviewed his chart.

"What is it? They said you know," Emily said.

"The Fraternitatem used your boy. They added magic to him. He's possessed with an evil soul. Did you let them do this?" Dr. Christine asked, her tone harsh.

Emily looked on in horror and shook her head. "I—I didn't know. I didn't protect him." She shuddered as tears burned her eyes.

"We'll take care of it." Dr. Christine summoned a brand-new crystal and held it to Shiloh's mouth. "Graham, hold his shoulders down."

When they thought he was secure enough, Dr. Christine chanted the exorcising spell. As the evil magic was being summoned to the crystal, Shiloh began to shake and quiver. His young body bounced on the bed as the black magical energy was syphoned from him. He groaned and fought against Graham's tight grip.

"Stop! Stop it! You're hurting him!" Emily screamed as she reached for the crystal. Graham reached for Emily's hands; she easily yielded as he pulled her from Shiloh. "She's hurting him," Emily murmured.

"No, Emily. She's removing the evil magic. She's saving him," Graham said.

When Dr. Christine finished the spell and the magic was removed from the boy, a thick, gray light glowed from the crystal.

Shiloh stopped shaking and bouncing against the bed. His muscles slumped against the sheets and he began to shake from cold.

Emily pushed Graham from her and grabbed Shiloh's hand. "It's okay, baby. Mommy's here."

Dr. Christine and Graham looked inside the crystal. The magic took on a form of a face with a nose and a mouth that seemed to be shouting at them.

"Do you think that's the man whose soul was taken?" Dr. Christine asked.

"It could be. I think maybe we should compare it to the magical signatures in the database. It might be useful."

"It just might."

CHAPTER 24

FABIEN FOLLOWED ANNIE across the path and stopped behind her as they came to the water's edge.

"Okay. Why are we here?" Fabien asked.

"Well. The next portal location appears to be South Africa, and I have a contact here who probably wants to go there." She took a step inside the water; Fabien followed reluctantly into the swamp.

Annie held her hand out until she felt that unmistakable chill. She glanced around the swamp and jammed her cursed athame inside. They ducked inside the whirlpool of air, their pants heavy with swamp water.

"Well, that was fun."

"My contact is this way," Annie said as she followed the narrow path to the left where she found Joseph working with a client. She pointed toward the portal and headed there.

When Fabien stepped behind the storage building, his eyes widened. "Yes. This is what I found in Greece." He reached out and touched the cool metal of the perimeter fence, his fingers grazing the painted glyphs.

Minutes later, Joseph joined them behind the building. "Annie Pearce, how are you?" he greeted her.

Annie introduced Joseph and Fabien. They shook hands.

"Now Annie, how can I help you?" Joseph asked.

Annie handed him the sheet of paper. "Fabien found a portal to the black market in Greece. That leaves two more, including this one." She held up the paper from Sturtagaard. Joseph glanced at the location.

"Where did that come from?"

Annie explained Sturtagaard's contact. "That said, I haven't established who his contact is. Anyway, I thought you might want to come," she finished.

"Of course. This is close to the South African Wizard Hall," he said.

They slunk out from their hiding spot and left the market separately; Annie and Fabien waited for Joseph at the edge of the swamp. "You sure nobody will suspect you?" Annie asked as they walked along the trail.

"Everyone is in and out. And if this helps get me away from the market, then it's worth the trip," Joseph said.

From a relatively isolated patch near the portal, they teleported to an empty acreage in South Africa. Being in a foreign territory, Annie had no jurisdiction and handed Joseph the paper from Sturtagaard. He studied the coordinates and their current location.

"We need to head west." He pointed and motioned for them to follow him through the thick trees, miles outside of Cape Town on a little-traveled plot of land. Annie held her hands out, feeling for a change in the air. "The Fraternitatem has left the smaller markets," Joseph said.

"It appears that the Fraternitatem might be making a move?" Annie asked.

"Yes. I was going to contact you in the morning and then there you were with this news," he said. The air began to change, grew chillier, hummed violently. Joseph stopped. "Here," he said.

Annie stared at the hazy anomaly. She felt the chill against her skin; goosebumps and itching coursed through her. She summoned her cursed athame and plunged it into the portal, which released a violent wind, reminiscent of the storm that erupted from the portal out of England— the one that could have collapsed with her inside. She stepped aside and watched the air whirl. It gained speed and lightning struck out at them.

Annie shook at the memories of the portal she had used to come home. She tensed her muscles and glanced inside.

"It's violent," Fabien said.

"It is." Annie held her breath as she stepped through, leaving one foot in South Africa, waiting for Fabien to step through. When he did, she entered the market and waited for the men to join her.

"That was something." Fabien joined Annie as they surveyed the market. It was smaller than the main market but larger than any other she had investigated. The air was humid, thick with stench of dung and smoke; a heavy layer hung over the market in a thick cloud. It was a comforting familiarity regardless of the evil that occurred there.

Annie turned and saw two small dragons hop across the silky dirt. When one coughed, a small puff of smoke flew from its mouth. To her left, a booth had several baskets on the table, each filled with dragon eggs.

"What really is the purpose of finding all of the portals?" Joseph asked. They walked along a wooden fence that spanned the perimeter of the market. As with the other markets, the wall was covered in seemingly haphazardly placed glyphs.

"To monitor traffic. Possibly to allow us to close the market portals, should we need to. I think once this is done, all Wizard Guards will need to monitor the black market situation more closely." Fabien said. They had made a complete turn of the market.

"Where do we think the portal's hidden?" Annie asked.

"There was a little corner, back that way. It might be a closet," Joseph suggested. They turned and followed the wall again until they discovered what looked to be a closet in the corner of the market. Though it appeared to be a door, there was no handle.

"Look for any hook or handle," Annie said. Fabien, who was six feet tall, felt along the top of the fence, while Annie sat in the dirt and checked the bottom and Joseph searched the sides.

"Got it." Joseph pulled the small latch out and yanked open the wooden door.

Behind the door was a brick wall with four distinctive glyphs that formed a large square. Annie recognized the portal and glanced across the market. Merchants took little note of them as Annie took out her athame and jammed it inside.

This portal was quiet. A light breeze blew outward from what looked like a transparent door exposing the main market. Annie glanced at Fabien and shrugged as she entered. The two men each followed.

"The market," Fabien said as he looked around. "It almost looks like the original."

"I need to make a quick stop," Annie said. Getting her bearings, she found the path to the right and took the passage to the end.

Arrowhead glanced up when she arrived and caught her eye before returning to his customer and the impending sale. Annie perused the items on his table, even after he finished with his customer.

Arrowhead bent down, picked up a box, and shoved it into a bag. "Here's your order as you requested."

Annie pulled out a pile of avrum gold and handed it to him. He didn't look at the pile, didn't count how much she gave him, simply pocketed the coins and returned to another customer at his booth.

Annie walked to the portal, shrunk her wares, and pocketed them.

"What was—" Joseph began.

Annie held her fingers to her lips to quiet him as they stepped through the portal. The smaller market had grown crowded, and though they tried to blend into the crowd as it moved in the same direction, several merchants caught sight of them as they re-entered.

"We've been discovered," Annie said. She grew uncomfortable as they followed the wall to the portal. They were being followed.

"Run!" Fabien shouted.

He grabbed Annie's arm and pulled her; she shot successive spells in front of them as Joseph cast spells behind them, knocking one of their pursuers to the ground. Two more men grew closer to them. Annie ducked as a fireball missed them, hitting the wooden fence. Fire quickly caught hold and began consuming the fence. Fabien pulled Annie out of the way as a purple hex was thrown at them. As they ran up to the exit, Annie cast a spell opening the portal; Fabien pulled her through.

"Shit!" Joseph shouted as he tumbled from the portal.

Annie shined a light on him. His shirt was covered in blood and he was missing part of his arm. "Damn. Where's your hospital?" she asked anxiously.

"Yours, now." Joseph gritted out through the pain.

Annie reached around Joseph and teleported to the U.S. Wizard Hall, outside the doors of the hospital. She whipped her hands out, sending the doors flying open, and summoned a wheelchair. A nurse ran from the hospital, helped Joseph into the chair, and wheeled him inside.

❦

Annie paced outside the emergency room.

"You got him here in time," Fabien said.

"I know. I shouldn't have brought him with. Should've just left him at his booth." Annie turned and walked in the opposite direction.

"And he would have found out and been upset you didn't ask," Fabien replied.

Cham ran through the front doors, finding Annie pacing. "How is he?" He looked toward the doors.

"I haven't heard yet." Annie stopped and leaned against the wall.

"I called his department manager. She's on her way."

Annie closed her eyes and told Cham about the two new portals to the main market.

"That's three of the four. Think Sturtagaard will cough up the last one?" Cham asked.

Annie nodded. "He'll play it out as long as he can. I expect he'll cough it up and offer something new to bargain for his life."

Cham touched her cheek. "Text me for anything new. I'm going to wait outside for the South African team rep." He waved to Fabien before heading back outside.

Fabien sat on the floor. "I've noticed just how hard you work here. How incredibly busy you are, with all the things you do." He looked at her.

"You have a smaller magical population. It makes for less stuff."

"I used to," he murmured.

"If you put yourself out here for us and the rest of the community, that might help you make a case for—" Annie turned as the emergency room door opened and Dr. Christine stepped through.

"Annie. He's fine. He's alive. His left hand is missing." Annie sighed as Dr. Christine handed her a crystal. "I have no idea what this magic is."

Annie glanced inside the pinkish rock, waved her hand, and searched through the magical signatures. The magic glowed an iridescent black.

"This is the second bit of magic we've never seen before. Where is the Fraternitatem getting this magic?" Annie asked.

"I think that is for the Wizard Guard to find out," Dr. Christine said.

"I'll take it back, see what we can see. Thanks." Annie pocketed the rock as Cham returned with a woman she didn't recognize.

"Annie Pearce, Fabien Arnault, Dr. Christine Andrews, this is Petra Johnson. She's the department manager for the South African Wizard Guard."

They shook hands.

"He's healing. His hand was shot off with a curse I've never seen before," Dr. Christine said. Annie showed Petra the crystal.

"That's quite disturbing," Petra said. She looked at Annie. "So, you're the famous Annie Pearce. Joseph is quite fond of you. He requested this job."

"I like him too. I appreciate all he's done for us."

Annie offered a wan smile. Petra looked as though she'd rather get this over with and leave the group.

"Well, if you'd like to see him, two of you can go in," Dr. Christine said.

Annie followed Petra into the ER.

They were taken to first room on the right where Joseph lay in a drug induced haze. He smiled when he saw them.

"Annie Pearce," he said.

"I am so glad you're okay. I was so worried." She kissed his cheek and squeezed his right hand.

"Petra, meet Annie," Joseph said.

"I have. You can come back anytime you're ready. You rest." Petra kissed his cheek. "We'll let you rest."

He closed his eyes and fell back into sleep, Annie led Petra from the room.

"I was hesitant to send him to do this job." Petra admitted as they walked past the ER entrance and into the hallway.

Annie observed the manager carefully. "He volunteered?"

"Yes. You were kind to him. When we had word the Fraternitatem of Solomon was coming, we decided a man inside would be the best way to help find the real market. He volunteered because of you." Petra stopped at the door where Cham and Fabien waited.

"He's a good man and I appreciate that he's here. He said the Fraternitatem is pulling out of the smaller markets."

Petra raised her eyebrows and looked at Annie. "They're moving quickly, then." She straightened her jacket. "I'll be staying in your hotel across the courtyard. I'd like to be here for Joseph tomorrow. I don't have many wizard guards, but please advise when you need us to mobilize." All business, Petra nodded once and headed to the hotel.

"Everything okay?" Cham asked when he saw Annie.

"Joseph's sleeping. He told me the Fraternitatem is pulling out of the smaller markets. Our time is running out," Annie said.

"I think we need to find that last portal. If anything, we can stop the flow in and out while we deal with the Fraternitatem," Cham said.

"I'll lean on Sturtagaard or have Robin lean on his contact." Annie startled a moment when she remembered what she had been doing earlier that day. She summoned the package from Arrowhead. "I saw Arrowhead. He's still in the main market. He gave me this." Inside the package were several poisonous leaves and, underneath those, a rolled scroll. She unrolled the paper and showed Cham and Fabien.

The Fraternitatem is pulling out of the smaller markets and it is assumed they are ready to make a play for complete control. If you are to send wizard guards to the market, send someone other than Annie. It is not safe here for her as they know she has taken their spies.

A

Cham looked at her.

"You don't have to say it. I'm done with the markets. We have other guards," Annie said.

"I volunteer my services," Fabien said.

"You're welcome any time."

"I will most definitely work with whomever you wish. For now, use me as you see fit. Having said that, you stay safe and I will see you in the morning." He half saluted her and headed out of the hospital for the hotel in the opposite corner of the courtyard.

CHAPTER 25

THE NIGHT PASSED slowly; Annie had persistent visions of hands and blood and Emily's face. When she finally fell asleep, it was only for a short time before she woke and checked the window for the position of the moon. She rolled out of bed, heaviness in her muscles as she took to the pavement for an early morning run. While the run kept her awake, she found herself emotionally exhausted and had difficulty focusing.

Cham had left before she returned, leaving her to ready herself for the day. She finished and found her way back to Wizard Hall, where she joined Fabien and Spencer as they sorted through Arden's notebooks, maps, and books.

"She's very wordy," Annie said as she closed her first notebook. "I'm not sure if this list of Fraternitatem members will help us now."

"Probably not. Even this map of the Cave of Ages is suspect. They could have changed something," Fabien pointed out.

"I think Bucky should get the list. It may help solve past cases," Spencer said as he pulled down another notebook.

"I think I'm going to take a walk," Annie said.

"Where do you want to go?" Spencer asked. With the Fraternitatem seemingly making a move, he had been assigned to trail Annie as her bodyguard.

"I'm not leaving the building. I'll be fine on my own," Annie said.

"You've been known to work around that before." Spencer frowned.

"I'm older and wiser. I need a break. I think I'll head down to see Dave. If that's okay?"

"You do what you need and then come find me. I'm a little tired of going through Dr. Blakely's notes. Thorough is an understatement." Spencer sighed.

Annie headed to Dave's cubicle on the second floor. They had been friends since high school; he had been her first real boyfriend. While it had been a messy breakup, they had found their way back to each other, if only as friends. It had taken many years, but now Annie would sometimes make her way to his cubicle for a laugh or a snack. Today, she needed a break and knocked on his cubicle wall. He looked up and smiled.

"Hey! I haven't seen you in awhile." He offered her a seat.

"Haven't you been in Colorado with the yeti for several weeks?" she quipped and rested her arms on the table with her chin in her hands.

"Yeah, I guess this was my fault. What's up?"

Annie rolled her eyes. "You're such a dork. How was the trip?"

He studied her carefully. "The trip was fine." He pushed his folder to the side and leaned against his desk chair.

"What are you working on?" she asked.

"I know you very well, Annie Pearce. What's going on?"

"I needed a break from research. Just thought I'd say hi."

Dave chuckled. "Fine. I'll let you stall. I'm working on plans to create a more permanent settlement in the Rockies, at the yeti site."

Annie glanced at him and assessed him for a moment: good looking, smart, and relaxed.

"What?" he asked.

Annie shook her head. "You have no worries in the world except doing your job, coming home, hanging out."

"And finding a wife. At least according to my mom." Dave smiled wanly. "So you came here to pick on me, or…?"

Annie chuckled. "I wanted to say hi. When I'm in your cubicle, I feel normal."

She looked at the pictures he hung on his wall. There were ones of him and Cham; Annie herself; Cham, Dave, and Janie at Great America the summer after her father died. She sighed and placed three sets of coordinates on the table.

"These coordinates show the location of portals that lead to the main market. There's a large selection of dragon eggs and a few dragons crawling about. They're up and running," Annie said.

Dave opened the sheet of paper and stared at the locations. "You are anything but normal. Look at what you've done. Some people might say you're a superhero."

Annie flushed and looked away.

"Sorry. I didn't mean to embarrass you. I just meant you work hard, and you're really smart, and you get what you want before most people know what they want."

"I just want to go home, have dinner, go for a run, drink a beer. I don't want to come home to my dead dad walking around the house and the Fraternitatem coming to kidnap me."

Dave looked at the coordinates again and pulled up his computer software, looking for the locations on a map.

"You've been to these?" he asked as he looked at the satellite pictures.

"Yes. Sturtagaard gave me two of them. Fabien Arnault found one in Greece. There's one more and I'm pretty sure Sturtagaard knows where it is," Annie said.

"Louisiana, Greece, and South Africa, interesting." He stared at the map of each area. "It's almost over and you can go back to being rather ordinary if you'd like."

Annie chuckled. "Yeah. I'm starting to make plans for that." She glanced down at her ring. It sparkled against her skin. She sighed.

"Think of the wedding. It's the end of the tunnel. Let me know when Sturtagaard comes clean with the portal. We're getting ready here to help you bring down the Fraternitatem. It's good to know we can get to the market."

"Glad to help," Annie said.

"You will get through this. You always find a way."

She blew a kiss, touched his hand, and headed back out.

᪣

Annie landed herself and Spencer just outside Sturtagaard's barn. The strong stench of smoke and water accosted them when they landed. Annie stared at the remains of the building; the ceiling had caved in, but the walls were mostly intact.

"What the hell?" she muttered.

Annie scanned the landscape. They were in the open, not a tree or building nearby.

Spencer walked along the perimeter of the building that no longer stood, his crystal out and collecting magic.

Annie took out a map, her crystal necklace, and a lock of Sturtagaard's hair, scrying for the vampire. For a second time, it landed on this location.

"The building is surrounded by magic I don't recognize," Spencer said as he held the crystal for her. She read what she could and shook her head.

She stomped around to the small open door. Water dripped from the top of the jamb. "I scried for him, it said he was here." Annie shined her flashlight inside. The car was covered in soot and ash; the vampire's living corner had been caved in.

"Annie, it's dangerous," Spencer yelled.

"Leave the door open. I'll teleport out when I'm done." She carefully maneuvered around piles of ash, mushy boxes, melted nails, and charred wood. Sturtagaard's corner had been destroyed in the fire. The sofa was gone, the chair, the stool—all piles of ash and garbage. The refrigerator no longer hummed and only a few burnt books remained on the shelves.

She stood at the center of his open living space and turned, examining each direction.

Spencer joined her, wiping water from his hair. "What are you looking for?" He tried to follow her gaze.

"I don't see any vampire ash, do you?" She felt panicked, as though his death would actually upset her.

Spencer glanced at the floor, beside the sofa remnant. He squatted down and touched what looked like a pile of ash. He sniffed it.

Annie glanced at him, wide eyed. "Is it?"

"I don't know. It would be a little anticlimactic if it was. What are you looking for?" He ran his crystal across the ash. There was no magic.

"The Fraternitatem is pissed because we have all of their spies. They killed Rathbone, maybe they found Sturtagaard."

"They saved us the trouble," Spencer said.

"Yeah. He was so looking forward to me killing him," Annie quipped. She walked around the perimeter of the eight-by-eight space, stopping at the bookshelf. "He was a reader. Proust, Shakespeare, Chaucer." She ran her hand across the bookshelf, covered in burnt books. She picked up the first and opened the cover. The pages were brittle and turned to dust when she touched it. She put the book back. "There should be more here. This was packed with books." She turned and looked around the space.

"The Fraternitatem must have found him. Besides Zola, he's the last living link to them that we had," Spencer said. He kicked at the burnt rug at his feet. "Do you think he hid something for you?"

"Yes."

Spencer knelt and pulled back the edge of the sodden rug. "Help me."

Annie removed the remnant of the table and pulled up her side of the rug. Beneath it was a plywood floor with a trap door.

"Thank you, Sturtagaard," Annie said under her breath as she pulled on the latch and turned on her flashlight.

"This building isn't safe," Spencer said.

Annie glanced around. "I know." She looked inside the small hole in the ground, about four feet deep and four feet wide, before jumping down. "Bless that bastard," she said.

Spencer lay on the sooty, wet floor and looked inside. Piles of books lined the far wall. They were damp and smelled of smoke but otherwise, as Annie touched them, still seemed pristine. Attached to the pile, Annie found a note in Sturtagaard's flowery handwriting.

Girl,

There is no way I would let them kill me. I'm reserving that pleasure for you. I also leave the books to you. You're too intelligent to read anything but.

> "Cowards die many times before their deaths;
> The valiant never taste of death but once.
> Of all the wonders that I yet have heard,

It seems to me most strange that men should fear;
Seeing that death, a necessary end,
Will come when it will come."

"What is that?" Spencer asked. "We need to get moving."

"It's from Sturtagaard. He left me his books." Annie read for Spencer the quote the vampire left for her. "Do you know that quote?"

"I couldn't tell you for sure, but I think it's Shakespeare."

"I don't have time for this." Annie held her palms out and shrunk the pile of books, shoving them inside her field pack. When the room was clear, she teleported from the small hole. They placed the rug back and left the barn.

"What's he trying to tell you?"

"I don't know. Between him, Rathbone's book, and Arden's stuff, I get the feeling we're on a very large wild goose chase," Annie said as they teleported back to Wizard Hall.

∽

Annie rebuilt Sturtagaard's entire book collection he had left for her; it filled the rest of her cubicle. She pulled out her phone, typed in the quote, and discovered it was from the play *Julius Caesar*. She searched for the book among the large stacks.

"What the hell?" Cham asked as he entered the already tight space.

"Sturtagaard's gone. The barn he was living in was set on fire. I don't know he did it or if the Fraternitatem killed him. We found a pile of suspicious ash. Found these books—they're his. They're probably original copies. He left me this note. I'm looking for the book it came from."

Cham read the note.

Annie found *Julius Caesar* and pulled it from the pile. "Got it." She sat back in her desk chair and looked at Cham. "Can I help you with something?"

"No. I just haven't seen you all day, and I was wondering if everything was okay. Dave said you stopped by."

She pulled open the book and stared at the title page. The book was originally published in 1700.

"These are old books. Original publications. He left me a small fortune," Annie said and looked up at Cham. "I did see Dave. I was feeling sorry for myself, and I wanted to see a friend."

Cham sat in the chair opposite her. "We're getting closer. Spencer and Fabian have sifted through the notes, Lial is reviewing the maps, and Emerson started reviewing the Fraternitatem's grimoire."

Holding her palms above the book from Sturtagaard, she searched for the quote while Cham glanced at her notes. When she found it, she read through the pages, sure the vampire wouldn't have marked up a nearly pristine antique book. Sure enough, she saw no markings, but in the space between the two pages, she found a loose piece of paper shoved tightly inside.

One set of coordinates was written on the scrap. Annie pulled up a map on her computer.

"Oh, shit," she said.

"What?"

"He left me some coordinates. And after what I think Rathbone's been trying to tell me, I don't think Sturtagaard's pointing me to the market either." Annie turned her computer screen.

"What is that?"

Annie pointed to the location on the screen. She couldn't understand why Sturtagaard had left her the coordinates for the Snake Head Letters.

CHAPTER 26

ANNIE BLAMED HERSELF for Joseph's missing hand.

If I hadn't brought him to the market...

She glanced inside his hospital room, where he slept peacefully, thanks to strong magical potions. She sat in the empty chair beside him and, for a few minutes, watched his chest rise and fall with each breath. When he didn't wake, she placed a card beside his bed.

"Hey, Annie Pearce," he said through a cloudy haze of medicine.

"Hi, Joseph. I didn't want to wake you."

"Nah, it's okay." He fidgeted with the bandages. "Have a seat."

"I am so sorry you got caught up in this. In my mistakes and problems." Annie reached for his good hand.

He closed his eyes and squeezed her cool fingers. "You are not to blame."

"It's become all about me and I'm so sorry." Annie sighed and wiped a tear from her cheek.

"No, Annie Pearce. This is all about the Fraternitatem gaining control. They were given an opportunity because of that vampire." Joseph fiddled with the bed and raised the head.

"You should sleep and heal."

"I see the weight of the world on your shoulders. You did not ask for this. Remember, the vampire caused this."

Annie squeezed his soft hand. "You are kind to deflect blame. But I've done so many things wrong. I could have stopped this."

Joseph stared at his bandaged arm. Annie felt a strong urge to scratch her legs and gave in.

"Were you there when Sturtagaard told the Fraternitatem about your powers?" he asked.

Annie glanced at him.

"Were you?" he asked more forcefully.

She shook her head. The itching grew stronger, so she scratched her thigh again. "No. It happened centuries ago," she admitted.

"So, how are you responsible?"

Annie offered him a wan smile, appreciating his attempt to make her feel better.

Then why do I feel so guilty?

"So, how are you responsible?" Joseph repeated. "You know this community. We're small everywhere. The fact that Princess Amelie's and your father's killer are the same, that's not unheard of. And yes, Rathbone worked for them, and they in turn killed one of their own in that Benaiah fellow. You weren't responsible for the market falling or Amelie returning as a vampire. You are smart, you are good at what you do. The past and your prophecy were because of Sturtagaard. It's cyclical energy pocket that is not under your control." Joseph closed his eyes again, the speech apparently having left him exhausted.

"I'll let you sleep." Annie pulled away.

He grabbed her arm. Though he lacked strength in his drugged state, it was firm as if he meant he wanted her to stay.

"So, how are you responsible, Annie Pearce?" he asked once more, then let go of her hand and drifted off to sleep.

§

Annie didn't say much when she and Spencer teleported to Tartarus Prison; the walk along the lane was quiet. Spencer was giving her space. She gave him several side-eyed glances.

"Sorry you're stuck babysitting me," she finally said.

Tartarus loomed large above them.

"I'm your partner. We're on a case." Spencer looked upwards at the tall gates and through to the courtyard where the giant was waiting for them.

Annie rolled her eyes. "A case? To see my mom?"

The giant opened the gates and motioned them inside. With so many storms in recent weeks, the courtyard was a lumpy pile of mud. They walked across a plywood walkway toward the doors.

"Hi, Beverly," Annie said as she cast her spell.

"Glad you got the message," Beverly said in response. "She wanted to talk to you."

Spencer followed with his own spell; they entered through the security gate.

"Thanks," Annie said to Beverly before they walked onward. They turned right and stopped outside the makeshift apartment for Emily and Shiloh. She glanced into the window on the side of the door. Shiloh was watching television while Emily read.

"Are you okay?" Spencer asked.

Annie shook her head. "When this is over, I hope she goes back to wherever it is she comes from and I never see her again."

Spencer placed a firm hand on Annie's shoulder as she knocked on the door. Shiloh hopped up and opened the door.

"Hi, Shiloh."

"Hi, Annie. What are you doing here?"

"Mom called me. Can I come in?" Annie asked.

The boy nodded and moved out of the way as Annie and Spencer entered. Emily sat on the sofa, wrapped in a heavy blanket, her feet tucked under her body. She looked at Annie, who sat down in the chair beside the sofa.

"Hi, Emily. I heard you wanted to see me."

Emily nodded. "You can call me Mom if you'd like." She fidgeted with her hands. "I know. I—I was trained to kill you."

Annie observed her mother carefully and glanced at the book she'd set beside her. It was a romance novel of some kind.

"You followed in your father's footsteps." Emily refrained from looking Annie in the eyes.

"I did." Annie felt tension between them. "Do you want me to call Sami? She really wants to spend time with you."

Emily didn't respond to the question. "Shiloh, come here. I'd like you to really meet your sister."

Shiloh, still holding his schoolwork, sat beside his mother and stared at Annie in what seemed to be curiosity or awe. It made Annie uncomfortable.

"Hi, Shiloh. The first time I met you, something wasn't right with you," Annie said. "It's nice to meet the real you."

"They wanted me to hurt you," he murmured. Spencer firmly held Annie's shoulder.

"I know. You don't feel like hurting me now, do you?" Annie asked.

Shiloh shook his head. "I didn't want to." He was so young. His eyes darted from her to Spencer and back again, as if he was trying to make sense of the impossible situation. Annie studied him and wondered if he would ever have a normal life.

"Are you getting what you need? Getting outside, enough food? Are you comfortable?" Annie asked. She was at a loss for what to say to the woman who birthed her. She knew Emily was her mother. It was obvious even just looking at her face, her hair, the lips, the eyes. They were just like Annie's, and yet, she couldn't generate the feelings she thought she should have toward her.

Maybe because she came here to kill me!

"I'm fine, Annie. Shiloh and I are just fine. Safe and warm. And Samantha can come any time." Emily pulled the blanket across her shoulders, fiddling with the soft fabric. "I hear Levi is here."

At the sound of his name, Shiloh jumped, his eyes wide in what looked like fear.

"Is Levi his dad? I saw you married him after Dad died. He's thirteen; the timeline isn't straightforward," Annie said.

"No. Levi... Levi was unavoidable. Shiloh's dad is someone else," Emily admitted.

While her admission deepened Annie's curiosity, she realized she wouldn't have known the father and it didn't really matter.

Though where was he?

"What did you want to see me about?" Annie finally asked.

Emily, for the first time since Annie arrived, looked at her youngest daughter, her eyes overflowing with tears. "I was wrong to leave when they told me you were in danger. I believed them. It made me an easy target." She began to shudder.

"Mom?" Shiloh asked her. He put his arm around her.

Annie dug deep to muster the feelings she thought she should have, but they didn't come. She found her compassion instead and sat on the sofa beside Emily. "I'm here because you asked and I promise we'll keep you safe." Annie looked at Shiloh, a worried young boy, still unsure of what was happening to his mother.

Annie pulled away and played with the remote, searching for the Witch News Network. "Is his father magical?" she asked. Braxton Borne appeared on the screen; she left the station on for Shiloh to watch.

"Yes. I was taken by magicals. I... fell in love with a magical."

Annie held her palm up. Magic floated from her hand. Shiloh looked at it with awe, as if he wasn't familiar with magic use or didn't have the opportunity to use it.

That's odd.

"Can you do this?" Annie asked him.

"I—I can't do much. Sometimes things happen," Shiloh admitted.

Annie sat on the coffee table across from him and held his hand up. "You have to think what you want and sometimes it happens. Or sometimes you can chant a spell." Annie summoned a clear rubber ball, with specks of glitter inside. She placed it on his palm. "Rise," she said as she aimed her palm at the ball. She hovered it over his palm. When she flicked her wrist, the ball began twirling. She added magic so that the ball spun faster.

Shiloh smiled. "Cool!" he said.

Annie stopped the magic and the ball fell to his palm.

"Think 'hover,'" she whispered.

Shiloh did as she said. The ball rose millimeters above his palm and fell again.

"And that's how the magic flows from you to the object. Good job," she said. Had he been raised away from the madness, the evil, he'd almost be away at school, already proficient in the magic.

She glanced at Emily who smiled proudly. "You're good with kids. Are you planning on having any after you marry?"

Annie breathed deeply. "Someday. I'll be teaching in the fall, actually." She glanced at Spencer, who had not heard her news, then returned to watching Shiloh. Each time the boy tried, the ball hovered higher in the air before falling again.

"I can feel the magic. It tickles," Shiloh said.

"Yeah, it'll do that. You keep practicing and I'll show you more tomorrow." She fluffed his hair and chuckled.

It seems so cliché. So normal.

"What else can I do for you?" Annie asked.

Emily turned and pulled the cushion away from the couch, lifting out a thick, accordion file folder with papers sticking out. She handed the folder to Annie. "I know you have Arden here. I'm glad you have compassion to protect her. I was a little frightened by her. She was a... she was—"

"I know. I met her months ago. She tried to kill my fiancé."

If the news surprised Emily, she didn't react. Emily moved in, closer to Annie. "Arden's been out for a very long time. I'm still in. Whatever she gave you will be old. These are the names. The real names of those who are working with the Fraternitatem. They are going to control the market."

Annie took the folder, opening it. "We have the Fraternitatem grimoire. Is that anything?" she asked as she pulled out a map.

"The spells will help you. You can use them to open doors and block their magic."

The map was hand drawn and not scaled accurately, but it appeared to be a complete map of the caves. "The books are code for this?" Annie held the map for her to see.

"Yes. It's how we communicate back and forth without anyone knowing," Emily admitted.

"So, you're basically helping us bypass those."

"They took me away from my girls. They took my life. I want to be free of them, of Levi. For the first time in years, I'm not being drugged into compliance." Emily placed her hands on Annie's.

Emily's hands were slight like Annie's own and had the same shaped nail beds, the same color skin. Annie looked at her mother again and realized that she and Emily were nearly an exact copy of each other except for Emily's red hair. Annie shuddered. While she hadn't felt anything for her long absent mother prior to meeting her, she was feeling her loss greatly now. She finally was starting to long for the life she should have had and yet her mother was only here to kill her. The conflicting feelings confused Annie.

Spencer pulled a chair beside her. "This will help. We've been deciphering Arden's notes." He took the folder and the map, attempting to straighten the papers inside. "I texted Cham. They know about this."

"Thanks. I think we need to get back to work." Annie wrote out her phone number and handed it to Emily. "If you need anything, call me."

Emily rose. The women were the same height, a fact not lost on Annie. She gave Emily a hug and turned to Shiloh. "Keep practicing, kid. I can see you're a magical genius."

Shiloh smiled and waved.

Annie closed the door and watched them from the window. They spoke in low tones as Shiloh showed Emily what he had just learned. Emily pulled him closer and kissed his long floppy hair, then glanced at the door, seeing Annie above his head. Annie waved and left. She stopped when they came to the front entrance to Ariana and Arden's apartment.

Spencer followed at stopped at the archaeologist's door. Annie looked through the window and observed the two women. They were drinking wine, laughing, and lightly touching each other's hands and forearms.

"They seem happy," Annie commented.

"Did you want to go in?" Spencer said.

Annie shook her head. "How long was she medicated? She seems so happy now that she's off the drugs."

"She was still taking the meds up until we sequestered her. We're not sure how she was drugged," Spencer noted.

"Unless Ariana was somehow involved. Though I can't see her doing that," Annie surmised. "I'll let them be. Ready?"

Spencer followed Annie out the door, waving goodbye to Beverly at the security desk. Outside the prison, the light was hazy and the sky was covered in a thin layer of clouds. She glanced back at the front entrance before exiting the gates that slammed shut when they left.

Annie leaned against the gate post. "Before I knew Emily was alive, I suppose I loved her. She was my mom and she died." The field across from the prison was an empty mass of high and wild grasses blowing in the late summer breeze. It could have been pretty in the right location.

"And you found out the truth," Spencer said.

"She was easily fooled, maybe a little naïve and stupid. I get that she originally thought she was helping me. But Dad saw her, and she stopped caring or was too brainwashed. I could accept she wouldn't come back with him because she couldn't—didn't—know better."

Spencer reached for her hand and led her down the path toward the teleportation spot amongst the trees. "You see her with Shiloh and she's a mom. She cares, she loves him, ruffles his hair, kisses his forehead. I can't imagine what it's like to know one thing about a person and see something else."

"It was easier when I could demonize and hate her. My feelings are all churned up and confused," Annie admitted.

"Give yourself a break. It's been a tough year. A lot of truths to accept and a lot of changes. You're a good person and a fabulous wizard guard with an amazing partner. It's almost over and then you can get on with your life."

They entered the open picnic area surrounded by thick evergreens. At the center, Spencer wrapped his arms around Annie and teleported her home.

CHAPTER 27

WHILE ANNIE HAD known Spencer for six years, they had only been partners for one year. They had grown close and enjoyed working with each other, but her surprise news of leaving the guard didn't seem to sit well with him. When he landed on her back porch, he didn't leave.

"What?" Annie asked. She sat on the built-in bench and offered him a seat.

"Nothing." Spencer sighed and joined her.

Annie raised her eyebrows.

"So, you're leaving me," he said.

She knew several things were coming to an end, but admitting it to Spencer made it real. She had wanted to tell him in private, explain how it all came to be.

"That wasn't how I planned on telling you. I had it all planned out—dinner, drinks,"

she began to explain. "If I could, I'd stay, but Cham—"

"I did figure you'd leave. I was just hoping it would happen after the wedding," Spencer said. "But you're still a wizard guard. And I'm assuming you'll be at Wizard Hall."

Annie nodded and held his manicured hand. It was soft yet strong. She had trusted Spencer's hands to protect her many times. "Educational liaison. I'll be at Wizard Hall and teaching a class at Windmere."

He took a moment to digest what she told him and smiled when it hit him. "Impressive. You'll have to explain the whole thing someday. I will definitely miss you," he said.

"Like you said, once a wizard guard, always a wizard guard. They can bring me in anytime they need extra guards."

"How much time until you move?"

"September 1, a few weeks."

"I'll miss you." Spencer hugged his partner and friend. He stood and smiled at Annie as he teleported himself home.

It was still hours before Cham and Jason would return home. Her visit with her mother and Shiloh left her anxious and restless. She sat to watch television, but it offered her little of interest. Instead, she found herself roaming her house, moving some objects, dusting others, and folding her laundry.

Returning to the first floor, she stared down the basement steps into the darkness. She felt her anxiety rise. She balled her fists tightly and then released them so that her magic billowed in the air. The magic swelled into a large ball above her hand and continued to grow as she continued to release energy. Her itching and anxiety eased.

She turned on the light and walked down the stairs, entering Jason's space. He had made up the hide-a-bed. His clothes hung on a portable rack. He had sifted through the family photos and frames and placed them on the side table and on the shelves surrounding the large television. She glanced at them, taking them in, letting the memories return.

Annie wanted to scream at how unfair it was, or punch something in hopes she would feel better, or maybe finally stake Sturtagaard. She found a picture of her and Kathy, the first Mother's Day after Emily "died." She called Kathy instead.

"Hi, sweetie. What's up?" Kathy said when she answered the phone.

Annie rushed straight into her thoughts. "When I was five, we had a Mother's Day tea in my kindergarten class. I was really upset because I didn't have a mom, I had a Kathy. I told my teacher that and she made me write Happy Mother's Day on my card. She didn't understand," Annie could feel the pain from that time; it was tight in her chest. She breathed deeply and shuddered.

"If I remember correctly, you brought the card home, crossed out

'Mother's' and wrote 'Kathy' on it." Kathy chuckled at the memory. "I'm guessing something happened today."

"I saw Emily. She suggested I call her 'Mom.' I—I know she birthed me, but when I think of a mom, I think of you." Annie blew out her breath.

Kathy was quiet for a moment. "I can see how Emily's return is churning you up inside. It can't be easy for a lot of reasons."

Annie summoned Emily's folder and placed it on the table. "I saw her interact with her son. I was so mad when I learned she was alive and seeing that makes me feel jealous of him. It's confusing."

"Sweetie. There are two ways to go. You could leave it as it is, not let her in, and watch her leave when this is over. Or you can open your heart and let her in."

"What would you do?" Annie asked.

"I—I don't know. I'd probably be confused, angry, distant. There's nothing wrong with leaving it as it is. You have to decide what you want. You have your mom and grandmother back in your life. You alone have the choice."

"What if I don't want her in my life? Either one of them?" Annie wiped the tears from her cheek and sat in the chair. Her sigh was as heavy as the pain in her chest.

"Oh, sweetie. It's your choice alone. You don't have to decide now."

Annie drummed her fingers on the folder. "She's helping us get them. Or so she's making it seem like she is. She gave us updated names, dates, places, maps."

Kathy was silent for a moment. "It's good that she's helping. Maybe she wants to make amends," she suggested.

"Maybe. I just don't want anything to come between you and me," Annie admitted.

"Annie. I helped raised you. I love you like a daughter. Even if you move past why your mom is here, and she stays in your life and you build a relationship, I will always be here for you. Did you have a prophetic dream?"

"No. Just a gut feeling. Things are changing really fast and I can't help thinking I'm going to lose someone," Annie admitted.

"Give me a half hour and I'll come over."

After hanging up, Annie felt no less anxious but calmed herself by perusing the items Emily had given her.

She started with the map of the Cave of Ages. She could picture the dark cavern with shimmering blue walls, Melichi's icy glare. The memories made her shake. She touched the narrow passages on the map as they trailed down the cliff. Additional caverns had been cut into the rock, splintered off the main tunnel. Annie could only guess they were individual apartments or rooms.

The main cavern wound its way down the mountain, ending in the hidden entrance on the back side of the cliff. It was out of view of the Cave of Ages and led into a clearing. She stared at the map and noted that Emily had written "rock formations."

"If we follow it upwards, it's a corkscrew. We'd go in blind. It'll be a bloodbath."

"What did you say, sweetie?" Kathy asked, walking in just in time to hear the backend of Annie's conversation with herself.

"Nothing," Annie said as she pushed the map to the side.

"What's all this with losing someone?" Kathy sat beside her and pushed Annie's hair behind her ears. "Tell me."

"I've been watching her with her son. It didn't affect me at first, but seeing it out in the open, I'm feeling…"

"Unwanted, unloved maybe? Wrongly, I might add. Whole picture, Annie. Whole picture here. Ryan and I helped your dad raise you and Sami. We finished raising you. I love you and Sami. I got my daughters with you." Kathy smiled through tears. "What I have with you will never change, even if you choose a relationship with Gloriana and Emily. We— you and me—we're always going to be."

Annie glanced away, at the map and pulled it back towards her. "Even with an army of wizard guards, we can't go after them. They have the upper hand."

"You don't want to lose anyone else you love in a battle." Kathy looked at the map. Her fingers trailed along the second entrance at the bottom of the mountain. "They built staircases like this in medieval buildings to benefit those coming down the stairs in case of attack because—"

"Most people are right-handed. It gave them the upper hand." Annie chuckled.

"If you go after them, you'll need to bring them out, down here. In the open. How would you do that?" Kathy inquired.

"Smoke bomb, firebomb. Something to cause an immediate evacuation. They probably have ways." She summoned a map of the world and looked carefully at the locations for the three known portals. "They built the portals. Why wouldn't they put a portal in the Cave of Ages?"

"Do you really think so?" Cham asked as he entered.

"It's a possibility. By the way, we can't go in after them." Annie explained what she discovered on the map from Emily.

"It looks like you're right. Arden's notes are a hodgepodge of stuff. I've gone through the copy you gave me of Emily's notes, and they seem more accurate. I was thinking of sending Jason in from our portal to see if he can find the other three entrances. Usually the magic only allows you to see the one you came through, but maybe he could track the magic and find the fourth," Cham said. He pulled out more notes from Emily and sat across from Annie. "This is a list of hundreds of people. She labeled them as assassins, porters, cooks, council members." Cham passed the sheet to Annie.

"We're meeting with the Middle Eastern Wizard Guard tomorrow. We can start planning with them," Annie said as she read each name, finding the one she knew. "Starla falls under contractors," she noted and passed the page to Cham.

"Well, there's the proof I need to fire her. I can't wait until you're in the new position. I need you to overhaul how we hire and train." He tossed the sheet back on the table.

Kathy squeezed her shoulder and began dinner. Feeling the magic bubble up again, Annie made a fist and squeezed tightly before releasing her fingers. Magic flew from her palm.

"It's still bothering you quite a bit," Cham said.

"Yeah, when I'm stressed." She looked at her hand and watched the tiny bubbles of magic rise from her palm. She repeated the action, releasing more magic.

Another name caught her eye. "Rathbone's on the list." Annie stopped for a moment, her mouth opened and closed. "So is Sturtagaard. Emily knew him. Damn it!"

"Why are you surprised?" Cham asked.

Annie rapped her fingers against the table. "Not surprised. Just another reason to be pissed." The magic flowed faster through her veins. She closed her eyes to stop the dizziness, though the world still felt as though it was spinning around her. She took long, slow breaths and only opened her eyes when Kathy placed spaghetti and meatballs on the table. For a moment, she ignored the magic and enjoyed a few hours of peace.

᷈

Annie stood outside Tartarus Prison, but she had no memory of teleporting to the island or walking the lane. She reached for the handle and walked through the gate and into the courtyard. A trail of golden, pink magic followed her.

Tonight's guard on duty was Evelyn and continued to work without acknowledging Annie as she entered the front door and through the security gate.

Emily's apartment was to the right. Annie stood outside the closed door and watched her mother and brother through the vertical plate of glass. At 10:30 p.m., the prison was silent while the night staff walked the halls or worked quietly at their reception desks. Vampires might be sitting sullenly in their cells planning their escape, while evil wizards dreamt of freedom that wouldn't come soon.

No longer outside the apartment, but inside with her mother and brother, Annie glanced back at the door; she didn't remember walking through.

Am I even here?

She turned back to her family; Emily and Shiloh sat on the couch watching the news. As they watched, Shiloh practiced floating the ball Annie gave him.

Annie smiled. He learned quickly.

"Shiloh, take a break. You can practice tomorrow," Emily said with a broad smile. Annie's stomach fluttered as she observed Emily's pride.

Cautiously, Annie strolled over, giving in to her curiosity. While Kathy had always been there for her, she had never lived with Annie and Samantha. For the first time, Annie realized there was some intimacy between mother and child that she had never experienced.

As she got closer to the sofa, Shiloh tensed. He turned and looked at Annie—or rather, through her. Annie tried to calm her own breathing. Shiloh couldn't possibly see her; she really wasn't there. Shiloh returned to the news, but somehow Annie felt like he knew someone was there.

Annie sat on the chair beside the sofa. Emily turned and looked at her; she, too, stiffened up.

"Is someone here?" Shiloh asked.

"We're in a magical jail. It could be a ghost," Emily said, still looking at Annie.

"Cool," Shiloh replied as if a ghost was normal and not something to be frightened of.

Emily walked to the chair where Annie sat. She reached out, rested her hand on Annie's shoulder, and held it there. Annie touched her mother's hand, causing Emily to startle and pull her hand away.

She surprised Annie when she set a book on the chair and bent over to retrieve it. "I don't know how you could be here, but if you are, I want you to know I was so glad to see you today," Emily whispered.

Annie felt herself being pulled from the chair and forced upwards toward the ceiling, entirely out of her control. Emily shuddered and returned to her son as they sat and continued to watch the news.

Annie flew up from her bed, sitting in the dark with Cham sleeping contently beside her. She could still feel her mother's hand on her shoulder and could smell a scent so familiar her heart began to pound. It was the same scent Kathy wore, the same scent Annie started wearing in high school, the smell of vanilla and strawberry. She lay back down and stared at the ceiling until it was time to get up.

CHAPTER 28

ANNIE WALKED PAST the Snake Head Letters once and peered inside. Seeing no one, she continued past the store. When she turned, she thought she saw an arm slip inside the alley several buildings from where she stood.

She hurried back to the Snake Head Letters and startled when she saw Archibald Mortimer waiting for her. "Whatcha waiting for, girl?" he grumbled. Annie scoped the street before entering. He glanced down the street and closed and locked the door before leading her to the back of the store.

"Good morning to you, too."

Mortimer grumbled and crossed his arms against his chest. Annie pulled out a scroll and passed it to Mortimer.

He unrolled the paper and stared at the coordinates. "Numbers?" he groused.

"Coordinates. For this store," Annie said.

"So what?" he asked.

"I found it in a book belonging to Sturtagaard. Know why he'd have it?"

Mortimer shrugged. "Nope," He passed the scroll back to her.

Annie walked to the first shelving unit and perused the books, though she wasn't interested in the section or in buying anything.

"Why haven't you staked the beast yet?" he asked.

"I thought I needed information from him," Annie glanced at Mortimer. He was looking toward the front windows.

"More and more customers are coming back here now that the Fraternitatem has gotten a foothold." Mortimer continued to watch the front windows. "The old market wasn't safe, per se, just safer than now. I hear you will be taken if you go back."

Annie froze. She knew she couldn't go back to the market, but hearing Mortimer state that fact made her anxious.

"I suppose that might be true," she admitted.

"Melichi ain't in charge of the market. He's too important for that. A bit of a wanker if you ask me. Thinks himself in charge of the whole Fraternitatem. I s'pect he won't be in the battle." It was unlike Mortimer to be this chatty. Annie watched him closely through a spot between two books. He began to wring his hands. "The Cave of Ages ain't safe either, girl. They ain't gonna come out and meet you, though I think you know that already."

Mortimer shuddered. Annie didn't think it was from the cold. She thought he might be afraid.

"Are they watching you?" she asked.

He shook his head. "Not what you'd think. No bugs. Just spies. They'll ask me what you wanted to know or what you bought. I will tell them you ordered a book weeks ago." He pulled out a large leather-bound book, the word *Magiks* scrawled on the cover.

"Magic?" Annie asked.

"I'll say you wanted to know about your powers and what they can do," Mortimer said as he rang up her purchase.

It came to one hundred and fifty dollars. Knowing she was being watched, Annie pulled out a wad of money. Years of experience told her to always be prepared when she came to the Snake Head Letters.

Slowly, she counted out two hundred dollars and passed it to Archibald Mortimer. "How many are out there?"

"'Bout two, I expect. They won't bug the store. Don't want to scare away the customers. They want information, though. Paying me lots to tell them."

"I'm sure you've obliged."

Mortimer shook his head and pulled out a thick sack cloth bag. He put the book inside, lifting half the pages when he did to show Annie that inside the sack held something important for her. "I haven't told them truthful things. Now go upstairs, through my apartment. There's an open window in the kitchen. You can teleport from there." He handed the bag to Annie.

"If I don't walk out of here, they'll know you're helping me escape," Annie said.

"I also have an open window in the customer bathroom. You suspected something and escaped. They still need me alive," Mortimer said.

"For what?" Annie asked. Mortimer knew things, knew people, but he was generally harmless.

He waved off her question. "Go now!" he ordered as he watched the front door.

Annie raced upstairs just as the front door to the shop burst open. She reached Mortimer's apartment, entered, and ran for the open window. The voices downstairs grew louder and several footsteps ran up the stairs. Annie closed her eyes and teleported away.

᚛

Annie stepped foot inside the courtyard of Wizard Hall. She glanced around the large, open space and considered the ease with which anyone with magic could enter. It no longer felt safe. She ran for the front entrance and stared at another new security guard, one Annie didn't recognize.

The guard looked at Annie with trepidation. "How can I help you?" she asked.

Annie whipped out her ID and simultaneously shot her spell into the lock box on the desk. "Sorry, I think I'm being followed!" she shouted as she ran through the doors.

Rather than heading to the fifth floor, she stopped in the security office, where Manny looked up as Annie slammed the door shut.

"Annie? What's the matter?" Manny asked, concerned.

"How much do you know about what's going on with the Fraternitatem?" Annie asked.

Manny stood and opened the top drawer of his filing cabinet. He pulled out a thick accordion file and dropped it on his desk.

"I know a lot. All those names you've been given, I have them now. All of those magical signatures we've got in the magical database are on the no entry list and that includes anyone who's been sent to Tartarus. There're a lot of people who can't get in here." He offered Annie a seat and poured hot water into a teacup. After preparing a mug of tea for her, he sat down. "What happened?" he asked.

Annie held the mug in both hands. She was still shaking from narrowly escaping the Snake Head Letters. She took a sip of the hot tea. It warmed her as it slid down her throat.

"I had to teleport from Mortimer's apartment above the Snake Head Letters. It's being watched and whoever's watching me almost caught me. I just wanted to make sure you know the situation," she said.

Manny nodded. "We're always aware of the situation with any department, especially the Wizard Guard and this case. My manager is given daily updates as they come in. This time the hospital, schools, and hotels are aware and have linked to our security system." He took out a pad of paper and pencil. "Did you see anyone?"

Annie shook her head. "Mortimer, over at the Snake Head Letters, was acting more unusual than normal—locking the door after I arrived, staring out the window. I thought I saw someone hide in the alley."

Manny made a call to his manager, the head of security for Wizard Hall, and explained the updated situation. After listening to and acknowledging whatever his manager was saying, he hung up.

"We expected that might happen. I hear you're not allowed in the market," he said.

Annie nodded.

"They're going to choke you out of every place you would go," Manny said.

Annie nodded again. Her stomach roiled, and she took another sip of peppermint tea and hoped it could settle the nausea in her gut.

"How do we stop them from getting in?" she asked.

"Show me your badge," he commanded.

She took out her wallet and handed him her Wizard Guard shield and ID.

"You and the rest of the wizard guards use this. Everyone else just has the ID."

Annie waited for him to say more; she already knew this.

Manny pulled her ID out and showed her the back. There was a square, gray chip at the bottom left corner. "Just like a credit card, this is a chip with a specific magical spell loaded inside."

Annie nodded. It was something else she knew.

"We are using this now on all visitor passes that have been vetted by both the Wizard Guard and the telecommunication departments. The Middle Eastern wizard guards are due to arrive at 1:00 p.m. They will be given these. The Fraternitatem, unless they steal it from someone, can't get into the building. They can, however, get into the courtyard," Manny explained.

"Who's guarding the courtyard?" Annie asked. She took another sip, her hands still shaking.

"I get why you're scared. We have a few security officers in the courtyard. They rotate between the doors. I know it's not ideal, but if we block off teleportation into the courtyard, we can have issues getting anyone in."

Annie put the mug down on the desk. "Sorry. It's not that I don't trust you."

Manny chuckled and waved her away. "Let me figure out a way to get you into the building safely. Just remember, you've got mad skills and powerful magic."

"Thanks for that. I need to get moving." Annie stood, nodded once, and smiled as she left the security office for the fifth floor.

⁓

Annie knocked on Cham's cubicle. He glanced up and his smile faltered.

"What's up?" he asked as she sat across from him.

"I stopped by to see Mortimer about the coordinates Sturtagaard left for me. He gave me this sack and a tome inside."

"What is it?"

"The Fraternitatem is watching me. They're staking out the Snake Head Letters. I heard them coming for me as I teleported from Mortimer's apartment. He told me to do that and gave me the book beforehand."

"They're controlling you," Cham said.

"Yes."

Cham texted a group and put his phone down. Within a few minutes, Spencer, Shiff, and Brite piled into his cubicle. Annie explained her morning to them.

"I'll find new ways for you to get from home to work and back again," Spencer said.

"And Manny is sure they can't get in?" Shiff asked.

"Yes. The meeting with Avraham, Sari, and Michael is today, and he says they've all been vetted and will receive special visitor passes that will allow them inside the building. After the meeting, I'll need someone to get me home," Annie said.

"I'll take you home. Shiff and I will stay," Brite offered.

"Thanks."

For the near future, Annie would be tied to Spencer as they worked their last case together. While he joined her in her cubicle, the rest of the team resumed their own work.

"Taking out their spies forced them to speed up their plan," Spencer pointed out.

Annie nodded and placed the tome from Mortimer on the desk. There was a sticky note with her name on the cover. "He gave me this to help me get out of the store with an item and then he routed me to his apartment."

"Okay. He's got a soft spot for you. What's in it?"

Annie shrugged. She opened the book and read the word *Magiks* again. "It seems very bland," she said as she scanned the pages quickly. Eventually, she came to a hollowed out middle, a square cut out of the pages. Several white quartz crystals were hidden at the center. She summoned her own crystal and ran it over the ones hidden. There was no magic. She removed them from the hiding spot.

"They're quartz. Nothing interesting about them," Spencer said.

Annie placed them on her desk and pulled out a handwritten note. The writing was shaky, with drag marks in ink.

She read the note:

Girl,

If you're reading this, I am either dead or will be soon. Not sure why I'm even gonna help you but I am, because you need it. Don't go to the Cave of Ages. Make them come to you. Not the market either. Stay out in the open. They're dangerous. Melichi doesn't run the market, Harrison Plank does. He's a mean bastard and he hired those that are tailing you.

Just remember. You have the magic.

Archibald Mortimer.

Annie's hands shook as she reread the message.

Someone entered the store!

She pushed the note to Spencer and looked at her hands. The magic began again to rise from her palms. Her skin itched unbearably.

He could be dead now!

"You said more than one person was tailing you?"

Annie shook her head.

"They probably snatched him." Spencer sounded worried.

Annie struggled to breathe normally as she processed what happened. She shot a spell to try and relieve some of her magic buildup. It flew upward and knocked a ceiling tile off of the grid.

"Damn, it's really strong," Spencer said in awe.

"I'm worried. It keeps building up," Annie said.

Spencer eyed her for a moment in apparent concern and then took out his phone. "We'll send someone to check on Mortimer."

Annie raised her eyebrows as Spencer texted the department scheduler. He watched the phone until he received a response.

"Lial and Eddy will go," he finally said.

CHAPTER 29

ANNIE PACED ALONG the window of the conference room, feeling much like a caged animal at the zoo. She was sequestered, hidden, and trapped by the Fraternitatem after their first attempt at her.

She shook as she waited for Cham to return with the Middle Eastern wizard guards. She thought of the group she met nearly a year ago when the original black market fell. While they had worked out of Israel, the small group was taxed with the entire Middle East region. She wondered how useful they could be in this final battle—but then again, she herself was trapped in a conference room, unable to leave without protection. Absently, she glanced at her phone for any word about Archibald Mortimer. Spencer watched her patiently.

His phone beeped and he scrolled through the message. "Eddy and Lial said the store was in shambles and Mortimer wasn't there. It didn't appear like a struggle happened. They also said he left you a note, demanding that you examine the entire tome."

Annie glanced at Spencer, confused by the cryptic message. "The one he just gave me?" She summoned the book, opened it to the compartment cut from the pages and removed the contents Mortimer had left. When the book was empty, she flipped through the pages.

Eddy, Lial, and Isaak entered the conference room. "You understood that?" Lial asked. Annie nodded as she continued through the pages, stopping when she found an additional envelope in Mortimer's handwriting.

"I guess this is what he meant. Did you scry for him?" Annie asked as she opened the envelope.

"We did. If the Fraternitatem has him, they've hidden him well. My guess is, he had an escape plan. What's in the envelope?" Lial asked.

Annie pulled out a document, written on the letterhead of a lawyer named William Beeker.

August 1, 2019

I, Archibald Mortimer, leave the Snake Head Letters building on Howard Street and all of its contents to Anne Elizabeth Pearce, effective immediately.

Signed.

Archibald Sigmund Mortimer

"What the hell?" Annie asked. She passed the note to Spencer. He read it, frowned, and handed it to Lial.

"That's the question. Why the hell did he leave you the store?" Spencer asked.

Annie shrugged. "I guess I'll call the lawyer and find out."

Lial passed her back the note. She stared at it again and placed it back in the envelope, hiding it inside the book.

In a few moments, Avraham, Sari, and Michael entered with Cham. They each took a seat around the large table.

"Annie, Spencer, Lial, good to see you. It's been some time," Avraham said.

"Glad to see you. Sorry it's such a difficult situation," Annie said and introduced Eddy and Isaak.

Annie hid her confusion and anxiety, smiling as Cham took his place at the head of the table and waved his palm to summon several folders. She distributed the files for the team.

"In these files, you'll find relevant names, places, dates. Emily King-Solomon gave up the most recent information. Arden Blakely also gave what she knew, though her information is considerably older." Cham let the Middle East wizard guards peruse the notes.

Avraham looked up. "This is thorough. This is everything we had hoped to get and couldn't. I understand you have several agents in your prison?"

Cham looked at Annie. She said, "That's correct. They were here to spy on me, to draw me out and get me away from any protection I might have had. The idea was to kill me and steal the power I received." Annie took in a deep breath. "Emily King-Solomon is my mother, who until three months ago I believed to be dead."

Sari, Michael, and Avraham glanced at her. "She's your mother?" Michael asked.

Annie nodded. "We think she was brainwashed and trained to kill me. Their plan was to have her come here, gain my trust, and trick me away. I have a feeling she's still going to try."

Cham, Lial, and Spencer stared at her. "Why?" Spencer asked.

"She's trying hard to gain my trust and get me to call her mom. But, she's been gone for twenty years and was brainwashed. I just keep thinking they expected we'd go after her before she came after me. I can't shake the idea that there might be a trigger, something that will get her to do what she was trained to do," Annie said.

"Like a word or sound?" Michael asked.

"Or an action or a scenario. Something that might happen to make her act."

"Not if we keep her in Tartarus," Cham said.

"She was trained by them. If a trigger word was said, I have a feeling she'd have a way to get out of there. Or find a way to get me there."

Cham stood and dialed his phone, leaving the conference room to make a call.

"What do you need from us?" Avraham asked.

"It's time to put a plan in place. It's your jurisdiction, so we need permission, based on our size versus yours, however, we'd like to lead the takedown." She glanced at Avraham, who led the Middle Eastern department. He nodded.

"As you remember, we have a disadvantage. If we walk up the cliff, they can see us. Instead, we can try and go through this back entrance." Annie showed them the location on the map.

"There is another way in. We always wondered about that," Michael said.

Annie pointed to the spiral staircase. "If we take this to them, we'll be sitting ducks on the way up. We will have to draw them out, to this area here." She next pointed to the land outside of the hidden entrance, which was flat with a scattering of large boulders.

"How do you suppose we draw them out?" Sari asked.

"My first thought is; we have three of the four portals to the main black market. We have someone trying to find the fourth right now. If we can find that, I think we need to shut three of the four portals down. That will squeeze their access to the market." Annie showed them the pictures of the portals and a map that showed their locations.

"Four quadrants on Earth. One portal in each quadrant. Very organized," Avraham said.

"And if we don't find the other portal?" Michael asked.

"Then we need to find a way to keep the Fraternitatem from leaving the desert. I don't want them entering the market; they could then use the portals to escape or hide."

"Okay. Let's say we find it. That doesn't tell me how we're going to draw them out," Avraham pressed.

Annie pulled out a map of the cliff. "My question is, how do they pump clean air in and stale air out? We could use smoke and stink bombs as well as spells to draw them out."

"Air ducts, vents of some kind." Avraham smiled. "Yes. That could work. I suggest we do surveillance. Examine the top and side of the cliff." He pulled the map toward him. "Maybe these lines up here."

"What about the main entrance?" Sari asked.

"We'll have to get someone inside to put a magical spell around the opening to block it off," Annie said.

"And who would do that?" Michael asked.

Cham entered. "The spells around Levi are enhanced. There's a camera on Emily at all times. No one except the Wizard Guard is allowed in to see them. If your thought is correct, you're not going back there. She could very well be trapping you. You said she was nice and encouraging last time you were there. You're going to have to find a way to not astral project there," he said.

The Middle Eastern team glanced at Annie with that revelation.

"You astral project?" Sari asked.

Annie nodded. "Not on purpose. It just seems to be one of those powers I've been told I have."

"No wonder they want your power. So, we block the portals to the new market and then what?" Avraham asked.

Cham sighed. "You know the area better than us. You've studied them. Can we set up some sort of protection in the area for us to hide?"

Avraham pointed to the map. "This outcropping of rocks should hide us. We'll get the lay of the land, see how we can keep them inside this area." He pointed to the transcripts provided. "There are so many names. I wonder how many are still members. If this is accurate, they outnumber all wizard guards on the planet."

It wasn't a comforting thought to Annie.

"We'll set up a video conference with all of the wizard guard units across the planet," Cham said. "Those without the technology will be on a phone call. I do have an issue. One of my guards is a mole for the Fraternitatem. We have her off on a case away from here and I have some-one trailing her now. She's doing what she's supposed to be doing for us, and it looks like she's being followed by the Fraternitatem. Just make sure you can trust whoever you bring into this. I don't know how many units have moles."

"We haven't had a new guard in two years and there aren't many of us," said Avraham. "I have with me those I trust the most. We'll take your lead and I'll pay attention to your concerns. We'll do early reconnaissance and verify if there are air vents on the cliff. If there are you should be able to toss bombs through those and not send someone on the inside. Either way, we'll send you pictures."

Cham turned and pulled up satellite images on the television behind him. "We have to assume they're watching you too. We do have these," he admitted.

"I appreciate your concern. But we are wizard guards, too. We need eyes on the ground. And we should be watching them," Avraham argued.

"Fair enough," Cham said. Once a wizard guard, always a wizard guard—they would want to control what they could.

Annie listened to the exchange. It was no longer about her and only her. It was about the Fraternitatem using her to get to the rest of them.

⊰

Lial sat beside Spencer in Annie's cubicle. "It's a mess there. It's hard to tell for sure, but I think it was tossed for effect, not because they were looking for something."

"I'm not so sure about that," Annie said as she held up the book from Rathbone. "I've been going through this book I found in Rathbone's cell. I took this one because it had the word 'Fraternitatem' in the margins and several letters were circled. I've gone through the entire book and discovered the words 'September 1,' 'Snake Head Letters,' and 'portal.'"

Spencer and Lial looked at her with curiosity. "A coincidence?" Spencer asked.

Annie grimaced as she held up a scroll. "Since we don't believe in them, no. And there's more. Sturtagaard left me his collection of books with a note quoting the book *Julius Caesar*. So I pulled that book and guess what I found?" She passed the scroll to Lial.

"Coordinates?"

"To the Snake Head Letters."

"Uh…" Lial's mouth dropped. "What the hell. You think there's a portal in that store? Where? I've never felt anything portal like."

Annie tapped her fingers on her desk, releasing nervous energy. "There's so much shit in that store. Who knows where one could be hidden. But based on Rathbone, Sturtagaard, and Mortimer leading me there, I can't help but think there's a portal there somewhere."

They all sat with their thoughts for a moment. Then Lial said, "While it would be convenient for Mortimer to have direct access to market, that doesn't fly with the theory of there being four portals across the earth."

Annie grimaced. "You have a point. But still, they want me to know there's something in that store. On another note, do either of you know a Harrison Plank?" She handed them the note from Mortimer.

"Not me," Lial said.

Spencer shook his head.

"Awesome." Annie texted Bucky and then dialed the lawyer, William Beeker.

"Hello, William Beeker's office," a female voice said.

Annie introduced herself and was immediately put on hold. A gentleman's voice came on.

"Ms. Pearce. I assume you found the letter from Mr. Mortimer," he said.

"Yes, I did. Do you know why he left me the store?" she asked.

"I do not know that. I tried to persuade him to leave it to someone… more suitable to its nature, but he insisted it be you," the lawyer said.

Annie tried again. "And he gave you no indication as to why?"

"No, Ms. Pearce. He did not. I would ask him, but he is gone, and I do not know where he is or when he plans on returning. He transferred the store to you. I have the rest of the paperwork in my possession. The building and land belong to you as well."

"I accidentally found the note. When was he planning on telling me?"

"Actually, I was instructed to personally bring the letter to you today. As you found his note now, I will forward this via the magical mail network to you at Wizard Hall. You will have the complete documentation today."

"Okay. Thank you, sir. I appreciate your help," Annie said and hung up. "That was useless. Can you get me back to the store? With the Fraternitatem watching me, I'm not sure I can get there safely."

"No. We'll go back and see what he's hiding for you. Why he couldn't have just given you whatever it was six months ago, before the black market crashed, is beyond me," Lial said in a huff.

"He's watching us and laughing," Annie surmised.

"I don't think so. He knows more about the Fraternitatem than he's ever let on. He's been dishing information out carefully. He was watched, too," Spencer suggested. "He's in trouble, but I have a feeling he's got a plan."

"They took away my access to information," Annie said. She rolled the rubber ball in her hand.

"We'll go. He left you the store for a reason. Your hypothesis that he's hiding a portal might not be so farfetched," Spencer said.

She watched Spencer and Lial leave for the Snake Head Letters.

᷍

Spencer and Lial exited the alley and strolled to the Snake Head Letters. As they walked, they surveyed both sides of the street; if any members of the Fraternitatem were still there, they were well hidden.

The door to Annie's new store was unlocked. The glass had been smashed and scattered across the floor.

"Almost can't tell the difference," Lial said as his shoes crunched against the glass. The store on a good day was almost as messy and disorganized.

Spencer turned on his flashlight and scoured the main floor, searching for the unmistakable signs of a portal or anything out of the ordinary.

Lial walked the aisles with a crystal, capturing the magic contained in the small bookstore. Colors spun from white to beige to purple and black. Most of the magical signatures he captured were old, barely registering as magic. He walked one aisle, turned, walked back toward the main aisle, and repeated the process again until he had covered the entire floor.

After scanning the front of the store, they examined the cashier desk, the shelves with the store records, the cash register, and the wall and corner behind the desk. When they finished, Lial and Spencer entered Mortimer's office and closed the door behind them.

"What a slob," Lial said as he sat down at the desk and began rummaging through the files and paperwork.

Spencer opened the first drawer of the filing cabinet and perused years of folders, stuffed so tightly he could barely stick a finger in to pull one out. He pushed the drawer shut and opened the next, which was not as crowded and easier to search. At the back of the drawer, he discovered several files on all the wizard guards.

"Huh. He's got files on all of us." Spencer continued through the files, finding the largest one, labeled with Annie's name. He pulled it out and dropped it on the already chaotic desk.

Lial pulled it open and his jaw fell. "He's been keeping track of her for years." He held up a copy of Annie's birth certificate.

They split the pile and quickly scanned the pages.

"The prophecy, the coven," Spencer said.

"He was in the business of knowledge," Lial responded.

"And he knew she was important." Spencer held up the Mortimer family tree. "He's related to Callum Wortham from the original coven. I wonder if Annie, Gibbs, and Brite met him."

"We'll have to ask. Until then, I'm not seeing why he left her the store," Lial said.

They continued to scan the horrendous pile of documents. "Actually, here. According to this, this location was chosen because of its magical properties. There's been a Mortimer business or house on this property for centuries." Lial pulled out the original deed to the land. He continued reading. "Uh... huh. That can't be right."

"What?" Spencer asked.

"The magical properties are due to the fact that this is supposedly the location where the portal was closed on the Day of First Sun," Lial said. "Annie found 'September 1' circled in Rathbone's book."

"I thought the portal was in Chicago," Spencer grumbled as he read through the notes.

"Chicago's across the street. But it does mean we assumed it was about fifteen miles down the road," Lial said as he pulled out additional pages. "This store's been in his family for years. If this really is the location of that original portal, Annie's joke about hiding a portal could be true."

"Is there a basement here?" Spencer didn't wait for an answer before he exited the office. He shined his flashlight on the walls, searching behind the heavy bookshelves and behind the cash register. He tapped the wall below the staircase and heard a hollow thud. He glanced at Lial. The two began tapping at the wall in search of a handle.

"Got it!" Spencer pulled a thin latch and the wallboard gave way. It led to a narrow, short staircase; both guards slipped inside and closed the door behind them.

They found themselves in a room approximately ten feet by ten feet with dirt walls and a dirt floor. Their flashlights illuminated the walls, the floor, and the air around them as they searched for any odd magical energy. They walked the perimeter and paced back and forth, feeling for cool air, listening for buzzing of magical energy.

Lial stopped at the direct center of the room. "It's here. It's strong and ice cold."

Spencer maneuvered a crystal around the chill. In the dim flashlight, they could see the outline of the magical energy. "It's definitely here." He showed Lial his crystal.

"If you believe in the story of the Day of First Sun, the portal opened to another dimension. When it was closed, it kept any other demons and evil things from entering the earth. So if we open it again, what do we risk coming out of it?" Lial asked. He touched the portal and shivered from the cold.

"Remember, that portal was closed permanently, though. All that would be left would be the energy—energy that's trapped inside this small room. It might not open to the other world, but maybe the Mortimer family was charged with protecting the energy," Spencer said. "The longer I stand here, the dizzier I get." He stepped away. As he did, he pulled some of the magical energy from the portal into his crystal and stared at it. "If this is from the Day of First Sun, it doesn't appear that old." He handed Lial the crystal.

Lial looked inside the crystal. "What if it's not 'normal' magic? Like the magic Annie has inside of her?"

Spencer glanced at Lial and shined his flashlight on the magic. It hung in the air as a hazy film and shimmered. "I see a portal. They kept it available to be accessed," Spencer murmured. "Why?"

"Do we dare?" Lial asked.

"Just get ready with magic in case something flies out." Spencer summoned his cursed athame and pierced the portal. It opened with a gust of violent wind. The air spiraled, forming a tornado. Air blew across the room, kicking up dirt and swirling it into a cone. It battered against their legs as they moved to look inside the portal. "What the hell?" Spencer stepped closer. The air battered against him; Lial hung on to him as he, too, stared inside.

A dragon limped across their field of vision. People walked past; one glanced at them, a quizzical look on their face. Spencer pierced the portal and it fell silent.

"Was that a market?" Lial asked.

"Looks like a market," Spencer said.

"If that's a portal to the market, that would explain how Mortimer remained hidden and kept tabs on everyone," Lial said.

"But what use would that be to Annie though? And why is this the only thing created from the powerful magic that's supposed to be here?" Spencer asked. "It's a little anticlimactic."

"It still doesn't make sense that this would be the fourth portal," Lial said.

Spencer shook his head vehemently. "Rathbone, Mortimer, and Sturtagaard led her. I can't believe it's for a portal to the market. Especially when there are three other portals out there." He stared at the hazy anomaly in the air and reached for it, jamming his cursed athame back inside. Air whipped across him, blowing back his hair, rustling his clothes. He glanced inside. "Whoa."

Lial looked inside, his eyes widened in surprise. "One portal, multiple locations. How the hell does that work? And is this what I think it is?"

They stared inside the main cavern of the Cave of Ages; the blue shimmer of the walls lit their faces. When they heard voices growing louder, Spencer thrust the knife through the portal again, closing it.

"Now that's worth protecting," he said, amazed.

"How does it work?" Lial asked as he reviewed the magic of the portal with his crystal.

Spencer glanced at his athame and pierced the portal again. This time it opened to the courtyard of their own Wizard Hall. They watched several members of the hospital staff smoking outside the front door.

"Now we just need to determine how to get to the location I want to get to," Spencer said as he closed the portal.

"Maybe we need something from that portal. A brick from Wizard Hall, dirt from the black market, something like that?" Lial suggested.

"I didn't have anything for the Cave of Ages, Wizard Hall, or the market," Spencer said. He reached out and touched the portal, which felt icy and filled with dread.

"Whatever that is, we need to figure out how to use it, because that's a game changer," Lial said.

CHAPTER 30

SPENCER RETURNED TO Wizard Hall nearly giddy and didn't bother to knock on Annie's cubicle; rather, he sat across from her and smirked a quirky grin that left her confused.

"What?" she asked.

"He left you a magical portal."

With raised eyebrows, Annie said, "That's hilarious. Where does it go to, Neverland?" She didn't understand his unusual emotion or what he meant by a magical portal, because all portals consisted of magic. Even Lial, who took up a place in the second chair, was laughing in a childlike manner.

"I'm not sure if it goes to Neverland. We'll have to check. But that's not the point. Mortimer left you something amazing." Spencer handed her his phone, a photo on the screen.

She squinted as she looked at the dim photo. All she could see was a small, dark basement. "Okay… what is it?"

Spencer's grin widened. "That's a portal. Mortimer is hiding it in a secret basement. And it is a game changer!"

Annie frowned. "Okay. What does it do?" She pushed aside her case folder, curiosity getting the better of her.

"The portal opened to the main market. I closed it and reopened to the Cave of Ages. Annie, it opened to Wizard Hall." Spencer said, excitement pouring from his voice.

Annie looked at him. "A two-way portal?"

"We don't know yet," Lial answered.

"But the portal opened to the Cave of Ages?" she asked.

"Yes, it did," Spencer said, still smiling.

"How is that possible?" she asked.

Spencer explained how the magical energy housed in the building was supposedly the true location of the portal from the Day of First Sun story. She glanced at him doubtfully and picked up the folder Lial tossed to her. Her name was scrawled across the cover.

"To sum up, the property has been in the Mortimer family for a very long time and they've been protecting the magical energy in this basement. By the way, the family dates back to the original coven through a man named Callum Wortham."

Annie grimaced at the name. "Callum, to say the least, was rather difficult. Along with the rest of the coven, he made everything more difficult than necessary." She stared at the family tree, at Mortimer's connection to the coven. "It shouldn't be a surprise; everyone knew the Mortimer family was an old one," Annie said. She read the name of Callum's wife. It sounded more like an old Norse name than an English one.

I wonder if he married a Viking?

"How long has the family had the land?" She pulled up more papers, scanning the data quickly.

Lial handed her the deed. "Long enough for them to know they owned hallowed land," he explained.

Annie held her breath. "That's not possible, is it?" She reviewed the copy of the prophecy, the deed to the building, the names and contact information in the folder. "Knowing this was coming, why did Mortimer wait so long to tell me?" she asked.

"Can only figure he was being watched, too. He probably had to dole it out slowly and in secret. But that's what he left you," Spencer said.

"I take back every nasty thing I have ever said or thought about that bastard," Annie said.

"In the meantime, we need to get you there without being discovered," said Spencer.

Annie nodded. "Keep this our little secret. I think this might help us greatly."

The library was busy, with employees and visitors wandering the stacks in search of books, scrolls, or other items. Annie and Lial shared a table in a far corner where she stared at the assortment of maps he had laid across the large table.

"I wonder if we could create a two-way portal with the magic," Lial pondered.

"We should probably learn how to reach the location of our choice first." Annie stared at the places on the maps where sticky notes highlighted several locations.

"Just you wait until you see it," Lial said. He continued to sort through the maps, finally pulling a scroll from the year 1640 and laying it across the others. "We were always taught that the Day of First Sun portal was in Chicago, as marked here. But according to this other map..." He pulled up a second map, this one from 1750, with a sticky note on a very specific location. "Here we see the magical energy in the Snake Head Letters, which is on Howard Street. Not too far off, as Howard Street borders Evanston and Chicago."

Annie stared at both maps and nodded. "The maps aren't an exact match. It could be a variance of about ten to fifteen miles, which would place the portal in the correct location at the store."

"It's really not a lot if you consider the circumference of Earth."

Annie drummed her fingers against the table. "The portal magic is different. You'd think it would be strong enough to feel it. I've never felt anything but disgust in the store. No humming, buzzing, weird magic," she said.

"If he was protecting it, there could be wards surrounding the building or inside the premises. It's a magic shop, so we might not have noticed. And besides, there's so much shit in there. Who knows what's on the walls or on the floor."

"Fair enough. So we have the maps to corroborate the portal. Then who created the port—" Annie stopped as a thought occurred to her. She pulled out Bega's Book of Shadows.

"What are you thinking?"

"My family, Mortimer's family, the Donaldsons, we all trace back to the ninth century. This is from my family member in that early coven. They made sure to pass down everything they could because they knew I got the power to fight a strong evil. They knew we would grow strong and survive. They saw an opportunity to assist, maybe?" She held up the Book of Shadows and opened it. As she had the more modern version at her house, she started with the end and worked her way backwards.

The portal!

"Well?" Lial asked expectantly.

Annie passed him the book. As Lial read the directions, he smiled.

"Archibald Mortimer gave me the best possible gift I could receive right now," Annie said. "I hope he got out. He said he was going to leave through the bathroom window. Has anyone heard anything?"

Lial shook his head. "We have people looking out for him, but nothing yet." He rolled up the two maps and handed them to her as he cleared the rest of the papers. "He knew it was coming and had a plan. If he made it, we'll find him. In the meantime, I'll meet you upstairs."

When Annie left, she took the maps with her and headed to Mrs. Cuttlebrink's desk.

"Find what you needed, Annie, dear?" Mrs. Cuttlebrink asked as she helped Annie check out the maps.

"I think so, Mrs. Cuttlebrink. I'll have these back to you this week," Annie answered.

"I hope that smile is for something really good."

"I think I was just handed a solution to a very complicated problem."

&

When Annie returned to her desk, she saw a note. *Conference room*, it said. She walked over and saw that Cham, Milo, and Spencer were waiting.

"What's up?" she asked as she placed the maps in front of them.

"Find something?" Spencer asked.

"Yes." Annie took her seat, just as Lial entered.

Cham flicked his wrist and closed the door. "Quickly. Eddy and Isaak have been watching Gloriana. So far, nothing. The night team also reported no activity. I'm afraid to take them off duty. Jason, Robin, and Fabien have been working the black market and managed to find the fourth portal that way. It's in the Pacific Ocean. We're close to closing three of them down,"

Annie smirked.

"Also, Brite and Shiff were pulled to help the Middle Eastern unit in assessing the location outside of the Cave of Ages. They're at their Wizard Hall now. Spencer just told me what Mortimer left Annie. I'm not ready to share this with anyone yet, at least until we can see it and figure out how it works," Cham said.

"I think we found the answer," Annie said.

Cham turned on the television behind him and dialed the phone, calling the Middle East Wizard Hall. Shiff, Brite, and the Middle Eastern wizard guards soon appeared on the television screen. In control of the computer, they switched the screen and showed the overhead view of the area.

"We did verify that there are vents in the cliff," Avraham began. "But most importantly, it's miles from the cliff to the rock outcroppings. We're going to have a time figuring out how to set the traps without them knowing. Even the opposite entrance, we can get in there and set off jinx bombs that would force them out from the main cavern."

"We're working on a theory that I don't want to discuss yet; in case it doesn't pan out," Cham said. He glanced at Annie, who still wore a smile on her face.

The screen switched to show the smaller entrance at the bottom of the cliff. It was rocky, with difficult access into the cave system but plenty of places to hide.

"If we have a way to get them out of the cave leading them to that entrance, we will have more protection," Michael said.

"That's actually good news. Let us work on a theory we have. If it works, we might be able to lead them out that way," Cham said. "If you don't need Shiff and Brite anymore, send them back. And I promise we'll have something for you by the end of the week." With the end of the call, Cham turned back to the team. "We originally thought we'd have to go through the smaller entrance to set off the magic, lead them out the large entrance. If we can do it through that amazing portal..."

❦

Cham looked over Kathy's shoulder as she prepared the arrest warrant for Melichi Davis, as per his name on Emily's list. She noted that he was the leader of the Fraternitatem of Solomon and listed his crimes: the murder of Benaiah Portman, and sending operatives to the United States against a magical agreement made with the U.S. Wizard Guard.

She signed the arrest warrant as an agent of the law department and stamped the parchment with the seal of the law department as well as the seal of the Wizard Council United States. When the document had dried, she handed the scroll to Cham.

"You're going to walk this to the Cave of Ages and expect Melichi to come?" she joked.

Cham chuckled. "No. I just wanted an official document," he said.

"How's Annie holding up?"

"She's practicing with the magic, trying to burn it off. It helps with the itching and her blood pressure. I think she's ready for this to be over."

"What about Emily. When this is over?"

Cham shrugged. "Annie's confused. She doesn't know what to think about her mom or Jason."

"Just be good to each other. It's going to be a rough ending, I'm afraid," Kathy said.

❦

Samantha watched Annie from behind the window in the wall separating the gym from the morgue.

Annie saw her and waved but remained inside the gym. She turned and shot a powerful spell at the practice dummy, blowing it to pieces. She hit a second and third consecutively, then looked at her hands. The magic had stopped trickling from her palms.

She turned quickly and stopped just as fast. Samantha was heading toward her.

"Hey."

"Hi, Sami. What's up?"

Samantha walked through the dummy stuffing, touching what was left on the stand. "Who cleans this up?"

"I'm not sure. They keep kicking me out before I can."

Annie turned and shot a spell toward the ceiling where a dummy was hanging loosely. The spell was different this time. It came from her hand and burned a hole in the dummy's stomach with pinpoint accuracy.

"That's scarily exact," Samantha said.

"Just takes practice." Annie's left hand flew out as she shot a spell into the first dummy; the spell was so strong it blew through the first dummy and landed on the one behind it, knocking it over.

"Does it help?"

Annie held up her hand. The magic was minimal, almost nonexistent. "I'm not itching," she said.

"That's something."

As Annie walked toward her sister, she held her hands out and collected the debris, pulling it into a large pile at the center.

"What's up?" Annie asked her again.

"Mom."

"You saw Mom and Shiloh?"

Samantha nodded. "I went with Kathy."

"And?"

Samantha fiddled with her hands, unable to look Annie in the eyes. "It was one thing to see her breakdown at the safe house. It's another thing to…" She walked around the stuffing and touched the nearest dummy stand. "I missed her every day. Every day for twenty years. Mother's Day lunches, growing up, buying my wedding dress, the wedding—I felt their loss, both Mom's and Dad's." Samantha wiped tears from her eyes. "I was so mad at you for not feeling it. And then I sat there with her and Shiloh. I saw how loving she was to him. How she guided him, even with the magic that you taught him. I could barely look at her, let alone talk to her. How do you sum up twenty years to the one person who should have been there with you, when she chose to leave?"

Annie smiled and wrapped her arms around Samantha. "It's one thing to hate her for leaving, regardless of the reason. But it's very confusing watching her mother him. But really, I don't remember Emily back then, so it's hard to miss something I don't remember. What now? I'm not giving up Kathy. She raised me."

"I get your viewpoint now. It was hard. She's—she's mom, but she's not *our* mom. She's *his* mom." Samantha lay her head on Annie's shoulder.

"And that boy is our half-brother," Annie said.

"So, what do we do? When you have the Fraternitatem, what then?"

Annie still believed there would be a moment that would trigger something in Emily. Though she had no proof or any reason to think so, she was fearful that her mother would still come after her. For now, Annie chose not to share that with Samantha.

"Don't worry about it yet. If we win, and the Fraternitatem is put away, I'm not sure what that will mean for Emily or Shiloh. One problem at a time. Okay?"

Samantha nodded. "You're not as okay with this as I thought."

Annie shook her head. "No, I'm not. I'm a mess, and the magic keeps going wonky, and I feel sick." She turned and shot a spell. The practice dummy slid across the floor and crashed into the wall.

"What do you mean IF we win?"

Annie pulled her arm around Samantha and walked her from the gym.

CHAPTER 31

THE PLAN WAS to keep Annie away from the Fraternitatem forever, if they could; if the Fraternitatem couldn't get to her, they couldn't kill her. And with that, moving her to the Snake Head Letters became an all-out project.

Shiff and Brite landed on the roof of the store, ducked below the perimeter wall and hid themselves behind the duct work. They scanned the rooftops beside them and across from them and crossed the rooftop in the shadows, positioning themselves in a darkened corner with a clear view of the street below.

"Across the street," Brite whispered as he stared at the roof directly across from them, where two men were watching the Snake Head Letters.

"They don't seem particularly concerned about being spotted." Shiff surveyed them through binoculars. There was enough light from the streetlamp that he could clearly see them eating.

"They don't look like they're really watching, either." Brite sat back and sent a text.

"The Fraternitatem had centuries to plan and they send *them*?" Shiff joked.

Brite chuckled to himself and scrolled through his phone. "Knuckleheads aside, the Fraternitatem picked the right location to spy on Annie and the magical community. I'd love to know how they convinced the owners of the stationery store to up and leave," he whispered.

"It's a stationery store. I can't imagine it was that hard. You can buy that stuff online a whole lot cheaper," Shiff noted as he continued to keep an eye on the shadows across the street.

∽

The Fraternitatem occupied the empty stationery store across from the Snake Head Letters. At the time, it seemed like the perfect location to spy on Annie Pearce and the magical community. Little did they know; other cases were keeping Annie away from the store. They would only see her three times in the four months of surveillance.

While Melichi had originally wanted to kill the owners and steal the shop, Levi King-Solomon convinced him rather easily to torment the owners with easy-to-perform "pranks." It started simply: scaring away customers with menacing stares, offering discounts to other establishments, letting loose a box of live rats that ran through the store and chewed up the merchandise. Each trick made Levi laugh louder, even as it made Melichi grimace and threaten him to get on with it. But in the end, the owners "with much sadness" closed up shop and retired.

Melichi hadn't thought of sending his best foot soldiers; they'd be needed for other things. Instead, he sent five two-person teams to spy on the Snake Head Letters, taken from a pool of dregs and thugs who thought they were better than they actually were. That decision was his first mistake.

The roof offered them a good view of the comings and goings of patrons. They could even see the items customers purchased—or they could if Mortimer didn't place the items in a bag. It was boring and tedious. To stave off the boredom, these low-level Fraternitatem members brought books, magazines, and food to keep themselves busy.

Their lackadaisical attitude toward the work was the reason why, on the day they finally saw Annie come into the store, the Fraternitatem missed her and the wretched owner of the establishment managed to escape.

When these men returned to the desert, they did so with their tails between their legs, their heads hanging in shame as Melichi reproached them. They were taken off of the surveillance team and sent to a remote corner of the desert to look for King Solomon's artifacts.

The team on the night Brite and Shiff watched was no better. They, too, found the work to be boring, useless, and a waste of time. They'd glanced down at the store, ensured it was empty, and returned to their musings, unaware of what was happening around them.

The men took sips from a shared thermos and ate their dinner in silence. Every few minutes, they checked the store front but quickly returned to their food. For a moment, the largest of the men thought he saw movement on the roof of the Snake Head Letters, so he picked up his binoculars but saw nothing. Deciding the store was abandoned and they were alone, he continued to attack his dinner instead. Neither man knew what happened when they were both hit with a jinx from behind.

꿍

Lial and Spencer landed on the roof of the former stationery store. They scanned their surroundings and noted that both men surveilling the Snake Head Letters were so preoccupied with their midnight snack, they hadn't heard the air rushing from the space the wizard guards now occupied.

Squatting out of view, Lial and Spencer raised their palms and cast jinxes at the two men. Their bodies jerked forward and slipped from their chairs. One of the men landed against the perimeter wall, his face smooshed against the dirty brick, while the other slipped to the floor. The wizard guards moved quickly, checked the pulse of each man, and searched their pockets for any form of identification. They texted their findings to Bucky, who was awaiting any new information at Wizard Hall. Then they each grabbed a man by the collar and teleported the Fraternitatem members to Tartarus.

꿍

"They're gone," Shiff whispered, once Lial and Spencer removed the men from the building.

Brite glanced off into the darkness. He was about to send his next text when he noticed a man and woman strolling down Howard Street. "Odd," he whispered. It was 12:30 a.m.; very few people were usually out at this hour.

The couple walked past the Snake Head Letters, heading east. They turned at the cross street and walked back down Howard on the opposite side, past the former stationery store.

"Awfully late for a causal stroll down this street," Shiff agreed.

The pair repeated their stroll several times, keeping the same speed and making no motion to turn away and return home. By the third pass, Brite grew anxious and texted Cham an update.

※

Cham read the text message, sighed. "There's a slight issue. Jason and I need to go now. Someone else will come for you."

"What it is?" Annie asked. Everyone knew she thought this was overkill.

"There's more than one surveillance team. Just let us take care of it. Okay?" He kissed her cheek and teleported from their house to the alley beside the Snake Head Letter.

Jason and Cham hid in the shadows of the alley and watched the pair pass, walking to the east toward the lake. They peered around the corner and watched as the couple turned at the corner, walked across the street, and headed back down to the west.

This team, a man and a woman, were only a slight bit more competent than the others. The two of them caught sight of Jason and Cham, who hadn't ducked back inside the alley quick enough. In a panic, they ran west, away from the lake.

"Damn," Jason said as he and Cham took up the chase. Running past the cross street, they let their jinxes fly. In quick succession, the jinxes hit their targets, jerking the man and woman forward until they were both on the ground. Cham and Jason lunged across the street. Cham ran to the nearest of the two, jamming his knee into the lower back of the tall, strong woman, who tried to shake him off. He yanked her arms behind her back and tied them with magical rope. He stood to help Jason and watched in surprise as Jason cast his own spell.

"Ghosts are just energy. You shouldn't have magic," Cham said. In the light of the streetlamp, he noticed for the first time the ravages of time that had appeared on his face. Jason's wrinkles had deepened and his hair was peppered with gray.

Jason pulled on the magical rope. "My magic came in. Promise me you won't tell Annie that I'm not a corporeal ghost."

"I can see it in your face. I'm sure she has too."

Jason frowned and held his finger to his lips. "If she knew for certain, she wouldn't let me go and protect her. Please just don't say anything."

Cham shrugged. "It's a bad idea." Both men cast jinxes, rendering the Fraternitatem members unconscious. Cham scanned the neighborhood, assessing if anyone else was lurking about. Deciding they were alone, Cham and Jason teleported the man and woman to Tartarus.

⚬

Spencer rushed from the prison and picked up Annie at her house. She was pacing the back hallway and nearly bounded from her house with nervous energy when she saw him.

"Two groups had eyes on the Snake Head Letters. Brite assures me no one else is on the street," Spencer updated her as he wrapped her in a hug.

"This is a lot of trouble to get me there."

"At least you'll be safe." Spencer teleported Annie across the miles to the Snake Head Letters.

The roof top was quiet; Shiff and Brite were waiting for her predetermined knock before exposing their location.

She knocked as they had agreed, and Shiff and Brite stepped out of the darkness.

"See, that wasn't so bad," Brite said.

Annie grimaced. "Easy for you to say."

"I'm going to sweep the store again to make sure it's still empty." Shiff said.

Annie rolled her eyes as he descended the staircase, his footsteps softening the farther down he walked. After a moment, they heard scuffling and a thump.

"Who's in the store?" Annie whispered.

Spencer's hand tightly gripped her shoulder, ready to teleport her from the rooftop. Below them, footsteps crossed the linoleum floor. A door squeaked closed, and then the person crossed again and walked up the staircase. After a moment, Shiff appeared in the doorway. While his lanky form was easily identifiable, Spencer didn't release his hold on Annie.

"Is someone else down there?" Spencer asked.

"I have him unconscious and tied up. We should have covered the broken window with more than a sheet of plywood. I've got a bookshelf across the door, so hopefully that'll slow them down. You okay?"

"Yeah. I'm ready to see this amazing portal," Annie said.

Shiff led them down the stairs, Spencer still holding Annie's arm, Brite keeping up the rear. When they reached the back of the store, Shiff's phone buzzed. He pulled it out of his pocket and read a text.

"Everyone's upstairs and coming down," he said. "So, how do we get in?" He glanced at Spencer who pulled on the hidden latch and pulled the door open.

Cham, Lial, and Jason joined the group and stared into the hidden basement.

"It's down there?" Cham asked.

Shiff shined the light inside. Spencer and Lial led the team into the tight space; Annie, Brite, Shiff, Cham, Lial, Spencers and Jason crowded themselves inside, standing in a circle around the portal.

Annie held the cursed knife, which was gleaming in the light from the flashlight.

"You just plunged the knife?" she asked.

"Yep. Just pierced the magic," Spencer said.

Annie plunged the knife into the portal and tightened her muscles as a powerful wind swirled out at her. Her hair flew around her head and she held her athame tightly as she glanced inside the portal. She found herself staring at the new main market.

"I'm at the market." Annie smiled, stepped aside, and let the others stare through the portal. When they finished, she removed the athame, closing the portal. She took a deep breath. "That's helpful," she said. "And you didn't do anything else when you opened the portal again?"

Spencer shook his head. Annie glanced at her knife and plunged it inside the magic once again.

For the second look, Annie found herself staring inside of the

Cave of Ages. Hearing footsteps clack against the stone, she closed the portal immediately.

"What's the matter?" Cham asked.

"It's the Cave of Ages. Someone was coming," she said. She reached out and touched the magic. "One portal, multiple locations. That is unbelievable magic." She pulled out Bega's Book of Shadows. "I thought that since the Mortimer family had this in the family for so long, maybe the other families knew about it too." She held it up.

"Did they?" Brite asked.

Annie nodded and opened the tome. "I looked up how I could focus the portal on where I want to go. And sure enough, according to the notes, all I have to do is focus and think of where I want to go."

To demonstrate, she thought of a safe location. She imagined the size and smell of the courtyard at Wizard Hall: the green grass, children laughing in the park. She jammed her knife inside the portal and looked inside, clenching her muscles as the wind whipped against her. She beamed broadly. "It works. Amazing."

The rest of the team took their turn looking into Wizard Hall courtyard, each astounded by the power of the portal.

Annie closed the portal and reopened it immediately, after deciding she wanted to view the market she was no longer allowed to enter. She pictured the dust and stench, the dragons that hopped across the silky dirt, the smell of burnt dung and flesh. She plunged her knife inside, pushed her hair from her face, and stared inside the portal. People, animals, and elves walked past; it was right where she had been aiming. She took a deep breath and closed the portal.

"Think about where you want to go." Annie handed Spencer the knife.

Spencer said, "Witches Brew," and plunged the knife inside. Through the portal, the backyard to their favorite magical bar. He closed the portal. "That's definitely helpful."

They each took turns, even opening a portal back to the side alley beside the Snake Head Letters and one outside the wizard hospital. Each opened portal was met with "Damn," "Amazing," and "No way!" Annie closed the portal again.

"Mortimer wants you to win," Cham said.

Wherever he is.

"I suppose that's true. I suddenly have a soft spot for the man." Annie glanced back up the stairs. "Can we put a blood lock on the door up there before we tell the Middle Eastern group about this? I don't want the portal to be abused."

"Who do you want allowed in?" Cham asked as he held Annie's hand.

She gave him the knife. "Me, and since I'm usually either with Spencer or Brite, make the others Lial and Shiff."

If Cham was upset she didn't choose him, he didn't show it. It was Annie's property, her choice to make.

Cham collected blood from her, Shiff, and Lial and set out to create the lock.

"Do we care how this was created?" Annie asked.

"I don't think it matters unless the magic can hurt someone," Spencer said. "You're sure you were in the Cave of Ages?"

Annie nodded. She touched the portal again and shivered at its chill. "I wonder if this can get me to the past."

"If you go back, you can count me out," Brite said.

"I'd go," Lial said. "Think of the answers we could learn, like who Jack the Ripper really was or who shot JFK."

"Maybe I was wrong about giving you access," Annie said with raised eyebrows and a smile.

Lial raised his hands. "I'm over it."

"Okay. The blood lock is done," Cham said. "I think, if it's okay with Annie since she's the new store owner, we should put a blood lock on the building until she decides what she's going to do with the place. This portal could be dangerous."

"I'm good with that. I trust everyone here for that lock." She held out her hand.

With that, they left the sub-basement. Annie closed the hidden door, now only accessible to a few people. She touched the latch as they made their way to create one more lock.

CHAPTER 32

ANNIE STROLLED THROUGH the aisles. The store was deafeningly quiet.

My store.

The thought that she now owned the Snake Head Letters made her chuckle and then made her sad. While she wasn't a fan of Archibald Mortimer, he had proved over the last year that he was capable of compassion.

As she walked the stack of books, she grazed the book spines with her fingertips, feeling the bumps and cuts across the leather bindings. She shined a flashlight along the walls, the shelves, the floor, searching for wards that might hide the magic.

The door rattled open as she glanced through the books, and the wizard guards from the Middle East followed Cham inside.

"Annie!" Cham called out.

She exited the aisle, her stomach roiling. She knew she was sharing the biggest secret she had. "Hi. I was just looking around. Welcome to the Snake Head Letters."

"Annie. Hello. Thank you. We hear you have a secret entrance into the Cave of Ages," Avraham said.

"We believe we do." She glanced at Cham before leading them to the hidden door. She poked her finger in the lock, triggering it open, and pulled the door away. "We recently learned of this. It should help."

The group followed Annie down the short staircase and stopped at the portal. Her flashlight illuminated the hazy anomaly for Avraham, Sari, and Michael to see. Avraham touched the portal magic. "This portal goes to the Cave of Ages?"

"It's a little better than that," Annie said. She murmured, "Wizard Hall," plunged her athame into the portal, and watched her guests' expressions as they stared inside the portal to the courtyard of the U.S. Wizard Hall.

"Isn't that the courtyard at Wizard Hall?" Michael asked.

"Yes, it is. we're not exactly sure how it works. All we know is, you think about where you want to go, and the portal opens there." Annie plunged the knife inside; the portal closed and the tornado stopped. "Windmere School," she murmured. Again, she pierced the portal, and they found themselves staring at the teleportation area for the wizarding school. After another moment, Annie cut the portal with the athame, closing it and reopening again to the Cave of Ages.

"Oh, my," Avraham said.

Quickly, Annie closed the portal, not wanting to show their hand and draw the attention of the Fraternitatem.

"How did you come by this?" Sari asked questioningly.

"It's a complicated story, but it was left to me by the previous owner of this store. While we have no idea how it works, we do know this will be our advantage," Annie said.

"It looks like the start of a plan," Avraham said.

⟨϶

While the Wizard Guards were in a good place with a powerful magic on their side and nine Fraternitatem members locked in Tartarus Prison, Annie found herself anxious and unsure of the portal.

What if they have the same portal? Or can use the portal energy we created when we opened a portal to the Cave of Ages?

She walked through the passageways of Wizard Hall, climbing down the stairs to the second floor. She swallowed the lump in her throat and knocked on Graham Lightner's cubicle wall.

"Annie, hi. Come in. How can I help you?" He pushed aside his paperwork and offered her a seat.

She sat, her thoughts jumbled as she tried to order them and ask her question. "You know about the portal?"

Graham smiled patiently. "Department manager meetings keep me up to date. Though Cham's been giving me more than what he gives in those meetings." He turned and shot a spell at the cabinet behind him, pulled a thick folder from the top drawer, and touched the cubicle wall, sending a muffle spell around his office. Once they were safely ensconced inside the magic, he passed his folder to Annie.

After reading the file, she looked at him.

"Annie, I'm the cleanup. The information is passed to my employees on a need-to-know basis. They only have the details that will affect them," he said.

"Have you ever seen a portal that could do what that one can do?"

Graham shook his head. "Having only heard about it, I can't say I've seen anything like that before. Cham told me about the magic. It's an unbelievably complex spell that I'm hoping is only possible because of the hallowed magic in that basement. But you're worried about something."

Annie nodded. *Traceable portal energy.* "We have a lot of Fraternitatem operatives in the prison, I fear the Fraternitatem could reach them—reach Emily—to come after me."

Graham nodded and pulled out a map of the island on which Tartarus was built. The island was three miles by five miles, hidden in the northern part of Lake Superior. "There are several locations in the United States that have a high concentration of magical energy. This you know," Graham said.

Annie nodded. "Wizard Hall was built on magical land. Windmere, Hayden, Spring Brook, and Mount Circle Schools of Wizardry were built over magical energy. I get the desire to build over the magical energy; it's easier on all magicals to draw energy from magical locations. We learned that in school." Graham nodded patiently, waiting for her to get to her question. "My concern is Tartarus though," Annie finally said.

"There's magic in the prison that doesn't allow for teleportation or portals. It's been that way for centuries."

"Are we sure? What about the magic in the Snake Head Letters? It's old and strong. We inadvertently opened several portals to the Cave of

Ages as we figured out what it did. What if the Fraternitatem can draw from that magical energy and reverse it, then use it to get to where they want to go. Like Tartarus?" Annie asked.

"The magic in the bookstore is old, proprietary of the coven. I don't expect the Fraternitatem will know how to use that energy before you are able to use the portal to get to them. The question really is then, could a portal open in Tartarus, built from somewhere magical?"

Annie shuddered.

"A prison break isn't unheard of as strategy goes," Graham continued. "Like you said, several of their operatives are locked away. My guess is that it would be an unnecessary use of their time to break them out. We assume there are hundreds if not thousands of operatives out there who do need our attention."

"Wishful thinking for us," Annie said.

"Go to the portal and see if you can get into the prison. If not, don't worry about it. Any of it. If you can get into the prison, a new plan will need to be drawn up. We can't have people getting in and out of Tartarus." He smiled at her.

"Thanks. I'll do that. Not sure if it helps, but I can't get rid of the nagging feeling in my gut," Annie said.

"Good news. We're close to closing three of the market portals."

"Which one are you keeping open?" Annie asked.

"Louisiana. It's the hardest one to get at."

"Remember the days when the demons opened portals willy-nilly because it was convenient for them?" Annie tried to joke, but there was a heavy feeling in her chest. The itching grew stronger throughout her body. She began to scratch.

"You okay?" Graham asked concerned.

"It's the stress and extra magic." She held up her hand. Graham stared in awe as the magic seeped from her palms. "If I don't expel it, I get dizzy," Annie explained. "I need to get rid of the energy."

"I heard you had a way to reduce the magic interaction," Graham said.

"Yeah. It's the best I could hope for until this is over," she said.

"I think you're correct about that," he agreed.

❦

Annie sat on a metal folding chair and stared at the hazy anomaly. In her beam of light, the portal was a soft, shimmering, hazy bit of magic. The more she looked at it, the more it seemed to beat with her heart.

She studied it closely. It felt as though she and the magic were becoming one; that the magic of the portal was the same as the magic that coursed through her. Sitting in the room beside the portal lessened the itching and made Annie feel strong and powerful. She ignored the fact that to feel this at peace, she had to sit in the basement of the Snake Head Letters. Regardless, it was hers now.

Annie thought of the teleportation area on the island where Tartarus Prison was housed. She pictured the lane that led there, the clearing, the field of dead grass, the picnic table. She jammed the knife inside the portal and looked past the tornado-like wind to the clearing. It was empty. The lone tree in the grasses had been downed, split in two by a perfect lightning strike. Annie closed the portal, feeling uneasy that a portal could be opened to the island.

The athame was cool and smooth in her hand. She turned the hilt several times as she walked around the portal, staring at the unevenness of the magical outline, at the pulse and energy it created. She thought of the inside of the prison, of the cell block in which Levi was being held, and then plunged the knife inside. She fully expected a windstorm, lightning, and a full view of his cell. But when the knife blade touched the magic, the haze pulsated as if it were trying to honor her request, but nothing happened. Annie removed the athame and breathed a sigh of relief. Tartarus was still secure.

The long weeks and the constant lack of sleep made Annie's hands shake as she closed up the hidden room. She walked the dark aisles of the store and stared at the dilapidated walls and floor. The windows were now boarded up and magically enhanced. The bookstore and the portal were as safe as possible.

"Well?" Spencer asked as he came down from the upstairs apartment.

"The portal couldn't connect to the inside of the prison. Just the teleportation area," she said.

She opened a random basket on the middle shelf and grimaced at the dingy artifacts inside. She touched a mason jar filled with poisonous leaves and another with a bouquet of herbs. There was a cursed statue inside. It buzzed against her skin, causing her to shudder.

"What am I going to do with this?" Annie waved her arms around as she spoke. Magic flew from her palms and knocked a ceiling tile to the floor.

Spencer pulled her away. "Well, we can't let anyone get a hold of that portal." He wiped dust from her shoulders.

"Yeah. I found out what I wanted to know. I guess it's time," Annie said as she and Spencer finished securing the building before teleporting away.

❧

Annie stared at Levi King-Solomon while he lay sleeping on the cot in his cell. In the week he'd been there, he had been generally belligerent and unhelpful.

Not surprising.

She knocked on the cell. The lump of a man remained on his side, facing the wall. His leg twitched.

"If we let you out, what will they do to you?" Annie asked.

Levi didn't acknowledge her. She summoned a stake and ran it across the metal bars, the pinging sound reverberating off the stone walls. She continued the annoying motions until he turned and glared at her.

"Well?" she asked again. "Will they kill you if you're released, or will they come and break you out?"

"I'm safer in here," Levi grumbled.

"Then, why protect them?"

He turned over and stared at the grayish-brown stone that surrounded him. "Will you let me out of prison if I speak?"

With evidence mounting against him, Annie knew he would never see the light of day. As a Fraternitatem of Solomon member, Levi had killed at least one person of which they knew. His future would be limited to spending the rest of his life either in Tartarus or in a nonmagical prison.

"You won't be leaving the prison. But if you speak, we have more comfortable cells—bigger, warmer, with better food, and possibly a window," she said.

Levi sat up. Any movement on the thin cot caused it to squeak. He frowned at Annie. "I clean up their messes. I killed Rathbone. There was one more I had to kill and then I was out of here. I was going to be set up for life away from all of them."

She trembled at his admission as he smiled coldly at her.

He was going to kill me.

"Were you really married to Emily?"

"Are you really that blubbering fool's daughter?" His voice was bitter, angry. There was clearly no love for Emily. In that instant, Annie felt sorry for her mother.

"You're obviously not Shiloh's father," she said. "But you married her for the plan. My guess it's you who kept her drugged and compliant."

He continued to smile a disturbing, empty smile. "Now you know," he said.

"No. What I have is confirmation that you're an ass who didn't care whose life you ruined." She kept her voice emotionless. Another piece of the puzzle fit into place. She was so angry at how many people had a hand in pulling her family apart.

CHAPTER 33

"THIS MIGHT BE the last time I see you," Jason said to Annie.

She had been unable to sleep or eat as she waited for morning to come. She had curled up on her window seat and stared into the darkened backyard. When he spoke, his familiar voice broke her heart just a little more. She motioned for him to sit on the bed, in the room that was once his.

"You've done an amazing job with the house. It's warm and cozy," he said.

Annie faced him. He had changed in the weeks since he returned. It wasn't just the gray in his hair or the wrinkles around his eyes and mouth. He was more hunched over and had put on weight around his belly. He was clearly alive and Annie knew he would die if he went to battle for her. Her eyes welled with tears.

"That's not what you want to talk about," she managed to say.

"No. I wanted to properly say goodbye."

She hiccoughed, then held her breath. He didn't belong here. It wasn't his time, and yet, he had come when she called, to protect her. She wiped her cheek, not ashamed to cry about him leaving.

"I know you've been very cautious with me here and I'd expect nothing less of you." Jason held Annie's hands. "Sami doesn't think like you. She accepted me a lot easier than you did. I expect this will be harder for her."

Annie knew he'd ask her to look after Samantha like he had done so many years earlier, as if Annie were better suited to caring for Samantha than Samantha was for her.

"I always protect her," she said through her tears.

"Coming back was not something I would have wished for. It's been so hard watching you with Kathy and Ryan and knowing I don't belong here." He stared at the ring on her finger. Even in the moonlight, it sparkled. "You are my strong, brilliant, beautiful daughter. I am so incredibly proud of—" His lips quivered as he held back his own tears. "It is truly a privilege to have known you."

Annie wrapped her arms around her father and kissed his cheek. His familiar scent and touch were so comforting to her. "I love you, Daddy," she said.

❧

As Annie waited for Spencer to pick her up, she paced her house, unsure how long it would be before she could return home. While Jason remained in the basement preparing, Annie glanced at her phone for the hundredth time. Just as she tucked it into her back pocket, it buzzed with a text from Bucky.

Harrison Plank is Melichi Davis.

She grimaced and texted acknowledgement before pacing again.

The back door squeaked open. Cham entered the kitchen. "Can't sleep?"

"Could you?" Anne said tersely, her anxiety showing through her voice.

"Sorry."

Annie created a small fireball and let it float above her palm. She dropped the magic and created a new one. "The itching's awful. How did it go with Starla?"

"She denied it. Said she didn't know what Antique Symposium was or how the money got in her account. I left her to stew in Tartarus, staring at stone walls. She called me back ten minutes later and admitted everything," Cham said.

"That was… easy." Annie stared out the back window into the yard. Cham wrapped his arms around her. "Did she tell you why?"

"She really believed she was doing good work for the Fraternitatem. They convinced her you messed up." He rested his head on her shoulder. "There's enough evidence for treason."

For several minutes, they watched out the window in silence. Annie felt safe with his muscles against hers.

"Spencer will be here soon." She glanced at her phone again.

"Please stay away as long as you can," Cham pleaded.

Annie shuddered. "I promise." Turning toward him, she placed her arms around his neck and looked at him sternly. "Promise me you will call me to end it if you need me."

"I hope we won't need you." He kissed her forehead as Spencer's distinctive knock echoed against her back door and Jason appeared in the doorway.

Annie took a deep breath. "I love you," she whispered and kissed him.

"I love you," he whispered back.

❧

The protection spells had been increased around the Snake Head Letters, allowing Annie, Spencer, and Jason to land on the roof unseen. Annie punctured her finger against the small needle in the blood lock, popping it open. Spencer led them down the dark staircase and past Mortimer's apartment to the first floor. At the hidden door, Annie again stuck her finger in the blood lock and pulled the door open.

Hidden safely inside the small basement, they sat on three metal chairs surrounding the portal. Annie let out the stale air in her lungs as she stared at the hazy anomaly, an ancient reminder of her magic, of all that had come before her and all that would come after. She reached out and shivered in the chill.

"And you're not going to the desert, correct?" Jason asked.

"If they need me, I'll have to go." Annie held her palm up. The magic billowed upwards and was consumed by the portal.

"I just don't—" he stopped.

Annie knew what he would say and held her hand up to stop him. "Dad, let me do my job." She took a deep breath and glanced at her phone. As they waited, wizard guard units across the planet were gathering in the desert. The clock on her phone ticked off another minute.

"Just promise me you won't go to the desert unless absolutely necessary. I came back to keep you safe. Let me do that," Jason said.

"I promise." She returned to her phone while Spencer scrolled through emails, if only for something to do while they waited.

News about the Fraternitatem operatives in Tartarus came through in emails. They had been moved to new locations within the prison and additional spells were placed on their cells. As each person was moved, Spencer showed Annie the notifications.

"The prison's still safe," he said. His knee bounced up and down.

Annie glanced at his phone without interest, her head churning with other thoughts. Beside her, Jason summoned his field pack and fiddled with the contents, checking that he had everything he needed.

Annie glanced at her phone. "We haven't been summoned yet," she said as they waited for word.

⁓

The list of assignments was neatly folded and stuffed inside Lial's shirt pocket. After spending hours with the list of wizard guards and a map of the desert, he had spread out the teams across a wide range and hoped it would be enough to keep the Fraternitatem from escaping. He held his breath when he entered through the temporary portal with another American wizard guard, Stephenson McKay.

"This is it," Stephenson said as Lial peered around the large boulder, surveying the rocky outcropping.

"Yeah. This is it," Lial responded. His heart beat rapidly and sweat poured from his forehead. Though the sun was low and still at the horizon, the desert was hot and the air hung heavy around them. He let out stale air and motioned for Stephenson to follow him. They slunk from the landing location and placed themselves in their hiding spot with a clear view of the wizard guards as they came to though the portal.

Lial surveyed the flat land though his binoculars, noting the hidden entrance to the caves and the clifftop where Cham and other managers were landing to watch the scene. He looked out into the desert. It was barren, though his eye caught a shimmering mirage.

"It begins," he murmured to Stephenson, who stood guard beside him.

The first team to cross through the portal was Shiff and Brite. They spotted Lial, nodded quickly, and teleported to their pre-assigned location. When they were hidden, Lial scanned the rocks for signs of the Fraternitatem. Once he ascertained that the wizard guards were still undiscovered, he texted the next group. Eddy and Isaak landed in the tight space behind a large boulder, nodded to Lial, and teleported again to their own location. As each new team entered the desert, Lial scanned the area before texting the next team. After the teams from South and Central America took their positions, Lial texted the Middle Eastern guards. He recognized Sari, Michael, and Avraham but not the five others who landed with them. As the plan had unfolded during the night, Avraham had been insistent that they take the location closest to the hidden entrance in the rocks. Of all the Wizard Guard units that had ever chased the elusive Fraternitatem, they had done it longer than any of them. Lial obliged and watched anxiously as they each took off for the boulders just outside the entrance to the Cave of Ages.

His heart grew heavy as he recognized the teams: Jory, Roland, Sabine, and Olivier from France, along with Marcus and Phillipe from Amborix. Lial fully understood the danger in what they were all taking on and he couldn't help feeling responsible for their safety.

Teams from Italy, Morocco, Canada, and Germany streamed through the portal at safe intervals, finding their places in the field. By the time all teams had found their assigned hiding spots, Lial was weary and hot; he wiped his wet forehead with his sleeve.

He sent the last text and the U.S. Wizard Guards entered two at a time, filling in the empty spots in the outcropping or taking the line between the outcropping and the desert; their focus would be to keep any nonmagical Fraternitatem members from escaping into the desert.

Lial scanned the landscape one last time. He checked the cliffs where upper management placed themselves, verified where the Vampire Attack Unit had hidden themselves, and noted Cham's location where he would view and direct the action if needed. Lial glanced at his watch; it had taken forty-five minutes for the groups to enter and set themselves in place. When no more were due to arrive, he sent the final text to Cham.

∽

The United States Wizard Council was the largest in the world and had multiple departments that could assist with such an operation as this. The Vampire Attack Unit was made up of several better-than-fair fighters, who had positioned themselves on the tops of several cliffs overlooking the field of engagement, just before dawn.

Graham Lightner lay on his stomach, viewing the scene through his binoculars. From his location behind the action, he could see each guard as they took their place and prepared for the fight to begin. Beside him, Guenther Grimm from Amborix lay in the dirt and observed.

"They're nearly set, it appears," Guenther whispered in case their voices could carry below.

"It's a large-scale cooperative operation," Graham said. He shifted his position and watched another section of the flat land.

"It's dangerous. We don't have an absolute number to match the Fraternitatem," Guenther said.

Graham chuckled. "You're a little late for that."

"Aren't we always?"

"I have faith in the wizard guards." Graham sat in the dirt, wiped dust from his clothes, and watched with intensity and unease as the next text update came.

৵

The phone buzzed in Annie's hand. Jason and Spencer glanced at her. "It's time."

Annie pulled out Jason's athame. He reached for it like it was an old friend and held his hand over Annie's.

"Please keep her safe," Jason said to Spencer.

They stood beside the portal and Annie thought of the Cave of Ages. Together, father and daughter jammed the cursed knife inside.

Through the heavy wind, Jason looked through the portal into the empty cavern and turned to Annie. It was so clear now that his face and body had caught up to the age he would have been now, had he not died nine years ago. It was most shocking on his head, where the salt-and-pepper hair was mostly salty in a frizzy, unkempt way. Annie wasn't positive if his wrinkles were as deep as they were because he was worried or just older.

"I love you. Don't ever forget it." Before Annie could answer, Jason jumped through the portal. As his second foot crossed the plane, the portal closed, dropping them in the darkness and quiet.

"I love you, too," she murmured.

"He'll be fine," Spencer said when the portal closed shut. He placed his hands on her shoulder to calm her.

"He won't be. He's human."

He squeezed her shoulder. "I guess ghosts don't age." He stared at the remnants of the portal. The chill radiating from it made him shudder.

"You saw that, too?"

"It doesn't mean he won't be fine. He should have his magic now."

Annie shook her head. "I conjured him because I was frightened, because I needed him. He came. I made him corporeal and he vowed to stay with me, to keep me and Sami safe. That hasn't changed. He will die to keep me away from them."

"He doesn't belong here. It isn't his time," Spencer whispered.

"It doesn't make it hurt less though."

"You had a month with him that you wouldn't have had otherwise. Most of us aren't so lucky."

Annie nodded and wiped the tears from her eyes. "I know. I appreciate your concern. Still, knowing I wouldn't have him for very long, doesn't lessen the pain."

"He is here to protect you. Let him do that, regardless of the outcome. You are very fortunate in that you know just how much your father loves you and what he would do for you."

Annie reached out for the portal with the athame.

One touch and I can help him.

She lowered her arm, sat on the chair, and waited for her text instead.

❧

Jason had last seen the shimmering blue walls of the Cave of Ages nine years ago, the night he was forced into the desert and up the narrow mountain path. It was a draining hike as he had been pushed and pulled in the heat. His only thought had been how he was going to get back home to his girls.

He clearly remembered the awe he felt when he stared at those shimmering blue walls. Even recollecting the awe, he couldn't forget the fear he felt when Melichi issued his stern warning that Jason drop the case and return the Chintamani stones. He had gladly given them up as long as he could return home.

It was then that he had seen her: the wife he buried twelve years prior, alive and seemingly well hiding behind the throne. It was the same throne he saw now, in the same location at the back wall. He had thought he imagined Emily standing there, but he soon learned it was really her. At that moment, everything changed. Seeing it again brought on an unexpected rush of emotions, from sadness to pure anger. He hadn't expected that.

The throne was intended as a display of power to create fear amongst those in the cave. Emily had hidden there, much to Melichi's dismay. She had been so young and so confused, almost sorrowful as she used the throne to distance herself from him.

After stepping through the portal to this place, Jason remembered the exasperation and anger at seeing Emily there and the hurt he felt when she ignored his pleas to come home. Every word uttered that night replayed in his head as if he was living it all over again. Every scent and emotion from the past invaded him and tormented him. He thought of Annie in an attempt to rid himself of the pain.

If he did his job as planned, Annie wouldn't have to come to the desert and use her magic to save them all. If he followed the plan, she would remain safe and hidden and away from the Fraternitatem. He held his breath as he scanned the cave and listened for voices or footsteps or any sign of life inside the walls. Determining he was alone, he ran for the large entrance of the cavern that overlooked the desert and the narrow, rocky mountain pass he had taken here the first time he visited.

When this is over, I should blow it to pieces.

Jason pulled out two crystals. He bent beside the entrance and embedded the first rock in the lower left corner where it met the floor. As his magic liquefied the rock, the crystal sunk inside until a dime-sized piece remained. He looked into the cave and ran for the opposite side, repeating the process.

Once both crystals were hidden in the mountain rock, he placed his palm above the nearest crystal and murmured the powerful spell. Magic burst from the crystal and searched out the other on the opposite side. The blocking spell buzzed inside the large entrance. Jason tossed a loose rock at the spell. It exploded on impact, flinging small particles of rock into the cavern. He hid himself behind a convenient boulder near the entrance and waited. When no one from the Fraternitatem took notice of the small explosion, he took one last look at the shimmering blue walls, turned on a small pink quartz crystal to light his way, and followed the tunnel deeper inside the mountain.

Jason had studied both Arden and Emily's maps of the caves, noting the differences and paying careful attention to what he would come across as he trapped himself in the rock. As expected, the first room he came to was empty, devoid of furniture, people, and animals. He continued on, examining the next five rooms along this passage and discovered them to be much of the same: dark, empty spaces.

Maybe the Fraternitatem isn't as big as we thought.

As he came to the next room, he expected more and was not disappointed. This room was a large cavern loaded with bookshelves storage boxes, baskets, books, scrolls, and artifacts. When asked, Arden was sure the room would still be there, but Emily's map hadn't shown this particular room. Jason sighed at the verification that Emily's map was less than truthful. He was not excited about what he was to do inside.

If I had time, I could save it all.

But there wasn't time for anything except the job he came here to complete. As much as it pained him to do this, the information found in this room would be risky if it found its way into the world. He summoned the first of several magical bombs and tossed it into the cavern. The glass bomb shattered on the table top and exploded. The force of the magic sent ancient tomes across the room and set baskets and books on fire. Rather than watching a millennium of work and knowledge become consumed in flames, Jason ran down the passage and turned left at the next junction.

Voices wafted from the first room on the right. He peered inside the nearly closed door and saw three Fraternitatem members working and laughing. He thought he heard Annie's name and would have liked to strike them down there and then. Instead, he slunk past them to the end of the short hallway where three rooms had been carved into the rock. The final room on the right was still open, so he slipped inside, closing himself in.

The walls were covered in pictures of Emily and Shiloh. This small, musty, drafty room must have been Emily's home for several years. Though Jason had known she was a member, he hadn't realized how far they had isolated her and the boy.

He glanced up at the thin vent in the ceiling. They had been carved into the clifftop, venting the entire cave system which allowed people to live and work inside the stone. Throughout the night, the Middle Eastern wizard guards and the VAU had covered the vents; Jason hoped the blocks would contain the smoke and fire.

With one last look at Emily's past, he exited the room and tossed the next bomb. He ran back down the corridor, past the occupied room, and turned left, deeper into the caves.

Smoke began collecting in the passages. He ignored the bitter stench as he made his way to the end of the cave system. A distant din of voices began to rise as the smoke billowed across the rocks, choking out the fresh air.

I'm almost done.

Jason stood at the final few inches of the passage. He glanced down the hallway, unable to see through the thickening smoke. He took a deep breath and dropped the largest of bombs he had with him. Before it hit the stone, Jason teleported himself away and landed in the Cave of Ages, behind Melichi's throne.

His lungs burned and his heart pounded. Jason peered out from behind the throne and listened for the sounds of people escaping. The magical fires continued to eat away the magical energy trapped inside the complex cave system. It continued, unsatiated, through the narrow passages, its only purpose to consume. With the room vents blocked off, the smoke had nowhere to go and continued to build up and hang in the air.

Panicked, shrieking voices echoed against the rock as Fraternitatem members made their way through the caves, running for the main entrance. The first man lunged for the fresh air beyond. He was thrown from the spell and landed on his back. His face, hands, and clothing had been scorched. When he fell, he bashed the back of his head and didn't move as his flammable clothes burst into flames. Many Fraternitatem members tried to beat the fire with their thick, heavy robes, but the fire was cursed. Only the anti-spell could quell the flames.

As the fire consumed their associate, they watched in horror, helpless to assist. Jason watched without guilt or sadness; he felt nothing.

He summoned a smaller bomb and tossed it into the center of the cavern where ten Fraternitatem members ducked from the exploding glass. The new spell billowed from the remnants on the ground. They looked at the spell in confusion. Jason pulled himself from behind the throne and stood for them to see. They all stared at him, unsure of who he was at first, until recognition dawned on them and their confusion turned to shock. The man they killed nine years ago was alive and well.

Melichi walked toward him. "How?" he demanded

"Her powers you want so badly," Jason said. "You best run off that way or the spell will kill you, much like your friend there." He pointed to the burnt corpse at the cave opening. Nine men ran for the hidden entrance.

Melichi watched them escape with a look of disgust. His face was scrunched and angry as he looked upon the dead Fraternitatem member and touched his face with the toe of his shoe.

"The spell is going to kill you if you don't leave," Jason said.

Footsteps echoed and bounded down the spiral cut corridors for the back entrance. In anger, Melichi whipped his hand out and cast the first of several jinxes. Jason ducked behind the throne. As he pulled his leg around, the magic hit his shin. In a split second, his pants were shreds of fabric, and blood oozed from his leg. The second spell splintered the top of the throne and Jason ducked from falling wood.

Jason knew he was no longer a ghost. Cham had known it too. While he had tried to keep the information from Annie, he was sure she knew it too. He wanted to make sure she wouldn't keep him away from what he needed to do. He believed he would die here, but he didn't care. This was no longer the time where he had belonged.

Jason gritted his teeth and cast a jinx that hit Melichi in the chest. The leader of the Fraternitatem flew through the air, narrowly missing the blocking spell on the main entrance of the cave.

Jason hobbled to Melichi as he lay sprawled on the ground. "Melichi."

The smoke was thickening in the cave. The stampede of people grew more distant as the Fraternitatem exited the cave. Jason was sure more would be coming as someone, somewhere set off an alarm.

Time was closing in on them. The Wizard Guard had intended on Jason joining the fight, something he knew was starting now. He stared at Melichi; the leader raised his hand.

Melichi's spell hit Jason's shoulder, burning through his shirt and to his flesh. Blood seeped from the wound, quickly saturating his shirt with blood. The pain stung deeply, and yet he held in his scream as he expended magical energy casting another spell. He put all of his anger and his fear into the jinx. It was so strong, the magic forced Melichi up against the wall, leaving him hanging for several minutes. Jason's arms trembled as he kept the man in the air; his legs weakened as his magical energy was drained. No longer able to hold Melichi in the air, Jason dropped the spell and Melichi crashed face first on the floor, cracking his teeth.

Melichi slowly rose. Blood poured from his mouth and his nose. His face was swollen. Jason met Melichi's glare and didn't release it as he threw his next spell. Melichi fell back to the stone, his eyes wide with fear.

Jason let him rise, keeping his eyes on the other man, then dropped a glass ball. Upon shattering, a billowing, poisonous gas rose in the air. Jason held his palm inside the magic gas and directed it at Melichi. The leader of the Fraternitatem of Solomon watched in horror as the flesh on Jason's hand burned in the magic. His arm shook from the pain and his skin blistered. Melichi scrambled for the exit.

Still holding the magic, Jason used his other palm and forced a heavy jinx into Melichi, dropping him to the floor. Jason didn't look back as he ran from the Cave of Ages.

⤙

Annie's phone buzzed. She jumped and stared at the screen.

"Crap. As much as we wanted one portal to control the flow, the portal between the Louisiana market and the main market is becoming unstable. They need me now."

Staring through the portal to the main market, Annie could immediately feel the chaos emerging from inside. Spencer held her arm as they passed through the magic. Three of the smaller markets had been closed and their portal energy removed, leaving only the Louisiana market open. The portal between it and the main market was packed with a horde of people, most of whom were entering the main market with only a small amount leaving.

"I thought they were going to clear out customers," Annie said as she glanced at the portal.

"It's a small Wizard Guard unit. Maybe they couldn't have gotten everyone out."

As the plan was discussed through the evening and late into the night, the South African wizard guards had set themselves up in a booth in order to monitor the flow of traffic. Joseph was known in the market, so it had seemed the best course of action at the time.

But now it was descending into madness.

"Damn. It's getting out of hand. We need to find them now," Annie said.

She and Spencer ran along the market perimeter, past an odd collection of individuals—merchants still selling wares to customers, stall owners packing up their belongings to leave, and more merchants preparing to fight for their lives and livelihood. People in each group watched in interest as Annie and Spencer made their way to the other side of the market.

Their first stop was to Arrowhead's booth, where he was busy protecting his property and helping last-minute customers. He spotted them but kept his attention on his customer.

"There's word that the Cave of Ages has been attacked," Arrowhead said once he finally joined them.

"We're aware," Annie said.

"Fraternitatem members have been called back to the desert."

Around them, panicked people streamed inside the market, talking rapidly with each other and pointing and motioning as if they had somewhere else to go.

"They seem to have found their way here instead." Annie tossed coins on the table. "What are the remaining customers looking for?"

"Protection spells, potions, amulets. Won't do any good though." He pulled an ugly amulet from inside his shirt.

"And the merchants?" Spencer added additional avrum to the pile.

"Those who are still here are ready. Don't make me regret siding with you," he said.

The Fraternitatem members were obvious as they marched through the market, wearing thick, red cloaks that swung as they ran. Several made their way along the perimeter wall to the back side of the market. "Is there a portal to the desert from here?" Spencer asked.

Arrowhead shrugged. "Not that I know of. If I see something, I'll pass it on. Keep yourselves alive." He returned to the last of his customers.

Annie led Spencer to Joseph's new booth, turning left at the next aisle. She caught his gaze and walked through the remaining stragglers to the empty booth beside his.

They ducked under the tent wall that separated the two booths. They were greeted by Petra, who was accompanied by two men and two women.

"Annie Pearce and Spencer Ray," Annie said, gesturing at herself and Spencer.

Petra introduced them to Mark, Steve, Shayna, and Lisa, all of whom were members of the South African Wizard Guard.

"Who's walking the market?" Annie asked.

"Richard and Char are out there now. We came in to wait for you. The portal is becoming unstable. That's why we called you," Mark said.

"We've also noticed the Fraternitatem members have been called back home. Why they came here is beyond us," Shayna added.

"They've been forced out of the cave system within the last thirty or so minutes," Annie said. "We saw a few Fraternitatem members heading toward the back of the market. Do you know if there's a portal to the desert back there?"

The team exchanged concerned glances.

"We've never noticed," Steve admitted.

"Noticed what?" Petra asked.

"Why Fraternitatem members are heading to the back of the market," Spencer said.

Petra frowned. "That's disconcerting. We'll look into that. Do you think your magic can stabilize the portal?"

Annie nodded. "I have it. I might as well put it to the test."

CHAPTER 34

THERE WERE TWO known entrances to the Cave of Ages. The newest one was carved into the cliff and hidden between two large boulders. Right outside of the door was a two-foot-deep space. Once the Fraternitatem made it past the boulders, they could enter the rocky outcropping and head for the desert. There wasn't much space to hide on either side of the boulders without being seen. Avraham, Sari, and Trey stood behind the rock on the left. Michael, David, Jenna, and Bryce took the other side.

"You okay?" Sari whispered to Avraham.

Avraham nodded and focused on the holding pen beside them. A large area had been prepared the night before and blocked off and hidden with magic. The giants, descendants of the hundred handers that had protected Hades in ancient Greece, had stayed to protect the location. It was clear that the giants could tell something was about to happen in the caves; they lumbered through the holding pen as they waited. Avraham sighed at the sight.

He continued to survey their location. The cave entrance was still blocked. Without binoculars, he couldn't see a single soul in the desert. He turned his attention back to the outcropping. He knew a good force of wizard guards was hiding out there, yet he saw nothing and felt truly alone, even with his fellow wizard guards beside him. Finally, he glanced again at his phone, knowing that Jason would be sent in once he and his team were placed.

Not much longer.

The first of the bombs were set off. Smoke and poisonous gas began to fill the cave system, starting the flood of Fraternitatem members. First, Avraham heard their panicked voices reverberating across the stone walls and floors.

Avraham signaled Sari, who sent a ready spell.

The sound of hundreds of feet stampeding to them came next. Sari's eyes grew wide as the sound became louder, more chaotic.

"Holy hell," she said as the thick, black smoke billowed out into the desert.

Avraham held his breath. His hands shook from raw nerves.

Not much longer after the appearance of the smoke, the first of the Fraternitatem lunged out of the cave. His thin, red cloak billowed around him. Across his back, the symbol of the Fraternitatem blazed in gold. The disoriented man scanned the desert in confusion. Avraham stepped out from behind the boulder and slammed the man with the first jinx. He crumpled to the sand and lost his grip on the basket he had been holding. Scrolls and papers scattered across the ground.

The giants were there immediately. The first pulled the man up and placed him over his shoulder, carrying him to the holding pen and locking him in. The second picked up the scrolls and stored them along the cliff face.

"Out in the open," Avraham murmured. While the lone man had been easy to contain, the next would not be.

The six wizard guards stood in a line, visible to the exit. Five giants stood behind them at the ready. They waited for the mass exodus.

It came quickly. Jinxes flew in the air. Some members were hit and immediately carted away; others, seeing their chance, pulled away and ran.

"Shit!" Avraham shouted as two members ran for the open desert.

Too many streamed from the cave in a chaotic hum of confusion and fear. They ran straight for the wizard guards, who jinxed as many as they could. It was too much for the remaining Middle Eastern wizard guards. Avraham raised his arm and shot off a spell, and the next wave of wizard guards revealed themselves and ran into the fray.

The desert air, no longer still, was alive with human voices and the buzz of magic as jinxes flew through the desert.

᪥

When Cham wasn't watching the rocky outcropping below him, he was watching the air vents along the cliff top for any signs that Jason had set off the bombs. When he saw tiny puffs of smoke and poisonous gas escaping through the cracks around the rocks that blocked the vents, he moved farther away, crossing and uncrossing his arms as his anxiety rose.

They'll be escaping soon.

He peered through his binoculars. The wizard guards were well hidden. Even the holding pen was not visible to the naked eye. On top of a cliff a mile away, Graham Lightner and others were waiting expectantly should they be called in to fight. Cham balled his hands into tight fists and returned his attention to the cave entrance below him.

He held his breath as the first of the Fraternitatem exited. Even after the man had easily been jinxed and carried away, Cham still felt uneasy. He glanced through the binoculars as additional members streamed from the cave.

Cham paced, but the sound of footsteps against the stone floor was loud through the vents. He stopped his pacing and watched the horde of people to see if Jason was among them.

He's still inside.

The first line of offense was quickly overwhelmed by the sheer numbers of the Fraternitatem escaping the fire and smoke. The next wave of wizard guards stepped out from behind their hiding spots and began tossing their jinxes at any Fraternitatem member they could find, felling many. The pile of jinxed bodies grew in the pen.

Cham returned his attention to the cave entrance. Smoke streamed outward, only dispersing as bodies exited. He saw several Fraternitatem members attempting to teleport, but when they failed to lift off, he knew all anti-teleportation wards were holding. While some members set out on foot, they were unprepared for desert travel. Cham knew his U.S. wizard guards could handle the flow from the outcropping; that was why they were stationed there.

Spells and jinxes were cast with dizzying speed. The movement of bodies in the fight whipped up a thick cloud of dust. Through the madness, Cham saw flashes of light and wisps of robes.

Beyond the fighting on the other end of the outcropping of rocks, a door opened inside the cliff wall. Several all-terrain vehicles exited. In their haste to escape, they nearly sideswiped the fighting. Cham texted Graham to warn him.

They won't get far, Graham texted back.

Cham returned to his observations. Two of the cars had been hit by magic. He smiled wanly.

∽

Brite leaned against the tall boulder and lay his head on the hard rock. From his location in the outcropping of rocks, he could hear the voices and footsteps as they exited the caves.

"It's starting," Shiff said. He looked at his partner, sadness in his eyes.

"Yeah. It's almost over." Brite reached for Shiff's hand. "We wasted all that time."

"I thought we were best friends, and then you left for the past and I knew it was more than that," Shiff said.

Brite glanced around the rock and watched the dust as it rose in the air, the shots of light as the spell rushed through the air.

"I wish I realized sooner," Brite admitted.

"If I don't make it, just know I love you. And when this is over—"

Brite looked at his partner. "Tell me when it's over." A deafening noise reverberated across the desert. Shiff and Brite glanced at each other. "I love you too," Brite said.

As the second team, they weren't to enter the fray unless called upon or it was deemed necessary. For now, the first team was containing the exodus of men and women.

"I'm sorry I pushed you away when I got back," Brite told Shiff, the man he realized he loved.

There's no more time.

A second explosion rocked the desert.

"Don't die on me!" Shiff said through gritted teeth. They rushed from their hiding spot and ran into a thick cloud of dust.

With low visibility, they were separated immediately. Brite slunk forward, his hands out, feeling for people or rocks. He followed the sounds of whizzing fireballs and shouts. He ducked low just as a fireball hit the rock beside him. He stared at the scorch mark across the rock and breathed out.

"Shit," he murmured.

Brite stepped slowly, his feet crunching in the coarse sand. He squinted as he made out the shapes around him. Heavy robes swished against the ground, and Brite headed toward the Fraternitatem member in full dress.

So focused on the robes, he was surprised when he was rushed from behind. His arms flailed around him as he fell face first onto the sand.

Damn!

His back stung from the spell. Blood saturated his shirt. He pulled himself up and scurried forward on his forearms and legs. A heavy weight jumped atop him and thick legs pinned Brite's arms against his sides. Brite felt pressure against his lungs as he struggled to remove his attacker from him. The man squeezed his legs tighter around Brite, forcing the air from his lungs until they burned. When Brite twisted his hand to cast a jinx, his attacker applied even more pressure around his waist. Dizziness overtook Brite and his stomach roiled as nausea gripped him. He struggled against the man.

His muscles went slack; he couldn't suck in enough air. But Brite couldn't release his desire to live, couldn't stop thinking of Shiff waiting for him. He popped his shoulder as he twisted his arm, just enough to aim his palm at his attacker. As his vision darkened, he shot off a jinx. The Fraternitatem member was struck with such force, he flew from Brite and landed against the rock.

Finally free of the attacker, Brite coughed up sand and dirt, delighting in the air. He rolled to his back and stared at the grayish cloud above him.

Sounds became clearer, his breathing easier. Brite gingerly pulled himself up and coughed again. He blinked several times. As his vision cleared, he saw the shadow of a body against a rock and crawled forward. When the dust cleared, he saw a tall man in Fraternitatem robes sprawled unconscious against the rock, blood streaming from the back of his head. Brite checked his pulse and looked into his eyes. For now, the man was alive. He tied the him to the rock with a strong, magical rope. Once the man was secure, Brite checked him for athames, amulets, and other weapons. He found two knives attached to his legs, pulled them from their scabbards, and placed them in his own pockets. When he found nothing else, Brite glanced at the man's unconscious face before running back to the fight.

⚜

The French Wizard Guard had once been a highly respected organization. It all changed after their overzealous and illegal use of memory modification spells on their own people was discovered. Now the French Wizard Guard was considered the lowest of the low in many magical circles.

While the remaining wizard guards still had their jobs, they were relegated to chasing vampires and demons. Real investigations were given to other Wizard Guard units in Europe, which left Jory and Roland in a limbo, doing boring, unfulfilling work. While they were grateful for the opportunity to work in the field doing something useful, it didn't erase the bitterness they still had over the last six months during which they were punished for the actions of others. Seeing Fabien on the battlefield made them bitter.

"Fabien's been helping them," Jory scoffed as he leaned against the rock.

"Did they hire him too?" Roland spat.

"Can't. He's on probation. It's against international law."

"They better give us something important after this."

"Maybe we'll transfer to the U.S. Anything's better than what we've been doing," Jory said. He peered around the rock after the first alarm was sounded and teams exited from hiding.

"Only if we get into this action," Roland said.

It hadn't taken much time for the second alarm to be blared across the desert. "They're breaking free!" Jory shouted.

They ran from their hiding spot toward the open desert, following several Fraternitatem members.

They crossed to the next boulder, where Roland was clocked in the nose by escaping adversaries. Blood poured down his face into his mouth. He threw a punch of his own, cracking the jaw of the woman who had hit him. Her head flew backwards and she groaned. Rather than waiting for her to go for him, he ran at her, leading with his shoulder and knocking her into the rock.

Taller and heavier than her, he pinned her into the stone as she kneed him in the groin. He yelped and backed away, bent over and nauseated. She limped off; Jory followed her as she headed into the desert.

◈

It would have been naïve to think the Fraternitatem had no vehicles at their disposal. It was becoming common knowledge that not all Fraternitatem members were magical and those who were not needed the ability to move around. Lial believed a vehicle garage had to be somewhere in the cave system, under the sand or in the other cliff. What he couldn't find on any of the maps was a way into a garage. While he watched the fighting from afar, he surveyed the cliff opposite him, searching for seams in the stone.

He wiped sweat from his forehead with the bottom of his already drenched shirt. He took a sip of water and proceeded to feel the bumps and the grooves in the rock. It was a long cliff. He glanced at the cliff with the Cave of Ages and back to the one where he stood. They were a mile apart. He wondered if maybe they had missed a subterranean tunnel beneath them, joining both cliffs.

Scratching, squeaking, and scrapping, the rock behind him shuttered and shook. Lial ran behind the next boulder and watched as the rock scraped against itself. Crouched low, he peered out as the stone door slid open.

Lial refrained from raising a signal; management would see the cars and he didn't want draw attention to himself.

I might be able to stop them.

He snuck around the rock and tossed a spell at the second all-terrain vehicle as it exited the garage, blowing out the back tire. The car fishtailed in the sand as it tried to gain traction. The wheels continued to spin without moving and soon stopped, holding up the exodus. The driver exited, stared at the destroyed tire, cursed loudly, and kicked the car. Other cars began to skirt around the disabled vehicle as the angry driver searched for the person who had caused the tire to fail.

Lial moved to the other side of the rock and aimed his next spell at the next car to exit the cave. The back window blew apart and glass shattered across the inside of the vehicle. The angry driver got out of the car, stared at the back window, and turned to the direction from which the spell had come. Lial ducked behind the boulder. His breathing grew heavy and his heart pounded wildly.

Voices grew louder around him. Someone issued orders. Lial knelt low and glanced around the rocks. Several women were walking toward him. He stepped out from behind the rock and cast successive jinxes at the group. One fell, stiff as a board, and another fell to her knees, unable to move.

A third woman, glared at Lial, raised her arm and pointed at him. He whipped his arm roughly toward her, casting a jinx. She flew backwards, landing on a moving car.

Lial had little time to keep the flow from streaming out of the cave. He summoned several magical bombs, decided it was now or never, and rushed forward. With magic streaming from his palms, he pushed the bombs into the cave. Made of glass, they shattered easily, and their toxic magic burst forth. Unable to teleport for the wards around the outcropping, Lial ran for the fighting, hiding himself inside the storm of dust and sand that swirled around them all.

Lial ran through the bodies, some unconscious and some dead. He saw one woman alive and awake whose gaze met his.

She sat up; he ran at her and jumped over her like a hurdler. She shouted after him and pulled herself up. Still shaking from the magic that knocked her out, she held her gun and pointed at him, but he had immersed himself in the fighting.

Once he was far enough from the cars, he stopped, his breath ragged. He glanced back toward the caves. Several more cars had clogged up the exit, their engines billowing black smoke. He leaned against the stone and chuckled softly.

Lial wiped his face, which was covered in sweat, sand, and dirt. He peered around the rock. Men and women were escaping the vehicle caves. Many of them had burns from an acidic spell on their hands, faces, hair, and clothes.

"You ruined everything!" a female Fraternitatem member screeched.

Lial turned and faced her. She had a gun pointed at his head. He held his arms above his head as if to surrender, his palms pointing out at her.

He stepped back, glanced at his location and ran.

I need to get to the edge of the no-teleportation zone.

Tired, hot, and parched to the bone, he ran for the edge of the outcropping where the wards had been removed so the wizard guards could teleport.

He didn't dare look, but he knew she was following. He could hear several gun shots as he ran.

He saw the marker flag.

Almost there!

As he leapt over the imaginary line and teleported away, he felt a burning pain in his back.

⁓

Annie and Spencer rushed for the decaying portal that separated the Louisiana market from the main market. Even with the anxious voices echoing across both markets, Annie could hear the portal crackle and hum like the air during a thunderstorm.

"Hey, wait your turn, bitch!" screamed a patron waiting to exit. Spencer glared at him and the man slunk back

Annie pushed forward, the magic inside her now ravaging through her veins; she itched and burned from every inch of her body. The closer she got to the portal, the more she could see it pulse rapidly in sync with her heartbeat.

It feels me.

Bolts of lightning shot from both sides of the portal. It singed whoever stood near. Even bits of sand turned to glass in the electric onslaught. Spencer held Annie's shoulders as she touched the edge of the portal. Lightning struck her palms and she pulled away.

"Shit," she murmured as she stared at her burnt skin.

She held her breath and blew out the air as she placed her hands against the magic for a second time. A summer thunderstorm began to build; wind swirled from the portal and battered Annie's body. She tightened her muscles as Spencer supported her from behind.

She fed the portal with the magic that didn't belong to her. It flew from her palms in an icy purple haze and seemingly calmed the overused portal. The more magic she added to it, the more relief came to her. The itching lessened.

"Anyone who wants in or out, do it now!" Annie shouted above the wind. No one chose to re-enter; rather, they began a steady stream out of the main market and back through to Louisiana.

The portal fed on the magical traffic as wizards and witches escaped. It began to spin like a washing machine. Annie's arms shook as the foreign magic drained from her. When it needed more, the portal consumed hers. She felt exhilarated and strong as the magic left her.

Behind her, a dragon blew out its fiery breath, setting the nearest booth on fire. The stench of burnt canvas assaulted Annie as she returned her concentration to the portal and keeping it stable. Her muscles burned and shook. Her head pounded.

"What are you doing?" Spencer asked.

"The portal can't hold this many people. It's going to explode," she said. Her knees buckled and she fell to the ground—and yet she still held the portal.

"You're going to get sick if you keep adding magic," Spencer said.

Annie shrugged. Her phone beeped in her back pocket. Spencer pulled it out for her and read the message.

"You need to go!" he shouted.

"If I let go, we might get trapped inside," she shouted back.

Spencer stuck his hand inside. His magic, not as strong as hers, could barely keep the portal stable.

"Go!" he shouted.

Though Annie was tired, the magic no longer itched beneath her skin. She joined the fray of the escapees and ran through the Louisiana market.

∾

"Where are they going?" Petra murmured.

She followed the swishing hems of the Fraternitatem cloaks toward the back of the market. They stopped in the farthest corner. She hid behind a booth and watched as they held their hands to the wall.

"What are they doing?" she wondered, just before one of the men jammed an athame into the wall, opening a portal. "Shit!" she hissed.

Petra ran for the back corner and threw successive jinxes at the members, trying to keep them from entering the portal. One of the men made it through before she could reach him. The second was hit by a jinx and fell. His lower body remained in the market, but his upper body was in... She rushed forward and looked inside the portal. It was the Israeli desert.

"This is how they got around," Petra said softly to herself.

She glanced into the rocky outcropping. A small cry escaped her lips as she looked on the fighting. She reached for the unconscious man and dragged him against the sand. She took one last look at the fighting, sighed, and closed the portal before imprisoning the unconscious man at her feet.

CHAPTER 35

LIAL CRASHED INTO the ground, his face in the dirt. His body burned hot and wet, and the stench of iron filled his nose. He groaned lightly and felt for the source of his pain. His hand came away from his side covered in blood.

"Crap. Damn." He gritted his teeth and raised his head taking in his location. He was in the teleportation clearing outside Tartarus. "Why am I here?" he murmured.

He rolled himself over, his arms tired and shaking. He glanced at the early morning sky, pondering how he got here and how he was going to get back to Wizard Hall. His muscles spasmed and his side burned.

Lial summoned his phone. The screen was blurry, appearing only as a burst of colors, a mash of spots. He pressed the button and spoke into the smartphone. "Tartarus Prison phone number."

He groaned as the world swirled in front of him in multitudes of dusty browns and greens. He tried to keep his eyes open, to keep himself awake. "I'm Lial Peng," he said through shallow breath. "I'm in the teleportation spot. I need help."

He neither said goodby nor did he hang up; the voice on the phone continued to ask questions as the phone slipped from his fingers. Blood saturated his shirt from his waist to his chest—the upper band on his pants were now soaked. He groaned as his eyesight blurred. He assumed this is what eternity felt like as he waited for someone to at least check on him.

Soon a security guard entered the clearing and rushed forward. "Hi

Lial. I'm Scott. I'll stabilize you and get you to the hospital." He wrapped a pressure bandage over the wound, took his pulse, and glanced into Lial's eyes. "We weren't expecting anyone from the battle. How'd you get here?" Scott asked.

"Don't know," Lial said. His breath was quick, his lungs burned as they grasped for oxygen, his wound stung. Colors danced wildly before his eyes, streams of colors like a snake through the grass, dots popping like bubbles. "So cold," he murmured.

"It doesn't matter. You got here and you'll be okay," Scott said when he finished with Lial's basic care. "You've lost a lot of blood. We're almost there." He gently picked up Lial and teleported him to the hospital.

※

Dust kicked up around Brite as he ran through the boulders chasing the billowing red cloak. The woman he was following inserted herself into the wild crowd of people trying to escape. Losing sight of the hem of her cloak, Brite continued in the direction she had been running. He flicked his wrist and the sand dispersed, giving him a quick glance at the chaos.

There!

He spied her running for the open desert. When his spell dissipated, the sand reformed into a thick fog around them. Brite headed after.

Fireballs whizzed by and spells flew through the air and caught his arm, scorching his sleeve. He patted the embers and continued to follow the swirl of the red cloak.

As he exited the sandy fog, he searched the landscape; it was open, expansive, deserted, and scorching. He spotted her along an empty river-bed and ran after her.

With his wider strides, Brite easily caught up to her and lunged, forcing her into the sand. She wriggled underneath him. He quickly realized he had underestimated her strength. She pushed up and rolled him off of her, surprising him. While he was on his back, she jumped on him, grabbed his neck, and squeezed.

His arms flailed as he reached for her and punched at her side. Her eyes were wild, and her scowl was harsh and angry. She punched him in the head, in the jaw, in the neck. The world grayed. He raised his palms and cast the jinx; she flew up, pulling him with her.

As they flew, she released her hold on him. He landed feet from her and rolled away. The taste of iron was strong in his mouth, and his nose felt stuffed and achy. He wiped blood and sweat from his face and stared at her as she glowered at him.

From his knees, he cast successive spells, each one strong enough to knock her backward. In Brite's anger, his frustration of what he had endured with Annie fueled him. One spell after the other hit the woman. Her body jerked, her head rolled backwards, and she slipped to the sand. And yet Brite couldn't stop, even as her bruised and battered body lay still in the middle of the desert.

He felt a hand on his shoulder. "She's unconscious. I think you're done."

At first, Brite didn't recognize the heavy French accent. He lowered his palms and glanced behind his shoulder. Jory held out a hand and helped him up. Brite shook violently, shivered in the heat, and turned his head to vomit.

Jory let him be as he examined the woman in the sand. "She's alive, but barely. We need to get her to the holding pen." He picked her up and threw her over his shoulder.

Jory held his hand for Brite, who hobbled close behind. They were still within the confines of the magical wards; neither could teleport in or out of this section of desert.

"I don't think I can make it. Too dizzy." Brite slipped to his knees.

Jory pulled a bottle of water from his jacket. "Here. Take this and don't move. I'll come back for you when I can."

Brite watched as Jory headed back to the rock outcropping, leaving him alone in the sand.

❧

Below him, in the canyon, more members of the Fraternitatem were attempting to escape through a hidden garage and out into the open desert to never be heard from again.

"Come on, Lial," Cham murmured. He watched from his perch. The wizard guards seemed outnumbered, and yet, the holding pen was filling up.

Cham felt bad he couldn't effect change from up there. Only Annie could do that. He stared at his phone.

I need her magical boost to end this.

They had thought they had enough juice, enough magic to do this without her, but the sheer number of Fraternitatem members pouring from the caves was much more than they expected.

He texted Annie.

As he was about to teleport into the canyon, he heard the groaning and grunting. Behind him, Jason dangled from the cliff top.

"Damn it." Cham rushed to the edge, pulled him up from under his arms, and lay him in the dirt. He examined Jason. The older man's hands were red and raw, burnt by the poisonous gas and magic. Cham summoned his field pack. "You're human again. You should have worn gloves," he chided. He opened a bottle of water, poured out the liquid, and warmed it above his palm before placing it on Jason's injuries.

Jason grimaced.

"Sorry," Cham said as he added more magic to the spell. While the magic reduced the size of the welts, he knew it must still burn and ache. Cham worried Jason's hands might permanently be damaged by the magic. "It's not working," he said after a few minutes. "I'm going to cover them and you can go to the hospital."

He gently wrapped Jason's hands in gauze, then looked back at the fighting, conflicted about whether he should stay by Jason or join the rest of the wizard guards.

"I need to get you out of here," he said.

"No. Melichi will try to find Annie. I need to go after him," Jason argued.

"I called her. She's on her way." Cham felt a sinking feeling in the pit of his stomach.

"I told you not to call her!" Jason pulled his hands away from Cham and stumbled as he pulled himself up. He looked out at the desert, the battle that was raging in the rocky outcropping.

"We need her!" Cham insisted.

He turned his attention to Jason but was startled to see Melichi, who stared at his father-in-law, a lopsided grin across his lips, his palms facing them.

"And this is how it will end for you," Melichi jeered.

"At least Annie's safe and the magic will never be yours." Jason ripped off the bandages, ignoring the pain in his burning hands.

Jason and Melichi released their magic simultaneously. It streamed from their palms and exploded; the force of the impact threw them backwards. Jason slid along the rocky cliff until he reached for a rock at the edge and held on tightly.

Melichi flew and landed against one of the stones that covered an air vent. Poisonous gas and smoke rose from the opening. He scampered away and lunged for Jason.

Cham blocked Melichi's path with a jinx when Jason staggered up. As Melichi cast another spell, Cham lunged for Jason, pushing him out of the path of the jinx.

"Ahhhhh!" Cham screamed as he crumpled to the ground. His leg, from the knee down, was blown apart by the black magic and oozed with blood, muscle, and sinew.

Melichi grinned and aimed his palms at Cham. Jason stumbled up, swaying slightly. With determination, he ran for Melichi, wrapping his arms around the man and pulling him over the cliff.

At just that moment, Annie arrived and ran frantically toward her father. "No!" she screamed.

"Annie," Cham murmured.

Seeing the pool of blood and Cham's missing leg, Annie ran for him. "I need to get you out of here."

"No. Stop this now," Cham pleaded. He breathed deeply as he tried to stop from fainting. "Please save them."

She looked into the desert. The wizard guards were holding their own, but the ranks were thinning. She could hear them shouting and screaming. The chaos made her heart break. She ran back to Cham, lay him flat, and shrugged off her jacket, using it to raise his healthy leg. She wrapped a tight bandage around his thigh to stop the flow of blood, then touched his ashen face.

"Don't die on me," she ordered.

"I wouldn't dream of it," he groaned.

She ran for the cliff's edge. Her muscles shuddered and spasmed—so much magical energy had been released from her that day. When she raised her palms, magic flowed with ease. She parted the sand that hung above the outcropping, exposing everyone.

From the high perch, Annie clearly saw the wizard guards, outnumbered by the Fraternitatem.

Not for long!

Annie wasn't completely sure what her magic could do, but it didn't mean she couldn't do what she wanted to do.

"Fraternitatem," she murmured as she cast the spell into the valley.

Magic rushed from her body as if it understood her desire. A steady stream of magic searched out the men and women in the Fraternitatem robes.

How?

It wasn't for her to worry about now. She knew only that she could think it and it would happen, much like the magic of the portal in the basement of the Snake Head Letters.

Annie remember when she sat beside the portal, how she and the portal magic seemed as one, as if they breathed together.

She no longer had control of the magic as it flew from her palms. It was as if a dam broke.

This is too much!

Behind her, Cham moaned in pain.

Annie's arms shook as her magic was depleted. It hummed and zinged as it stretched out across the desert, searching out for the Fraternitatem as though murmuring the name would force the magic to find them.

I know it will.

Her magic hovered over the outcropping of rocks. Then it flew from the desert, searching for Fraternitatem members not in the desert: those that were in the markets, those that had hidden in their homes, those in Tartarus Prison.

Mom!

The magic continued to search for every member of the Fraternitatem of Solomon. All of the men, women, and children who had magically pledged themselves to the group or who had signed a contract in lieu of magic if they had none. The magic contained Annie's fury and anger as it sought out anyone under the umbrella of the Fraternitatem. Wherever they were, they'd be rendered incapable of movement. Annie didn't care that this could potentially expose magic to the nonmagical world. It was too important.

Her legs trembled and her hands shook uncomfortably. She held the magic as long as she could, but it was too much. She fell to her knees and let the magic go. She stared at the motionless Fraternitatem members across the sand.

Cham moaned again.

Summoning what little energy she had, she scrambled to him, he was sweaty and ghostly white. Wrapping her arms around him, she teleported him away.

CHAPTER 36

THE MAGIC STOPPED.

The dust settled.

Magical energy still buzzed in the desert.

Giants and wizard guards worked side by side in silence as they pulled Fraternitatem members from the rocks and locked them into the holding pen, which was quickly filling with unconscious people.

The jinx had been an awesome sight as it flew from the mountaintop and covered the desert. Annie had delivered the spell with such strength and accuracy, only Fraternitatem members were effected.

Shiff returned to the middle of the rocks frantically searching for Brite. He stopped at an unconscious Fraternitatem member and dragged him back to the holding pen. He couldn't stop looking around for Brite even as he ran an injured wizard guard to the medical station, where staff had been waiting.

Shiff continued to cross the two-mile-by-two-mile wide rocky land until he had scoured it four times. He hadn't found Brite yet and he was ready to drop from exhaustion.

He pulled one more man from the path and carried him over his shoulders. His arms and shoulders ached and shook, while his legs felt as though he was walking through gelatin. He handed the man to the giants.

Shiff glanced up toward the cliffs where Cham and other teams had waited for the fighting to begin, where Annie had shot off the strongest spell he had ever seen. As he returned to the rocks, he saw other members of the Wizard Guard and members of the VAU as they assisted with the cleanup.

He recognized the team from Amborix, the teams from the satellite offices in the U.S., but he still didn't see Michael.

I wonder if Michael took someone to the Hall.

Shiff leaned against a large boulder, put his head against the hard rock, and took a sip of water. He turned and saw the hem of two more red cloaks lying in the sand. Gingerly, he pulled himself from the rock and found Roland kneeling beside a man and a woman. Roland glanced up and grimaced. Blood had dried from his forehead to his chin.

"I need help," Roland rasped.

Shiff examined the woman, checking her pulse and looking into her eyes.

"The spell was strong," Roland said. He stood carefully and pulled up a short thin man, placing him over his shoulder.

"It was. It knocked them out cold," Shiff replied.

They were silent as they trekked to the holding pen to deliver the unconscious pair.

"Have you seen Michael Brite?" Shiff asked before he re-entered the rocks.

"No. I was wondering where my partner, Jory, was." They stopped at the first large boulder. "That spell was something. I hope Annie is okay."

"It was so focused. So strong. I'm sure she's fine," Shiff said, though he was trying to convince himself. He had seen the magic she wielded, how quickly the magic felled only the Fraternitatem members, as if she could think it and it would be. Remembering the power frightened him and he didn't know why. He shuddered as he and Jory moved on to the next red cloaks, pulling them from the desert.

Brite lay in the sand. The heat and sun burned his skin, and his mouth was dry. He imagined what it would be like to see Jory come back for him, for anyone to find him, for that matter. Several times he looked toward the fighting and thought he saw someone walking toward him, but each time it was merely a mirage that shimmered in the sunlight.

He shivered in the heat. Closing his eyes, he took a sip of the last of the water. He turned his gaze back toward the outcropping, where he could see movement but nothing more clear than that.

What happened?

Brite shook as he waited until he finally saw Shiff's form glide across the sand. He closed his eyes, grateful that Shiff found him, and smiled. When he opened his eyes, ready to greet him, Shiff wasn't there.

He began to cry. All his hopes and dreams seemed to float away from him, leaving nothing but his fear. He heaved as he cried, and yet, no tears fell. Not in this heat, not now.

"Sebastian," he murmured.

Two arms reached down for him and pulled him up. He floated upwards, afraid to open his eyes in case he saw that he was no longer in the desert, that maybe there was an afterlife and he was now in hell.

His head rolled toward a taut body. The stench of body odor and burnt embers filled his nose. The arms that held him shook violently. Brite opened his eyes.

"I'm sorry it took so long," Jory said, his voice gravelly and tired. He limped away from the fighting.

"Where are we going?" Brite managed to ask.

"To the teleportation line. It's time to go home." Jory's knee buckled and he held Brite tighter.

Brite glanced up at Jory and smiled as the other guard carried him out into the desert where the protections wards had been taken down. When they arrived, Jory glanced back at the outcropping of rocks and teleported Brite from the desert.

⟋

Scott rushed Lial to the Wizard Hall hospital, bursting through the doors. "I need help!" he shouted.

The medical team was prepared for any wizard guards that entered; extra staff had been brought in. Dr. Christine was the first to meet him.

"Oh, my," she said. "I need nonmagical medicine, now."

She stared at Lial in Scott's arms and summoned a stretcher. She and Scott placed him gently on his back. She did a basic assessment, checking his pulse and eyes and listening to his heart; but she could feel from his skin that it was too late. She shook her head.

"He didn't make it?" Scott asked tearfully.

"No." She summoned a crisp, white sheet and placed it over Lial. As the director of Black Magical Medicine, she worked with the Wizard Guard a lot. She knew them all personally. When Lial was wheeled to the morgue, she let herself cry.

⁓

Annie landed outside the hospital doors, cast a spell, and threw the glass doors open. They bounced against the wall. One shattered with the force.

Nauseated and worried, she held Cham in her arms. He lay unconscious. His leg pumped blood profusely around his protruding shinbone.

Dr. Christine flew from the emergency room with a stretcher. She stopped short when she saw Cham on the ground and Annie covered in his blood.

"Help him," Annie murmured.

Dr. Christine, along with an orderly, pulled Cham up and lay him on the stretcher, racing him inside.

Annie stumbled after them but was stopped in the waiting room.

"You look like you need help too," a medical student told her. He gently led her back inside.

"I need to see Cham," she murmured.

"In just a bit," the medical student said as Annie fell to her knees.

⁓

Annie turned quickly. Her eyes popped open. She blinked several times as the light from above blinded her. It took her several moments to figure out where she was and what had happened. Her father's face clouded her memory. She couldn't stop picturing his arms around Melichi as he pulled the man from the cliff.

Dad!

She felt nauseated as the memory returned. It felt like she was living it all over again. Her brain struggled to remember more. Her eyes darted across the room as she took in the sounds, the footsteps across the floors, the monitors beeping wildly.

The hospital! Cham!

She raised her hand. It was hooked to an IV. Weak and exhausted, she pulled herself up and swung her legs over the side of the bed. She held her breath as she yanked the tape from her skin, held the needle firmly, and pulled it from her arm.

She ignored the blood as it spurted across her arm and hopped off the bed. The world spun in front of her and she slipped to the ground.

"Annie!" Cham's younger brother, Danny, a fourth-year medical student, rushed up to her. "You need treatment," he said and helped her to the chair.

"I don't need treatment. I need to see Cham!" she shouted. She whipped the nasal cannula from her nose and tossed it to the floor.

"You need fluid. I'll go find him. He's got to be in the waiting room," Danny said as he stabilized her back on the bed.

"Cham. He's here. He… he…" Her skin began to crawl with magic; she feverishly scratched at herself.

"Let me get you to bed." He glanced at her hand where the IV needle had been. "You pulled it out. I'll start with the other hand."

She pulled her arm away. "You're not listening. I need to see him. His leg is horribly injured!" she screamed, clenching her fists. Magic billowed from her palms.

"He—let's get you to bed," Danny said as his hands shook.

"I want to see him now!" she screamed.

Danny knew better than to fight her. He led Annie from the room. She stumbled against him. Dr. Christine exited Cham's room toward Annie's panicked cries.

"You can barely stand. You're going to stroke out with the magic. Back to bed," she instructed.

"No! I need to see him *now!*" Annie screamed and pulled from Dr. Christine. The doctor waved for a wheelchair and sat Annie down.

"What happened to him?" Danny asked, each word filled with worry.

"Call your family. He lost most of his leg and is bleeding profusely. We're prepping him for surgery," Dr. Christine advised. "Come, Annie.

I'll let you see him and then you need treatment. I won't have you stroking out. He needs you now." She wheeled Annie inside Cham's makeshift room.

Cham lay unconscious. Tubes poked out from his arms and nose, and monitors beeped and flashed.

"He can't hear you and you need to get stable," Dr. Christine said.

"No. No. No!" Annie shrieked.

Dr. Christine held her shoulder firmly. "Now, Annie," she said.

Annie slumped in the chair, too tired to fight, and let herself be wheeled from the room. As they left, Don and Marina rushed into the emergency room, followed by Kathy, Ryan, Samantha, and John.

"Annie, how is…" Marina could barely keep from crying.

Magic billowed from Annie's hand at an alarming rate. She trembled.

"Cham is in good hands. Please try to calm yourself," Dr. Christine said.

Behind her, the surgical team wheeled Cham from his ER room to the operating room. Marina cried out. Annie sobbed as she watched him being taken away. Her magic continued to flow from her hands, gathering around her head, and wrapping her in light. The world swirled around her.

She could hear monitors beeping around. Graham entered the area and spoke with Ryan. Annie strained to catch their conversation, but the stress overtook her and the world went blank.

"No. He's still in surgery. We don't know how long it will be," Ryan said into the phone. He placed himself away from the group as he spoke to Graham Lightner. While Cham was indisposed, Ryan took to directing the final stages of the battle with the Fraternitatem. Hundreds of members were being housed not only in Tartarus but also, the wizard prisons in several other countries. The cells everywhere were filling fast.

The VAU enlisted the help of the Zoology Society and other departments in the Wizard Hall as they collected as many artifacts as they could. Robin Price was cataloging and packing them as they were brought in. Dead and injured wizard and witches were brought to the hospital for treatment or prepped for burial. Ryan only listened half-heartedly to the updates as he looked on at the family and friends assembled.

John Chamsky tried his best to comfort Samantha. She was near catatonic as she came to terms with the death of her father for the second time in nine years. Danny and Jimmy Chamsky sat with their parents as they attempted the same. Marina would cry and stop and then start again as they waited for word that Cham had come through the surgery.

Ryan glanced inside Annie's room. She was unconscious, which he thought was a blessing as Cham fought for his life. There would plenty of time for her to come to grips with everything that happened.

Ryan walked the corridors and found an empty spot near the nurse's station. "Thanks, Graham," he said. "Use whatever department you need to help clean up. Have you heard from the guards at the market?"

"Annie kept the portal open long enough for people to get out. Spencer kept the magic up when she left. There are about seventy-five Fraternitatem trapped inside the market. Petra Johnson has a pretty good handle on the inside. Whatever Annie did knocked out all Fraternitatem members everywhere."

Ryan knew he should be more upset, but he smiled as Graham gave him the report. Annie's magic had done what she asked of it and they had won. The Fraternitatem of Solomon had been torn apart that day. For that he was happy. For everything else, there would be time to deal with the sadness and the pain.

"And what do we do if there were Fraternitatem members not in the market and not in the desert?" Ryan asked, though he thought he knew the answer.

"Bucky Hart and the telecommunications department are on the lookout for weird illnesses or people just keeling over unconscious."

Ryan nodded. "Thanks, Graham. Keep me apprised. I'll take over the wizard guards until Cham is healthy enough to do so."

After ending the call with Graham, Ryan strolled back to Annie's room and watched as Kathy and Dave sat beside her, holding her hands, moving hair from her face. Kathy glanced up, tears welling in her eyes, and then she glanced back down at Annie.

Ryan returned to the waiting room to offer what little comfort he thought he could to the family members there.

❦

Emily and Shiloh packed the few things they had with them. It was the day they had waited for, the end of the Fraternitatem and the day they could return home.

"Are we going home, Mom?" Shiloh asked as he placed the last comic book in his backpack and zipped it up.

"We'll go back to the townhouse first. After that, anywhere you want." She smiled and touched his red hair.

Early that morning, Emily and Shiloh had been informed about what happened in the desert. Emily had worked very hard to seem genuinely upset by her daughter's injuries, by Jason's death again, and by Samantha's reaction—but in truth, Melichi's death was what she reacted to. No one was any the wiser.

She glanced at her son. She was finally free to raise him the way she wanted to, away from the Fraternitatem. But then, her anxieties kicked in. She hadn't lived as an adult on her own in many years.

Can I do this?

She knew she'd return to the townhouse first, at least for a few weeks as she figured out her next step.

When they were packed, they exited the room at the same time Arden and Ariana left theirs. The two women were also being sent back home now that their lives were no longer in jeopardy from the Fraternitatem. Arden looked surprised when she saw Emily and merely smiled and nodded.

"Hi, Dr. Blakely," Shiloh said with a smile.

"Hi, Shiloh," she said quickly before she and Ariana were rushed from the entrance hall and led to the teleportation location.

Shiloh appeared dejected.

"It's okay. You and me, kid. Ready?"

Shiloh nodded as they, too, were led back out into the world for the rest of their lives to begin.

CHAPTER 37

"WHY DIDN'T YOU tell me you were human?" Annie asked Jason as he sat down beside her.

"You wouldn't let me go if you knew. I couldn't help you if I didn't go to the desert," he said.

"I watched you die," Annie cried. Even here, wherever here was, she couldn't shake that moment when she saw Jason go over the cliff's edge.

"But I saved Cham and that's more important."

"You didn't tell me you were human," Annie said again.

Jason glanced at his daughter curiously. "You knew, though, didn't you?"

Annie nodded. "I'm sorry, Dad. I never should have brought you back."

Jason shrugged. "You did and I saw my girls again. I'm grateful for that."

Jason held Annie's hand and stared at the hole from the IV needle. "He'll be okay. It will be a struggle at first, but you're both strong. He'll be fine," he told her.

"Mom's still coming," Annie said. She yawned, aware of her exhaustion.

"Yeah, she will. Be careful."

Annie yawned again. "I will." She glanced at her hands. For now, the magic was calm; she felt no itching.

"I'm going to miss you, Dad."

"I'm always with you. Don't forget that," Jason said as Annie began to stir.

Annie felt as though her spirit was re-entering her body. Warmth covered her as she flickered her eyes open. She blinked rapidly in the blinding light.

"Welcome back," Dave said as she glanced around the room. Beside her, Kathy held her hand.

"Cham's doing well. He's out of surgery," Dave continued. He fiddled with the hospital table, pushing it closer to her. "Are you hungry? The nurses made me promise I'd get you to eat."

Annie shook her head. She reached for the bed controls and lifted herself up. Once she was more comfortable, she closed her eyes. Cham's face and her dad's face intermingled in her thoughts. She trembled as her eyes filled with tears again.

"Oh, sweetie." Kathy rubbed the back of her hand.

"I'm sorry. I'm not in the mood," Annie murmured.

"Annie. I'm so sorry about your dad." Dave held her right hand, which was free from the IV.

She shivered from exhaustion, from the magical energy loss. "And Melichi?"

"No one could have survived that fall. I'm really sorry."

Annie began to shake. "Can I have a warm blanket, please?" Kathy nodded and left for the nurse. Annie rolled to her side and glanced at Dave. "I knew he wasn't coming back."

"How?"

Annie shook her head. "He wasn't a ghost anymore."

"He was human again?"

Annie nodded. "He started aging. Ghosts don't age." She felt the tears rising up again.

Kathy returned with a warm blanket that quickly eased Annie's shivering.

When Dr. Christine finished with Cham's parents, she came to Annie and sat down beside her. "I'm glad you're awake." She touched Annie's hand and watched magic slowly billow from her palm. "Itching much?"

"A little. Can I see Cham?" she murmured.

"He's awake and will only see you," Dr. Christine said.

Annie nodded. She let Dave and Kathy help her from the bed and into a wheelchair. Her head fell sideways. She could barely make eye contact when she saw Don and Marina in the waiting room. Her heart broke when she saw Sami in the far corner.

Annie entered Cham's room. While he seemed small and frail in the hospital bed, he was sleeping peacefully in his drug-induced haze. Her eyes traveled to his legs. She could see the outline of his right leg, firm and straight, ending in his foot lying on the side. Beside it was only a flat thin blanket where the left leg below the knee had been.

She took up his hand and rubbed his palm with her thumb like he always did for her.

When his eyes fluttered open, Annie said, "Hi, baby." She couldn't think of anything else to say with the lump in her throat.

"Hi," he murmured as he squeezed her hand weakly.

Annie pulled herself up and sat on the bed beside him, kissing his forehead, his cheek, his mouth.

"Hi," she said.

His eyes opened. He touched her hair; the large tube sticking from his hand grazed her cheek. The machine in the room beeped rapidly and slowed. Annie sucked in air and held her breath for a moment.

"I love..." he began, but the sedative made him sleepy, his mouth didn't work.

"Don't talk. Just rest. You've been injured."

"Lost leg..." he murmured.

She squeezed his hand and watched him sleep.

CHAPTER 38

THE SOUTH AFRICAN wizard guards had watched in awe as Annie's spell had reached the Fraternitatem, leaving everyone else in the market untouched. While the Fraternitatem lay frozen on the ground, the wizard guards had assisted everyone else out of the market through the Louisiana portal.

"Now what?" Joseph asked Petra as they stared at the fallen enemy.

"Open a portal to Tartarus Prison in the U.S. and get them transferred out."

The VAU had left the desert and entered the new market. They worked quickly as they opened a portal to the teleportation location outside of Tartarus Prison. Eight hours after everyone in the Fraternitatem had been brought to the overcrowded prison, Petra and her wizard guards stood at the center of the black market.

"Do we shut it down?" Joseph asked. The fifty-year-old had attempted to make a living at the market, a rough, rowdy, deadly place. He looked on at the empty booths. Some were burnt from wayward spells or dragons shooting out fire spray. Others were still filled with merchandise, their owners putting things right, cleaning off the dust and debris as if nothing had happened.

"No. But we watch it. And never allow absolute power to corrupt it. Well, at least more than it will naturally be." She motioned him to follow her and he held his arm with his missing hand against his chest as walked through the booths with her. Their team had begun finding hidden

Fraternitatem members throughout the booths and corralling dragons, elves, and other magical creatures lost in the stalls. "Is this too much for you?" Petra asked.

Joseph laughed. "No. It is where I should be. So, how shall we monitor the market?"

It was Petra's turn to laugh. "I suspect the U.S. Wizard Guard has some ideas on that. I have some of my own. One of which would have a permanent booth installed here." They walked to Joseph's booth and looked inside.

"This is where you'd like me to work?" he asked cautiously.

"No. Not you directly. I'll request a rotation of wizard guards to take turns. People from all throughout the world. That should be fair. We should know what happens here."

She climbed over the table separating the passageway from the inside of the tent and began to clear away the debris. Joseph stood on the other side, straightening the wares with his good hand.

He didn't notice at the time, but an elderly gentleman was limping toward him. The gentleman stopped at their booth and examined the items on the table.

"How can we help you?" Petra asked.

The man looked at her blankly.

"Sir, can I help you?" Petra asked again.

"Annie Pearce did this?" he asked

"Who are you?" Petra asked.

"Not important." He glanced at the booth across the aisle, which had been charred at the edges. Items had fallen from the shelves. "I told that girl to run away. Good thing she didn't listen." He struggled to breathe and leaned against the table.

"Sir, can I help you with something?" Petra asked him again.

"Nah. I just wanted to see for myself what that girl did."

"If you give me your name, I'd be happy to tell her you asked about her," Joseph offered.

He waved his hand at them, tossed an envelope on the table and shuffled away for the last time.

"Who was that?" Joseph asked. He picked up the envelope and looked at the writing on the front.

To: Annie Pearce

From: AM

"AM?" Joseph asked.

"Better get that to Annie."

⁂

While Cham slept in the Intensive Care Unit, Annie walked the halls and read the names on the doors. Of the ten severely injured wizard guards, she only knew Michael Brite and Jory Poulin. She touched the name plates as she walked past. Her heart was heavy for the men that had been lost, especially Lial Peng. Annie sighed as she stood outside of Brite's room. She wasn't sure what to say to him.

"You did it."

The heavy French accent was familiar to her. She turned and saw Fabien standing beside Jory's room, a card and flowers in his grip.

"I guess so." She assessed him. He was battle worn, with a large cut across his cheek and two black eyes. "How was the fight?" she asked.

"Came out alive, Annie Pearce. Caught a few Fraternitatem." He smiled and wiped sweat from his forehead.

"Thank you," Annie murmured.

Fabien held up the flowers and pointed to the door. Annie nodded and watched him enter Jory's room. She held the handle to Brite's room but remained there for some time, not wanting to disturb the private conversation inside.

"He'll be okay," Dr. Christine said as she walked up to Annie.

"That's good to know." Annie glanced at his name on the nearly closed door.

"You need to rest."

Annie looked at her hand. While the magic still floated from her palm, it was only coming in small puffs. "I know. I'm fine right now."

The magic is mine now.

"You need to rest. You're exhausted. In time, we'll find a way to rid you of the magic permanently."

Annie leaned against the wall. "No. You won't. It's mine now." She watched it puff above her palm. When she closed her fist and opened it quickly, the magic sputtered at her command.

"It looks like you can control it now."

Annie nodded and placed her hands under her arms to hide them. "Thank you for saving Cham's life. All their lives." She was grateful that eighty-nine of the one hundred and three wizard guards had made it home that night.

"It's my job. And part of that job is to get you back to your room."

"Some died."

"I know. Annie. It's not surprising in a battle. You know that." Dr. Christine gave Annie a hug. Annie shivered in her arms. "I don't mean to make light of this, but you need to concentrate on yourself right now. Get back to bed and sleep. And then you can mourn for... everyone."

Annie acquiesced and let Dr. Christine lead her to her room and help her to bed.

"Please sleep," Dr. Christine sad softly. "You need to get your strength back."

Annie nodded absently and let herself settle for the night.

∽

Shiff watched Brite sleep fitfully, restlessly. He moaned in his sleep and his leg twitched. While Shiff didn't know how close his partner had come to death, he knew at least that the battle had done this to him and that he had been that way for hours.

In his worry, Shiff paced from one end of the single room to the other. He stretched his arms, his back, his legs. He, too, was sore. When he heard noises elsewhere in the hospital, he felt his blood pressure spike. He felt dizzy, hungry.

He turned to the window and watched the purple and orange against the sky as the sun set.

Brite groaned again.

The battle in the desert filled Shiff's thoughts. Annie's powers were strong. He wasn't sure if he should be scared or look on her with awe.

Brite's groans grew louder as he woke. Shiff sat on the edge of the bed and picked up the other man's hand. It quivered in his. They had been wizard guard partners for seven years, first becoming close as friends and now as something more. He saw it when he looked at his partner. The feelings were growing for both of them.

He watched him wake and found a washcloth and water, wetting it and placing it on Brite's parched lips.

What happened to you?

All Shiff knew was that Jory had found Brite and brought him here, though Jory himself wasn't much better off. Shiff sat with Brite, waiting for him to wake rather than bothering Jory to find out the details.

There was time.

Brite's eyes flitted open and darted across the room as he came to the realization of where he was.

He coughed.

"Hey. You're awake." Brite licked his lips. Shiff gave him the wet towel. "You were found in the desert. Jory brought you in."

Brite nodded and closed his eyes. "Did we win?" His mouth was dry and his throat sounded sore.

"Yeah. Annie's powers were scary amazing." Shiff said. He used the towel and wiped Brite's face. The sand left streaks against his cheeks.

"I knew she would be," Brite murmured.

Shiff fumbled with the hospital bed's controls until Brite was upright, then helped him drink from the plastic hospital cup.

"Thanks," Brite said. He lay back against the bed and stared at the ceiling.

"I thought I lost you," Shiff whispered. Tears welled in his eyes when he remembered the desert, the feeling of not finding Brite, the relief in learning he was taken away.

Brite reached for his hand. "You told me not to die."

"I'm glad you listened." He smiled at Brite. "I was so worried."

"I have too much to live for." Brite attempted to sit up. Shiff fiddled with the bed controls some more. "Did everyone make it?" he finally asked.

Shiff averted his gaze and looked at his hands.

"Who died?"

"Not now. Just... maybe tomorrow when things are brighter."

Brite nodded and closed his eyes. "Tomorrow," he murmured. "Is Annie okay?"

"Yes. You should rest. I'll tell you everything tomorrow."

"Will we be?" Brite asked.

"That depends." Shiff offered a relieved smile. "We've never had a proper conversation about it."

Brite opened his eyes. "I'm no longer confused about us. I'm sorry how it was when I came back from the past. It was..." He sighed.

"Overwhelming."

Brite chuckled lightly, then coughed from the effort.

Shiff handed him the water and helped him take several sips. Brite shook his head when he was done.

"I know I love you. I'm here now because of it," Brite said, his voice growing stronger and less grave.

Shiff moved closer and kissed his partner gently on the lips. After a moment, he pulled away and touched his cheek. "Tomorrow is the first day of the rest of our lives."

"Yes, it is." Brite raised the blanket to his chin and smiled at Shiff before letting sleep take him again.

Shiff stayed by his side until morning, long after the sun came up.

Graham Lightner pulled together a field pack. The VAU had expected emergency calls to be intercepted by the telecommunications department, alerting them of unconscious Fraternitatem scattered across the planet. The evening after the battle, Max White walked the first of the calls to Graham's office.

"Hi, Graham. I have something for you," Max said.

"Does that mean we found one?" Graham pushed his field pack aside.

"New Orleans. Male, approximately forty years old, six foot six, two hundred and fifty pounds. He was found in an alley, unresponsive. The call came about ten minutes ago. Here's what Bucky's been able to find." Max handed him a thin file.

After perusing the data, Graham glanced at Max. "I'm surprised we haven't found more."

"I just sent two calls to the Middle Eastern Guard before I came. If I had to guess, I'd say the Fraternitatem has tight control over the members and kept them close. But I'm not paid to guess," Max said.

"Well, Max, I'd take your guess. Thanks for this. My team and I will take care of it."

Max nodded quickly and exited. Graham sent a text.

Within twenty minutes, his team of six was back at Wizard Hall and in Graham's cubicle. "We have one. He's at Tulane University Hospital." He described the man and his condition.

"What's the play?" Skye Allen asked.

"I need two at Tulane to reverse the spell." Graham held up a thin folder. Skye and one other raised their hands and took the folder. Graham continued. "Reverse the spell and find any blood samples taken. All magic needs to be removed from the blood. Two more need to get to the Middle Eastern Wizard Guard. Give them the spell reversal and implore them to do the same. Bucky—" Graham pointed to Bucky leaning against the wall in the corner of the cubicle. "Two need to go with Bucky and work on all medical records for the three in question. Work on the protocol to make the changes so if more of these unfortunates appear on our radar, we can move in quickly. Any questions?"

With that, the department split into three teams of two and headed off to reduce the risk of exposure.

CHAPTER 39

IN TOTAL, FOUR wizard guards died in the desert. A joint funeral was held for them in the courtyard of the U.S. Wizard Hall. Four pyres burned, and Annie cried when Lial was consumed in the fire. She would miss him. On that day, she decided she was done feeling guilty for events that took place long before she was born. It was time, she knew, to move on with her life.

With that, she sat on the dock at the edge of the island that housed Tartarus and looked into the lake. She found peace here as the water lapped against the shore, wetting the sand.

In her lap were two letters, one of which was from Archibald Mortimer. Not much of a man of words, he simply wrote:

Girl, I told you to run and hide. Glad you didn't.

A. Mortimer

She had smiled when she read it the first time; now it made her chuckle.

The second letter was addressed to her in Sturtagaard's flowery handwriting. She had grimaced when she read it but did as he requested and sat at the dock in the lake, waiting for him.

When she heard his footsteps, she didn't turn. She swung her legs like she used to when she was a kid. She enjoyed the sun as it beat down on her skin.

Sturtagaard limped as he walked. At one point, his shoe caught in the space between the wooden slats of the dock and he nearly fell. Annie stifled a laugh. When he reached the end, he lowered his lanky body and sat beside her. The chill off his skin made her shudder.

Sturtagaard handed her a stake.

Annie glanced at the stake and returned her gaze to the lake as it shimmered in the sun. "I'm not in the mood."

"None of this would have happened if I didn't tell them about you. That makes you in the mood," Sturtagaard quipped.

It no longer mattered to her anymore. What was done was done. She was grateful for the time she had with her father again and felt a little guilty she hadn't spent the time more wisely. But, it wasn't Jason's time. Losing him again didn't hurt any less; the pain pierced her heart in a way she couldn't explain.

Annie stared at the stake, which was carved into such a point that she wouldn't have to push hard to pierce his breastbone. "Why don't you just go off and do whatever it is that you do?"

"I've lived my life. I've lived other people's lives. I'm done," Sturtagaard admitted.

"Killing you doesn't change what happened. I actually don't care about you anymore," Annie said. She returned the stake to him. Since she returned from the desert, the magic billowed from her palm at a slower pace, but it still followed her. She made a fist and released the magic until it dissipated. She was certain now that it would never go away.

"I have no place to go," Sturtagaard said.

Annie laughed. "I don't care."

"I need to be done of this earth," Sturtagaard said.

"Then kill yourself. I'm done with you." Annie stood and left the vampire alone to stew in whatever emotions he had.

⁌

"Have you seen Mom yet?" Samantha asked.

"No. Between the funeral and Cham, I haven't stopped by the townhouse," Annie explained. She paced the den as she spoke on the phone. She didn't want to talk to Samantha about their mom.

"She's leaving. The Wizard Council said she was brainwashed and therefore won't be charged with a crime. She was given permission to go back to Israel and the Middle Eastern Wizard Guard will check on her periodically," Samantha said.

"Okay. I guess that's good for them." Annie cleared her things from the sofa. She had taken to eating meals in front of the television. She carried her dirty dishes to the kitchen.

"You're okay letting her go?" Samantha asked, nearly crying.

"Sami, she came here to kill me. I'm having trouble with the whole thing. Just because she's leaving doesn't mean you can't see her," Annie said.

"Annie, you need to talk to her. You can't just let her go," Samantha pleaded.

"Sami. My heart is broken. Dad is gone. I can't. I just can't see her. Have you seen Zola at all? I haven't seen her since I left for the desert."

"I—come to think of it, I haven't seen her either. Have you called for her?"

The doorbell rang. Annie peered through the peep window. "Actually, I'll have to do that later. Emily's at the door. I'll call you later."

"Be nice," Samantha said.

"Always."

Annie placed the phone on the stair and let her mother in. Emily nervously entered the house where she once raised her children. She glanced up the stairs and into the front room.

"Hi, Mom. Come on in. Have a seat."

Emily nodded and sat on the sofa, still taking in the house and the changes Annie had made. "I remember when we bought this house. Your dad and I looked at, I don't know, maybe twenty different places. I loved this one." She smiled at the memory. "You did a good job updating it."

"Thanks. Is there something I can help you with before you go?" Annie asked as she sat on the ottoman opposite her mother.

"I'm leaving and I wanted to say goodbye. Can't a mother do that?"

Annie smiled cautiously. "Of course. I'm sorry I haven't had a chance to see you." She glanced at the door. "Um. Where's Shiloh?"

Emily smiled. "He's getting ready for our trip."

"Too bad. I'd love to say goodbye."

Emily reached for Annie's hands. Annie felt her mom's hands trembling in her own.

"I want a relationship with you," Emily said. "Sami agreed. You can come out for a visit. We'll take you all over. Shiloh really wants to get to know you."

Annie pulled away. "I—I suppose we could work something out. Why didn't Shiloh come?"

In her heart, Annie knew she wanted nothing to do with Emily and Shiloh; it was much too painful. But her gut told her not to upset her mother in case there really was a trigger.

"Shiloh is a boy. He's confused. I thought it best if he remained at home and packed." Emily began to cough.

"You okay? Can I get you something?" Annie asked.

"I could use a glass of water," Emily said. "I feel parched."

Annie nodded and headed to the kitchen. She filled a glass with water from the spout on the refrigerator. When she turned, Emily was in the kitchen. Annie startled.

"I really like it here. It's so comfortable. So big," Emily said as she took a sip of water. She stepped closer to Annie, who looked at her with curiosity and careful observation.

"When are you going back home?" Annie asked. She kept a watchful eye on Emily's face; her demeanor changed. Annie felt a cool chill from her mother. Emily didn't blink as she remained focused on her youngest daughter.

Sami, call for help! Annie shouted in her head.

Emily drained the glass and handed it to Annie, though she could have placed it on the counter herself. As Annie took the cool glass, Emily whipped out her hand and stuck something sharp into Annie's neck. The glass slipped from Annie's fingers and shattered on the floor as she fell.

≪≫

Opening her eyes, Annie found herself on the ground, unable to move. She blinked rapidly, confused for a moment by her predicament. Her eyes darted around her kitchen until she found Emily above her, smiling.

"They told me you'd be blindsided." Emily chuckled and knelt beside Annie, touching her cheeks and smashing them into weird shapes.

Annie would have cringed if she could have moved her head. "What did you do?"

Emily showed her an empty syringe. "It's filled with a potion that quickly renders a person paralyzed. Easy peasy." She dug in her pocket and pulled out a vial for Annie to see. "And this potion will give you a heart attack, one that won't be detectable." Emily waved the small vial in front of Annie before donning rubber gloves. Annie's eyes widened as Emily opened the jar.

Sami, help me! Sami!

Annie mentally screamed at her sister, hoping her telepathy would work and her second request would inspire Samantha to do something. Emily dropped the stopper on the vial. Annie tried to glare at her mother, but her face was nearly frozen now.

"What was the trigger?" she mumbled. Her lips were barely able to move; she couldn't take in a breath to raise her voice.

Emily's smile was cold, emotionless, unreal. "I was told that under no circumstances were you allowed to live. You cost them everything. Most of them are in jail. The rest will be back."

Annie held her breath as she looked from her mother to the vial and back again. Her panic grew so strong; she began to whimper. Emily grabbed Annie's chin and pried her mouth open.

Samantha! Emily's going to kill me!

Annie screamed in her head, hoping against hope that her telepathy could reach her sister in time. Annie's eyes darted from Emily to the hallway door. Unable to move and barely able to speak, she tried again to twist her head away from her mother's grasp.

While Annie lay incapacitated, Emily prepared a small dropper of potion for her and held it for Annie to see. "This will kill you. All I have to do is…"

Annie closed her eyes and concentrated on the vial, the stopper that was nearly at her lips.

My magic. The telepathy? Can I use my powers without my hands?

Annie imagined herself jinxing Emily, concentrated her whole being on that one act. Emily flew against the cabinet doors and bounced to the ground.

The front door burst open. Annie heard footsteps running for the kitchen. While Spencer jumped over Emily to reach Annie, Shiff ran to restrain Emily.

Spencer checked Annie's pulse and looked into her eyes. "What did she do?"

Shiff pulled Emily up and began to tie her legs and hands together.

"Did Sami call you?" Annie asked. She closed her eyes. Her tears fell quickly.

Spencer wiped the tears as they trickled down her neck. "Just in time, it seems. Can you tell me what Emily did?" He gently touched her cheek.

"Syringe paralyzed me. Potion… heart attack," Annie struggled to say. Spencer scanned the ground, found the syringe and sniffed the contents. He glanced at Annie and then at Emily, whom Shiff had left slumped against the wall, tied with magical rope, a smile on her face.

"Do you see a small vial or bottle?" Spencer asked. "Annie said it was meant to give her a heart attack."

Shiff took to his hands and knees, searching for the vial. He found it open and drained of the liquid. "Did you use this on her?" he shouted in Emily's face.

Emily smirked.

"No," Annie whispered.

Spencer turned back toward her. "Good. I need to get you out of here." He looked back at Shiff. "She didn't give the potion to Annie yet."

Shiff closed the lid of the potion and bagged it. "Where's the boy?"

Emily still smiled but said nothing of Shiloh's location.

"I can't worry about Shiloh. Get her back to Tartarus. Annie needs the hospital."

Shiff pulled Emily from the ground and dragged her back to the prison, while Spencer gently lifted Annie and teleported her to the hospital.

∽

"Can you move?" Dr. Christine asked.

"Yeah." With the remnants of the potion, the Wizard Guard lab had easily made the antidote to the poison. But Annie still felt dizzy, weak, and in need of sleep.

"What was the trigger?"

Annie glanced up and smiled. Cham was being wheeled in. His missing leg still surprised her.

"She was told under no circumstances was I allowed to live," Annie said.

Cham reached out held her hand. She looked at him.

"I'm supposed to take care of you," she said.

"Yeah, yeah. You always have to have the last word." He turned the chair to get closer to the bed and kissed her hand. "It's over."

She knew he was trying to make it better. While Cham had forgotten for a moment that Jason hadn't planned on surviving, he still tried to save him. For that action, he lost his leg. He was trying to be brave for her, and she for him.

"Yeah. It's definitely over." Annie heard a noise and looked at the door. "Come in, Sami."

Samantha cautiously walked in and sat on the other side of the bed. "You were right," she said.

"I'm always right," Annie teased. "You need to be more specific."

Samantha chuckled. "You are a smart ass."

"Agreed. What was I right about?"

Samantha took Annie's free hand. "About Dad, about Mom. I should have trusted your instinct. You knew this was going to turn out badly."

Annie turned her head, grateful she could move it again. "Optimism is good too."

Samantha chuckled. "Mom came to kill you. There's nothing optimistic about that."

"I knew she would. I never trusted her. She tried to get me to like her, call her Mom. I couldn't."

"And Dad?"

"He was here to save us. He did that and I will forever be grateful. My heart aches, though. I lost them both all over again." Annie felt contemplative. She rested her head against the bed. "You should go back to bed," she said to Cham.

"Not yet. You need me now; I'll need you later." Cham held her hand tighter.

"It'll all hit me in a few days. Or maybe it won't. If it happens, I might fall apart then. I'm alive and engaged and can step into the future knowing that she can't come after me and that I'm safe."

"You're my brave, baby sister. You did good."

For the moment, Annie would hang on to that.

CHAPTER 40

THE HOUSE WAS quiet when Annie returned from the hospital; Cham wouldn't be released for another week.

"Zola!" she called out. Annie realized she hadn't seen Zola for days. Her fairy hadn't been there for the battle, didn't come for her when her mother tried to kill her, and she didn't even come when Annie was in the hospital.

"Zola!" she called again. It was odd for her not to respond to Annie's calls. The last time it happened, Zola had been kidnapped and held hostage in the dungeon of the original black market. In her panic, magic rose from Annie's palms. She made a fist and sent the magic billowing in air.

She texted Samantha. *Is Zola with you?*

No. I still haven't seen her.

Annie strolled through the house. The bedrooms were empty and clean; the front room and den had been picked up and dusted. She walked the stairs to the basement and stopped. She held her breath. Jason's clothes were folded neatly on the sofa and his items were laid out on the shelf beside the bed. Pictures Annie had never seen lined the television stand.

She sat on the couch and touched his T-shirts, which were neatly folded like an Aloja fairy would do.

On the coffee table in front of her, she saw an envelope with her name scrawled across it. She recognized Zola's handwriting. With shaky hands, she opened the envelope.

My darling Annie,

It pains me that I have been absent to you in your most dangerous hours, but I had to ensure you had a long, long life. You were right. I made a deal to spare your life.

When I returned home to the Fates and bargained for your life, they promised me that if I did as they asked, you would most certainly return from the past alive and well. But it came with the highest of costs. They took Gibbs from you. In order to save you, he would have to die in your place. I am so sorry. But if I had the choice to make all over again, I wouldn't hesitate to make it. I would do it wholeheartedly.

But it came with a higher cost to me and to you. The worst thing that can happen to an Aloja Fairy is to be removed from their charge. For my insolence, I was taken from you. Our ties have been cut. I was ordered to return home, and I will no longer be allowed a charge. I will live out my long life alone. That is my penitence.

I will always love you. Be good to your sister and to Cham. Love wholly, be wise, and be strong. You are my brave girl, and I will never stop loving you.

Zola

Always keep my amulet close to you. Always.

Annie pulled Jason's flannel shirt from the pile, wrapped herself in it, and cried.

❧

The Wizard Guard's best tracker had died in the desert. Shiff was sure Lial would have found the boy by now. Feeling a deep sense of guilt at the thought, he put down his scrying crystal and placed his face in his hands as he rubbed his stubble.

"Any luck?" Spencer asked. He dropped a flimsy paper bag on the table and sat across from Shiff at the conference room table. The smell of fast food wafted out.

"Nothing. I went with the VAU to physically search the townhouse and looked for any hiding places in the walls, under the floors. The house was stripped. No sign of Shiloh. I did bring a bunch of his things from home to search for him, though. And I'm guessing Emily was less than helpful."

Shiff watched Spencer as he fiddled with the scrying crystal. "She's suddenly catatonic after flipping out when I arrived. Where else has the VAU been?"

"They were at Gloriana Worthington's. She hasn't seen her grandson. Actually, she didn't realize she had one. Annie never told her. But she did willingly let the VAU check all of the outbuildings on her property and gave them several locations of interest to the family." He crossed off the townhouse location and the Cave of Ages on the map.

"He's not at the Cave of Ages. The Middle Eastern guards went in and found nothing. Antique Symposium, maybe," Spencer suggested.

"It's on the list. You and I can go. I'm starting to worry about him. He's thirteen and alone now."

"I can't imagine Emily had many options. She hadn't lived in the U.S. in twenty years and can't teleport. He's got to be in the city somewhere. I say let's go to Antique Symposium."

They teleported onto the roof of the townhouse and entered, taking one more look though the building just in case the boy had returned home. It was as empty as when the VAU had opened it the first time. They exited the house. The courtyard was empty in the middle of the week. Next, they followed the path Emily would take every morning for work.

"Such a waste," Shiff said as they walked past Shiloh's favorite convenience store, glancing inside for his red hair.

They continued on and turned where Emily had turned the last day she had worked for the Fraternitatem. Spencer and Shiff glanced around the street. There was minimal street traffic and only one person walking toward the main road.

At Antique Symposium, Shiff stood guard as Spencer magically popped the lock and opened the door, letting themselves in. The door opened to a small entrance. A staircase went up to the right and a hallway wandered off to the left. They opened the first door on the left, but it was empty. Spencer shined his flashlight against the walls and floors. Both wizard guards ran their hands across the walls, searching for a hidden door.

After crossing the room, they exited and entered the next two rooms on the left, coming out of each with no new information. Beyond the first three rooms was a large kitchen area, refrigerator, stove, sink, and microwave. Spencer opened the closet door. It was lined with shelves and packed with empty boxes.

"This is very bizarre," Spencer commented. He turned and saw Shiff at an open basement door.

"Yeah, it is. I hear something," Shiff said.

Spencer texted the VAU and followed Shiff down the rickety wooden stairs. Both illuminated the walls and floors of the cellar. Rock walls were covered in dirt and cobwebs, and a heavy old furnace was silent and cold in the corner. They both ran their lights behind the mechanicals.

"Shiloh! Shiloh are you here!" Spencer shouted.

Shiff opened an armoire. It was empty. "Shh," he said.

They walked the perimeter of the basement. After a minute, they heard something banging into wood. Shiff ran for a coal bin and yanked up the lid. It was empty, except for a thick layer of coal dust that had been there for decades.

Spencer held a finger over his lips as he slunk slowly along the back wall. He stepped down where the floor had sunk. Shiff walked away from him toward one side of the room, wiping cobwebs from his hair and shirt. Together, they walked the perimeter of the room again, meeting at a door that was hanging askew, a light shining below from a crack in the floor.

Someone banged on the door. "Mom! Mom!" The voice was scared and panicked.

Spencer texted Graham Lightner, who found himself on the second floor. He and Sky Allen teleported themselves to the basement. Spencer pointed at the door.

"MOM!" the boy cried.

"Shiloh! My name is Spencer Ray. I work with the U.S. Wizard Guard. I'm friends with Annie and Samantha. Can I come in?"

"Where's my mom?"

"Can I come in? I'll explain it then."

"I can't open the door. It's locked."

Spencer held his palm at the handle and twisted his wrist, popping the lock. He opened the door. The room was dimly lit and consisted of a bed, a desk, and a bookshelf filled with comic books. The remnants of two meals lay on the floor, half eaten.

"What the hell," Spencer murmured.

"Where's Mom?"

"She tried to kill Annie. She's back at prison." Spencer said. He held his hand out to the boy, who sheepishly took it.

"I can see Annie and Samantha?"

Spencer nodded. "What did your mom tell you when she left you here."

He shook his head and began to cry.

"Okay. It'll be okay," Spencer reassured him. "Let's get you somewhere safe." He and Shiff walked Shiloh out, and teleported him to the only family he had left.

⋘

Annie stopped crying when she read Spencer's text. She sprayed water on her face and waited for her brother to arrive. It was the final straw for her, the one that released her from conflict about her mother. It wasn't enough that her mother tried to kill her; Emily had also left her son to die without a second thought.

Annie's hands shook when she opened the door, unsure if Shiloh, was brainwashed to kill her. It was a chance she would have to take as she stared down at his thin frame and his dirty, tear-stained face.

"Hi, Shiloh. Come in."

He cautiously followed her inside, staring at her home—a real home with furniture and walls and wood floors. Shiloh must not have had these things, growing up with the Fraternitatem as his family.

"She left me to die," Shiloh murmured. Annie wrapped a blanket around his shivering body and held him tightly. "She's the bad one. Not you," he said.

"Something happened to her when she finally saw Samantha and me. Everything she had been brainwashed to believe left her conflicted. She knew it was wrong, but she couldn't stop. Her mind isn't well. You are safe here. I promise you that."

He wiped his eyes. "Can I stay here?"

Annie looked at him. His eyes were hers, as were the curve of his lips and the shape of his face. Without wanting to hurt him, she said, "As long as you need."

As much as she had hoped she would never have to see Emily and Shiloh again, Annie knew two things in that moment: First, she couldn't send him away. Second, her life would forever be changed.

ONE YEAR LATER...

THE PORTAL HAD been an unexpected surprise. It had also become a burden to Annie, a lifelong responsibility that she would have, as well as her children and their children. She hadn't taken the inheritance of the Snake Head Letters lightly.

Annie stood outside the once-dingy storefront. The bricks had been cleaned, the trim replaced and repainted, and a new front window installed. A stronger door hung straight, without a jingle in the handle. She poked her finger in the blood lock, closed the door behind her, and locked it up again.

The inside had undergone the most changes. The walls had been painted and a new wood floor gleamed. While the Snake Head Letters no longer existed as a business, the store had bookshelves along the east wall, that contained books, artifacts, maps, and other miscellaneous scrolls. Tables and chairs had been placed in the room, as well as a few sofas and overstuffed chairs. It was more like a library or a meeting space for secret organizations. That always made Annie chuckle.

She crossed the floor. As much as the magical community had relied on this store and what Mortimer could do for them, any former patrons now had to rely solely on the black market for their magical needs. Annie was okay with that.

Her fingers grazed the glass and wood display case on the west side of the room. It contained her personal memorabilia relating to her ancestors, as far back as the original coven. While it could have been stored at

Artifact Hall, Annie had decided to keep it close, near the portal for which she was now responsible. She took a seat at the desk in the far corner, in the space that now acted as a combination library and artifact hall. The space now had the sole purpose of protecting the portal, studying it, and, in very rare cases, using it.

The heavy oak desk had a phone and a pile of phone messages and mail for First Coven, Inc. The similarities to the Fraternitatem of Solomon weren't lost on Annie. She just hoped they did a better job with their task than the Fraternitatem had.

Annie glanced up when the door swung open and Emerson Donaldson walked through the door. As the Donaldsons were one of the original covens that came from England, Emerson had been invited to join First Coven and given priority when it came to access to the space. It was Annie's peace offering to Emerson after realizing it wasn't the young woman's fault her family withheld information. Other members of her family had been arrested and convicted of treason as a result, but Emerson had never been involved and did everything she could to make up for their mistakes.

"Good morning, Annie," Emerson said cheerfully.

The young woman was still the best researcher in the Wizard Guard and had recently decided that being a full guard wasn't her skill set. She transferred to the library as an assistant librarian at Wizard Hall and now acted as a liaison between the Wizard Guard and Artifact Hall. The last year had tested her resolve and she had moved on from her family's mistakes. Annie and Emerson hadn't looked back.

"I don't know if you saw this or not. It was attached to the door." Emerson handed her an envelope addressed in Sturtagaard's flowery hand.

Annie made a face. "Thanks." She pocketed it.

"What do we need to do this morning?" Emerson asked.

"Just a check on the portal. These messages need to be sorted and answered." Annie glanced at her watch.

"Are you heading back to Wizard Hall? I can stay and handle those before I head to work."

Annie smiled at Emerson and handed her the messages. "For a few hours and then I'm off for the next two weeks. Wedding stuff." She walked to the metal door under the staircase.

The First Coven had been a distraction for Annie as she attempted to pick up the pieces of her life. Between Cham's injury, planning the wedding, and getting to know her half brother, it had been a long year. Over that time, she had worked with Emerson and other descendants of the original coven to clean and restore the Snake Head Letters and to create the foundation to protect and monitor the magic inside. In that time, Annie and Emerson had become friends. Annie no longer blamed Emerson for what had happened with the prophecy or her trip to the past, and in turn, she gained a good friend and ally.

Still, Annie and Shiff were the only two wizards with access to the portal. She pricked her finger in the blood lock and opened the strong metal door. The two women entered the room, which still was made up only of rock walls, dirt floor, and the portal. As always, the portal pulsed when Annie entered.

"It still senses you," Emerson said. She ran her crystal across and around the magic, taking readings.

"How's it doing?" Annie asked as she reached out to touch the magic. Goosebumps trailed up her arm and the itching under her skin stopped.

"Same as last week. It's no longer gaining strength, and thankfully, it's not losing any. I think we're managing it well."

"We'll have to note that when we have our meeting. It's good to know the charms and wards are working."

After Annie and Emerson closed up the portal, Emerson took her place at the desk and began to make her calls.

"See you at the hall," Annie said and left the building.

Before teleporting away, Annie pulled out Sturtagaard's note and stared at his handwriting. She had let him live after he asked her to stake him. Annie knew the vampire was miserable, living in his pain and agony. That gave her a great deal of pleasure. Though she rarely thought of him, there were those times when he entered her thoughts, and his pain brought her some justice and she'd smile at least until the thought passed.

Annie began to tear at the envelope in half but quickly changed her mind. Hating that he knew her so well, she opened his letter.

Annie,

Meet me at the warehouse. I have something to discuss with you.

Sturtagaard

She saw the note for what it was, another game perpetrated by Sturtagaard, and yet, she couldn't resist. He knew she couldn't.

Rather than heading for work, Annie teleported to the warehouse where it had all begun for her and Sturtagaard on the day she sought out Jordan Wellington in the death of Princess Amelie. Sturtagaard had been there, inserting himself into the case like he would on several others.

Annie landed in the alley between the two factories and looked up to the open loft window that was waiting for her. She sighed and teleported into the building. The loft hadn't changed since she had been there last; it was still clean and fresh and, Annie thought, likely used very little.

Unsure she was alone, she glanced out the window and listened for employees. The warehouse sounded abandoned. She leaned against the wall and waited.

Minutes later, Sturtagaard climbed the staircase. His heavy footsteps pounded against the wood, the sound reverberating off cement walls. When he entered the loft, she continued to stare off into the alley. Irritated, the vampire cleared his throat.

Annie shrugged. "You asked me to come. I'm here."

He sauntered over confidently. Annie turned and he tossed her a stake, the same one he had offered her a year ago.

She caught the stake midair and held it for him. "I told you I didn't care anymore."

He shook his head. "I tried by myself. I can't do it."

"Why? Why now?"

"I've lived long enough and I don't scare you. You won." He looked dejected.

"Well, duh. I'm smarter than you." Annie said.

He no longer pushed her buttons and that was the final straw. Resigned to his death, he walked to her. That familiar chill radiated from the vampire's skin. He pulled an envelope from inside his wool overcoat.

"What's this?"

He shrugged and stood before her, his hands out, his arms wide open. "Do it. End my misery."

She glanced inside the envelope. There was close to ten thousand dollars inside.

"Why?"

"Do it," he said.

Annie flipped the stake. When it smacked against her palm, he didn't flinch.

She thought for a moment of the direction her life was heading. Two weeks from now, she'd be married. In the future, she expected there might be a kid or two. She didn't want to look over her shoulder and worry that he'd be there waiting.

Maybe it's time for Sturtagaard to go.

Her emotions swirled around her in conflict. She had been so angry at him for what he had done to her family, for giving her to the Fraternitatem and taking away her mother and her father. She had wanted him dead. The whole wizard guard had wanted him dead for all the things he had done over the past millennium. But for Annie, knowing he was miserable gave her great pleasure, and she didn't think killing him would be as fun.

She observed him carefully. Sturtagaard had lived with so much fury for so long, with no end to his suffering. He had once been a man with a wife and child, who both died savagely. Sometimes their faces snuck into Annie's dreams at night, and she'd wake in a cold sweat.

Maybe ending his misery, would make the dreams stop.

She stared at the stake.

"Please."

In all the years Annie had known the vampire, she had never heard him beg or cry or kneel before her, so absolutely needing something from her. Even a bag of blood usually rendered nothing but jeers.

If I hold on to my anger, I'll be no better than him.

Annie took a step closer until she was so close, she shivered in his chill. She plunged the stake into his chest, piercing his heart. She stepped back as his body burst into flame.

The flames were fierce and angry as they consumed his demon flesh, washing away the unclean thing he had been for over eleven hundred years.

She held her breath. Sturtagaard remained on his knees, silent and stoic. The fire continued to eat away at the demon, releasing the human. His eyes lightened to his original blue, and his fangs curled up and disappeared. He smiled, an honest, fearless, human smile. The sneer she was so accustomed to was no longer there.

"Thank you," he said, then cried out from the pain.

Annie watched him die with the same intensity with which he watched her; she dared not look away in case there was something he had left to say. Slowly, he melted—his hands, his arms, his chest, his face—until nothing of the vampire was left except a pile of ash.

His final cries echoed around her. She shuddered and stared at his remains for some time. When enough time passed, when the sun was directly above her, she cleaned up Sturtagaard's remains, tucked them safely inside her field pack, and teleported through the window.

❧

Annie's boots clicked against the stone floor, echoing around her as she walked to the only cell in this wing. She slowed her pace as apprehension washed over, just like it did every month when she visited her mother. Even after a year of monthly visits, seeing her mother was just as raw as it had been the day Annie came to her after Emily tried to kill her.

She sighed and reminded herself she was only there to ensure her mother was still locked away, unable to harm her children again.

She stopped before the cell doors, took a deep breath, and walked in front of the metal bars.

Emily was reading a book, lounging in a comfortable club chair. Her legs hung over the high arm rest. She looked up when Annie jangled the bars.

"Annie!" she shrieked, delighted to see her youngest daughter had come for a visit.

After she tried to kill her, they were unsure of what they should really do with Emily. For all intents and purposes, she had been kidnapped and brainwashed and most likely wouldn't have wanted to kill Annie had it not been for the Fraternitatem of Solomon.

Unfortunately for Emily, she had gone through with the plan to take

Annie's life. Annie had made the decision that she'd rather lock her mother away in Tartarus Prison rather than an nonmagical one.

The cell had been set up much like an apartment with a bed, two comfortable chairs, and a television that only ran from five to ten at night. There had to be some consequence for attempted murder; though from Annie's perspective, this didn't seem like much of a punishment.

"Hi, Mom," Annie said. She whipped her wrist across the bars; they slid open, disappearing inside the rock wall. She stepped inside as Emily offered her a seat.

"What are you doing here? Did I forget you were coming?" Emily sat in the chair beside Annie and smiled expectantly.

"No. I had business to take care of and I thought I'd see how you were doing."

Annie felt nothing when she looked at Emily. She never expected she would. She would, though, protect her mom. Annie summoned a bouquet of flowers and handed it to her.

"These are beautiful." Emily walked to the small sink and reached for a glass. After filling it, she placed the flowers inside and put the bouquet on the table beside Annie.

"What's the weather like outside. They told me it was July... July, that's your birthday."

"It is," Annie said curtly, though she smiled at her mother as she said it. If Emily read her coolness, she didn't react to it. "The weather's lovely."

"Are you doing anything fun?" Emily giggled. It was off putting. Annie didn't want to discuss anything of consequence or share anything personal with her.

"Just dinner and cake," Annie said as she fidgeted with her fingers.

"Well, have fun. I would so like to join you." Emily sat and stared through Annie to the bars on the door and sighed.

The Wizard Guard, the VAU, and the hospital had spent the last year debriefing her, in an attempt to undo twenty years of brainwashing. The process had been incredibly slow. In the end, Emily would either be lucid or far more confused than when they started. Once in a while, her assassin tendencies would reveal themselves.

Like she did every month, Emily began to tear up. Annie knew she'd be asking about Shiloh. Annie held the edge of her chair in anticipation.

"How's Shiloh?" Emily asked.

Annie thought carefully, before she answered. "He's good. He's in summer school, catching up in math and science." Shiloh, of all of them, was much more conflicted where his mother was concerned. He was young and loved her and yet she had left him to die in the basement of Antique Symposium. He was working very hard to overcome what had been done. As of yet, he had no desire to see her.

"Tell him I love him and miss him terribly."

Annie handed Emily a picture of Annie with Sami and Shiloh. Emily smiled and wiped away her tears. Her lucidity didn't last, though. As Emily sat, her body tensed, she clenched the edge of her chair as her smile turned to a look of disgust.

"I should have killed you," she said.

Annie held her breath. Her grip on her own chair was so tight, her knuckles were white. This wasn't a one-off incident. Every time Annie visited, her mother said the same thing, and yet, it took her breath away and filled her with fear every time.

But as quickly as Emily made her pronouncement, she settled back and lovingly placed the picture on the table. "I'm so glad you're here. When can I see him?"

Emily asked the prison guards every day when she could see her children, and every day her children told the prison no. In her mental state, she seemed unaware that she had asked already and unaware they hadn't come to visit.

Emily stuck her hand inside her sweater pocket and held out a picture for Annie. "This is Shiloh's father."

Annie stared at the picture of a tall young man with clear blue eyes and light-brown hair. Both he and Emily had wide smiles on their faces. They looked truly happy as they held their baby son.

"What happened to him?" Annie asked as she put the picture on the table. It was the first time Emily had been willing to speak of him.

"Jeff worked in the lab. He arranged to get my body out of there, keep me safe. He brought me to the Fraternitatem. I couldn't help but fall in love with him." Emily held the picture and smiled, a tear sliding down her cheek.

"He's dead?"

Emily nodded and stood, walking to her cot to lie down. She wrapped herself in the blanket. Annie knew her mother's brain had just gone somewhere else that was safe, that wasn't here, and that didn't involve her children.

Annie pocketed the photo and left her mother alone in the cell, keeping her safely inside where she was unable to harm any of them again.

~

Annie stared at the list of all employees that worked in the lab twenty years ago, the one that Perkins gave her a year ago. She found a Jeff Silver working there. Even though it most likely no longer mattered, Annie texted Bucky and asked him to look for the man. She sent along a picture of him.

"How was your day?" Cham asked as he entered the den.

"Do you want the weird or the weird?"

"Hit me." Cham walked to the couch as smoothly as if he wasn't wearing a state-of-the-art prosthetic leg, then sat beside her.

"I saw Mom." Annie glanced at her phone.

"And how was Emily today?"

"Much of the same. Loving, homicidal, worried about Shiloh." Annie handed him the picture of Emily, Jeff, and Shiloh.

"Is this who I think it is?" Cham asked as he stared at the picture.

"Supposedly, that's Shiloh's dad, if that's what you were asking."

Cham handed the picture back. "Bucky's looking for him?"

Annie nodded. "She claims he's dead." With perfect timing, her phone rang. "Hey Bucky," she said, answering it.

"I wish they were all this easy," Bucky said. "Emily never married him; she was technically still married to Jason. They had a baby named Shiloh and Jeff died when Shiloh was about four. Was there something you wanted in particular?"

"Not really. I just want to keep Shiloh safe. I don't want to be looking over my shoulder worrying someone will come for him or us."

Annie could hear the sounds of Bucky typing on his computer. "Well, if that's what you want, you shall have," he said. "According to the death certificate, he died of cancer. I just pulled up the old autopsy reports and did a quick comparison. He's the same man in the picture you sent. I think you can relax."

"Thanks, Bucky." Annie ended the call and turned to Cham. "The dad is dead, so no chance someone's coming after Shiloh."

Cham kissed her. She sunk against him, always grateful when he could protect her. Sometimes she just wanted to be taken care of, and today was one of those days.

"And the other weird?" he asked.

She summoned a large bag and placed it on the ottoman.

"A bag of ashes. What's that?"

"Better question is, who's that?" Annie smirked. She couldn't help how light she felt without the vampire.

Cham looked at her with raised eyebrows. "Sturtagaard?"

Annie laughed. "He begged."

Cham let out a loud and long laugh, his own stress seeming to melt away. It was followed by footsteps that entered the house and headed to the den.

"Hey, Shiloh. How was magic school?"

He held his palm up, summoned a puddle of water, and floated it above his hand, warming it. When he was done, he gracefully poured the water back into the bottle.

"I think it was good." He smiled broadly.

For the last year, Shiloh had lived with Annie and Cham. This was partially because shortly after Shiloh's rescue, Samantha had announced that she was pregnant. Between the pregnancy and the baby boy she gave birth to, she had her hands full. The other reason Annie had been chosen to take care of Shiloh was that she was a teacher and far better trained to catch him up on magic.

"You think I can go to Windmere this fall? Please?" he mock begged.

Annie laughed. "You, my dear, are a nut. Your evaluation is next month. After that, you can go."

"Awesome!" he shouted and pumped his arm. He grabbed his backpack and headed upstairs to his room.

"Don't forget! Grandma Gloriana is coming for dinner soon!" she reminded him.

"I know!" he shouted back he entered his room.

"You think he's okay?" Cham asked.

Annie nodded. "I think he's as okay as he can be for now. School should help. Being around kids his age will be good for him."

They sat in silence. Annie chuckled when he blared his speakers. After a moment, Shiloh began to sing along to his favorite song. Annie leaned against Cham as they watched the news, content in the course their life had taken and how it all seemed to fit into place.

"Two weeks until you're a married lady. Are you ready?" Cham asked a few minutes later.

"You have no idea how ready I am."

The End

IF YOU ENJOYED The Wizard Hall Chronicles, please leave a review. I always appreciate the help help and I hope you enjoyed the series and Annie Pearce's journey. I enjoyed writing it and sharing with you.

For more information about me and any upcoming books, you can find me at:

www.Sherylsteines.com

Facebook: Sheryl Steines Author

Twitter: https://twitter.com/SherylSteines

Instagram: SherylSAuthor

Amazon: The Wizard Hall Chronicles
https://www.amazon.com/s?k=the+wizard+hall+chronicles&ref=nb_sb_noss

www.ingramcontent.com/pod-product-compliance
Lightning Source LLC
Chambersburg PA
CBHW030807260626
47169CB00001B/226